LICKS OF LOVE

Also by John Updike

―――――

POEMS

The Carpentered Hen (1958) • *Telephone Poles* (1963) • *Midpoint* (1969) • *Tossing and Turning* (1977) • *Facing Nature* (1985) • *Collected Poems 1953–1993*

NOVELS

The Poorhouse Fair (1959) • *Rabbit, Run* (1960) • *The Centaur* (1963) • *Of the Farm* (1965) • *Couples* (1968) • *Rabbit Redux* (1971) • *A Month of Sundays* (1975) • *Marry Me* (1976) • *The Coup* (1978) • *Rabbit Is Rich* (1981) • *The Witches of Eastwick* (1984) • *Roger's Version* (1986) • *S.* (1988) • *Rabbit at Rest* (1990) • *Memories of the Ford Administration* (1992) • *Brazil* (1994) • *In the Beauty of the Lilies* (1996) • *Toward the End of Time* (1997) • *Gertrude and Claudius* (2000)

SHORT STORIES

The Same Door (1959) • *Pigeon Feathers* (1962) • *Olinger Stories (a selection,* 1964) • *The Music School* (1966) • *Bech: A Book* (1970) • *Museums and Women* (1972) • *Problems and Other Stories* (1979) • *Too Far to Go (a selection,* 1979) • *Bech Is Back* (1982) • *Trust Me* (1987) • *The Afterlife* (1994) • *Bech at Bay* (1998)

ESSAYS AND CRITICISM

Assorted Prose (1965) • *Picked-Up Pieces* (1975) • *Hugging the Shore* (1983) • *Just Looking* (1989) • *Odd Jobs* (1991) • *Golf Dreams: Writings on Golf* (1996) • *More Matter* (1999)

PLAY

Buchanan Dying (1974)

MEMOIRS

Self-Consciousness (1989)

CHILDREN'S BOOKS

The Magic Flute (1962) • *The Ring* (1964) • *A Child's Calendar* (1965) • *Bottom's Dream* (1969) • *A Helpful Alphabet of Friendly Objects* (1995)

John Updike

LICKS
OF LOVE

SHORT STORIES
AND A SEQUEL

Ballantine Books • *New York*

A Ballantine Book
Published by The Ballantine Publishing Group

Copyright © 2000 by John Updike

"Licks of Love in the Heart of the Cold War" first appeared in *The Atlantic Monthly*; "Oliver's Evolution" in *Esquire* (as a piece of "snapfiction"); "Scenes from the Fifties" as a small individual volume published by Penguin Books, Ltd. *The New Yorker* first published the other nine stories and portions of "Rabbit Remembered." The latter could not have been written without the kind advice of Martha Ruggles, LICSW. Information was also gratefully received from Ted Bernhard, Carole Sherr, John Schrack, Jack De Bellis, and Robert McCoy. The stories written in much the order they have here.

www.ballantinebooks.com

Library of Congress Control Number: 2001118795

ISBN 0-345-44201-6

This edition published by arrangement with Alfred A. Knopf, a division of Random House, Inc.

Manufactured in the United States of America

Cover illustration by Chris Ware
Cover design by John Updike and Chip Kidd

First Ballantine Books Edition: December 2001

10 9 8 7 6 5 4 3 2 1

Contents

LICKS OF LOVE

The Women
Who Got Away

PIERCE JUNCTION was an isolated New Hampshire town somewhat dignified by the presence of a small liberal-arts college; we survived by clustering together like a ball of snakes in a desert cave. The Sixties had taught us the high moral value of copulation, and we were slow to give up on an activity so simultaneously pleasurable and healthy. Still, you couldn't sleep with everybody: we were bourgeoisie, responsible, with jobs and children, and affairs demanded energy and extracted wear and tear. We hadn't learned yet to take the emotion out of sex. Looking back, the numbers don't add up to what an average college student now manages in four years. There were women you failed ever to sleep with; these, in retrospect, have a perverse vividness, perhaps because the contacts, in the slithering ball of snakes, were so few that they have stayed distinct.

"Well, Martin," Audrey Lancaster murmured to me toward the end of a summer cruise on a boat hired out of

Portsmouth in celebration of somebody or other's fortieth birthday, "I see what they say about you, at last." The
"at last" was a dig of sorts, and the "they" was presumably
female in gender. I wondered how much conversation went
on, and along lines how specific, among the wives and divor-
cées of our set. I had been standing there by the rail, momentarily alone, mellow on my portion of California Chablis,
watching the Piscataqua River shakily reflect the harbor
lights as the boat swung to dock and the loudspeaker system
piped Simon and Garfunkel into the warm, watery night.

My wife was slow-dancing on the forward deck with her
lover, Frank Greer. Audrey had materialized beside me and
my hand went around her waist as if we might dance, too.
There my hand stayed, and, like the gentle buzz you get
from a frayed appliance cord, the reality of her haunch
burned through to my fingers and palm. She was a solid,
smooth-faced woman, so nearsighted that she moved with a
splay-footed pugnacity, as if something she didn't quite see
might knock her over. Her contact lenses were always getting lost, in somebody's lawn or at the back of her eyeballs.
She had married young and was a bit younger than the rest
of us. You had to love Audrey, seeing her out on the tennis
court in frayed denim cut-offs, with her sturdy brown legs
and big, squinty smile, taking a swing and missing the ball
completely. Her waist was smooth and flexible in summer
cotton, and, yes, she was right, for the first time in all our
years of acquaintance I sensed her as a potential mate, as a
piece of the cosmic puzzle that might fit my piece.

But I also felt that, basically, she didn't care for me, not
enough to come walking through all of adultery's risks and
spasms of guilt, all those hoops of flame. She distrusted me,
the way you distrust a competitor. We were both clowns,
bucking to be elected Funniest in the Class. Further, she was
taken, doubly: not only married, to a man called Spike, with

the four children customary for our generation, but involved in a number of murky flirtations or infatuations, including one with my best friend, Rodney Miller—if a person could be said to have same-sex friends in our rather doctrinairely heterosexual enclave. She had a nice way of drawling out poisonous remarks, and said now, to me, "Shouldn't you go tell Jeanne and Frank the boat is about to dock? They might get arrested by the Portsmouth fuzz for public indecency."

I said, "Why me? I'm not the cruise director."

Jeanne was my wife. Her love for Frank, in the twisted way of things back then, helped bind me to her: I felt so sorry for her, having to spend most of her hours with me and the children when her heart was elsewhere. She had been raised a French Catholic, and there was something noble for her about suffering and self-denial; her invisible hairshirt kept her torso erect as a dancer's and added to her beauty in my eyes. I didn't like Audrey mocking her. Or did I? Perhaps my feelings were more primitive, more stupidly possessive, than I knew at the time. I tightened my grip on Audrey's waist, approaching a painful pinch, then let go, and went forward to where Jeanne and Frank, the music stopped, looked as if they had just woken up, with bloated, startled faces. Frank Greer had been married, to a woman named Winifred, until rather recently in our little local history. Divorce, which had been flickering at our edges for a decade while our vast pool of children slowly bubbled up through the school grades toward, we hoped, psychological health, was still rare, and sat raw on Frank, like the red cheek he had been pressing against my wife's.

Maureen Miller, in one of those intervals in bed when passion had been slaked but an awkward half-hour of usable time remained before I could in decency sneak away, once told me that Winifred resented the fact that, in the years when the affair between Frank and Jeanne was common

knowledge, I had never made a pass at her. Winifred, sometimes called Freddy, was an owlish small woman, a graceful
white owl, with big dark eyes and untanned skin and an
Emily Dickinson hairdo atop a plump body that tapered to
small and shapely hands and feet. If my wife held herself
like a dancer, it was her lover's wife who in fact could dance,
with a feathery nestling and lightness of fit that had an embarrassing erotic effect on me. Holding her in my arms, I would
get an erection, and thus I would prudently avoid dancing
with her until the end of the evening, when one or the other
of us, in an attempt to persuade our spouses to tear themselves apart, would have put on an overcoat. Otherwise, I
was not attracted to Winifred. Like the model for her hairdo,
she had literary ambitions and a dogmatic, clipped, willfully
oblique style. She seemed in her utterances faintly too firm.

"Well, I won't say no," she said, not altogether graciously,
one night well after midnight when Jeanne suggested that I
walk Winifred home, through a snowstorm that had developed during a dinner party of ours and its inert, boozy aftermath. Couples or their remnants had drifted off until just
Winifred was left; she had a stern, impassive way of absorb-
ing a great deal of liquor and betraying its presence in
her system only by a slight lowering of her lids over her
bright black eyes, and an increase of pedantry in her fluting
voice. This was before the Greers' divorce. Frank was absent
from the party on some mysterious excuse of a business trip.
It was the first stage of their separation, I realized later.
Jeanne, knowing more than she let on, had extended herself
that night like a kid sister to the unescorted woman. She kept
urging Freddy, as the party thinned, to give us one more tale
of the creative-writing seminar she was taking, as a special
student, at our local college, Bradbury. Bradbury had formerly been a bleak little Presbyterian seminary tucked up
here, with its pillared chapel, in the foothills of the White

Mountains, but it had long loosened its ecclesiastical ties and in the Sixties had gone coed, with riotous results.

"This one girl," Winifred said, accepting what she swore was her last Kahlúa and brandy, "read a story that must have been *very* closely based on a painful breakup she had just gone through, and got nothing but the *most* sarcastic comments from the instructor, who seems to be a real sadist, or else it was his way of putting the make on her." Her expression conveyed disgust and weariness with all such transactions. I supposed that she was displacing her anger at Frank onto the instructor, a New York poet who no doubt wished he was back in Greenwich Village, where the sexual revolution was polymorphous. He was a dreary sour condescending fellow, in my occasional brushes with him, and disconcertingly short as well.

These rehashed class sessions were all fascinating stuff, if you judged from Jeanne's animation and gleeful encouragement of the other woman to tell more. A rule of life in Pierce Junction demanded that you be especially nice to your lover's spouse—by no means an insincere observance, for the secret sharing did breed a tortuous, guilt-warmed gratitude to the everyday keeper of such a treasure. But even Winifred through her veils of Kahlúa began to feel uncomfortable, and stood up in our cold room (the thermostat had retired hours ago), and put her shawl up around her head, as if fluffing up her feathers. She accepted with a frown Jeanne's insistent suggestion that I escort her home. "Of course I'm in no condition to drive, this has been *so* lovely," she said to Jeanne, with a handshake that Jeanne turned into a fierce, pink-faced, rather frantic (I thought) embrace of transposed affection.

Winifred's car had been plowed fast to the curb by the passing revolving-eyed behemoths of our town highway department, and she lived only three blocks away, an uphill slog in four inches of fresh snow. She did seem to need to take my arm, but we both stayed wrapped in our own thoughts. The snow drifted down with a steady whisper of its own, and the presence on the streets, at this profoundly nocturnal hour, of the churning, scraping snowplows made an effect of companionship — of a wider party beneath the low sky, which was glowing yellow with that strange, secretive phosphorescence of a snowstorm. The houses were dark, and my porch light grew smaller, receding down the hill. In front of her own door, right under a streetlamp, Winifred turned to face me as if, in our muffling clothes, to dance; but it was only to offer up her pale, oval, rather frozen and grieving face for me to kiss. Snowflakes were caught in the long lashes of her closed lids and spangled the arc of parted dark hair left exposed by her shawl. I felt the usual arousal. The house behind her held only sleeping children. Its clapboard face, needing a coat of paint, looked shabby, betraying the distracted marriage within.

There was, in Pierce Junction, a romance of other couples' houses — the merged tastes, the accumulated furniture, the framed photographs going back to the bridal day and the premarital vacation spots. We loved being guests and hosts both, but preferred being guests, invasive and inquisitive and irresponsible. Did she expect me to come in? It didn't strike me as at all a feasible idea — at my back, down the hill, Jeanne would be busy tidying up the party wreckage in our living room and resting a despairing eye on the kitchen clock with its sweeping red second hand. Tiny stars of ice clotted my own lashes as I kissed our guest good night, square on the mouth but lightly, lightly, with liquor-glazed subtleties of courteous regret. Of all the kisses I gave and received in Pierce Junction, from children and adults and golden retrievers, that chaste crystalline one has remained unmelted in my mind.

When I returned to the house, Frank, surprisingly, was sitting in the living room, holding a beer and wearing a rumpled suit, his long face pink as if after great exertion. Jeanne, too tired to be flustered, explained, "Frank just got back from his trip. The plane into the Manchester airport almost didn't land, and when he found Freddy not at their home he thought he'd swing down here and pick her up."

"Up and down that hill in this blizzard?" I marvelled. I didn't remember any car going by.

"We have four-wheel drive," Frank said, as if that explained everything.

Maureen could be a raucous tease. Her rangy body was wide but not deep—she had broad hips but shallow breasts—and all summer she bore around the base of her neck a pink noose of sunburn, freckled and flaking, from working in her garden in a peasant blouse and no sunhat. A redhead, she remained loyal to the long, ironed hair of the flower-child era years after the flower children had gone underground or crazy or back to their parents. When I described these events to her, leaving out the odd physiological effect which holding Winifred in my arms always produced, Maureen laughed and tossed her mane as if about to devour me with her prominent white teeth. "Jeanne is incredible," she said. "Imagine setting a date with your boyfriend at one in the morning in the faith that your husband would be off sleeping with the guy's wife! It sounds as though the snowstorm held everything up—that's why she kept egging Freddy to stay."

"I can't believe," I said, as primly as I could while wearing no clothes, propped up in her bed with a cigarette and a glass of red vermouth, "that things are as cold-blooded and as, as *set-up* as that. My guess is he swung by because he thought the party was still on."

"But he could see there weren't any cars!"

"Ah," I said, in modest triumph, "Freddy's car *was* out front, plowed in."

"Plowing, that's the theme," Maureen said. " 'If ye had not plowed with my heifer'—what?—'ye had not found out my riddle.' " She and Rodney had met at a summer Bible school, and Rodney still retained the well-combed, boyish shine of a future missionary. "Anyway," she went on gaily, giving the bed such a bounce that I spilled vermouth into the hairs of my chest, where—damn!—Jeanne might smell it, "I can see you feel you let Freddy down, but don't. She's screwing that odious little New York poet, everybody at Bradbury says."

"I wish you wouldn't tell me all this. I'd like to keep some innocence."

"Martin, you *love* it, you love knowing *every*thing," she told me, and nuzzled at the spilled vermouth with a faceless, thrusting, leonine seriousness that rather frightened me. I fought her off by finding her ears in all that hair and using them as handles to pull her head up from my chest. Her face, thus tugged back, with uplifted upper lip and slit eyes, reminded me of Winifred's held to be kissed in the snow, and of a death mask. Maureen's was not a female body that hid its bones, its lean doomed hunger. Laughing but hard-eyed, spiteful though playful, she said, "Rodney says you're just like a woman, you're so nosy."

This hurt me and aroused me. Rodney and I were severely discreet, talking about nothing but our chaste sports— golf, poker, tennis, skiing. We didn't even talk politics, at the height of Vietnam and then through Nixon's prolonged downfall. Yet it was stirring, to think of Maureen and Rodney talking about me, in their marital intimacy. "Like a woman, am I?" I said, growling and wrestling her under, to reverse our positions in the bed, that guest-room bed I knew so well, a mahogany four-poster, with a removable pineapple topping each post. Maureen's shrieks of resistance and amusement rang through the oak-floored rooms of her Victorian house and out, I feared, into the street.

Pierce Junction was a town of secrets that kept leaking out, like sawdust from a termite-ridden beam. There were all these tiny wormholes, with a flicker of life at the end of each. When Jeanne learned of my affair with Maureen, she reacted with a surge of fury that surprised me, since I had been putting up with her and Frank for years. Unforgivably, she demonstrated her anger by storming over to the Millers' and telling Rodney everything. Maureen, with her pious streak, worked Wednesdays and Saturdays at a Methodist home for delinquent children in Concord, and it was the telephone company's efficiency, listing non-local calls by town and number, that had given our liaison away. When I try to recall our passion, it comes not with X-rated images from our hours in bed but with a certain dull taste, the madeleine of an especially desolate minute in an idle day, the longing that made me, of a dull and hollow afternoon, insatiably crave the sound of her voice—lower and huskier over the phone, more thoughtfully musical, than it seemed when we were face to face. Her voice momentarily pushed aside the sore dread in which I lived in those years; her voice and its quick inspirations of caustic perception painted the world, which seemed to me rimmed with a vague terror, in bright fearless colors. Hearing Maureen reassuringly laugh, as if we were all caught in a delicious, precarious joke, slaked a thirst that weighed in my throat like an iron bar. Without her in it somewhere, at least as a voice over the telephone, the world lacked a center. I *had* to talk to her, though the phone bill did us in.

The hunger was not only mine, but pervaded our circle with the pathos of unsatisfied need: poor Jeanne and Frank, stealing that silly half-hour in the blizzard. Maureen for me was like a campfire whose light makes the encircling darkness seem absolute, and whose heat becomes a sharp chill a few paces from its immediate vicinity.

Jeanne didn't come back from her interview with Rodney for hours. Not immediately, but after some days had worn us down to skeletons of weary honesty, she confessed that, Maureen being absent, she had slept with him, in some delirium of revenge, though he had been reluctant.

"One of Maureen's sadnesses," I told her, "was always that he was so faithful, so satisfied by her. Or so she thought."

"How funny of her. You remember that period when Winifred and Frank were just breaking up, and Freddy was wildly on the make? I was terrified she was going to seduce you, that snowy night. Well, Rodney was the only man around here who didn't disappoint her—who lived up to her self-image. Apparently she is very sexy. Rodney said he was rather put off by his sensation that at that point in time— I sound like Nixon—she would fuck anybody. I wish he hadn't told me—even Frank doesn't know, and I hate having a secret from *him*."

"Such beautiful scruples," said I.

"Go ahead, mock. I deserve it, I guess."

"My martyr. My Jeanne in the flames," I said, hardly able to wait until I could take her to bed and discover how her new knowledge, her fresh corruption, had enriched her.

Yet we did divorce, in painful piecemeal, as did Maureen and Rodney. I moved to Nashua, but would return to Pierce Junction to visit the children, take Jeanne's temperature, and play my old games. One poker night, rather than let me drive back to Nashua full of beer, Rodney insisted that I sleep in his bachelor shack, up in the hills, at the end of a mile of dirt road. While waiting for my turn to use the bathroom, I saw a note carelessly left on his cluttered desk. The rounded upright handwriting, with its "a"s oddly like "o"s, struck me as momentously familiar; Audrey Lancaster had been the secretary of a conservation committee I had once served on. *Another fool's errand,* it read. *Did I misunderstand, or has Friar Lawrence goofed again? Now my van is dusty and my legs full of mosquito bites from an hour on your porch. Some damn bird in your woods was trying to deliver a message in clear English but couldn't quite make it out of birdsong. Yours, sort of. Yes?* Unsigned. A blue-lined page torn, with an anger visible in the tearing, from a college notebook. A thumbtack hole where it had been pinned up outside. It brought me thrillingly close to Audrey, as close as we had been the night I had rested my palm on her haunch. She had come up that gloomy dirt road through the forest like a big smooth salmon upstream, and ignominiously driven back down again. Her literary allusion seemed more like Winifred, somehow.

When Rodney emerged innocently from the bathroom, wearing little-boy cotton pajamas and a fleck of toothpaste on his chin, I hated him as never in those years of entering his big house near the college, past the lawnmower and the oil cans in his garage, through the kitchen where he gobbled breakfast every day, past the shelf of his golf trophies, toward the mahogany guest bed. While some of us burned on the edges of life, insatiable and straining to see more deeply in, he sat complacently at the center and let life come to him—so much of it, evidently, that he could not keep track of his appointments.

Down in Nashua, as the Seventies dwindled into Jimmy Carter's inflation and malaise, I lost track of the ins and outs of life in Pierce Junction. The possibility that Maureen and I might get together on a respectable basis had been early dismissed by her. Too many children, too much financial erosion, too much water over the dam. "Don't you see,

Marty?" she told me. "We've *done* it. We'd look at each other and all we'd see would be evidence of our *sin!*"

The quaint last word shocked me with the possibility that she—and Jeanne, and all the women—had been suffering in our sexual paradise, stressed and taxed by the divergence from monogamy. I felt insulted. So it was with, among other things, a pang of vengeful satisfaction that I heard of her sudden death, in a car driven late at night along Route 202 by, of all people, Spike Lancaster, a beefy, loud, hard-drinking restaurateur whose plain deficiencies had given Audrey, in our little set, a halo of forbearance. Spike and Audrey had nothing in common but bad eyesight. Maureen died, and he, the driver, came out of the crash with minor injuries and a rakish reputation that probably didn't hurt business in his roadside restaurant—called, actually, the Lucky Shamrock.

I could hardly believe that, after sublime us, Maureen could have taken up with this brute, this simpleton. Served her right, getting her neck broken, that slender neck springing with its pulse from a circle of summer sunburn. These ugly, unworthy thoughts lasted only a second, of course—a lightning flicker of amoral neurons before the gentle rain of decent sadness began. But her death, and this final scandal, with its black skidmarks and shattering of safety glass, did shut down Pierce Junction for me.

Jeanne and Frank married, and I edged into a second life, with a second wife and new children. My own children continued to grow, went to college, married, and moved away. I had fewer and fewer reasons to return; when I did, the town's geography, little changed, seemed to contain the same old currents, but the wires were different. The faces, and the old wormholes, if they still existed, were out of sight, running through younger lives. When I thought back to our hectic, somehow sacred heyday, it was, as I say, less in terms of the women closest to me than of those in the middle distance, relatively virginal, who had taken the siren call of the unknown with them as they disappeared over my horizon.

A mall had sprung up between Nashua and Pierce Junction, on the site of a dairy farm whose silver-tipped silos I still expected to see gleaming at that particular turn of the highway. Instead, there was this explosively fragmented glitter—chain stores in postmodern glass skins, and a vast asphalt meadow paved with cars. Intending to buy a grandchild a birthday present at one of those toy emporia with the queerly reversed "R," I was traversing the insistently musical reaches of an enclosed arcade lined, in its parody of an old-time Main Street, with windows of name-brand goods and dotted with underpatronized kiosks offering tinselly jewelry, exotic herbal teas, and candy and yogurt-coated pretzels in cloudy plastic bins. Suddenly I saw in the middle distance an unmistakable walk—splay-footed, wary, yet determinedly forward and, to my eyes, enticingly youthful. I ducked into a Gap outlet and, concealed amid shelves of softened denim and earthtone turtlenecks, gazed out as Audrey, plumper and gray but still supple, passed. The contact lenses that she was always losing had given way to cheerfully clunky thick glasses. She was squinting and smiling and talking with animation, moving that flexible murmurous wide mouth of hers.

Her companion, wearing trousers and a feathery short white hairdo and a quilted down vest, for a moment seemed a complete stranger, a solemnly pouting small man. But then, with a stab of recognition that set off a senile stir of excitement behind my fly and jumped me a step farther back from the window, I saw; there was of course no mistaking the barrel-shaped owl body, the hooded dark eyes, the dainty extremities. Winifred. She and Audrey moved with the dreamy mutual submission of an old married couple. They were holding hands.

Lunch Hour

DAVID KERN had not lived in Pennsylvania for forty years, but he always attended his high-school class reunions, which were held once every five years. The basic treasure of his life was buried back there, in the town of Olinger, and he kept hoping to uncover it. Julia Reidenhauser, on the other hand, hadn't attended a reunion for decades, not since those first low-budget get-togethers the class committee put on at the Wenrich Grove picnic grounds and the Schenktown VFW, when they all could still fit into their high-school clothes and still meant most of the real world to one another. "Julia is here this year—with Doris, of course," Mamie Kauffman told him.

Mamie had grown round as a muffin and her little clever dimpled hands—she had been "artistic" and had hoped to become a fashion designer—were bent by arthritis, but she still had the starry-eyed sweetness, the touchingly relieved happiness to be here, to have *arrived*, that she had when her mother would walk her hand in hand to the old elementary school on the Alton Pike, and boost her up onto the three-foot retaining wall that separated the asphalt playground from the sidewalk. It wasn't a playground, exactly; although the children played on it at recess it had no swings or slides or basketball hoops, just a few half-erased white lines and circles painted on it. Only the teachers knew the games and rules that went with these markings. The asphalt encircled the building like a broad moat, and was strictly divided into the boys' and girls' halves, with a cement walkway, front and back, as the dividing line. Everything was symmetrical and strict at the old elementary school except for the bobbing, squirming, tittering, runny-nosed, queasy-tummied, nervous-bladdered students, kindergarten through sixth grade.

"You're kidding," David said, but knew she wasn't; Mamie's eyes, smaller than the eyes she had had in grade school, glittered mischievously with this gift she was giving him. She was class secretary and had been the heart of the reunion committee ever since there were reunions, plotting how to inveigle each one of the hundred and twelve class members to attend. "How did you get her to come?" he asked.

Mamie took an unexpected offended tone. "I didn't. I'm through with begging, David. I used to beg Julia, and about a dozen others that I knew would have a swell time, if they deigned, but now I figure, send out the invitations and let those that want to come come. We're all adults, God knows." They were all over sixty; they had graduated forty-five years ago, the June the Korean War started. Seven of the hundred twelve, by the secretary's accounting, were already dead. Yet all around him, through a mist of gray hair and wrinkles and body fat, David saw children's faces, rising essentially unchanged up through the grades. Mamie added, "Betty Lou says Doris begged her to—she didn't want to come all that way from Schenktown alone. And I guess Julia's over her time of troubles, with her health and husband and all."

Time of troubles? Mamie had never left Olinger—in fact, she lived two blocks from her mother, who was still alive— and assumed that David, who had gone away to college, and then into the Army, and then to New York City, and for thirty years had commuted to the city from Connecticut, knew more than he did of local news. He did remember Ann McFarland telling him, back at the fifteenth reunion, that Julia had said she would come only if she could lose ten pounds, and she hadn't managed to, and so had proudly stayed away. She lived in Schenktown, six miles from Olinger, and hadn't entered the school system until the ninth grade. She was not a slave to the old Olinger magic the way Mamie and Betty Lou and Ann were.

David's mother had always marvelled at the good opinion Olinger people had of themselves. It was not as if it were the richest suburb of Alton, or the prettiest, or the "Dutchiest." In Pennsylvania Dutch country, Dutchiness could be measured, not just by counting the number of decorated barns and whitewashed old inns in a town, but by a certain sullen air of resistance to all the things—malls, self-serve gas stations, discount outlets, housing projects for the elderly and less fortunate—that diluted the way things used to look. Busloads of tourists came out from Baltimore and Philadelphia to see how things used to look. Olinger had a pre-Revolutionary limestone house at its center, and a nineteenth-century track for harness races had preceded the curving streets of a rather posh section, Oakdale, developed in the Thirties and extended up the sides of Shale Hill after the war; but the town was not especially Dutchy, even with the multiplication, it seemed to David upon each return, of mass-produced regional kitsch—decal hex signs, dolls in Amish costume.

Someone driving from Lancaster to Alton would pass through Olinger as a segment of a continuous strip of commercial enterprise. In David's boyhood, the town had trailed

off into cornfields, an old grist mill, a creek full of water-
cress, a great stone quarry both dangerous and enticing in its
emptiness. Now all such mysterious, underpopulated terrain
was filled with shopping centers, car lots, aluminum diners,
and fast-food franchises. Still, Olinger retained, at least in
the minds of his generation, a distinct sense of itself as a sane
and blissful medium between the laughable rural innocence
of a one-street, two-factory town like Schenktown, tucked
into bleak stretches of corn stubble and abandoned apple
orchards, and the urban horrors of Alton, a big depressed
industrial town now increasingly dominated by its citizens
of color. The people of Olinger were proud of being where
they were, and David still felt his initial departure, set in
motion by his mother, as a loss. She had talked his father
into moving out of Olinger into an old farmhouse some
miles to the south when David was fourteen.

Though tending to hang back shyly at these reunions,
he stood up and looked for Julia. The reunion was being
held in a function room of an Alton restaurant, festooned
with the class colors, maroon and gold. Blown-up photos
from the happy days—duck tails, bobby socks, the smoke-
filled luncheonette—had been hung about. A long buffet
table was being set up. The bar was busy and noisy. He
found Julia standing not far away, in the center of the room,
with a few old admirers and the inseparable Doris Gerhardt.
Good-natured, ginger-haired Doris had been perhaps the
shortest member of their class, and one of the first to get
married. Both women kissed him, which David had not
expected. While Doris's kiss, delivered strenuously upward,
was warmer and more pressing, Julia's had certainly occurred,
a moist female moment in the center of his lips. The Connecticut courtesy kiss, an antiseptic brushing of the cheeks,
didn't exist here. Julia had put on at least ten pounds since
high school, but her tallness and elegantly erect posture

made light of it. Her hair was white yet still abundant and somehow high, springing from her forehead in a soft combed crest, and then falling away toward her wide shoulders. She had a hook nose and gray-green eyes with a dark quiet to them: a German beauty, sallow-skinned, carrying herself as if simply being herself was quite enough. She had gone out for no extracurricular activities that he could remember. In the yearbook she had listed as her main ambition "to get out of school." In class she was stately and impervious, except when called upon to recite; when she stood, her face flooded with a blush that sent an erotic shiver across the rows. Her smile had an engaging helpless air to it, as if to say, "Well, what can one do?" *Was kann mer duh?*

David, who upon entering the reunion had been nervous, jittery, trying too hard to get back into the Olinger groove, was aware of feeling altered in the presence of Julia and little Doris. He became another self, calmer and taller. "How are you both?"

"Oh, we can't complain too much," Doris said.

"Maybe you can't, but I can," Julia said, brushing back her thick hair with a languid gesture. "I spend half my time at the dentist and the rest at the chiropractor."

"You look great," David said. "You both look great." And then he interrupted their stilted but smiling pleasantries to call his wife out of another conversation—she had attended enough reunions with him to have her own acquaintances in his class. He wanted her to meet Julia. The two women shook hands and looked at each other with a quizzical blandness. David wondered why he had forced this little encounter, and why he felt so uncharacteristically relaxed and *at home*. Then he remembered: lunch hour. To these Schenktown girls he had been another country person, a normal person. They had not minded his being torn from Olinger, by a mother with absurd ideas; they had seen him as he was, a man-to-be.

. . .

His family's move had occurred when he was in the ninth grade. The farm wasn't in the Schenktown direction, but to the southeast instead of the southwest of Olinger and Alton. The idea of going to school in the district in which they now lived horrified him, as a descent into a chasm of strange rural offspring, smelling of hay and dung. But his father taught in Olinger, and it was easy to arrange that David continue in the school; they commuted back and forth together, in an old black Chevrolet. After school, David killed time on the school grounds or at the luncheonette up the street. He had gone from being an Olinger boy to being a waif, a homeless bumpkin clinging to the status of a student. Of all his class, he came from farthest away.

But in truth Olinger had begun to slide from him before the move. Beginning in about the fifth grade, school would be full of chatter and gossip concerning weekend events that had excluded him—gatherings in somebody's basement, or down at the quarry, or at the roller-skating rink at the Alton amusement park. There was a gang, and he was not in it. He had lost the trail that he had been following since the walks to kindergarten, and the summers spent at the Olinger playground, and the bicycle trips in a pack all over the town, with the knot of boys and girls he had known all their lives. Of the girls, some were prettier than others, with more spunk and energy, and of the boys, some had more of the magic ingredients—confidence, knowingness—that made for popularity, but the distinctions hadn't mattered so much as they came to matter in seventh and eighth grades. By ninth grade, David almost felt he might as well live in the country, where he could read mystery novels all afternoon, and practice set-shots at a hoop his father had nailed to the barn wall for him, and hoe in the "organic" garden his mother had planted up past the shaggy orchard slope.

In the tenth grade he got his driver's license, and access to the family car as it sat on the school lot. He found himself in the same orbit as Julia and Doris. There was an old hat factory in Schenktown, and though felt hats would soon fade from daily use in America, enough prosperity had been generated to afford Julia the use of a green Studebaker convertible and Doris that of a Willys station wagon, with all-steel sides instead of varnished wood, which was still a novelty in 1948. The cars liberated them not only from the school bus but from the high-school cafeteria. While most of the students walked home for lunch in the compact blocks of Olinger, and the others were dished up fried Spam or chicken à la king in the cafeteria line, Julia and Doris and David and some Schenktown boys like Wilbur Miller and Morris Hertzog drove up and down the Alton Pike in one or another of their cars, looking for the perfect hamburger. Luncheonette or diner food cost a few dimes more than cafeteria fare, but, just as David's parents had agreed that the country high school wasn't good enough for him, they provided the five-dollar weekly allowance for his non-cafeteria lunches. Looking back, he marvelled at their generosity and his selfishness: a teen-age predator, hungry for hamburgers, acceptance, and gasoline.

The school allotted a class period, fifty-five minutes, for lunch. After finding and eating the hamburgers, they would still have time to drive around. In that Pennsylvania of the late Forties, before the transformations of the postwar boom had really taken hold, pure countryside lay five minutes from Olinger in every direction except along the trolley tracks toward Alton. Hilly, twisting township roads connected lonely farmhouses and an occasional grocery store with two rusty red gas pumps outside, advertised by a Pegasus. David remembered standing in the rear seat of Julia's Studebaker, battered by wind, and then lying back across the folded convertible top onto the sun-warmed metal of the trunk and watching the dazzling alternation of sky and tree branches scud overhead.

Little cemeteries of tilted sandstones, mysterious thick groves of planted evergreens, rickety farm stands that would have appeared deserted but for their fresh yellow squashes and orange pumpkins and the bonneted old woman keeping an eye on things from the porch; collapsing stone spring-houses, the overgrown ruins of old iron forges, creeks making brown foam with their chuckling small waterfalls; fields of corn, of rye, of tobacco, of cattle, of peach and apple trees in blossom or bent low with fruit—all this poured around the noontime travellers, who were oblivious to most everything but one another and the sensation of speed. When David was the automotive host, in the old black Chevrolet, he had a trick, safer than it looked but infallibly producing shouts and screams from his passengers, of putting the car in neutral at the crest of a hill and getting out on the running board and steering through the window. The chance of meeting another car was not great. The roads, laid out in dirt for horse-drawn farm wagons, had been paved before the war. Soon enough they would be broadened, and the curves straightened at the cost of a little dormered farmhouse or stone-sided dirt-ramp barn, but for now they formed an empty maze that called these licensed adolescents out, out from the high school with its crammed halls and classrooms, its perfumed and slick-haired mobs in angora sweaters and corduroy shirts and saddle shoes and penny loafers, its whispering seethe of romance and breakup and calculated misbehavior, and its merciless gradations of worth by Olinger standards—the shining ins and the shadowy outs, the attractive and admirable versus the many more who were neither.

Reunions revealed that keenly felt structure of implacable

discriminations to have been a poor predictor of adult performance. It was the comically tongue-tied yokel, invisible in
class, who moved to Maryland and founded an empire of plant
nurseries and parked a silver Jaguar in the lot of the reunion
restaurant. It was the forlorn, scorned daughter of a divorced
mother—a monstrous thing in those days—who had become
a glamorous merchandising executive out in Chicago. The
class cut-ups had become schoolteachers and policemen,
solemn and ponderous with the responsibility of maintaining
local order. The prize for newest father—his bouncy fourth
wife, in a low-cut satin minidress, indistinguishable from his
third, five years ago—went to a boy who had never, as far as
anyone could recall, attended a dance or gone out on a date.
The class wallflowers, an almost invisible backdrop of colorless femininity against which the star females had done their
cheers and flaunted their charms, had acquired graceful
manners and a pert suburban poise, while the queens of the
class had succumbed to a lopsided overdevelopment of the
qualities—bustiness, peppiness, recklessness, a cunning chis-
elled hardness—that had made them spectacular.

Julia had been spectacular but seemed unaware of it or, if
aware, dismissive of it. Her characteristic expression, that
worried smile which asked, "What can you do?," alternated,
in David's observation, with a faintly grim, masculine intent-
ness, as when she was driving her convertible fast, her chestnut hair flattened back from her forehead and rippling
furiously, or when she was smoking a cigarette at lunch. Her
lower jaw would move out under the cigarette and her eyes
would narrow like a man's. The way she always travelled
with an attendant, little Doris, enhanced the powerfully
exotic impression she made on the class élite. The good-
looking, dynamic girls courted her, and enrolled her in their
circle almost against her will. She shrugged off as ridiculous
the boys who professed, along the wriggling grapevines of

gossip, their love for her. She had no sex life, that David could see; perhaps it was back in Schenktown. The boys, Wilbur and Morris, who came along on their lunchtime drives had a countrified softness and tact of manner, as if life were innocent of undercurrents—as if these devil-may-care lunchtime excursions were not an exhilarating exercise in bonding, in nerve, in escape from the order imposed back in Olinger High and the surrounding tight community of semi-detached brick houses. There was something negative, something refusing about Julia that David liked, without being tempted to improve upon the pleasant sexlessness between them. If she had ever kissed him before this forty-fifth reunion, he had forgotten it.

Their rural mobility brought its social rewards. Julia's Studebaker or Doris's station wagon would show up on a weekend at David's farm, that farm with which his mother had expected to place an irrevocable remove between her family and the town. They would carry him away, in a nest of passengers that included not just the stolid Schenktown pals but such prizes as Mamie and Betty Lou and Ann, and the boys they deemed acceptable. By way of Julia's magnetism and the power of the American automobile, he had made his way back in, into those mysterious, pointless, indispensable get-togethers that had begun to exclude him in the fifth grade. The group went bowling, played canasta in clouds of cigarette smoke, watched infant television, drove to a pond where there was a dock and diving board—flimsy excuses, all of them, for being together and staying together, on the edge of those possibilities they felt, dimly, approaching to shape and limit their lives. It was a little late for him; he was plotting a life for himself after Olinger, following his mother's lead after all. But he was happy to be in a gang again, and took with him into the world the pride of membership, of acceptance.

Until tonight he had not distinctly seen how much that acceptance had been a prize Julia had passed on to him, not valuing it greatly herself. Of her life once she made her escape from school he knew little and needed to know nothing—a Schenktown husband, a row of children, a dose of the illnesses and disappointments that give life its final fatal flavor. She had tasted it all even as a teen-ager. Well, *was kann mer duh?* All we have in the end is our posture. The erect way she carried herself in those vanished, clattering halls had made her breasts, in an old-fashioned edgy bra and fuzzy sweater, jut out sharply, above a stomach as tautly flat as if she had taken a deep breath to sing.

So that was why he had felt relaxed and tall and grateful, known for what he was, seeing Julia Reidenhauser again. But why had he felt that sharp impulse to introduce her to his wife? He watched his wife move about in the motel room on the edge of Alton, slowly undressing, draping her bra on a towel rack, fussing at the provincial inadequacies of the accommodations—instant coffee in the bathroom but no shower cap or bath oil—yet sweetly calm and somewhat absent beneath this skin of irritation. A woman was a circle whose center was slightly elsewhere. David wondered if he would live to see the fiftieth reunion. Mamie had spoken into the microphone about it, her voice with its childish lisp curling around a vision of something extraordinary— a cruise on the Chesapeake, a weekend in Bermuda even, which aren't as expensive as you would think, off-season. She wanted them all to write her with their ideas. "And please include your present correct address, for the class list. Things don't get forwarded any more; the parents that used to do it are . . . are gone." Help, she was saying, we are sinking into the sea of the generations. There was no more Olinger High School: the name had been swallowed up by a regionalization in the Fifties, and the high-school building itself, with its waxed oak hallways and wealth of hidden asbestos, had been razed in the Seventies. At their twenty-fifth reunion, the door prizes had been yellow bricks salvaged from the rubble.

"Maybe this will be the last one I'll drag you to," David announced to his wife.

She gave him a harassed, dishevelled, lovable look. "Miss your fiftieth? Why? I don't mind them. They're nice people, really. They just have never gone anywhere."

"I think they think they're already there. How did you like Julia?" Julia had left, with Doris, before the dancing began, and the post-dinner drinking. First, Butch Fogel had shown an old movie his father had taken on eight-millimeter film, of a Memorial Day parade in 1937, and then of a clambake on the vacant lot next to the Lutheran church. David had been rapt, spotting as they flickered by an old Sunday-school teacher brandishing a cigar, and the bald doctor who had aided his birth and used to come visit with his little unfolding black bag, and (for a piercing split-second) David's youthful father mugging for the camera, and then the fat town policeman who at Christmas always dressed up as Santa Claus to hand out red-wrapped boxes of Zipf's chocolates. David looked for himself in the swiftly panned throngs, but he would have been only five, and would he have recognized himself anyway?

"Which was she?"

"The tallish one with the hook nose and the crown of white hair."

"She seemed a bit above it all."

"That was her approach. But she wasn't, really." It came to him why he had wanted them to meet, to touch each other: he was proud of knowing both of them, both these women. Until Julia, he had only known growing girls.

New York Girl

IN THOSE DAYS New York seemed as far from Buffalo as Singapore does now. I used to take the train, all eight stultifying hours of it, or drive, on Route 17, stopping off in Corning and Binghamton, where we had clients, and then coming down through the Catskills into Westchester County. I used to stay at the Roosevelt or the Biltmore, easy walks with a suitcase from Grand Central Station. Once you were in New York, you were on another planet, a far shore; it cried out for you to establish another life. Time, at home so filled with the needs of the house and of the children and of the wife—Carole kept counting her gray hairs, and childbearing had given her varicose veins—time was here your own, hours of it, and no one told you how to fill it, once the day's appointments had been kept. Extruded nonferrous metal, mainly aluminum alloy, was our product. Combination storm-window manufacturers were our big customers, but in the Sixties a sideline had developed in metal picture frames, and this brought me into contact with the lower echelons of the art world. I visited galleries to see what they needed, and in one of them, on an upper floor on West Fifty-seventh Street, I met Jane.

She wasn't plain, but she wasn't a conventional beauty either. There was something asymmetrical about her; not just her smile but her whole bony face, with its high cheek-bones and powdered-over freckles, seemed a little tugged to one side. When she gestured, her arms and hands appeared too long, with an extra hinge to them somewhere. Her gestures involved a lot of sudden retraction and self-stroking, as if she were checking herself for loose parts. She kept flipping back her long ironed hair, a dull reddish color that reminded me of pencil shavings and the cedary fragrance that arises when you empty the sharpener. She wore a beige knit mini-dress and black pantyhose; her hips were wider and her thighs fuller than one would have expected from the bony top half of her body, and this added to her touching aura of being out of kilter, there in the merciless brightness of the display space. The white walls held hasty abstractions, blue pigments smeared upon white-primed canvas, all the same size and framed in thin cold-rolled steel, like a row of bathroom mirrors.

"I'm not here to look at the paintings," I apologized. "Just the frames. To get an idea of what you need."

"I guess inconspicuous is what we need," she said, fluttering one long hand at the cruel wall and then quickly resting the same hand on the ball of her shoulder and giving it a squeeze. "A lot of the artists can't stand any frames, they say it creates a mind-set, they want it to look *rough*, and are fighting the rectangle in any case. But we find," she said, relenting with a heart-catching crooked smile, "the customers are reassured if there's a frame. It shows it's *fin*ished; the artist *means* it."

"I'm interested more in the flanges," I said, but she knew already that I was interested in her. I had gone stupid; a mist of a kind had arisen between us. In those benighted days such an interest was considered not an affront but a datum, to be factored into whatever one's life equation was at the time. Jane and I were both in our early thirties, a time for fresh calculations. Back in Buffalo I had survived, with my family, a tumultuous infatuation and an explosive dénouement; in the aftermath I had adjusted downward my estimate of how much happiness I could extract from the world, and of how much I could offer any woman not my wife. I was wised-up and shy. But, then, New York was another world—an infinity of restaurants and apartments and elevator shafts and human appetites. I wasn't due home until late tomorrow night.

"For the flanges," Jane said, after a gawky hesitation and an alarmed stare that for a second burned through the mist, "you maybe need to come into the storage room." There, in a crammed but not totally disorderly clutter of unframed art and unassembled frames, of T-squares and knives and a scarred worktable, we sat on tippy tall stools and each smoked a cigarette.

"What do *you* do, Stan?"

I described my job, as a would-be engineer turned sales-man of alloy extrusions. I described my eight-room house, my three-child family, my two-car garage in Eggertsville, and the new red Toro snow-blower with which I tried to keep a path open through the fabled snows off Lake Erie. "Now tell me about you."

She smoked like someone who had never smoked before, bringing the cigarette to her lips with a flattened hand, the fingers tensely curved backward. She stabbed out the butt in a clunky green ashtray as if she were crushing a stubbornly vital insect. "No time for that, sweetie," she said, dismount-ing from the stool with an awkward hop. Her shoes at the end of her long full-thighed legs were a startling shiny scarlet, like red nails on black fingers. "I hear people out front. Maybe they're stealing the art. I should go encourage them." She added, "I have a child, too. A nine-year-old boy. No husband, no car, no snow-blower, but a dear hopeful child."

This time her hesitation and her stare had a clear import: it was my turn to make a move, and quickly. It was my turn to be awkward. "Would you, would you like to have dinner tonight? Or do you have better things to do? I bet you do."

Somewhat to my disappointment—I foresaw complications—she was not busy. "Sounds good to me," she said, brushing her hair back from one ear in a thoughtful way. "How about to you? You don't sound too sure."

"What about the boy?"

"I'll get a sitter."

"Really? On such short notice?" In Buffalo, sitters were inscrutable pubescent girls, off in a thirteen-year-old's dream world, or else grandmotherly women, widows and spinsters, who were highly valued and had to be signed up weeks in advance. I did feel dubious, but the haze between Jane and me had thickened.

"Really," she insisted. "Eight o'clock too late for you? I'll feed him and tuck him in. Here's the address—it's a walk from here. Don't be shy, Stan. It'll be fun."

Jane lived on the West Side, twenty blocks north of where she worked. That night, or one not long thereafter, I was amazed to discover that a number of cabs were cruising those streets at three in the morning. I had been fearful, stepping out onto Columbus Avenue, drowsily emerged from the warmth of her bed. Our whispers of farewell still hissed in my ears; her last kiss was evaporating under my nose. My whole body felt as defenseless as a slug's. I had left because of the boy, so he wouldn't find me there when he

awoke, and because of my wife, who might have been tele-
phoning the hotel, frantic with some domestic emergency.
Carole had a nervous, clinging streak beneath her practical-
minded aplomb. I had led her into multiple motherhood and
then kept hitting the road.

Now I had my own emergency: the empty straight streets
stretched to vanishing points all around me; a mugger—
did we call them muggers then?—could have been waiting,
switchblade ready, in any of the upright dark doorways,
behind any of the brownstone stairs. But an all-night drugstore gleamed two blocks away, and fits of traffic animated
the avenue. Within a minute or two, a taxi materialized with
its roof light signalling rescue. The driver and I were usually
chatty on these returns to my hotel; he was pleased to have a
fare and my tongue was oiled by sexual triumph and a sense
of escape. Those rides through the almost deserted city
had a clean, clicking feeling: I was back on track. Pulling up
at the hotel, paying the cabdriver, walking in my warm
dishevelment past the noncommittal desk clerk, into the elevator, down the windowless corridor, into the still, expectant
room, I rejoined a self who had been here all along. The bed
was cool and tightly made, with a mint on the pillow.

Sometimes Jane came to my hotel. Once, when I had left
the room dark in anticipation of her arrival, she asked as I let
her in, "Is this where the orgy is?" Another time—the same
time? how many times were there?—we couldn't open the
door when it was time for her to leave. It was absurd and
frightening; an invisible enforcer had trapped me with the
living evidence of my crime. This was after 2:00 a.m., long
past time for Jane to leave the orgy and to send the babysitter home. A woman in the apartment below would sit for
her at short notice. A sisterhood of single New York women
existed, egging each other on in the long-odds mating game.
Men—useful, unattached, heterosexual men—were scarce,

scarcer here than in the hinterlands; Jane taught me this to her disadvantage, for I rarely worried, in the months between my trips to the city, that she would not be there for me, as glamorous and game as ever.

The mystery of the locked room was never completely solved. The moral standards of hotel management in those years of imminent sexual revolution were obscure to me; I stammered guiltily, calling the main desk. For what seemed many minutes of waiting, Jane and I were prisoners together, fully dressed and physically weary. Finally, a black maintenance man turned the latch from the outside with a master key. He fiddled bemusedly with the obdurate inner knob and chatted with us as if we were the most ordinary, consecrated daylight couple who had ever required his expertise. We made a small society, at that odd hour; he and Jane hit it off, especially, vying in theories on the mechanical puzzle. She said, "I thought it might be like a subway turnstile—you needed a token." It was a revelation to me, this wee-hour camaraderie of New Yorkers, and the city's genial way of folding my adultery into its round-the-clock hustle.

Carole and I had met in college—the University of Buffalo, before its SUNY connection. A math major, she was bright, methodical, compact, and rounded. She had thick glasses and thin, serious lips. I saw at a glance that she would be a trustworthy partner and mother to my children. My estimate was sound; she was all I could reasonably ask for in a helpmeet. We both studied too hard for much of a formal courtship; we just palled around for two years and in senior year agreed to get married. So to stop at one of Manhattan's corner flower shops and buy an armful of red roses or lavender gladioli was to play a rôle, that of a swain, for the first time. I played opposite the veteran Italian actress behind the counter, with her faint mustache and frayed sweater and

tightly wound iron-gray bun into which a yellow pencil
had been thrust at a dramatic angle. In the burning lime-
light, all my senses were heightened a notch: I registered
with a feverish keenness the petalled colors massed with
their reflections in the black display window, and the chill
that wafted out of the glass-doored refrigerator where the
cut flowers were stored, and the angry deft gesture with
which my co-star plucked the pencil from the back of her
head and scribbled the receipt before sending me out into
the street with my green-paper cone of blooms. Bearing
flowers enrolled me in the city's anonymous army of lovers.
A few bright doorways up Columbus Avenue, I would stop
at the liquor store for a quart of Wild Turkey—the most
expensive brand of bourbon within my sense of possibilities.
At home Carole and I drank Jim Beam, and not much of it.
But I was somebody else here, a sugar daddy from Singapore. Flowers and liquor—what else could I take Jane to
clothe my gratitude? Sex paid for, however inadequately,
was better—clearer, more naked, more of a rush—than
married sex that we expect to sneak up on us for free. I did
not drop in at the liquor store often enough—four or five
times a year—to warrant a greeting from the dour brothers
who owned it, but after a year I could see something flicker
across their wary faces, a suspicion that they should know
me, that I was familiar. My courtship glow made me stand
out, perhaps. I might have been a young husband, new to
the neighborhood and still dazzled by the delights of
cohabitation.

A surely imaginary happiness bathes my memories. Once,
in January, I stood at Jane's front windows looking down at
the tops of a row of buttonwoods as a slanting wet snow
laid crescents of white on each little round pod, while the
apartment at my back overflowed with the plangent human

pealing of the Swingle Singers performing Bach fugues—a
record Jane had received at Christmas, I didn't ask from
whom—and I was joyful to the point of tears. My body,
wrapped in a loose wool bathrobe of hers, felt stuffed with
the spiritual woolliness of contentment. At my back, just off
the kitchen, she was setting up our breakfast. Paraboloids of
orange juice and a cylinder of marmalade glowed with inner
light. The scent of toasting English muffins intersected the
sight of the diagonal snow adhering to the buttonwood
pods. The morning moment kept overflowing, on and on,
Bach going at it again and again, never getting enough. Jeffrey, Jane's son, was with a friend or his father so that, this
once, we had the apartment to ourselves. I had spent the
night, daring the phone back at the hotel not to ring. Jane
was close enough to my size so that I could wear her blue
robe. I could never have gotten into a robe of Carole's; she
was petite and neat. What I loved in Jane was her excess, her
muchness—the hips so wide she walked with a seesawing
lurch, the cedary hair that was always falling into my face,
the angular downy arms, the legs that stretched to the corners of the bed. It was a single bed; we had slept badly, snor-
ing in each other's faces, dodging elbows.

Her ex-husband was an artist, not successful enough to
supply child support or for me to have heard of him but not
so unsuccessful that he had to abandon an artistic image of
himself. I hated and envied her world of artists—their lofts
and debauches, their self-exemption from the ruck of ordinary labor, their otherworldly charm. Jeffrey, nine and then
ten, was doe-eyed and gravely polite, perhaps because I usually saw him when he was being put to bed, at the moment of
my departure with his mother. His tiny room's one tall window looked south, upon the lights of midtown mounting in
rectangular masses higher and higher—an Arabian Nights

view that made me abjectly grateful to have been granted, a
marauder from upstate, my small illicit purchase upon such
display, such splendor.

Jeffrey was precocious at school, and Jane was proud of
that. Occasionally he and I talked; my impression was of a
sly docility toward me, a guarded hope. His mother's loneli-
ness was the air he breathed, and I gave him a brief change
of air. He was blonder than she, English-looking, with a
pointed chin and pale skin and rosy cheeks; only his owlish brown eyes and black eyebrows gave evidence of a darker
strain, his father's. He had read lots of Tolkien and C. S.
Lewis; at school he was having a little trouble with how to
add unlike fractions. Of the men in the margin of his life I
must have been the only one with a degree in engineering.

"You make the numbers so nicely!" he exclaimed, when I
began to instruct him in common denominators.

"You've got to. If they're not clear they're worse than useless. That kind of '4' you make, with the closed top, looks
too much like a '9.' "

"But, Stan, the '4's in books all are closed like that."

"Books get away with a lot we can't get away with in real
life," I told him, paternally. It was enchanting, somehow, to
be called "Stan" by a child the age of my own children. I was
momentarily a member of this family, but the membership
was woven of angel hair, insubstantial, with none of the
weight of real family ties. I was temporarily magical, to go
with their magic, so precariously poised in mid-air here,
between the tops of the buttonwood trees and the ranks of
burning skyscraper lights.

Jane's apartment was furnished cheaply; unframed out-of-
series prints were tacked to the walls, and instead of end
tables she simply used stacks of art books and catalogues. I
felt unprecedentedly nimble in this apartment, light-footed,
stealthy, stealing happiness from these rooms and then glid-

ing out the door, into the elevator (how loud its doors and gears seemed, in that solidly sleeping building!), and on to the barren streets that with mysterious quickness yielded a roaming cab, its third eye blazing.

Adventures! Adventures with Jane. We had to eat. After the maintenance man finally let us out of my hotel room, we were both famished and found an all-night Automat on East Forty-second Street. It was like entering a Hopper with a Petty girl on my arm. Escorting Jane into any restaurant felt luxurious. We never phoned ahead—I didn't like fencing with the fruity, accented voices at the name places, La Côte Basque and so on—but New York abounded with half-empty no-name restaurants where they were happy to see you; the maître d' beamed at the sight of Jane, in her miniskirt and falling cedar-red hair. I remember a pricy Swedish smorgasbord in the East Fifties, and a steak place with Texas decor and big windows overlooking Third Avenue, and a fish place with wooden tables somewhere south of Washington Square. Broadway plays took too long to waste our precious time together on, but she did lead me to an "underground" movie somewhere in the dreary Thirties, and to a play in the Village about a group of dope addicts sitting around waiting for their "connection" to show up. I kept hugging her during the play; its message of hopelessness, of addiction, seemed to be directed at us, and to enlist us in the scattered troops of rebellion in those pre-Vietnam years. But she pointedly did not respond, as if asserting, while her straying hair tingled against my cheek, that my romantic sense of it all let me off too easily.

The art movie had no plot that I can remember; there was a lot of grainy slow panning and some jumpy surrealistic collage, including a quick, repeated act of fellatio that caused Jane to exclaim softly at my side, "Uh-oh." The act was faked with photographs of a dildo and a young woman's face, not matter-of-factly enacted for the camera as it would have been a few years later. For the time, it was daring, as was Jane when, in bed, not without awkwardness, she startled me by suddenly dipping her head to touch her lips to the tip of my erection, like a small girl yielding to the impulse to bestow a kiss on the bald head of a favorite doll. The kiss was quick and light and seemed to startle her as much as it did me; it remains in my mind an isolated moment, lit by a flower-shop glow—the moist sheltered intimacy, the expectant soft petals. I didn't press her to repeat the gesture; it had derived from an overflow of feeling I was in no position to force. I could take, but I couldn't demand.

What did she get from me? A lesson in chopsticks. We had wandered into a rather overdecorated, underlit Chinese restaurant on Lexington Avenue, with gold wallpaper and royal-blue banquettes. Chopsticks were provided in little paper sheaths, but Jane reached for the knife and fork also set beside the plates. I asked her, "Your other dates let you get away with that?"

She blushed and bristled defensively. "My other dates, as you call them, don't take me to Chinese restaurants that often."

I tried not to be curious about her life in the long stretches when I wasn't there; it would have been painful for me to know too much, and painful for her to confess that there wasn't much to know. "Not classy enough, I suppose," I accused her, defensive in turn. Back in Buffalo, a Chinese meal out was a manageable treat for the kids or an easy way to see the boring couples Carole liked. I told Jane in a gentler voice, "Chinese food and silver shouldn't mix. There's no big trick to it." I unwrapped her chopsticks and took her long, freckled, loose-jointed hand in mine. She seemed

faintly frightened. I saw myself for a second in the mirror
of her female mind: I was a man, frightening, with big hands
that could inflict a bruising blow. Of the chopsticks, I
explained, "You rest one of them here, against that finger, so
the thumb holds it in place, and hold the other between
these two, like a pencil. Feel the mobility? With this pinch-
ing motion you can pick up anything, from a single grain of
rice to a chunk of sweet-and-sour pork."

"I can do it!" she announced, after a while. "This is
wonderful! Oops. Damn."

"Rice is the hardest. Sort of put them together. Chinese
peasants use them like a shovel."

"Over thirty," she said, "and I never thought I could manage the damn things. I'd watch other people twiddling away,
and they seemed so debonair. *Thank* you, Stan."

I accepted her thanks proudly. I doubt whether Jeffrey
really got the hang of common denominators, but I want to
think that to the day she dies Jane can handle chopsticks
because of me.

I am losing her. The mist that arose when we first met,
surrounded by glaring blue scrawls, threatens to swallow all
the details. The chopsticks, the taxicabs in the depths of
night, my excited impersonation of a man buying flowers for
a sweetheart—what else can I remember? We must have
talked, thousands of words, but of what? Our expertise was
in quite different areas, and if we talked too long about
our marriages, we would trip over the fact that hers was
ended and mine was not. Once, when, after a longer absence
than usual, I entered her, she breathed in my ear, "He's
home," which almost unmanned me, it seemed so sad an
untruth. My home was in Eggertsville, with the three children, the ensemble furniture, the Saturday-night dinner
parties, the Sunday-morning men's tennis group for me and

the Methodist choir for Carole. Jane's appeal was exactly that she was *not* home, that she was a splendid elsewhere.

New York City did not miss me; it did not occur to me that she might. Yet, explaining away a weepy mood—Jeffrey had a fever, she did not think she should leave him with Brenda from downstairs, so we sat together in our clothes, in the room with the view of the tops of the buttonwoods— Jane let drop, "Yeah, but you haven't been racing downstairs every day to the mailbox hoping for a letter from Buffalo."

Her letters to me, directed to my office at the plant, embarrassed me, as well as putting a funny look on the face of the department secretary as she delivered one, addressed in Jane's sprawling round handwriting, to my desk. The struggles of the gallery to survive, her glimpse at an opening of Robert Motherwell or some other giant, Jeffrey's progress at school—the details of her world, when I was not there, seemed meagre and unreal. The details of my own might estrange her by painting a life less lonely than hers. In Buffalo I had everything I needed for a life, except for her, my New York girl, tucked into my consciousness like a candy after dinner, like a mint on my pillow. "I have nothing much to say," I told her. "Except that I adore you."

" 'Adore' implies a distance, doesn't it?" Jane had a stern face she reserved for people who came into the gallery just to loiter on a cold day. She clumsily stubbed out her cigarette, smoked down to the scarlet filter, in a fashionably rough clay ashtray on her stack of art books. She had caught Jeffrey's cold and kept clearing her throat.

"You don't want to hear," I assured her, "about which child of mine has had his bicycle stolen or which dog has died."

"I don't?"

"Or how Carole's station wagon had a flat tire doing the

car pool, or how drunk so-and-so got at so-and-so's rather dreadful dinner party."

"This woman you almost left Carole for—you still see her?"

"Althea Wadsworth. Sometimes, at big occasions. We all put a good face on it. Life must go on."

"I suppose that's what it must do, yes."

I was not comfortable with the tug of this conversation and went to the front windows, wondering if this was the last time I would ever see these treetops. To the north, there were few skyscrapers, just a low recession of streets and domestic windows. It might almost have been Buffalo, along Seneca Street.

"For this Althea person, you really put yourself out. You tried to leave Carole for her."

It displeased me that Jane knew these women's names. I suppressed the impulse to explain that I had seen how Althea functioned as a suburban housewife and mother—that I could envision her fitting into Carole's slot. I knew all the furniture she would bring with her. Jane's furniture was impalpable—it was the city itself, the universe of anonymous lights.

"I did, and I swore I'd never try it again. It was too painful, for everybody."

Jeffrey began to cough in the other room—a dry, delicate, only-child cough—and Jane went into him. I heard murmuring as she rubbed his back. She began to sing. I had never heard her sing. She had a sweet voice, reedy but true, with an unforeseeable hillbilly twang to it. "You are my sunshine, my only sunshine," she sang softly to Jeffrey. "You make me happy when skies are gray."

After a while, the boy asleep, she came back to me, and unhurriedly, moving about with the high-haunched ungainly grace of a deer, she took off her clothes. We made love on her foam-rubber sofa, with its shaky chrome legs, and afterwards we ate six toasted bagels and two half-pints of cream cheese. This may have been the last time I slept with her, but I'm not sure. We phased out gradually. The extruded-aluminum business was facing an onslaught of fresh foreign competition—from South Korea and Taiwan, after all we had done for them—and Buffalo became more involving and complicated, both at work and on the social front, and I stopped rigging trips to Manhattan.

Althea and I had been married for close to fifteen years when I saw Jane again, in Rochester. Rochester, of all places, in the middle of winter, at one of the entrances to the downtown mall, where they have the totem pole and the clock with little puppet shows. Christmas was over, and the season's snowfalls had been compressed to a blotchy corrugated ice, hard as iron. Jane was accompanied by a blond child I took for Jeffrey; but of course Jeffrey would be in his twenties, I realized. The boy was tugging at her, against the tilt of her crooked smile, and I could hardly talk, since the old mist between us had arisen, plain as she had become. She had put on weight. Her middle-aged face was round and red beneath a wool knit cap, and she was wearing one of those black quilted winter coats that suburban matrons had taken to wearing as work uniforms. Dog hairs and what looked like a few bits of straw were clinging to it.

"Jane, my God," I said, reeling backward from the firm, even complacent hug she bestowed, through our wraps. "What are you doing here?"

"I live here," she announced. "In Irondequoit, actually. We bought an old farm."

We? I put off exploring that. "How—how long?"

"Oh, ten years. This is Tommy."

"Where's Jeffrey?"

"In Taos, trying to be a painter, the poor darling. God, it's been bliss for me to get away from *art*ists. What selfish boyish shits they all are. Ken works for Kodak—he's a chemist. We met the way you and I did—he was trying to sell the gallery some process."

"Not a process, I just wanted to look at flanges. But can you stand it, Jane, out of New York? The city, I mean."

She put a great black-mittened hand on mine, and even through the wool-lined leather I felt the rightness of her touch, the velvety rightness come back to me, a texture of youth, when the world still bristles with options. I felt in her presence the fear of death a man feels with a woman who once opened herself to him and is available no more.

"I hated New York, I was dying to get out of it. You knew that, Stan. It's what made you shy."

"I—"

But the strange child was tugging her toward some keenly imagined pleasure within the mall, and her hand was yanked awkwardly away. Flipping that hand in mid-air, she urged, "Don't say a thing, sweetie. Be happy for me is all you have to do."

My Father on the Verge of Disgrace

It FILTERED even into my childhood dreams, the fear. The fear that my father would somehow fall from his precarious ledge of respectability, a ledge where we all stood with him. "We all"—his dependents, my mother, her parents, myself. The house we lived in was too big for us: my grandfather had bought it in 1922, when he felt prosperous enough to retire. Within the decade, the stock-market crash took all his savings. He sat in one corner of the big house, the little "sunroom" that looked toward the front yard, the hedge, and the street with its murmuring traffic. My grandmother, bent over and crippled by arthritis, hobbled about in the kitchen and out into the back yard, where she grew peas and kept chickens. My mother had her nook upstairs, at a little desk with wicker sides, where she did not like to be interrupted, and my father was generally out somewhere in the town. He was a tall, long-legged man who needed to keep moving. The year I was born, he had lost his job, as salesman in the mid-Atlantic territory for a line of quality English china. Only after three years—anxious years for him, but for me just the few buried smells and visions retained by my infant memory—did he succeed in getting another job, as a high-school teacher. It was as a schoolteacher that I always knew him. Wearing a suit, his shirt pocket holding a pack of cigarettes and a mechanical pencil and a fountain pen, he loomed to me as a person of eminence in the town; it was this sense of his height that led, perhaps, to my fear that he would somehow topple.

One of my dreams, borrowing some Depression imagery from the cartoons in the newspaper, had him clad in a barrel and, gray-faced, being harried down the Town Hall steps by the barking apparitions of local officialdom. The crowd began to throw things, and my attempt at explaining, at pleading for him, got caught in my throat. In this present day of strip malls and towns that are mere boundaries on a developer's map, it is hard to imagine the core of authority that existed then in small towns, at least in the view of a child—the power of righteousness and enforcement that radiated from the humorless miens of the central men. They were not necessarily officials; our town was too small to have many of those. And the police chief was a perky, comically small man who inspired fear in no one, not even in first-graders as he halted traffic to let them cross the street to the elementary school. But certain local merchants, a clergyman or two, the undertaker whose green-awninged mansion dominated the main intersection, across from a tavern and a drugstore, not to mention the druggist and the supervising principal of the school where my father taught, projected a potential for condemnation and banishment.

To have this power, you had to have been born in the town, or at least in the locality, and my father had not been. His accent, his assumptions were slightly different. This was

Pennsylvania, and he was from New Jersey. My mother came from the area, and she may have married my father in hopes of escaping it. But the land of six decades ago had more gravity than it does now; it exerted a grip. Fate, or defeat, returned my parents to live in my grandfather's big house, a house where only I, growing up day by day, felt perfectly at home.

I was proud of my schoolteacher father. If his suit was out of press, and his necktie knotted awry, I was too new to the world to notice. He combed his hair back and, in the style of his generation, parted it near the middle. In our kitchen, he would bolt his orange juice (squeezed on one of those ribbed glass sombreros and then poured off through a strainer) and grab a bite of toast (the toaster a simple tin box, a kind of little hut with slit and slanted sides, that rested over a gas burner and browned one side of the bread, in stripes, at a time), and then he would dash, so hurriedly that his necktie flew back over his shoulder, down through our yard, past the grapevines hung with buzzing Japanese-beetle traps, to the yellow brick building, with its tall smokestack and wide playing fields, where he taught. Though the town had some hosiery and hat factories tucked around in its blocks of row houses, the high school was the most impressive building on my horizon. To me it was the center of the universe. I enjoyed the gleams of recognition that fell to me from my father's high visibility. His teaching colleagues greeted me on the street with a smile; other adults seemed to know me and included me in a sort of ironical forbearance. He was not a drinker—his anxious stomach was too tender for that—but he had the waywardly sociable habits of a drinker. He needed people, believed in their wisdom and largesse, as none of the rest of us who lived in the house did: four recluses and an extrovert. Imitating my mother, I early developed a capacity to entertain myself, with paper and the images it could be made to bear. When school—the elementary school, at the other end of town, along the main street—took me into its classes, I felt, in relation to my classmates, timid.

He called me "young America," as if I were more bumptious than I was. He pushed me about the town with a long stick he had made, whose fork gripped the back of my red wagon, so that all I had to do was sit in it and steer. No more births followed mine. My bedroom was a narrow back room, with a bookshelf and some framed illustrations, by Vernon Grant, of nursery rhymes. It overlooked the back yard and adjoined my parents' bedroom. I could hear them talk at night; even when the words were indistinct, the hiss of unhappiness, of obscure hot pressures, came through the walls. *"That son of a bitch,"* my father would say, of some man whose name I had missed. *"Out to get me,"* I would hear. Who could this enemy be, I would wonder, while my mother's higher, more rhythmic voice would try to seal over the wound, whatever it was, and I would be lulled into sleep, surrounded by my toys, my Big Little Books, my stacks of drawings crayoned on the rough dun-colored paper supplied at school, and the Vernon Grant figures presiding above the bookshelf—a band of cheerful, long-nosed angels who lived in giant shoes and tumbled downhill. Paper, I felt, would protect me. Sometimes in my parents' room there were quarrels, stifled sobs from my melodious mother and percussive rumbling from my father; these troubles were like a thunderstorm that whipped and thumped the house for half an hour and then rolled off into the sky to the east, toward Philadelphia.

One center of trouble, I remember, was a man called Otto Werner, which Otto pronounced as if the "W" were a "V." Among the Pennsylvania Germans, he was exceptionally German, with a toothbrush mustache, a malicious twinkle in his eye, and an erect, jerky way of carrying himself. He, too, was a schoolteacher, but not in our town's system. He and my father, on weekends and in the summer, travelled to Philadelphia, an hour and a half away, to accumulate credits toward a master's degree. Having a master's would improve my father's salary by a few sorely needed dollars.

The first scandal that attached itself to Otto concerned his standing on the steps of the Furness Library at the University of Pennsylvania and shouting, "*Heil*, Hitler!" The United States was not yet in the war, and a pro-German Bund openly met in our local city of Alton, but still it was an eccentric and dangerous thing to do. Otto was, my father admitted, "a free spirit." However, he owned a car, and we did not. We once did—a green Model A that figures in my earliest memories—but somewhere in the Thirties it disappeared. In a town so compact one could walk anywhere within fifteen minutes, and in a region webbed with trolley tracks and train tracks, the deprivation did not seem radical. Once the war came, those who owned cars couldn't buy gas anyway.

A worse scandal than "*Heil*, Hitler!" had to do with a girl at the high school. My father carried a few notes from Otto to her, and it turned out they were love notes, and he was aiding and abetting the corruption of a minor. The girl's parents got involved, and members of the school board were informed. Not only could my father get fired, as I understood it: he could go to jail for his part in this scandal. As I lay in my bed at night I could hear my parents talking in a ragged, popping murmur like the noise of something frying; I could feel the heat, and my father twisting in his agony, and the other adults in the house holding their breath. Had there been trysts, and had my father carried the notes that arranged them? It was like him; he was always doing people unnecessary favors. Once he walked out into a snowstorm to go and apologize to a boy in one of his classes with whom he had been impatient, or sarcastic. "I hate sarcasm," he said.

"Everybody in this part of the world uses it, but it hurts like hell to be on the receiving end. Poor kid, I thought he stunk the place up to get my goat, but upon sober reflection I believe it was just one more case of honest stupidity." His subject was chemistry, with its many opportunities for spillage, breakage, smells, and small explosions.

The scandal with the girl somehow died away. Perhaps the notes he carried were innocent. Perhaps he persuaded the principal and the school board that he, at least, was innocent. There had been a romance, because within a year or two the girl, graduated now, married Otto. The couple moved to the Southwest but occasionally would visit my parents. When my mother became a widow, living alone in a farmhouse ten miles from the town, the couple would visit her, as part of their annual Eastern pilgrimage. Though fifteen years younger, Mrs. Werner went plump early, and her hair turned white, so the age difference became less and less scandalous. They had bought a Winnebago and would pull up alongside the barn and Otto would limp across the yard to greet my mother merrily, that twinkle still in his eye. My mother would be merry in turn, having forgotten, it seemed, all the woe he once brought us. In trying to recall the heat in the old house, the terror he had caused, I have forgotten the most interesting thing about him: he had only one leg. The other was a beige prosthesis that gave him his jerky walk, a sharp hitch as if he were tossing something with his right hip. Remembering this makes him seem less dangerous: how could the world ever punish a one-legged man for shouting "*Heil*, Hitler!" or for falling in love with a teen-ager from another school system?

The country ran on dimes and quarters. A hamburger cost ten cents, and I paid ten cents to get into the movie house, until a war tax made it eleven. The last year of the war, a month before V-E Day and Hitler's vanishing—poof!—

from his underground bunker, I turned thirteen, and old Mrs. Naftziger in the little glass booth somehow knew it. An adult ticket cost twenty-seven cents, and that was too much for me to go twice a week.

The economics of my grandfather's household seemed simple: my father brought home his pay every other week in a brown envelope, and the money was dumped in a little red-and-white recipe box that sat on top of the icebox. Anybody who needed money fished it out of the box; each lunchtime I was allowed six cents, a nickel and a penny, to buy a Tastykake on the way back to elementary school. My grandfather did the packaged-food shopping at Tyse Segner's store, a few houses away. Tyse, who lived in the back rooms and upstairs with his wife, was a man of my grandfather's generation—a rather ill-tempered one, I thought, considering all the candy he had behind his counter and could eat for free whenever he wanted. My mother, usually, bought fresh meat and vegetables at Bud Hoffert's Acme, two blocks away, past the ice plant, up on Second Street. Bud wore rimless glasses and a bloody apron. My grandmother did the cooking but never shopped; nor did my father—he just brought home, as he said, "the bacon." The little tin recipe box never became so empty that I had to do without my noontime Tastykake. I moved a kitchen chair next to the icebox to stand on while I fished the nickel and the penny from the box, beneath a clutter of folded dollars and scattered quarters. When the tin bottom began to show, more coins and bills somehow appeared, to tide us over, and these, it slowly dawned on me, were borrowed from the high-school sports receipts.

My father was in charge of them, as an extracurricular duty: at football games he would sit at a gap in the ropes, selling tickets and making change from a flat green box whose compartments were curved to let your fingers scoop up the coins. At basketball games he would sit with the box at a little table just inside the school's front portals, across from the glass case of silver trophies and around the corner from the supervising principal's office. The green box would come home with him, many nights, for safekeeping. The tickets fascinated me— great wheels of them, as wide as dinner plates but thicker. They came in two distinct colors, blue for adults and orange for students, and each ticket was numbered. It was another kind of money. Each rectangle of the thin, tightly coiled cardboard possessed, at the right time, a real value, brought into play by a sports event; money and time and cardboard and people's desire to *see* were magically interwoven. My father was magical, converting into dollars and quarters and dimes the Tuesday- and Friday-night basketball crowds and the outdoor crowd that straggled out of the town's streets onto the football field on Saturday afternoon. (It was easy to sneak under the ropes, but many grown-ups didn't bother, and paid.) The tickets, numbered in the hundreds, were worth nothing until he presided at his little table. He always made the balance right when he got his paycheck, or so he assured my mother. She had begun to get alarmed, and her alarm spread to me.

My memories of their conversations, the *pressure* of them, have me leaning my face against the grain of the wooden icebox, a zinc-lined cabinet whose dignity dominated our kitchen as it majestically digested, day after day, a succession of heavy ice blocks fetched in a straw-lined truck and carried with tongs into the house by a red-cheeked man with a leather apron down his back, to ward off the wet and the chill. I could feel the coldness on my cheek, through the zinc and oak, as my parents' faces revolved above me and their voices clung to my brain.

"Embezzlement," my mother said, a word I knew only from the radio. "What good will you be to any of us in jail?"

"I make it square, right to the penny. Square on the button, every other week, when I get my envelope."

"Suppose Danny Haas some week decides to deposit the receipts on a Friday instead of a Monday? He'd ask and you'd be short."

Danny Haas, I knew, taught senior-high math and headed up the school athletics program. A short man who smoked cigars and wore suits with broad stripes, he was one of the righteous at the town's core. My tall father and he some-times clowned together, because of their height discrepancy, but it was clear to me who had the leverage, the connections, the power to bring down.

"He won't, Lucy," my father was saying. Whenever he used my mother's name, it was a sign that he wanted to end the conversation. "Danny's like all these Dutchmen, a slave to habit. Anyway, we're not talking Carnegie-Mellon bucks here, we're talking relative peanuts." How much, indeed? A ten-dollar bill, in those days, looked like a fortune to me; I never saw a twenty, not even when the recipe box was fullest.

"Nobody will think it's peanuts if it's missing."

My father became angry, as much as he ever did. "What can I do, Lucy? We live poor as dump dogs anyway." The phrase "dump dogs" had to be one he had brought from his other life, when he had lived in another state and been a boy like me. He went on, venting grievances seldom expressed in my hearing. "We've got a big place here to heat. We can't all go naked. The kid keeps growing. My brown suit is wearing out. Mom does what she can in her garden, but I've got five mouths to feed." He called my grandmother "Mom" and exempted her, I felt, from the status of pure burden. My mother's work at her wicker desk produced no money, my grandfather in his pride had bought too big a house, and I— I didn't even go out and shovel snow for neighbors in a storm, because I was so susceptible to colds. My father was warming to his subject. "Count 'em—five! *Nihil ex nihilo,* Dad used to say." "Dad" was his own father, dead before I was born. "You don't get something for nothing," he translated. "There are no free rides in this life."

My mother feebly used the word "economize," another radio word, but even I could feel it was hopeless; how could I go without my Tastykake when nobody else in my class was that poor? My father had to go on stealing from the school, and would someday be chased in his barrel down the Town Hall steps.

During the war things eased a bit. Men were scarce, and he got summer jobs that did not aggravate his hernia; he was made a timekeeper for a railroad work crew. The tracks were humming and needed to be kept up. In the history books our time in the war seems short: less than four years from Pearl Harbor to V-J Day. Yet it seemed to go on forever, while I inched up through the grades of elementary school. It became impossible to imagine a world without the war, without the big headlines and the ration tokens and coupons and the tin-can drives and Bing Crosby and Dorothy Lamour selling War Bonds at rallies. I reached seventh grade, a junior-high grade, housed in the grand yellow brick building where my father taught.

I was too young for chemistry, but there was no missing his high head and long stride in the halls. Sharing the waxed, locker-lined halls with him all day, being on his work premises, as it were, did not eradicate my anxiety that he would be brought low. The perils surrounding him became realer to me. We students filled the halls with a ruthless, trampling sound. My father was not a good disciplinarian; he was not Pennsylvania-German enough, and took too little pleasure in silence and order. Entire classes, rumor reached me from the upper grades, were wasted in monologues in which he tried to impart the lessons that life had taught him—you don't get something for nothing, there are no free rides.

These truths were well illustrated in the workings of chemistry, so perhaps he wasn't as far off the point as the students thought. They played a game, of "getting him going," and thus sparing themselves classwork for the day. He would suddenly throw a blackboard eraser up toward the ceiling and with a boyish deftness catch it, saying, "What goes up must come down." He told the momentarily silenced students, "You're on top of Fools' Hill now, but you'll come down the other side, I promise you." He did not conceal from them his interest in the fruitful possibilities of disorder; so many great chemical discoveries, after all, were accidents. He loved chemistry. "Water is the universal solvent," I often heard him pronounce, as if it were a truly consoling formula, like "This, too, will pass away." Who is to say his message did not cut through the classroom confusion—the notes being passed, the muttered asides of the class clown, the physical tussles at the rear of the room?

He was the faculty clown, to my discomfort. His remarks in assembly always got the students laughing, and, in the spring, in the annual faculty-assembly program, he participated in a, to me, horrifying performance of the Pyramus and Thisbe episode of *A Midsummer Night's Dream*. Gotten up as a gawky, dirndl-clad, lipsticked Thisbe, in a reddish-blond wig with pigtails, my father climbed a short stepladder to reach the chink in the Wall. The Wall was played by the thickset football coach, Tank Geiger, wearing a football helmet and a sheet painted to resemble masonry.

I had noticed in the privacy of our home how my father's legs, especially where his stockings rubbed, were virtually hairless compared with those of other men. Now the sight of his hairless legs, bare for all to see, as he mounted the ladder—the students around me howling at every mincing step he took upward—made me think his moment to topple had come.

Mr. Geiger held up at arm's height a circle-forming thumb and forefinger to represent the chink in the wall; on the opposite side of the wall, little Mr. Haas climbed his ladder a step higher than my father, to put his face on the same level. "O, kiss me," he recited, "through the hole of this vile wall." Mr. Geiger mugged in mock affront, and the auditorium rocked. My father, in his high Thisbe voice, answered, "I kiss the wall's hole, not your lips at all," and his and Mr. Haas's faces slowly met through the third teacher's fingers. The screams of disbelieving hilarity around me made my ears burn. I shut my eyes. This had to be ruinous, I thought. This was worse than any of my dreams.

But the next day my father loped through the halls with his head high, his hair parted in the middle as usual, in his usual shiny suit, and school life continued. "Burning," went another of his chemical slogans, "destroys nothing. It just shuffles the molecules."

When he was not in his classroom, I discovered, he was in the boiler room. There was a faculty room, with a long table, where the teachers could sit and rest in an idle class period; but they couldn't smoke there, and many of the male teachers took their time off in the boiler room, a great two-story chamber beneath the towering smokestack. A subterranean passage led into it from the school basement, past the woodworking shop, but as a mere student, a seventh-grader, I only entered, in search of my father, from the outside. You crossed a stretch of concrete enlivened by a few basketball backboards fastened flat onto the bricks, opened a resistant metal door, and stepped, with a hollow sound, onto the landing at the head of a flight of studded steel stairs. In front of you, across a dizzying gap, were the immense coal-burning furnaces that warmed the school. You could see the near furnace take a great sliding gulp of pea coal from its hopper, and the mica viewing-portals shudder with orange incandescence, and bundles of asbestos-wrapped steam pipes snake across the ceiling. Dwarfed by the downward perspective, a few male teachers sat and smoked around a card table, in company with the school janitors.

His coat off, and the full length of the parting in his hair visible, my father looked youthfully happy, sunk to the concrete bottom of this warm volume of space. The rising heat intensified my blush of shyness as I descended, breaching the male sanctuary with my message. Why I was intruding I have forgotten, but I remember receiving a genial welcome, as if I were already one of these men who had filled the glass ashtrays to overflowing and whose coffee cups had left a lace of brown circles on the card-table top. As a teacher's child I was privileged to peek behind the formal stage-set of education's daily theatre. It was a slight shock to see, on the stained table, a deck of worn pinochle cards, held together by a rubber band. Teachers were human. I was expected to become, eventually, one of them.

At the war's end, we moved from the house that was too big to a farmhouse, ten miles away, that was too small. It was my mother's idea of economizing. The antique small-town certainties I had grown up among were abruptly left behind. No more wood icebox, no more tin toaster, no more Vernon Grant nursery rhymes framed above my bed, no more simply running down through the yard to the high school. My father and I were thrown together in a state of daily exile, getting into the car—we had to acquire a car—before the frost had left the windshield and returning, many nights, after dusk, our headlights the only ones on the pitted dirt road home. He still took the ticket money at the basketball games, and, as another extracurricular duty, coached the swimming team, which, since the school had no pool, practiced at the YMCA in Alton's dingy and menacing downtown. The ten-year-old car we acquired kept giving us adventures: flat tires, broken axles, fearful struggles to put on tire chains at the base of a hill in the midst of a snowstorm. We sometimes didn't make it home, and walked and hitch-hiked to shelter—the homes of other teachers, or what my father cheerfully called "fleabag" hotels. We became, during those years of joint commuting, a kind of team—partners in peril, fellow-sufferers on the edge of disaster. It was dreadful and yet authentic to be stuck in a stalled car with only four dollars between us, in the age before ATMs. It was—at least afterwards, in the hotel, where my father had successfully begged the clerk to call Danny Haas to vouch for us—bliss, a rub against basic verities, an instance of survival.

I stood in sardonic, exasperated silence during his conversations with hotel clerks, garage mechanics, diner waitresses, strangers on the street, none of whom were accustomed to encountering such a high level of trust. It was no mistake that he had wound up in education; he believed that everyone had something to teach him. His suppliant air humiliated me, but I was fourteen, fifteen; I was at his mercy, and he was at the mercy of the world. I saw him rebuffed and misunderstood. Flecks of foam would appear at the corners of his mouth as he strove to communicate; in my helpless witnessing I was half blinded by impatience and what now seems a fog of love, a pity bulging toward him like some embarrassing warpage of my own face.

He enjoyed human contact even at its least satisfactory, it slowly came to me. "I just wanted to see what he would come up with," he would explain after some futile tussle with, say, the policeman in charge of the municipal garage to which our non-starting car had been towed, parked as it had been in a loading zone by the railroad platform; the cop refused to grasp the distinction between my father's good intentions and the car's mechanical misbehavior. "I used to land in the damnedest little towns," he would tell me, of his days selling china. "In upstate New York, West Virginia, wherever, you'd just get off the train with your sample case and go into any store where you saw china and try to talk them into carrying your line, which usually cost a bit more than the lines they had. You never knew what would happen. Some of them, in these dumps at the back of nowhere, would come up with the most surprising orders—tall orders. This was before the Depression hit, of course. I mean, it hit in '29, but there was a grace period before it took hold. And then you were born. Young America. Your mother and I, it knocked us for a loop, we had never figured on ourselves as parents. I don't know why not—it happens all the time. Making babies is the number-one priority for human nature. When I'm standing up there trying to pound the periodic table into their jiggling heads I think to myself, 'These poor devils, they just want to be making babies!' "

My own developing baby-making yen took the form, first, of learning to smoke. You couldn't get anywhere, in the high-school society of the late Forties, without smoking. I had bought a pack—Old Golds, I think, because of the doubloons—at the Alton railroad station, while my father was coaching the swimming team. Though the first drags did, in his phrase, knock me for a loop, I stuck with it; my vagabond life as his satellite left me with a lot of idle time in luncheonette booths. One winter morning when I was fifteen, I asked him if I could light up a cigarette in the car on the way to school. He himself had stopped, on his doctor's advice. But he didn't say no to me, and, more than thirty years after I, too, quit, I still remember those caustic, giddying drags mixed with the first grateful whiffs of warmth from the car heater, while the little crackling radio played its medley of farm reports and Hit Parade tunes. His tacit permission, coming from a schoolteacher, would have been viewed, we both knew, as something of a disgrace. But it was my way of becoming a human being, and part of being human is being on the verge of disgrace.

Moving to the country had liberated us both, I see now, from the small-town grid and those masters of righteousness. The shopping fell to us, and my father favored a roadside grocery store that was owned and run, it was rumored, by a former Alton gangster. Like my father, Arty Callahan was tall, melancholy, and slightly deaf; his wife was an overweight, wisecracking woman whose own past, it was said, had been none too savory. My father loved them, and loved the minutes of delay their store gave him on the return to our isolated country home. Both Mr. and Mrs. Callahan took him in the right way, it seemed to me, with not too much of either amusement or gravity; they were, all three, free spirits. While he talked to them, acting out, in gestures and phrases that had become somewhat stylized, his sense of daily peril, I would sit at a small Formica-topped table next to the magazine rack and leaf through *Esquire*, looking for Vargas girls. I would sneak a look at Arty Callahan's profile, so noncomittally clamped over his terribly false teeth, and wonder how many men he had killed. The only gangsterish thing he did was give me ten dollars—a huge amount for an hour's work—for tutoring his son in algebra on Saturdays, when I was old enough to drive the car there.

We had traded in our car for a slightly newer and more dependable one, though still a pre-war model. By the time I went off to college I no longer feared—I no longer dreamed—that my father would be savaged by society. He was fifty by then, a respectable age. Living his life beside him for five years, I had seen that his flirtation with disgrace was only that, not a ruinous infatuation. Nothing but death could topple him, and even that not very far, not in my mind.

The Cats

WHEN MY MOTHER DIED, I inherited eighty acres of Pennsylvania and forty cats. Eighty-two point five acres, to be exact; the cats were beyond precise counting. They seethed in a mewing puddle of fur at the back door, toward five o'clock, when they could hear her inside the kitchen turning the clunky handle of the worn-out can opener that jutted from the doorframe, beside the sweating refrigerator. One Christmas, when she was in her seventies, I had bought her a new can opener, but in time it too went dull and wobbly under its burden of use; I thriftily wondered whether or not it would last her lifetime. In her eighties, she as well was wearing out, as each of my visits to the farmhouse made clear. Walking to the mailbox and feeding the cats were the sole exertions she could still perform—she who had performed so many, from her girlhood of horse-riding and collegiate hockey-playing to the days when, moving her family to this isolated farm, she had led us by working like a man, wielding the chain saw and climbing the extension ladder and swinging herself jubilantly up into the wide tractor seat.

She had been born here, in the age of mule-drawn plows. Neither my father nor I had understood her wish to return to this wearying place of work, weeds, bugs, heat, mud, and wildlife. She had led us in imposing some order—renovating the old stone farmhouse, repairing the barn, planting rows of strawberries and asparagus and peas, mowing a lawn back into the shadow of the woods. But, after I moved away and my father died, the fertile wilderness threatened to reclaim everything. Even the windowsills, the next owner of the house discovered, were rotten and teeming with termites and wood lice. From inside the attic, the shingle roof looked like a starry sky. Not only did my mother allow mice and flying squirrels to nest in the house, she fed them sunflower seeds—whose shells, the new owner discovered, tumbled by the peck from their caches in the woodwork. The house in my mother's last years smelled of stacked newspapers that never made it to the barn, and of cat-food cans in paper bags, and of damp dog. Her overfed dog, Josie, was going lame along with her mistress; she never got any exercise. It was pathetic, how happy old Josie was to accompany me to the barn with the papers, and out to our mountain of tin in the woods with the loathsome cans.

Was it my imagination, or did my mother hum as she revolved the handle, like some primitive, repetitive musical instrument? She emptied one gelatinous cylinder of cat food after another into the set of old cake tins that served the cats as dinnerware on the cement back porch. Feeding these half-feral animals amused and pleased her—quite improperly, I thought. Their mounting numbers seemed to me a disaster, which grew worse every time I paid a filial visit, in spite of the merciful inroads of various feline diseases and occasional interventionary blasts from the shotguns of interested neighbors. Some neighbors threatened to report her to the humane society, and others, furtively, dropped off unwanted kittens in the night.

Being my mother's son, I could follow her reasoning right into this quagmire. If you didn't feed the cats, they would eat all the birds. She loved birds, that was why she had begun to feed the cats. Sitting right in the house with its closed windows, talking away on the sofa, she would cock her head and say, "The towhee is upset about something," or, "The mockingbird is telling a joke," or, at night, coming into my room in her white nightgown, her eyes going wide as if scaring a child, "Listen to Mr. Whipporwill."

In deference to my asthmatic tendencies she had never let the cats in the house, but on the day after she died they could hear me through the screen door as I churned away with the can opener. I spoke aloud to them, much as she had. "I know, I know," I said. "You're ravenous. The lady who used to feed you is dead. I'm just her son, her only child. I don't live here, I live in New Jersey, I teach Eurolit at Rutgers, I have a four-bedroom house, an elegant wife called Evelyn, and two grown children, one of them with a child of her own. I don't want to be here, I never did. And if you can think of a better place, go to it, because, my fine feline friends, *the dole is ending*. The cat food is down to its last case, and I'm here for just two more days. What are you going to do then? Beats me—it's a real problem, frankly. Well, you shouldn't have gotten sucked into the system."

When I put the brimming cake tins, which smelled disagreeably of horse meat and pulverized fish, down on the bare cement, the cat bodies clustered around them like the petals of a fur flower. Yet the older cats managed, in the skirmish, to make way for the kittens among them. The calico kittens had mottled, wide-browed faces like pansies. The black-and-whites suggested Rorschach tests, or maps of a simpler planet than ours. My mother used to name the cats that came to the porch, and would say of one, "Isabel is a rather lackadaisical mother," or of a wary, beat-up piebald tom, "Jeffrey has a limp today. His boots must pinch."

The cats that stayed in the barn didn't earn names. When I opened the top half of a stall door, light glinted from eyes in the straw as if from bits of pale glass, and a violent slither sent several cats squirming under the partition into the next stall. The pan I set down would be empty, though, an hour later. The barn cats paid for their shyness with relatively dismal lives; they were prone to the diseases of the inbred, and a probe of the straw, left over from the days when cows bedded here, would turn up a dried cat corpse—a matted pelt as stiff as a piece of leather, the dead animal's head fixed in an eyeless snarl.

Toward the end, my mother had been too frail to make it down to feed the barn cats, so my pan was only half consumed the first night. The barn cats that had not perished or fled had become porch cats. "What are we going to *do*?" I asked the prowling animals as I returned from the barn in the early-September dusk. "I can't give up my whole civilized life just to keep feeding you ingrates."

Moving here when I was a boy had indeed felt like the loss of civilization. No phone, no electricity, no plumbing: a terrible regress. Amish workmen came and hammered snug a bright cedar-shingle roof and rather nicely built in the living room what none of the house's previous inmates had needed—a bookcase. In time plumbers came and rendered the privy obsolete, and the electric company marched its tall creosoted poles down through the old orchard. Television entered the house, and instead of listening to weather reports and corn prices and country music on the Alton radio station we were watching the Philadelphia news, first in black-and-white and then in color. But I could never shake my impression that the farm was a trap, set backward in time, from which my clear duty was to escape.

· · ·

I asked my neighbor to the south, Dwight Potteiger, "What shall I do about all the cats?"

He grows sweet corn and snap beans for market and is second in charge of the township school-bus fleet. He confided to me, "I used to ask Irma, 'What's David going to do, in case you pass on, with all the cats?' She'd say, so serene-like, 'Oh, Davey will find a way. He always has. He's kept me here in style for twenty years.' "

She had become a widow in her sixties. My contributions to her upkeep, added to my father's pension and their savings, had been barely adequate and, now that she was dead, seemed quite niggardly. Dwight's remarks were also irritating in that, though Irma had been her name, she had never much liked it and had resented people's calling her by it. When I once asked her what she did want to be called, she looked offended. *"You,"* she said, "may call me 'Mother.' "

"She had a way of exaggerating," I said.

"Well, now, one thing she didn't exaggerate any was the size of that herd of cats. I can't imagine what-all money she put into cat food. This last year or two, she'd call me up after shopping, and I'd go carry the cases for her into the kitchen."

"Thank you," I said. Dwight was the son I should have been.

"A week or so, she'd have another trunkful to lug in." Was he airing a bottled-up grievance, or trying to bring her back to life for me?

As apologetically as I could, I said, "They were company for her, of a sort."

"They were stark wild," Dwight said. "If I'd show up in the evening, they'd scatter off the porch like they'd never seen a man with a beard before." His beard had alarmed me, too, when he first began to grow it—in this part of the country beards were left to Amishmen and to ancestors in stiff-leaved photograph albums. This beard had a surprising amount of red in it, among bristles of gray and brown. It gave its wearer a mischievous-looking authority, and seemed to amplify his voice.

"She began to feed them, you know," I wearily explained, "to keep them from eating the birds."

He chuckled. "That was the theory, I know from her own lips. But I used to tell her, 'Irma, I still wouldn't say your place here is any paradise for our fine-feathered friends.' She didn't appreciate my saying that. Then she'd motion me to be quiet and say, 'Listen! There's the mockingbird, thanking me.'" He laughed at that, or at the accuracy of his imitation.

"But—" I shifted my weight, my mother having been made real enough for me for the moment.

He went on, beaming in his beard, "I know for a fact she lost a couple nests of swallows, when the cats figured out how to climb the old stable doors. Barn swallows are hard to discourage, but Irma's finally did stop coming back."

I hurried on, away from such sadness. "My question is, Dwight, what do I do about them? The cats. I can't just leave them to starve in the landscape."

I was begging, he could see. Though I knew he thought it, he did not ask, "Why not?" He was indulging my fancies, as he had indulged my mother's.

"I have to get back to New Jersey," I said, "after I see the lawyer in town and the pastor up at the church and the undertaker again."

Now he shifted his weight, standing there. "Well, I could take the shotgun and go over at suppertime, when they gather on the porch. That would take out a few, and then the others might get the clue and skedaddle. If you'd like, I could ask Adam to come down with his woodchuck rifle and we'll run a pincer operation. We need owner's permission, but you're giving that, isn't that right?"

"I sure am. We have to do *some*thing." Adam Schwab was the neighbor to the north, a plump orchard-keeper with a multitude of children and now grandchildren. We were, we three proprietors, about the same age, in our late fifties. They had been boys here when we moved. I had tried playing with them, but they had had stunted ball-handling skills. Their opaque, slow-moving earthiness had frightened me— reminded me of death.

"I would be *very* grateful," I emphasized, and in my own ears my voice sounded citified, weak, patronizing.

Dwight said, "We don't want you worrying, over there with all those other smart folks at Rutgers." I could not accept my neighbor's favor without submitting to his needle. My mother, once my father had ceased to negotiate for her, had shown a good grasp of these country transactions: a little "kidding" for every kindness. She rented fields to her neighbors, and they helped her out in blizzards and mechanical crises. If she could not stay on the land, it would likely go under to a developer, and the neighborhood would be changed forever, with septic tanks and fast traffic and higher taxes and a lowered water table. It had suited me, too, to keep her on her farm, out of my life. I had begun to worry, though, how she would survive this coming winter. She took any decision out of my hands by dropping dead at the kitchen sink, frying herself a pork chop while the Channel 4 evening-news team was chattering in the living room.

Next morning, as I fed them, I told the cats, "Eat up, sweeties—your days are numbered." I had half expected to have rifle shots ring out in my sleep, but the day broke still and dewy. The cement porch was decorated with wet paw prints. A continent of gray cloud was moving up into the sky beyond the telephone poles and the surviving orchard trees. When we moved here, there had been a pump on this porch, and all our water had been drawn up into pots and buckets. At first, it had been a challenge to my strength to work the metal handle through the first dry shoves, before the water began to flow. By the time we got plumbing and an electric pump, the action had become as automatic as turning on a faucet. Like turning the can-opener handle, pumping had its own catchy rhythm, its mechanical song.

My mother had set out a few potted geraniums at the corners of the porch and hung wind chimes from an overhead hook. She had seen them in one of the innumerable catalogues she received, and had ordered them; the idea amused her. It was a fortunate gift in life, it occurred to me, to be easily amused. These chimes, and inquisitive scratchings from inside the walls, had not kept me from sleeping, though I had feared they would. The day's appointments clarified my future: I would get back to New Brunswick by nighttime and in two more days would bring my family here for my mother's funeral, with a U-Haul truck to take away what of her furniture we decided not to give to the auction house. Heading up the road with Josie in the car, I swung into the Schwabs' and asked Adam if he would keep an eye on the house. He and his wife live in a little new ranch house close to the road; his parents still live in the sandstone house, a twin to my mother's, down by the barn that he has turned into a fancy fruit outlet. He smiled as he said he would, implying that it wouldn't be necessary. This part of the world might be changing, but people didn't yet go around robbing the houses of the recently dead.

"I really appreciate," I said, "your helping Dwight shoot the poor cats."

He looked puzzled. "I haven't heard any about that, but

it's I guess not so big a problem," he said, as if he were reassuring my mother that he could get her tractor started.

When, two days later, at dusk, my family arrived in a station wagon and I in a lumbering, half-orange rental truck, the number of cats gathered on the back porch seemed no smaller than it had been, though visibly more frantic. They yowled upward, showing their curved fangs, their arched rough tongues, the rosy membranes of their throats. A few kittens were staggering with weakness, yet joined in the common mew of protest, of need. I kicked my way through the crowd but, once safely inside, gave my son, Max, a twenty and asked him to drive to the grocery store in Fern Hollow and buy enough cat food to see us through. He looked alarmed and said he always got lost in Fern Hollow. My wife overheard us and came over protectively. "Max hasn't been to that store more than three times in his life," Evelyn said. "When we came to visit we always went to the supermarket in Morgantown. Why can't he go *there*?"

"It's two miles further and closes at five-thirty. Also my mother thought the little stores should be patronized to keep them in business."

My wife sighed and rolled her eyes upward. "Your mother is dead, darling. We can buy at the big store if we want to."

"It's *closed*, I just told you. We can't stay here with these cats yowling all night."

"Maybe they'll stop yowling once we turn off the lights," she said. "Isn't it time they faced reality?"

"*I'll* go, dammit," I said, thinking they would all protest at having me, the leader of our mourning party, leave them alone in the old stone house, with its rustling rodents and airless, ill-lit rooms. We were all still in the kitchen, where my mother's antique hand-wound mantel clock had stopped ticking and chiming. Its melancholy, gulping gong had kept watch over my insomnia on many a boyhood night.

Hiram, my daughter's husband, said, "I'll go for you, Dave, if you'll tell me the way."

He was being kind, but he is also unctuous and prematurely balding, with a Princetonian complacency that makes me want to kick him. I let my irritation with the others taint my reply: "It would take too long to explain. There are about six forks and none of them are marked."

"*He's* the country boy," my wife told Hiram with a collusive smile. "Let's let him go." To me she said, "You love those windy old roads. You can commune with your mother." My mother had not been pleased by my marriage at an early age, and her displeasure had leaked into the open, as things in families will. "And you can pick up milk and orange juice for our breakfast and maybe bread for toast. I guess we can get by on your mother's stale cereal."

Nancy, my daughter, said, "I'll come with you, Dad."

"Isn't it Peter's suppertime?" Evelyn asked.

Peter was my grandson, two years old.

Hiram said, "I'll put him in his jammies, Nance. You keep your dad company."

"I want Peter to come," she said. "I want him to see what an old-fashioned country store looks like."

"It's not *that* old-fashioned," I said, defensively. They treated this working rural area as if it were a theme park. So I had turned on my only ally, my daughter. The cats' crying was getting on my nerves. They were scraping and scratching against the screen door in their hunger.

"Car ride, yukk," Peter said.

"*No*body come," I decreed. "Cat food, orange juice, milk, doughnuts."

"We don't believe in doughnuts," Hiram quickly said.

"O.K., no doughnuts," I snapped.

"Get them only for yourself," Evelyn told me, as if they might bring me illicit but delicious mother-comfort.

"Pretzels," I proposed instead. "Anybody here who doesn't believe in pretzels?"

It was a relief, as it always had been, to get out of the house and into the car and onto the rolling freedom of the leafy roads. Newish ranch houses, built in homely mixtures of wood and sandstone and vinyl siding, added their window lights and mowed yards to the scattered habitations that I remembered. My mother used to recall being allowed to ride in the gig with her father when he caught the train into Alton at the Fern Hollow station, and then, though she was only nine or ten, bringing the gig back to the farm by herself. Of course, the horse knew the way. In the darkness, thinking of a little beribboned girl bringing a horse and carriage through three miles of forest and tobacco fields, I missed one of the forks. Rather than turn around, I took what I remembered as a shortcut, but it led to a dead end at a forsaken gravel pit. I began to sweat, with the claustrophobia of my youth. It took forever, it seemed, to backtrack and find Fern Hollow. But Stoudt's Keystone was still open, with its two gas pumps and side porch loaded with horse feed and sacks of fertilizer. Behind the counter, Roy Stoudt nodded in recognition, though I was disguised in a city shirt and blazer. When I told him what I wanted, he said, "I was wondering how those cats would manage."

"Not so well. The neighbors promised to shoot some but they haven't yet. I need just a case, to tide us over." I pictured the kittens staggering with hunger and said, "Maybe two cases."

"Your mother favored the beef mix and the seafood medley."

"Fine. Anything."

"She used to say they turned up their noses at pork; they were Old Testament cats. She was a funny one. You never quite knew when she was pulling your leg."

"Yeah, that was a problem for me even." At Rutgers, I

would have said "even for me." The local lilt was not hard to slip into. Stoudt's Keystone was a long dark store, its floorboards hollowed by wear, with gleaming nailheads where generations had shuffled past the cash register. It still sold little tubes of flypaper and plugs of chewing tobacco. I had trouble deciding, amid the abundance of packaged carbohydrates, which brand of pretzels to buy. I settled for a bag that claimed, *NEW!: Lo Fat, Lo Sodium.*

As he rang up my purchases, Roy went on, "She used to say to me, 'My boy thinks I'm crazy, feeding all these cats, but it's my only luxury. I don't drive a Mercedes, and I don't wear mink.' "

"I never said crazy. I may have said misguided."

"She did trap some and take them down to the humane society," he pointed out. "It was just nature kept getting ahead of her." There was a slyness mixed in with his amiability; I felt how much of a local joke she and her cats had been. "There," he said. "I've given you the discount for quantity I used to give to her."

"You don't have to do that." I could have bitten my tongue. I could hear his response coming, like the pedantic distinction, made much of in the third grade, between "can" and "may."

"I know I don't *have* to, David, but I *want* to. She was a good customer," Roy said. "We'll miss your mother around these parts. She was of the old school."

The cat-food section of Stoudt's Keystone would certainly miss her. I said what I should have said in the first place. "Thanks a lot for the discount, Roy."

Outside, under the moth-battered lights, bits of abandoned railroad gleamed in the parking lot, where it hadn't paid to wrest the iron tracks from the blacktop. They crossed the little road, pointing on either side to tunnels of darkness. The woods had still not fully reclaimed the right-of-way;

the rails were gone but the spalls and creosoted ties had been left and discouraged growth. Through that dark gap my grandfather had once sped to Alton, over stony creeks and iron bridges, sparks flying.

Back in the house I had inherited, cat shadows slinked to the edges of the porch and the human heads were clustered around the television set. As I revolved the can-opener handle, I tried to remember the song my mother used to hum. It had an old-fashioned lilt to it, like "Let Me Call You Sweetheart," but wasn't that. From the living room Nancy, still hurt about my not urging her to come with me, called that the pretzels were tasteless. "They've taken out the fat and the salt," I explained. "For your *good*." When I was a boy, some summer evenings after work, my father would bring home not only a bag of pretzels but a carton of tri-color ice cream. "I should have brought you back some ice cream." As a boy I would use pretzels to fork in the ice cream: the combination of tastes improved both.

"Goodness," my wife said, from the overstuffed wing chair my mother used to sit in, watching one inane program after another. "You are really reverting."

The morning of the funeral, I began to clean out my mother's crammed desk and found a little note on brittle blue stationery in an envelope addressed simply DAVID. It said, in her small backslanted handwriting:

In the event of my death I wish to be buried in the simplest possible ceremony, in the least expensive available coffin. Instead of flowers, I ask that contributions be directed to the
Boone Township Humane Society
R.F.D. 2, Box 88
Emmetstown, Penna.

I had done it all wrong. Flush with my inheritance, I had bought her the second-most expensive casket in the undertaker's basement, cherrywood with shiny brass rails to carry it by, and had arranged with the Lutheran pastor for the usual Lutheran service, with a catered lunch afterwards. The announcement of the death in the Alton paper had said nothing about giving money to the humane society. Nor did her note say anything about what I was to do with the cats.

After the burial service, Dwight sidled up to me on the cemetery grass and said, "I haven't been able to come over with the rifle these last days—we're getting the buses ready for the school year, there's been a ton of maintenance. And Adam has the early peaches coming in. But we'll get to it, absolutely."

The sight of the cherrywood coffin, with its brass fittings, sinking into the clean-sliced earth was still gleaming in my brain. I said, "Dwight, maybe it's too much to ask. Why don't you and Adam forget about it, and I'll try to think of something else. It's not your problem."

"No, now, we wouldn't want to do that," he said consolingly. He looked strange, in a navy-blue churchgoing suit under a noon sun on a weekday. Adam had brought his entire family, including three grandchildren, getting them out of the orchard and into their good clothes. A few other neighbors were there, and Martha Stoudt from down in Fern Hollow—she was the caterer. Roy had stayed behind the counter at the store. Three of my female high-school classmates showed up, touchingly, and a business associate of my father's, a fellow-accountant, who I thought had long ago died. In fact, though older than my parents, he was wiry and tan. He spent half the year in Florida, and didn't lack for dancing partners down there; this last was confided with a wink. Senility showed only in his tears, which refused to dry up in the outdoors, even with the early-fall sun beating down and a dry wind blowing on the cemetery hill. All the grief the rest of us were too distracted to feel flowed, it seemed, through his unstoppable rivulet.

Martha Stoudt and the pastor's wife and I had been too optimistic about the funeral attendance; there were high-heaped platters of potato salad and cole slaw and sliced bread and cold cuts waiting for us in the church function room. The food held us fast like flies; we murmured and circled, though the farmers were anxious to get back to their farms and my high-school friends back to their jobs. All three former girls worked in welfare administration, as it had turned out—government-sponsored mothers to the nation's hordes of orphans. "It will all be *fine*," June Zimmerman reassured me. She had been the prettiest of the three forty years ago, when she weighed half of what she did now. "They *are* learning English," she all but sang. "They *know* they must, to get out of service jobs. It just takes a generation or two, the same as it did for our people." Prodigiously bosomy, she had long outgrown the bobby socks and pleated, flippy cheerleader's skirt in which I still saw her. In her eyes, perhaps, I was a newborn orphan.

As for my mother, it is strange, once a life is over, how little there is to say about it. I could feel her in the room, polite but taking sardonic note, for future reference, of our collective failure to quite rise to the occasion. People had always struck her as inept, compared with animals. It galled me on her behalf that the minister, in the very strenuousness of his oratorical attempt to evoke what had made dear departed Irma so special, had forgotten to signal the organist to play "A Mighty Fortress." How many Lutherans get buried without, one last time, "A Mighty Fortress"? I felt it as a scandal, albeit minor. Ignominiously my living kin gathered up all the uneaten food and went back to the forlorn house, with its rotting sills and teeming population of invited pests. The cats, though it was not their dinnertime, were swarming hopefully on the back porch; some of the barn cats had ventured up to the house and made gray streaks in retreat across the lawn as our car pulled in.

The house was stuffy and still inside. Evelyn went around tugging open the sticky windows, in contravention of my mother's theory that closed windows sealed the coolness in. She and Nancy and her family were dying to get back home; we had left it to a neighbor to feed fat old Josie, along with our own sleek cocker spaniel. Max and I were to stay a day or two—whatever it took—and load up the truck and get the house clean enough for the realtor to show. Everywhere we looked, from the refrigerator full of cold cuts and potato salad to an attic holding a half-century's worth of broken furniture, crockery wrapped in ancient brown newspapers, albums of ancestors whose names nobody now knew, and *Life* magazines of special historical interest, we were overwhelmed. Nancy put Peter down upstairs for his nap. Evelyn had a headache, Max and Hiram turned on the television set, and I escaped by getting in the car and driving to Emmetstown. My mother's note had offered a clue.

Four miles of back roads, crossing and recrossing a creek on rattling bridges, brought me to the outskirts of Emmetstown, where a homely stencilled sign pointed the way to the humane society. I had been here a few times with my mother, delivering trapped cats. The society had lent her two galvanized Havaharts a dozen years ago. She would bait them with liver pâté. On various weekend visits I had helped her lug her awkward catch. Tomcats and new mothers were the hardest to carry, as they made the long cage pitch back and forth in their terror, hurling their bodies against the dropped doors and trying to bite and claw their way through the wire mesh. We set them on the humane-society counter and a stocky, pale teen-age girl would take them away and ten minutes later, looking slightly paler, would bring them back empty.

In the years since I had been here, there had been some refinements. From the concrete-floored rear of the complex there still drifted animal smells and yowls, but the front room looked more like an office, with framed certificates and prints of wildlife. The high bare counter was gone and a walnut desk occupied the center of a shag-carpeted floor.

Here sat a broad-shouldered bland woman with "big" bleached hair, inflated and teased with an out-of-style styl- ishness. Her pale face lifted to me when I came in. Before I could introduce myself, she said, "I was sorry to read about your mother, David. She was a real nice lady. Such lovely manners, even when you could tell she was upset."

Falling in with this intimacy, I asked, "When did you see her upset?"

"Oh, with the cats. Having to bring them in to be, you know, disposed of, when they were a lot like pets to her. She would say goodbye by name, sometimes. She used to say it was the tamest that trusted her enough to take the bait—the really wild ones never got caught."

"It was horrible, the way they multiplied."

"Well, they will, if you feed them." She added, as I grap- pled with this Malthusian truth, "That's the nature of the beast." Seeing me still baffled, she said, "It's hard."

"Yes," I agreed. "Hard. Do you have any ideas as to what I should do?"

"About the cats?"

"Absolutely." What else? My other problems—dealing with Evelyn, selling the European canon to students with attention spans the length of TV commercials—were out of a humane society's range.

She thought and said, "Well, do you still have the traps?"

"I haven't looked, but I guess they're still in the barn."

"I ask because your mother hasn't been in for a couple of years at least."

"She got too weak to do it. A trap with a fighting cat in it isn't so easy to handle."

"Oh, don't I know." She spoke with an increasing gentleness, as if to a disabled man. Though her fingernails were short and unpainted, her face was made up with that faintly excessive care of minor officialdom—of small-town postmistresses and small-city lawyers' secretaries. I suddenly knew that this composed executive woman was the stocky girl of years ago, the teen-age executioner. She had assumed that I recognized her at once, as she had me. A young male minion in dungarees and ponytail opened the door to the fragrant beyond, said a few unintelligible words, received a confirming nod, and closed the door.

Lamely I continued, "I think she got overwhelmed and couldn't see beyond dishing out the cat food every day. There's an absolute *mountain* of tin cans in the woods!"

She thoughtfully scratched below her fair little ear and I caught a whiff of her perfume. "You know, David," she told me, "a population like that is self-limiting. With the inbreeding and the crowding, cats like that are very susceptible to disease. There's even a kind of cat AIDS that's around now."

"Great; but there's still a lot of live ones yowling around the back door. My family's come down for the funeral and they're scared to go outside. I can't just walk away, the cats'll migrate to all the neighbors! One of the neighbors promised to shoot some, but that's a nuisance for him and I doubt now he'll do it."

She changed the angle of her listening head, and her professional patience seemed momentarily strained. "What I started to suggest was, if you still have the traps in the barn, you could set them and bring in one or two every day. The ones you don't eventually catch will be so feral they'll keep to the woods."

"But I can't *stay!*"

She blinked at my fervor. Somehow she had seen me as replacing my mother on the property, its eighty-two acres of milkweed and horseflies and red mud, as if my whole life had been killing time until I could take possession.

"I live in New Jersey!" I insisted. "I have to get back to my house, my job."

"You're putting your mom's place up for sale?"

"I have to! I can't take care of it! Already the buildings are falling down."

She pursed her lips slightly as she took this in. "It's considered a nice place around here, but if you can't, well, you can't. Your mother wouldn't want you to do the impossible." Yet a loyalty to my mother drove her, after a pause, to go on, "Though I know she always spoke of you as the one who'd take charge. She'd say to me, 'Amy, I know the neighbors think I'm crazy, but I'm just holding the fort for Davey.' How many days *can* you stay, then?"

"Two at most, this time."

As a good professional she hid her shock at my feckless haste. "So, then. Bring the borrowed traps in, and we'll cross them off your mother's card. Otherwise I'll have to charge you."

"Fine. Super. I'll do it tomorrow." I hoped she didn't expect me to bring them in loaded. I didn't have any liver pâté, for one thing.

"And then," she said, "you know, David, we have a man who does some trapping for us. He lives not far from here, and works out in your area, at one of the new discount outlets in Morgantown. He could set the traps at your place on his way to work and pick them up on his way back."

"That sounds wonderful. *Wonderful.* How much does he charge?" Like a frontiersman packing a firearm, I had brought a checkbook, just in case.

"Oh, nothing to you. It comes under township wildlife control. He does it as a kind of hobby."

"Wonderful," I repeated once more. "It sounds almost too good to be true. Let me write a donation to the humane society. It's what my mother would have wanted." I didn't explain how I had failed to secure donations instead of funeral flowers. I pondered the proper amount. A hundred dollars seemed not enough for the magnitude of the service. I envisioned waves of cats, gathered like gray sheaves into cages set out in the dawn dew and harvested at twilight. Even two hundred seemed modest. I wrote a check for two hundred fifty, which came to about six dollars a cat. The amount startled her, I could tell by the arch of her plucked and pencilled eyebrows. "And here's my number in New Jersey if you ever need it," I said. "Could I have your card, so I can maybe call to check on progress?" I didn't want her, and her offer, to get away.

"Of course, David." She had stiffened; she had at last realized that she was a stranger to me—someone simply to use. The card said, "Amy Stauffer, Director, Boone Township Humane Society," with the same address as on my mother's note to me. The clue had cracked the case. I drove back to the farmhouse exhilarated, making the tires squeal on the winding Emmetstown road. Once, the thought of my high-school flames would stir my recklessness behind the wheel; now I was in love with Amy Stauffer.

Through the next two days, Max surprised me by being a great help in the packing up. While I stood around in the

midst of my inheritance paralyzed by the imagined importance of everything, all these artifacts fragrant of my past
and my ancestry, he made decisions. Keep this, take that. He
did the heavy lifting, and broke nothing; I looked at him
with newly respectful eyes. He might turn out all right after
all. He was just a child of his times, in less of a hurry to leave
home than I had been. When he and I drove away in the
loaded U-Haul truck, we left the rest of the funeral meats
in the woods, as a last feast for the cats. "O.K., kitties," I told
them as they mewed up at my face. "Now you're on your
own."

   In the months to come, as fall activity was renewed at
Rutgers, I avoided going back. I was afraid of getting sucked
in. Everything was handled over the telephone. It was
almost eerie, to see society smoothly bring into play its per-
fected machinery for the transfer of property. My lawyer,
another old high-school classmate, arranged for the estate
assessment and sent me forms to sign and return. The realtor kept me apprised of prospects and offers. When I asked
him if he, on his latest showing of the house, had noticed
any cats around the back porch, he pretended to search his
memory before saying, "Why, no!" Their mewing, furry,
hungry substance had vanished like the matter of a dream.
My mother's meagre treasures—the rose-pattern china, the
pine corner cupboard, a curly-maple sewing table, two lace
tablecloths, some Navajo silver-and-turquoise jewelry from
my parents' single trip west, six ladderback dining-room
chairs—found their niches in our home or our daughter's,
with a few pieces promised to Max when and if he ever
settled down. Little Peter wanted the wind chimes. Josie
inherited her yellow plastic dog-dish. In Pennsylvania, the
auction crew came into the house, cleaned it out of every
tattered piece of furniture and memorabilia, including *Life*

magazines from V-E and V-J Days, and in late October sent me a respectable check for the proceeds at auction. In early November the realtor had found a retired couple from Philadelphia whose bid was in the bottom end of my asking range, but who promised to keep renting the fields to Adam and Dwight. The buyers vowed they had no intention of developing the acreage but refused to sign a covenant without a sharp reduction in the price. I backed down. The farm could take its chances, like the rest of us. We set the date of the signing for the week after Thanksgiving.

I felt guilty, selling the place. My mother had believed it to be a piece of lost Eden and wanted me to live on it for my own good. Pathetically, she would argue that I could still teach at Rutgers, with a readjustment of my schedule that would bunch my teaching into a few days in the middle of the week. "What about my wife?" I asked.

"Tell Evelyn," she said, "that I've never felt right, as a woman, off this place. There's magic in the soil, I do believe it. Two days away, and I used to get the most terrible cramps."

"My kids, Mother. They've been raised New York–suburban."

This was before Nancy had married and Max had dropped out of Dartmouth. "It's not too late to fix that," my mother said. "When they were smaller they used to love it here."

I sighed, and we dropped the subject, knowing that I was the problem. I was the one to whom the farm meant poison ivy and crabgrass, and bush-whacking that would be invisible the next summer, and indoor plumbing that was forty years out of date, and a pack of asthma-inducing cats at the back door.

I didn't call Amy Stauffer for weeks, and when I did she sounded vague. "I know he went out and looked the situation over," she said.

"But did he trap any?"

"He has the traps right now in his other truck, I think he told me. Anyway, he didn't see any cats."

"None? What time of day was he there?"

"I guess around their dinnertime," she said, with an audible smile in her voice. I saw her clearly, stolidly sitting at her tidy desk in Emmetstown, with the wild ducks on the wall and the door leading back to the concrete-floored cages— a genie whom I had conjured up but could not quite control, through some little glitch in interstate communications.

"I'd be happy to drive over," I told her, "but I don't see how it would do any good."

"No, David," she said sadly, as to a former lover. "I don't either."

Yet the persisting fact of the cats gnawed at me; at night I would wake up, with my mother's ghost wavering in the room, over where Evelyn had dropped her white bathrobe on the back of a chair, and want to scream, in shame and helplessness. The runny-eyed kittens, staggering with hunger. Why had they been called into life? My mother, with more courage than I had, used to drown them, pressing one bucket down into another bucket half filled with water and their peeping cries. My mother's humming returned to me, marking waltz time with the handle's rhythmic chunking noise, and with it came the whole sweet-and-sour aroma of the kitchen, the way she had shaped it with her life, all those mornings of rising alone, making coffee and pouring cereal, and ceremoniously feeding the cats, while the mantel clock sounded its gulping gong. Thriftily, she would squeeze slivers of used soap together, to make a motley bar which sat in the bathroom dish like a rebuke to her only, stingy son.

One morning, before I was really awake, Amy, taking pity, called me. "Well, he's been busy," she told me. "He must have brought two or three in every evening now for nearly two weeks. But, as he says, the others get more and more wary, so it may be a case of diminishing returns."

"Still, that's terrific progress. I'm *very* grateful. At that rate there can't be too many left."

"That's right," she said, "and the young ones you can count on dying of natural causes, especially now that we're having frosts."

I couldn't quite bring myself to say that I was grateful for that, too.

At the beginning of hunting season, Dwight called and told me he and Adam had posted my land. Did I mind? He knew, of course, that one of my mother's eccentricities was to leave her land unposted, to the annoyance of her neighbors. "They just want the shooting for themselves," she had explained to me. "Especially they don't want Philadelphia blacks coming out here and finding any land to hunt on. One year, when I still had legs under me, I walked around and tore Dwight's signs down myself. No Hunting, except for him—it made me see *red*."

"No," I said. "I don't mind."

"I'm glad to hear it, Dave," Dwight's distant voice said. "If I see any of those cats still around, I promise they won't live to tell the tale. Hunting season is hard times on cats. Hunters see them as competition."

The last days of owning the farm were strange. It was as if I had a phantom limb; I could feel it move, but not see it. The papers were being signed the first day of December, and I thought I should go over the day before, check out the house and barn for any last remnants of our years there, and spend the night in an Alton motel. Thinking there might be a little last-minute brush-clearing or dirty lifting, I hung my suit in the car and put on a wool-lined olive-drab jacket, from an Army-surplus store, that my father used to wear on weekends, and that my mother inherited and would wear in winter, with not too bad a fit. I hadn't had the heart to leave it for the auctioneers to clear away. I put on the jacket and threw a pair of loppers and work gloves in the car.

But by the time I got away from my wife and my students, and made my way around Philadelphia, not many hours of daylight were left. The place when I pulled in was still— as still as a picture. Green was gone from everything but the pines and the two glossy holly trees, the male and the female. The orchard grass was an even slope of tan striped with shade. The woods beyond stood tall and silvery, the stalks of darkness between the trunks thickening. The region was called Firetown and as a boy I had imagined it had to do with the way the day's dying sun made the tops of the trees in the woods flame.

When I slammed the car door, it echoed off the barn wall in a way I had forgotten. When we first moved here, I used to stand in the yard and shout, marvelling at the echo, like the voice of a brother I didn't have.

The absence of an owner showed in a dozen little ways. I had paid a boy to keep the lawn mowed, but he had lazily left tousled fringes along the edges, and where the black walnut had dropped its pulpy shells on the lawn hadn't bothered to mow at all. I carried the loppers, though I doubted I would find much to do—perhaps just check the fragile weeping cherry tree for fallen branches, or cut some raspberry canes out of the hosta beds my mother had planted when we were new here. Busywork, to salve my conscience and the wound left when a piece of your life is removed.

As I drifted in my inherited coat across the lank grass, a few shadows filtered out of the orchard and flickered toward the house, eagerly loping. Several more materialized from the direction of the woods. These cats had survived. They thought I was my mother and that good times had returned.

Oliver's Evolution

His parents had not meant to abuse him; they had meant to love him, and did love him. But Oliver had come late in their little pack of offspring, at a time when the challenge of child-rearing was wearing thin, and he proved susceptible to mishaps. A big fetus, cramped in his mother's womb, he was born with in-turned feet, and learned to crawl with corrective casts up to his ankles. When they were at last removed, he cried in terror, because he thought those heavy plaster boots scraping and bumping along the floor had been part of himself.

One day in his infancy they found him on their dressing-room floor with a box of mothballs, some of which were wet with saliva; in retrospect they wondered if there had really been a need to rush him to the hospital and have his poor little stomach pumped. His face was gray-green afterwards. The following summer, when he had learned to walk, his parents had unthinkingly swum away off the beach together, striving for romantic harmony the morning after a late party and an alcoholic quarrel, and were quite unaware, until they saw the lifeguard racing along the beach, that Oliver had toddled after them and had been floating on his face for what might have been, given a less alert lifeguard, a fatal couple of minutes. This time, his face was blue, and he coughed for hours.

He was the least complaining of their children. He did not blame his parents when neither they nor the school authorities detected his "sleepy" right eye in time for therapy, with the result that when he closed that eye everything looked intractably fuzzy. Just the sight of the boy holding a schoolbook at a curious angle to the light made his father want to weep, impotently.

And it happened that he was just the wrong, vulnerable age when his parents went through their separation and divorce. His older brothers were off in boarding school and college, embarked on manhood, free of family. His younger sister was small enough to find the new arrangements—the meals in restaurants with her father, the friendly men who appeared to take her mother out—exciting. But Oliver, at thirteen, felt the weight of the household descend on him; he made his mother's sense of abandonment his own. Again, his father impotently grieved. It was he, and not the boy, who was at fault, really, when the bad grades began to come in from day school, and then from college, and Oliver broke his arm falling down the frat stairs, or leaping, by another account of the confused incident, from a girl's dormitory window. Not one but several family automobiles met a ruinous end with him at the wheel, though with no more injury, as it happened, than contused knees and loosened front teeth. The teeth grew firm again, thank God, for his innocent smile, slowly spreading across his face as the full humor of his newest misadventure dawned, was one of his best features. His teeth were small and round and widely spaced—baby teeth.

Then he married, which seemed yet another mishap, to go with the late nights, abandoned jobs, and fallen-through opportunities of his life as a young adult. The girl, Alicia, was as accident-prone as he, given to substance abuse and unwanted pregnancies. Her emotional disturbances left herself and others bruised. By comparison, Oliver was solid and surefooted, and she looked up to him. This was the key. What we expect of others, they endeavor to provide. He held on to a job, and she held on to her pregnancies. You should see him now, with their two children, a fair little girl and a dark-haired boy. Oliver has grown broad, and holds the two of them at once. They are birds in a nest. He is a tree, a sheltering boulder. He is a protector of the weak.

Natural Color

FRANK SAW HER more than a block away, in the town where he had come to live, where Maggie had no business to be, and he no expectation of seeing her. Something about the way she held her head, as if she were marvelling at the icicled eaves of the downtown shops, sparked recognition. Or perhaps it was the way the low winter sun caught the red of her hair, so it glinted like a signal. His wife used to doubt aloud that the color was natural, and he had had to repress the argument that if Maggie dyed it she dyed her pubic hair to match. It was true, Maggie considered her hair a glory. When she let it down, the sheaves of it became an enveloping, entangling third presence in the bed, and when it was pinned up, as it was today, her head looked large and her neck poignantly thin, at its cocky tilt.

She was with a man—a man taller than she, though she was herself tall. He moved beside her with a bearlike protective shuffle, half sideways, so as not to miss a word she was tossing out, her naked hands gesturing in the February sun. Frank remembered her face whitened by shock and wet with tears. Each word he reluctantly pulled from himself had been a blow deepening her pallor, driving her deeper into defeat. "I can't swing it," he had said, with both their households in turmoil and the town around them scandalized.

"You mean," she said, her face furrowed, her upper lip tense in her effort to have utter clarity at this moment, "you want to go back?"

"I don't want to, exactly, but I think I should."

"Then go, Frank. Go, darling. It makes it simpler for me, in a way."

He had thought that a lovely, pathetic bit of female bravado, an attempt to match rejection with rejection, but in fact she had carried through with her divorce, whereas he had kept his family intact and had moved to another town. That was more than twenty years ago. The children he had decided not to leave had eventually grown up and left home. The wife he had clung to had maintained a self-preserving detachment, which as they together advanced into middle age became a decided distance, maintained with dry humor and an impervious dignity. He had opted for a wife, and a wife she was, no less or more.

As for Maggie, she had recovered; she had a companion, and at a distance looked smart, in a puffy pea-green parka and black pants that made her legs appear theatrically long. Shocked by the spark glinting from her hair, Frank ducked into the nearest door, that of the drugstore, to spare himself the impact of a confrontation, of introductions and chatter. It was somehow an attack on him, to have her striding about so boldly in his town.

While he roamed the drugstore aisles as if looking for a magic medication or a perfect birthday card, he slowly filled with fury at her, for going on beyond him and making a life. Sexual jealousy of a wholly unreasonable sort raged in him as he blindly stalked between the cold tablets and the skin lotions, the sleeping pills and stomach-acid neutralizers. He skimmed the array of condoms, displayed, in this progressive, AIDS-wary age, like a rack of many-colored candies, each showing on the box a shadowy man and woman bending their heads conspiratorially close. It occurred to him, as his blood pounded, that sex has very little to do with kindness. He had been rough with Maggie, cruel, in the heat of their affair. It had been his first, but not hers. She had told him in the front seat of his car, with that serious, concentrating stare of hers, "That time when Sam and I were separated, I was an absolute whore. I'd sleep with *any*body."

The sweeping solemnity of the confession would have made him smile, had he not been awed by the grandeur of her promiscuity as he tried to imagine it. She seemed to swell in size, there beside him in the front seat of his Ford station wagon, parked on a dead-end lane between towns. That early-spring meeting, hurriedly arranged by phone, was like an interview, she in winter tweeds from shopping in Boston, he in his business suit. He didn't ask for details. She volunteered a ski instructor in Vermont, a scuba instructor in the Caribbean—handsome, carefree young fishers of women. She didn't say if she had slept with any of their neighbors, but he imagined some, and thus his heart was hardened before their own affair had begun. He was obliged to sleep with her now. It was a kind of race, in which he had fallen dangerously behind. The men she had slept with were each still in her, a kind of investment, generating interest while he had been chastely admiring her from afar. Part of Frank's gift to her was the heightened value that his innocence had assigned her. Because she was so experienced, they were never quite equal. She ran risks, coming to him, the same risks he did, of discovery and a disrupted family, but he considered her marriage too damaged already to grieve for, whereas his own was enhanced by his betrayal, his wife and children rendered precious in their vulnerability. Returning to them, damp and panting from his sins, he nearly wept at their sweet ignorance. Yet he couldn't stop. He led Maggie on, addicted to her and careless of their fate, until the time came to disentangle his fate from hers. She herself had said it: "You're *hard* on me, Frank."

He thought she might mean just the vigor of his lovemaking. They were both in a sweat, in her sunny bed with its view of a horse-farm riding ring, and she, underneath him, was doubly drenched. They had begun seeing each other in April; they were discovered and cut off before autumnal weather arrived. He remembered her in bright cotton frocks, animated at parties afloat in summer lightness, all her animation secretly directed at him. She was warm with Ann, his wife, and he was hearty with Sam, her husband, though even here there was inequality. She seemed genuinely to like Ann and, when with Frank, would wonder aloud how he could ever think of leaving his lovely wife. Each tryst, on the other hand, strengthened his impression that Sam—big, red-faced, his heavy head lowered with clumsy, shortsighted menace—was unworthy of her, and her remaining in her marriage was a sign of weakness, a meek acceptance of daily pollution.

"You have anything better to offer?" Maggie had once challenged him, having pinched her lips together and decided to take the leap. Her eyes in this moment of daring had been round, like a child's.

He felt attenuated, strained, answering weakly, "You know I'd love to be your husband. If I weren't already somebody else's."

"The beautiful prisoner," she said, gazing off as if suddenly bored. "I do think we should stop seeing each other."

"Oh my God, no. I'll die."

"Well, it's killing me. You're not being mature. When a gentleman has had his fun with a lady, he takes his leave."

He hated it when she pulled sexual rank on him. He wanted to learn but not to be instructed. "Is that how Sam would act?"

"Sam's not so bad as you think," she said, brushing away, with a sudden awkward hiding motion, tears that had started to her eyes, sprung by some image touched within the tense works of this suspended situation.

"Good in bed," Frank suggested, hating the two of them. In bed: this very bed, with its view of trim stables and fenced pastures.

She ignored the jealous probe. She said, reflecting, "He has a sense of me that's not entirely off. In his coarse way, he has manners."

"And I don't?"

"Frank," she exclaimed in an exasperation that still let the tears stand in her eyes. "Why does everything always have to come back to you?"

"Because," he could have answered, "you have made me love myself." But there were many things he could have said to Maggie, before communications between them suddenly ceased, Sam blundering in with bullish fury and lawyerly threats, Ann receding with a beautiful wounded pride. Frank found himself Maggie's enemy, having failed to become her husband.

In the freezing winter and raw spring before he and his family had moved from that town to this one, six miles distant, there was a long social season in which they all continued to rotate in each other's vicinity. Sam moved to a bachelor rental in yet another town, three miles away—not so far as to be out of reach of sympathetic gestures from their large communal acquaintance. Frank and Ann hunkered down in embattled, recriminatory renewal of their vows, mixed with spells of humorous weariness. And Maggie found herself marooned in her big house with the two children, an eight-year-old girl and a six-year-old boy. Their formerly shared friends, forced to choose among these explosive elements, opted for the intact couple over the separated one. Sam, though his face seemed redder than ever and his eyes were narrowed as if his face had been pummelled, established himself as willing to co-exist in the same room with Frank, and even to exchange a few forced courtesies. But Ann fled the one occasion, the annual Christmas-carol sing in the historical-society mansion, where Maggie had dared appear. Maggie showed up late, in a dazzling sequined long-sleeved green top and a long scarlet velvet skirt. Frank smiled at the audacity of the outfit; Ann gave a whimper and whirled from the room, straight down the hallway, hung with old daguerreotypes, toward the front door, prized for its exemplary Federalist moldings and fine leaded fanlight. Chasing her out with their coats into the cold, Frank said, "That was a cruel thing to do."

"Not as cruel as trying to steal my husband."

"That isn't what she tried."

"Well, what did she try? Fucking as a spiritual exercise?"

"Please, Ann. People are looking out of the windows." Though in fact the choruses of "Good King Wenceslas" rolled obliviously out the tall windows onto the snowy sidewalk. The town had seen worse spats than theirs, including a Unitarian-Congregationalist church schism in the 1820s. "Put on your coat," he said stiffly, and led her by the arm to where their car was parked, the station wagon in which Maggie had solemnly told him she had been an absolute whore, but whose interior now was awash in the childish odor of candy-bar crumbs and spilled milkshakes. In truth, the marriage had in the short run fattened on the affair: Ann was impressed that he had made a conquest of the spectacular Maggie, and Frank was moved by his cool wife's flare of jealous passion. It was as if Maggie, in her bereft, ostracized state, were a prize they had jointly dragged home. "If you can't hold it together in public," he told her, "it means she can't go anywhere where you're apt to be."

"We're *trying* to get out of town, we've got realtors coming out of our *ears*," Ann said with comical vehemence. "I'm *damned* if I'm going to take the children out of school before it ends in May. They're heartbroken we're moving in any case." As the car heater warmed, drowning in its gases the sour-milkshake scent, and the rumpled blocks of the old town rolled by, she conceded, "I'm sorry. That was not a good-sport thing to do. But just seeing her physically, after talking about her for weeks and weeks, it came over me how you'd seen her . . . how you knew every . . . and she looked so great, actually, in that grotesque outfit." Ann went on, "Pale and tense, but it's taken a few pounds off her. Wish I could say the same."

He reached over and squeezed her plump thigh through the thickness of her winter coat. "Different styles," he said, obliquely bragging. They were united, it seemed to him, in admiration of Maggie—two suppliants bowed beneath a natural force. Though rapprochement on such a basis was bound to decay, for a time it made for a conspiratorial closeness.

In the meantime, Maggie was crossed off party lists. She pursued her daily duties in majestic isolation, visited by only a few gossip-hungry women and oddball men sensing an opportunity. Frank was divided between acquiescence in her exclusion—her power over him, the grandeur she had for him, left no room for pity—and an impossible wish to reunite, to say the words to her that would lift them above it all and put them back in bed together. More experienced than he, she knew there were no such words. A few months after the Christmas-carol sing, the town fathers sponsored an Easter-egg hunt on the sloping common, this side of the cemetery. In the milling about, while parents chased after frantic, scooting children on the muddy brown grass, he managed to sidle up to Maggie, in her familiar spring tweeds. She gave him an unamused stare and said to him, as if the words had been stored up, "Your wife has ruined my social life. And my children's. Sam is furious."

Such a petty and specific grievance seemed astonishingly unworthy of them and their love. Startled, Frank said, "Ann doesn't scheme. She just lets things happen." As if, after all this silence between them, they had met to debate his wife's character. Maggie turned away. Sick with the rejection, he admired the breadth of her shoulders and the wealth of her hair, done up in a burnished, glistening French twist.

To a tourist travelling through, one New England town looks much like another—white spire, green common, struggling little downtown—but they have considerable economic and spiritual differences, and their citizens know what they are. Frank and Ann had, after a six-month struggle with real-estate agents, moved to a town where the property lines were marked by walls and hedges and No Trespassing signs. The friends they slowly made were generally older than they, a number of them widowed or retired. The lives, the winterized summer houses, the grounds maintained by lawn services were all in a state of finish. The town they had moved from had been a work in progress, with crooked streets laid out by Puritan footsteps and boundary lines marked by lost boulders and legendary trees whose stumps had rotted to nothing. The young householders had tried to do their own maintenance, leaving ladders leaning against porch roofs and two sides of a house unpainted until next summer. The yards were hard-used by packs of children; there was a constant coming and going of Saturday-afternoon tennis or touch football turning into drinks before everyone rushed home to shower and shave for that night's dinner party. You lived in other people's houses as much as you could; there was an ache to being in your own, a nagging unsuppressible suspicion that happiness was elsewhere. Driving back from taking the babysitter home, Frank would pass darkened houses where husbands he knew were lying in bed, head to murmuring head, with wives he coveted.

Out of this weave of promiscuous friendship, this confusedly domestic scrimmage, Maggie had emerged, touching his hip with hers as they stood side by side at a lawn party's busy, linen-clad bar, or exclaiming, in an involuntary, almost fainting little-girl voice, "Oh, don't go!" when he and Ann stood up at last to leave a dinner party that she and Sam had given. And when, at one of the suburban balls with which the needs of charity dotted the calendar, his turn came to dance with Maggie, they nestled as close as the sanction of alcohol allowed, and at the end she gave his hand a sharp, stern, quite sober squeeze. It took very clear signals to burn through his fog of shyness and connubial inertia, but she had enough expertise to know that, once ignited, he would blaze.

How gentle and patient, in retrospect, her initiation of him had been. Their meetings took place mostly in her house, because Sam worked in Boston and Ann didn't. Frank remembered, rounding the rack of condoms into a realm of packaged antihistamine capsules, how the driveway of her house, which sat on the edge of town, next to a horse farm and riding stable, was hidden behind a tilting tall stockade-style fence and a mass of overgrown lilacs. Sam would talk of replacing the fence and pruning the lilacs but didn't do it that summer. Approaching, Frank needed to slow for the hairpin turn into the driveway; it was a dangerous moment when his car might have been recognized on the road— several of their friends' children took riding lessons—and he would hold his breath as, half hidden behind the great straggly lilacs, he would glide across the crackling gravel and into the garage. Maggie would have swung up the garage door for him, which took some strength in this era before electronic controls. She would be waiting for him behind the connecting door into the kitchen, in a bathing suit or less. His eyes would still be adjusting from sunlight. She would bound into his arms like a long, smooth, shivering puppy. He stared at the Sudafed and Contac, his whole body swollen by a stupid indignation at having lost all that.

At last, making a few distracted purchases by way of paying for the shelter, he dared leave the drugstore. He looked down the street and saw with relief that the vista of icicled shops held no red glint. Heart pounding, as if he were being pursued by an enemy, he made his way to his car and returned to his house. It was a weather-tight box, a well-built tract house on a two-acre square of land. The foundation-masking shrubs newly planted when they moved in now looked overgrown, crowding the brick steps and front windows. In the kitchen, Ann, in her tan loden coat, was unpacking bags of groceries into the refrigerator; her face as she turned to him wore a slant expression, brimming with wary mischief. "I saw an old friend of yours in the Stop & Shop." The giant bright supermarket was part of a mall that had arisen in the farm country, slowly going under to development, between the town they had left and the town where they lived.

"Who?" he asked, though from the peculiar liveliness of her expression he had already guessed.

"Maggie Linsford. Or whatever her name is now." Maggie had taken back her maiden name after her divorce from Sam, and Ann could never be bothered to remember it.

"Chase," Frank said. "Unless she's remarried."

"She wouldn't do that to you. What's in that bag in your hand?"

"Razor blades. Sudafed. And I got you some of that perfumed French bath gel you like. 'Dorlotez-vous,' the label says."

"How sweet and silly of you. I have scads of it. Don't you want to hear about Maggie?"

"Sure."

"She was with this man, she introduced him, in that rather grand way she has, as 'my friend.' He reminded me of Sam—big and red-faced and take-charge."

"Good."

"Frank, don't look so sick. You're thinking back twenty-five years."

"No, I was thinking about 'take-charge.' I guess he was. Did she seem pleasant?"

"Oh, effusive. I always liked her, until you came between us. And she me, no?"

He wondered. At the height of their affair their spouses had seemed small and pathetic beneath them, like field mice under a hawk, virtually too small to discuss. "Sure," he said. "She admired you very much. She couldn't understand what I saw in her."

"Don't be sarcastic. You're no fun, Frank. I bring you this goodie, and you look constipated."

"What did the two of you discuss, effusively?"

"Oh, winter. Food. The appallingness of malls. Apparently a new one is going in on the land of the old riding stable next to that place she had with Sam. She complained there wasn't any gluten-free flour or low-fat cookies in the whole supermarket—maybe she's trying to slim down her beefy friend—and I told her we had a new health-food store just open up here, a charming idealistic girl we were all trying to give business to. She said she'd drive right over. If you were hanging out in the drugstore, I'm surprised you didn't see her."

He saw he must confess; there was no evading feminine intuition. "I did. I saw this flash of red hair down below the post office, and ducked into the drugstore rather than talk to her."

"Frank dear, how silly again. She would have been nothing but pleasant, I'm sure."

"I didn't like the look of the thug she was with."

"If she had been alone, would you have gone up to her?"

"I doubt it."

Ann put the last package into the refrigerator and closed the door, hard enough so that a magnet in the shape of a pineapple fell to the floor. She didn't pick it up. "Your reacting so skittishly doesn't speak very well for *us*."

Infidelity, he reflected, widens a couple's erotic field at first, but leaves it weaker and frazzled in the end. Like a mind-expanding drug, it destroys cells. He told Ann, "I felt nothing. I felt repelled."

"A 'flash of red hair'—I'll say. She's dyeing it an impossible color these days."

"You always said she dyed it."

"And she always did. Certainly now."

"I don't think so. Not Maggie."

"Oh, you poor thing, her hair would be as gray as yours and mine if she didn't dye it. She looked cheap, cheap and whorish, which is something I couldn't have honestly said before. You were smart not to allow yourself a look up close."

"You bitch. I know Maggie's hair better than you do." Ann

froze, not certain from his expression whether or not he would come forward and strike her; but she was safe, he was not even seeing her. The woman he did see, stepping naked toward him across a sun-striped carpet, was the one who, as long as he loved her, he must hate.

Licks of Love in the
Heart of the Cold War

KHRUSHCHEV was in power, or we thought he was, that month I spent as cultural ambassador and banjo-picking bridge between the superpowers, helping stave off nuclear holocaust. It was September into October of 1964. We had a cultural-exchange program with the Soviets at the time. Our State Department's theory was that almost any American, paraded before the oppressed Soviet masses, would be, just in his easy manner of walking and talking, such an advertisement for the free way of life that cells of subversion would pop up in his wake like dandelions on an April lawn. So my mission wasn't as innocent as it seemed. Still, I was game to undertake it.

My happy home lies in western Virginia, which isn't the same as West Virginia, though it's getting close, on the far side of the Blue Ridge. Washington, D.C., to me spells Big City, and when the official franked letters began to come through it never occurred to me to resist something as big and beautiful as the pre-Vietnam U.S. government. As to Russia, it's just one more mess of a free-enterprise country now, but then it was the dark side of the moon. The Aeroflot plane from Paris smelled of boiled potatoes, as I recall, and the stewardesses were as hefty as packed suitcases. When we landed at midnight we might have been descending over the ocean, there were so few lights under us.

The airport was illuminated as if by those dim bedside lamps hotels give you, not to read by. One of the young soldiers was pawing through a well-worn *Playboy* some blushing fur-trader ahead of me had tried to smuggle in, and my first impression of how life worked under Communism was the glare of that poor centerfold's sweet bare skin under those brownish airport lights. The magazine was confiscated, but I just don't want to believe the travelling salesman was sent to the gulag. He had a touch of Asia in his cheekbones—it wasn't like we had corrupted a pure-blooded Russian. The State Department boys swooped me out the customs door into a chauffeured limo that smelled not of boiled potatoes exactly but very deeply of tobacco, another natural product. My granddaddy's barn used to smell like that, even after the cured leaf had been baled and sold. I—Eddie Chester, internationally admired banjo-picker—knew I was going to like it here.

On the airport road into Moscow in those days there was this humongous billboard of Lenin, leaning forward with a wicked goateed grin and pointing to something up above with a single finger, like John the Baptist pointing to a Jesus we couldn't see yet. "I love that," my chief State Department escort said from the jump seat. "To three hundred million people—'up yours.'" His name was Bud Nevins, cultural attaché. I saw a lot of Bud, Bud and his lovely wife, Libby, in the weeks to come.

Already, Washington had been an adventure. I had been

briefed, a couple of afternoons, by a mix of our experts and refugees from the Soviet Union. One portly old charmer, who had been upper-middle management in the KGB, filled a whole afternoon around a long leather table telling me what restaurants to go to and what food to order. Smoked sturgeon, *pirozhki*, mushroom pie. His mouth was watering, though from the look of him he hadn't been exactly starved under capitalism. Still, no food like home cooking; I could sympathize with that. Those Washington people, they did love to party. After each briefing there would be a reception, and at one of the receptions a little black-haired coffee-fetcher from that afternoon's briefing came up to me as if her breasts were being offered on a tray. They were sizable pert breasts, in a peach-colored chemise that had just out-grown being a T-shirt.

"Sir, you are my god," she told me. That's always nice to hear, and she shouldn't have spoiled it by adding, "Except of course for Earl Scruggs. And that nice tall Allen Shelton, who used to fill in on banjo with the Virginia Boys; oh, he was *cute*! Now, have you heard those new sides the McRey-noldses have cut down in Jacksonville, with this boy called Bobby Thompson? *He* is the future! He has this whole new style—you can hear the melody! 'Hard Hearted.' 'Dixie Hoedown.' Oh, my!"

"Young lady, you know I'm not exactly bluegrass," I told her politely. "Earl, well, he's beginning to miss notes, but you can't get away from him, he's a giant, all right, and Don Reno likewise. Nevertheless, my above-all admiration is Pete Seeger, if you must know. He's the one, him and the Weavers, brought back the five-string after the war, after the dance bands had all but turned the banjo into a ukulele."

"He is folksy and *po*key and phony, if you're asking me," she said, with that hurried overemphasis I was beginning to get used to, while her warm black eyes darted back and forth around my face like stirred-up horseflies. "And a traitor to his country besides."

"Well," I admitted, "you won't find him on *Grand Ole Opry* real soon, but the college kids eat him up, and he does sheer, sincere picking—none of that show-biz flash that sometimes bothers me about old Earl. Young lady, you should calm yourself and sit down and listen sometime to those albums Pete cut with Woody and the Almanacs before the war."

"I did," she said eagerly. "I did, I did. *Talking Union. Sod Buster Ballads.* Wonderful true-blue lefty stuff. The West Coast Commies must have loved it. Mr. Chester, did you ever in your life listen to a program called *Jamboree* out of Wheeling?"

"Did I? I got my first airtime on it, on good old WWVA. Me and Jim Buchanan on fiddle, before he got big. 'Are You Lost in Sin?' and 'Don't Say Good-bye If You Love Me,' with a little 'Somebody Loves You, Darlin' ' for a rideout. Did I catch your name, may I ask?"

"You'll laugh. It's a silly name."

"I bet, now, it isn't. You got to love the name the good Lord gave you."

"It wasn't the good Lord, it was my hateful mother," she said and, taking a deep breath that rounded out her cheeks like a trumpet player's, came out with "Imogene." Then she exhaled in a blubbery rush and asked me, "Imogene Frye. Isn't it silly like I said?"

"No," I said. It was my first lie to her. She seemed a little off-center, right from the first, but Imogene could talk banjo, and here in this city of block-long buildings and charcoal suits that was as welcome to me as borscht and salted cucumbers would have been to that homeless KGB colonel, locked out forever as a traitor from the land he loved.

"I *loved*," this Imogene was saying, "the licks you took on 'Heavy Traffic Ahead.' And the repeat an octave higher on 'Walking in Jerusalem Just Like John.' "

"It wasn't an octave, it was a fifth," I told her, settling in and lifting two bourbons from a silver tray a kindly Negro was carrying around. I saw that this was going to be a conversation. Banjos were getting to be hot then, what with that *Beverly Hillbillies* theme, and I didn't want to engage with any shallow groupie. "Do you ever tune in," I asked her, "WDBJ, out of Roanoke? And tell me exactly why you think this Bobby Thompson is the future."

She saw my hurt, with those hot bright eyes that looked to be all pupil, and hastened to reassure me in her hurried, twitchy way of talking that I was the present, the past, and the future as far as she was concerned. Neither of us, I think, had the habit of drinking, but the trays kept coming around, brought by black men in white gloves, and by the time the reception was breaking up the whole scene might have been a picture printed on silk, waving gently in and out. The Iron Curtain experts had drifted away to their homes in Bethesda and Silver Spring, and it seemed the most natural thing in the free world that little Imogene, to whom I must have looked a little wavy myself, would be inviting me back to her apartment somewhere off in one of those neighborhoods where they say it's not safe for a white man to show his face late at night.

Black and white, that's most of what I remember. Her hair was black and soft, and her skin was white and soft, and her voice had slowed and gotten girlish with the effects of liquor and being romanced. I was on the floor peeling down her pantyhouse while she rested a hand on the top of my head for balance. Then we were sitting on the bed while she cupped her hands under those sizable breasts, pointing them at me like guns. "I want them to be even bigger," she told me so softly I strained to hear, "for *you*." Her breasts being smooched made her smile in the slanted streetlight like a round-faced cartoon character, a cat-and-canary smile. When I carried the courtesies down below, this seemed to startle her, so she stiffened a bit before relaxing her legs and letting them spread. The men she had known before didn't do this, back then before Vietnam took away our innocence, but ever since my days of car-seat courtship I've liked to press my face into a girlfriend's nether soul, to taste the waters in which we all must swim out to the light. I strove to keep my manly focus amid the jiggling caused by government-issue alcohol, and my wondering what time it was, and the jostling of my conscience, and the distractions of this environment, with its sadness of the single girl. Black and white—her little room was sucked dry of color like something on early TV, her bureau with its brushes and silver-framed photos of the family that had hatched her, an armchair with a cellophane-wrapped drugstore-rental book still balanced on one arm, where she had left it before heading off this morning into her working day, her FM/AM/shortwave portable radio big enough to pick up stations from Antarctica, her narrow bed with its brass headboard that was no good to lean on when we had done our best and needed to reminisce and establish limits.

"Lordy," I said. This was something of a lie, since when the main event came up I had lost a certain energy to the good times behind us, beginning hours ago at the party. I had felt lost in her.

She touched my shoulder and said my full name tentatively, as if I wouldn't like it. "Eddie Chester." She was right; it sounded proprietorial and something in me bristled. "You really are a god."

"You should catch me sober sometime."

"When?" Her voice pounced, quick and eager like it had been at first. The pieces of white beside her swollen pupils glinted like sparkles on TV. Her propped-up pillow eclipsed half her face and half a head of black hair mussed out to a wild size.

Mine had just been a manner of speaking. "Not ever, it may be, Imogene," I told her. "I have a week of gigs out west, and then I'm off on this trip, helping keep your planet safe for democracy."

"But I'll see you when you come back," she insisted. "You must come back to Washington, to be debriefed. Eddie, Eddie, Eddie," she said, as if knowing repetition galled me. "I can't ever let you go."

Imogene's magic essences had dried on my face and I longed for a washcloth and a taxi out of there. "I got a wife, you know. And four little ones."

"Do you love your wife?"

"Well, honey, I wouldn't say I don't, though after fifteen years a little of the bloom rubs off."

"Do you kiss her between the legs, too?"

This did seem downright forward. "I forget," I said, and pushed out of the bed into the bathroom, where the switch brought back color into everything, all those pinks and blues and yellows on her medicine shelves; it seemed she needed a lot of pills to keep herself functional.

"Eddie, don't go," she pleaded. "Stay the night. It's not safe out there. It's so bad the taxis won't come even if you call."

"Young lady, I got a hired car coming to the Willard Hotel at seven-thirty tomorrow morning to carry me back to western Virginia, and I'm going to be there. I may not be the future of banjo-picking, but I take a real professional pride in never having missed a date." Putting on my under-wear, I remembered how the taxi had gone around past the railroad station and then the Capitol, all lit up, and I figured we hadn't gone so far past it I couldn't steer myself by its tip, or by the spotlights on the Washington Monument.

"Eddie, you *can't* go, I won't let you," Imogene asserted, out of bed, all but one sweet fat white leg caught in the sheet. Her breasts didn't look quite so cocky without her holding them up for me. That's the trouble with a full figure, it ties you to a bra.

I crooned a few lines of "Don't Say Good-bye If You Love Me," until my memory ran out, though I could see Jim Buchanan's face inches across from me, squeezed into its fiddle, at the WWVA microphone. And then I told Imogene, as if still quoting a lyric, "Little darlin', you ain't keeping me here, though I must say it was absolute bliss." This was my third lie, but a white one, and with some truth still in it. "Now, you go save your undying affection for an unattached man."

"You'll be killed!" she shrieked, and clawed at me for a while, but I shushed and sweet-talked her back into her bed, fighting a rising headache all the while, and let myself out into the stairwell. The street, one of those numbered ones, was as still as a stage set, but, stepping out firmly in my cowboy boots, I headed toward what I figured was west— you get a sense of direction, growing up in the morning shadow of the Blue Ridge—and, sure enough, I soon caught a peek of the Capitol dome in the distance, white as an egg in an eggcup. A couple of tattered colored gentlemen stumbled toward me from a boarded-up doorway, but I gave them both a dollar and a hearty God bless and strode on. If a man can't walk around in his own country without fear, what business has he selling freedom to the Russians?

Bud Nevins got me and my banjos—a fine old Gibson mother-of-pearl-trimmed Mastertone and an S. S. Stewart

backup whose thumb string always sounded a little punky—
into Moscow and put us all to bed in a spare room of the big
apartment he and Libby and three children occupied in the
cement warehouse where the Russians stashed free-world
diplomatic staff. Mrs. Nevins was a long-haired strawberry
blonde beginning to acquire that tight, worried expression the wives of professors and government officials get,
from being saddled with their husbands' careers. You get
those pecking-order blues. The bygone Soviet summer hadn't
done much to refresh her freckles, and a bitter white winter
lay ahead. This was late September, shirtless apple-picking
time back home. The bed they put me in, the puff smelled
old-fashionedly of flake soap, the way my mother's laundry
used to when I'd help her carry the wicker basket heavy with
wet wash out to the clothesline. Ma and I were never closer
than around wet wash.

As he put me to bed Nevins said there was something
already come for me in the diplomatic pouch. An envelope
lay on my pillow, addressed to me care of the embassy APO
number in a scrunched-up hand in black ballpoint. Inside
was a long letter from Imogene, recounting her sorrowful
feelings after I left, guessing I was still alive because my
death in her neighborhood hadn't been in the papers and
she had caught on the radio a plug for an appearance of
mine in St. Louis. She recalled some sexual details I wasn't
sure needed to be set down on paper, and promised undying
love. I just skimmed the second page. Her words weren't
easy to read, like the individual letters wanted to double
back on themselves, and I was dog-tired from those thousands of miles I had travelled to reach the dark side of the
moon.

Now, I've seen a lot of friendly crowds in the course of my
professional life, but I must say I've never seen so many lovable, well-disposed people as I did that month in Russia.

They were, at least the ones that weren't in any gulag, full of
beans—up all night and bouncy the next morning. The
young ones didn't have that shadowy look American children were taking on in those years, as if dragged outdoors
from watching television; these young Russians seemed to
be looking directly at life in its sunshine and its hazard. I was
sorry to think it, but they were unspoiled. Grins poured
from the students I would play for, in one drafty old classroom after another. Converted ballrooms, many of them
seemed to be, or not even converted—they just hauled the
czarist dancers and musicians out and moved the Communist
desks in. There were dusty moldings and plaster garlands
high along the peeling plaster walls, with the walls still
painted pastel ballroom colors, and plush drapes rotting
around the view of some little damp park where old ladies in
babushkas, so gnarled and hunched our own society would
have had them on the junk heap, were sweeping the dirt
paths with brooms that were just twigs wrapped around a
stick. You used what you had here. People owned so little
material goods they had to take pleasure just in being alive.

I had worked up a little talk, allowing time for the transla-
tion. I would begin with the banjo as an African instrument,
called *banza* in the French West African colonies and *banjer*
in the American South, where in some backwaters you could
still hear it called that. Slaves played it, and then there were
the travelling minstrel shows, where white performers like
Dan Emmett and Joel Walker Sweeney still used the traditional black "stroke" or "frailing" or "claw-hammer" style of
striking down across the strings with thumb and the back
of the index-finger nail (I would demonstrate). Then (still
demonstrating) I would tell of the rise of the "finger-picking"
or "guitar" style, adding the middle finger and pulling *up* on
the strings with metal picks added to those three nails, and
ending with bluegrass and traditional folk as revived by

my hero Seeger. When I had said all that in about half an hour, with samples of what we think minstrel banjo sounded like and some rags from the 1890s the way Vess L. Ossman and Fred Van Eps left them on Edison cylinders and ending with a little Leadbelly, they would ask me why Americans oppressed our black people.

I got better at answering that one, as I strummed and picked and rolled through those echoing classrooms. I stopped saying that slavery had been universal not long ago and the Russians had had their serfs, that several hundred thousand white men from the North had died so that slaves could be free, that a hundred years later civil-rights laws had been passed and lynching had become a rarity. I could tell, as I stood there listening to myself being translated, that I was losing them, it was too much like what they heard from their own teachers, too much pie in the sky. I changed to saying simply yes, it was a problem, a disgraceful problem, but that I honestly believed that America was working at it, and music was one of the foremost ways it was working at it. Listening to myself talk, I'd sometimes think the State Department knew what it was doing, bringing a natural patriotic optimist like me over here. Ever since JFK had got shot, my breed was harder to find. They must have had a pretty fat file on me somewhere: the thought made me uneasy.

It felt best when I played, played as if for a country-fair crowd back home, and those young Russian faces would light up as if I were telling jokes. They had all heard jazz, and even some Twist and early rock on tapes that were smuggled through, but rarely anything so jaunty and tinny and jolly, so *irrepressible*, as banjo music going full steam, when your fingers do the thinking and you listen in amazement yourself. Sometimes they would pair me with a balalaika player, and one little Azerbaijani, I think he had some Gypsy blood, tried my instrument, and I his. We made an act of it for a few days, touring the Caucasus, hill towns where old men with beards would gather outside the auditorium windows as if sipping moonshine. When they had advertised ahead for a formal concert, the crowds were so big the Soviet controllers cut down on the schedule.

The translator who travelled with me varied but usually it was Nadia, a lean thin-lipped lady over forty who had learned her English during the war, in the military. She had lost two brothers and a fiancé to Herr Hitler, and was wed to the Red system with bonds of iron and grief. She looked like a skinny tall soldier boy herself, just out of uniform—no lipstick, long white waxy nose, and a feathery short haircut with gray coming in not in strands but in patches. Blank-faced, she would listen to me spiel, give a nod when she'd heard all she could hold, and spout out a stream of this language that was, with all its mushy twisty sounds, pure music to me. The more she and I travelled together, the better she knew what I was going to say, and the longer she could let me go before translating, and the more I could hear individual words go by, little transparent phrases through which I seemed to see into her like into the windows of a town as your train whips through. We travelled on trains in the same compartment, so I could look down from the top bunk and see her hands remove her shoes and her mustard-colored stockings from her feet. Then her bare feet and hands would flitter out of sight. I would listen, but never hear her breathing relax; she confessed to me, toward the end of my stay, that she could never sleep on trains. The motion and the clicking stirred her up.

An inhibiting factor was Bud Nevins being in the compartment with us—there were two bunks on two sides—and if not Bud, another escort from our embassy, and often a fourth, an underling of Bud's or a second escort from the Soviet side, who spoke Armenian or Kazakh or whatever the language was going to be when we disembarked. Sometimes I had more escorts than would fit into one compartment; and I expect I often got the best night's sleep, with everybody watching everybody else. Nadia was as loyal a comrade as they made them but seemed to need watching anyway. As I got to know her body language I could tell when we were being crowded, politically speaking.

After a while my tendency became to bond with the Communists. When we arrived at one of our hinterland destinations, Nadia and her associates would bundle me into a Zil and then we would share a humorous irritation at being tailed by an embassy watchdog in his imported Chevrolet. When we all went south, Bud came along with that willowy strawberry blond of his. Libby had, along with her worried look, a plump pretty mouth a little too full of teeth. For all their three children, they hadn't been married ten years. Out of wifely love and loyalty she wanted to join in what fun the Soviet Union in its sinister vast size offered.

Somewhere in backwoods Georgia—their Georgia, even hillier than ours—we visited a monastery, a showpiece of religious tolerance. The skeleton crew of monks glided around with us in their grim stone rooms. The place had that depressing stuffy holy smell, old candle wax and chrism and furniture polish, I had last sniffed thirty years ago, in the storage closet of a Baptist basement Sunday school. Among the monks with beards down to their bellies was a young one, and I wondered how he had enlisted himself in this ghostly brotherhood. Demented or a government employee, I decided. He had silky long hair, like a princess captive in a tower, and the sliding bloodshot eyeballs of a spy. He was one kind of human animal, and I was another, and when we looked at each other we each repressed a shudder.

Outside, a little crowd of shepherds and sheep, neither group looking any too clean, had gathered around the automobiles, and when Nadia made our identities and friendly mission clear to them, the shepherds invited us to dine with them, on one of the sheep. I would have settled for some cabbage soup and blini back at the Tblisi hotel, but the Nevinses looked stricken, as though this chance at authentic ethnicity and bridge-building would never come again, and I suppose it wouldn't have. Their duty was to see that I did my duty, and my duty was clear: consort with the shepherds, scoring points for the free world. I looked toward Nadia and with one of her unsmiling nods she approved, though this hadn't been on her schedule. Or, who knows, maybe it had been. By now I saw her as an ally in my mission to subvert the rule of the proletariat, no doubt deluding myself.

We climbed what seemed like a mile at least and sat down around a kind of campfire, where an ominous big kettle was mulling over some bony chunks of a creature recently as alive as we. The shepherds loved Libby's free-falling hair and the way her round freckled knees peeped out of her modified miniskirt as we squatted in our circle of rock perches. A goatskin of red wine was produced; as stated before, I'm no connoisseur of alcoholic beverages, but this stuff was so rough that flies kept dying in our cups, and a full swig took the paint off the roof of your mouth. After the goatskin had been passed a few times, Libby began to relish the shepherds' attention, to glow and giggle and switch her long limbs around and come up with her phrases of language-school Russian. Those shepherds—agricultural workers and livestock supervisors was probably how they thought of themselves—had a number of unsolved dental problems, as we saw when their whiskers cracked open in a laugh, but there was a lot of love around that simmering pot, a lot of desire for international peace. Even Bud took off his jacket and unbuttoned his top shirt button, and Nadia began to lounge back in the scree and translate me loosely, with what I heard as her own original material. The lamb when it was served, in tin bowls, could have been mulled somewhat longer and was mixed in with what looked like crabgrass, roots and all, and some little green capers that each had a firecracker inside, but as it turned out only the Nevinses got sick. Next day they had to stay in their hotel room with the shades lowered while the Communists and I motored out to entertain a People's War veterans home that had an excellent view of Mt. Elbrus. The way we all cackled in the car at the expense of the Nevinses and their tender capitalist stomachs was the cruellest thing I saw come to pass in my month in the Soviet Union.

Uzbekistan, Tajikistan, Kazakhstan: you wondered why the Lord ever made so much wasteland in the world, with a gold dome or blue lake now and then as a sop to the thirsty soul. But here's where the next revolution was coming from, it turned out—out from under those Islamic turbans. When my banjo flashed mother-of-pearl their way, they made the split-finger sign to ward off the evil eye. They knew a devil's gadget when they saw it.

Whenever I showed up back in Moscow I got solemnly handed packets of letters in Imogene's cramped black hand, pages and pages and pages of them. I couldn't believe the paper she would waste, as well as the abuse of taxpayer money involved in using the diplomatic pouch. She had heard me take an eight-bar vocal break on my Decca cut of "Somebody Loves You, Darling," on the station out of Charlottesville, and decided it was a code to announce that I was leaving my wife for her. "I am altogether open and YOURS, my dearest DEAREST Eddie," she wrote, if I can remember one sentence in all that trash. "I will wait for as LONG as it takes, though KINGDOM COME in the meantime," if I can recall another. Then on and on, with every detail of what she did each day, with some about her internal workings that I would rather not be told, though I was happy she had her period, and all about her unhappiness (that I wasn't there with her) and hopefulness (that I soon would be), and her theory that I was in the air talking to her all the time, broadcasting from every frequency on the dial, including the shortwave that brought in stations from the Caribbean and the Azores. If she caught the Osborne Brothers doing "My Lonely Heart" and "You'll Never Be the Same," she knew that I was their personal friend and had asked them to send her the private message, never mind they recorded it in the early Fifties. I couldn't do more than skim a page here and there—the handwriting got smaller and scrunchier and then would blossom out into some declaration of love printed in capitals and triple underlined. Just the envelopes, the bulky white tumble of them, were embarrassing me in front of Bud Nevins and the whole embassy staff, embattled here in the heartland of godless Communism. How could I be a cultural ambassador while shouldering this ridiculous load of conceited infatuation?

Imogene was planning where we would live, how she would dress in her seat of honor at my concerts, what she would do for me in the bedroom and the kitchen to keep my love at its present sky-high pitch. Thinking we were in for a lifetime together, she filled me in on her family, her mother that she had maligned but who wasn't all bad, and her father who was scarcely in her life enough to mention, and her brothers and sisters that sounded like the worst pack of losers and freeloaders on the DelMarVa Peninsula. Her outpourings would catch, my fear was, the vigilance of the KGB, X-raying right through the diplomatic pouch. I would lose face with Nadia, that steel-true exemplar of doing without. Those innocent-eyed gymnasium students would sense my contamination. The homely austerity of Soviet life, with that undercurrent of fear still humming from Stalin, made the amorous delusions of this childish American woman repulsive to me. As my month approached its end, and the capitalist world put out feelers to reclaim me, Imogene's crazy stuff got mixed in with business cables from my agency and colorless but loving letters from my wife with enclosed notes and dutiful drawings from my children: this heightened my disgust. I would have sent a cable—CUT IT OUT, or YOU AIN'T NO BLUE-EYED SWEETHEART OF MINE—but by some canniness of her warped mind she never gave a return address, and when I tried to think of her apartment all I got was that black-and-white feeling, the way she fed me her breasts one at a time, the very big radio, and the empty street with the Capitol at the end like a white-chocolate candy. I had simply to endure it, this sore humiliation.

They had saved Leningrad for me to the last, since it was where the Communists, still remembering the Siege, were the toughest, and I might run into the most hostility from an audience. But as soon as my Gibson began talking, the picked strings all rolling like the synchronized wheels, big and little, of the Wabash Cannonball, the smiles of mutual understanding would start breaking out. I am not a brave man, but I have faith in my instrument and in people's basic decent instincts. St. Petersburg, as we call it again, is one beautiful city, a Venice where you least expect it, all those big curved buildings in Italian colors. The students in their gloomy old ballrooms were worried about Goldwater getting elected, and I told them the American people would never elect a warmonger. I was always introduced as a "progressive" American folk artist, but I had to tell them that there wasn't much progressive about me: my folks had been lifelong Democrats because of a war fought a hundred years ago, and I wasn't going to be the one to change parties.

Then, just as I was about to get back onto Aeroflot, Khrushchev was pushed out of power, and all the Soviets around me tightened up, wary of what was going to happen next. This whole huge empire, think of it, run out of some vodka-soaked back rooms by a few beetle-browed men. Nadia—my voice, my guide, my protector, closer to me for this month than a wife, because I couldn't have done without her—complimented me by confiding, somewhere out on the Nevskii Prospekt or in some hallway where no bugs were likely to be placed, "Eddie, it was not civilized. It was not done how a civilized country should do things. We should have said to him, 'Thank you very much for ending the terror.' And then, 'You are excused—too much adventurism, O.K., failures in agricultural production, and et cetera. O.K., so long, but *bolshoi* thanks.' "

There would be a moment, toward the end of a long public day in, say, Tashkent, when her English would deteriorate, just sheer weariness from drawing upon a double set of brain cells, and her eyelids and the tip of her long white nose would get pink. We would say good night in the hotel lobby, with its musty attic smell and lamps whose bases were brass bears, and she would give me in her handshake not the palm and meat of the thumb but four cool fingers, aligned like a sergeant's stripes. And that was the way we began to say goodbye in the airport, until we leaped the gulf between our two great countries and I kissed her on one cheek and then the other and hugged her, in proper Slavic style. Her eyes teared up, but it may have been just the start of a cold.

Bud told me in the airport, so casually I should have smelled trouble, "We took you off the APO number two days ago, so your mail won't show up here after you leave. It will be forwarded to your home."

"Sounds reasonable," I said, not thinking it through. I

suspect Bud foresaw the complications, but he was a diplomat, a pro at saying no more than required.

Coming back, the last leg, out of Paris, I had an experience such as I've never had in all my miles of flying. We came down on the big arc over Gander and Nova Scotia and, five miles up, I could see New York from hundreds of miles away, a little blur of light in the cold plastic oval of the plane window. It grew and grew, like a fish I was pulling in. My cheek got cold against the plastic as I pressed to keep it in view, a little spot on the invisible surface of the earth like a nebula, like a dust mouse, only glowing, the fuzzy center of our American dream. Just it and me, there in the night sky, communing. It was a vision.

After I cleared customs at what had been Idlewild until recently, I phoned home. It was after ten o'clock, but I was powerfully glad to be again in the land of the free. My wife answered with something else in her voice besides welcome, like a fearful salamander under a flat rock. "Some letters for you came today and yesterday," she said. "All from one person, it looks like."

How bright, I was thinking, this place was, compared to the Moscow airport. Every corner and rampway was lit as harsh as a mug shot, the whole place packed with advertisements and snack bars and sizzling with electricity. "Did you open them?" I asked, my heart suddenly plunked by a heavy hand.

"Just one," she said. "That was enough, Eddie. Oh, my."

"It wasn't anything," I began, which wasn't a hundred percent true. For, though in one part of me I was not happy with Imogene for making what looked to be an ongoing talking point in my little family, on the other hand you can't blame a person too hard for thinking you're a god. You have to feel a spark of fondness, remembering the way she held up one breast and then the other, each nipple looking in that black-and-white room like the hole of a gun barrel pointed straight at your mouth. You can go to the dark side of the moon and back and see nothing more wonderful and strange than the way men and women manage to get together.

His Oeuvre

Henry Bech, the aging American author, found that women he had slept with decades ago were showing up at his public lectures. He could sense them in the auditorium even when it was dark. Clarissa Tompkins, for instance, slipped in late at a reading in New Jersey, in an old suburban movie theatre converted to cultural uses, after the house lights were dimmed and he had already launched himself into one of the prose poems from his miscellany *When the Saints* (1958), evoking an East Village junk shop. Lifting his head to project the phrase "a patina of obscure former usage annealing a contemporary application of very present dust," savoring the sibilance in that clinching duet of words, he saw her silhouette against the dull glow cast by the old-fashionedly ornate sign to the movie house's ladies' room. Clarissa glided out of the island of amber light into the dark rows at the back, but there had been no mistaking the upswept hairdo, taffy-colored in his memories, that enlarged her already sizable head, a head poignantly balanced on her petite, breastless frame. After lovemaking in the Tompkinses' splendid Fifth Avenue apartment, with its view of the Reservoir, they would have a naked picnic on the deep-napped Oriental at the center of the living room, a little further burst of taffy color innocently flared as she sat cross-legged, devouring her half of a turkey sandwich that the cook had made before leaving for the afternoon. Amidst the opulence of her apartment Clarissa was thrifty. One sandwich was cut in two, one teabag served two cups. Her face beneath all that bouffant hair looked tiny, and as she scrunched it into her half-sandwich it almost disappeared—the small straight nose, the myopic green eyes usually straining to see but now vaguely swimming in her orgasm's aftermath. At each bite, her plump upper lip would leave a cerise blur at the rim of white bread. Her lipstick was messy and indelible; Bech usually needed a full cleanup, not with just a washrag but with paper towels dabbed in vodka, before he dared confront the elevator, the doorman, the avenue.

What had led her to show up in New Jersey, at this community college wedged in the suburban wastes north of Newark? How had she known of his reading? He lost his place, wondering, and a silence stretched above the faces listening in the shadows before he found his spot on the page and went on: "One warily inspects, bending forward, a mostly wooden apple-corer, a piece of carved intricacy suggesting a torturer's device out of Borges or Kafka, that had somehow, through a chain of canny and, one hopes, profitable transactions made its way from an underheated Vermont attic to this stuffy, jumbled trading post in nether Gotham." He disliked the sentence, more wordy than he had ever noticed before.

Mr. Tompkins had been a patron—the chief patron, indeed—of an avant-garde publication with the austere name of *Displeasure*, to which Bech had been a faithful contributor. Clarissa had seen in him, perhaps, a noble savage—

a woolly-haired, thick-bodied bohemian beyond all bour-
geois scruples. The Fifties had been a boom time for noble
savages, more or less modelled on Henry Miller, before
the Sixties brought in such a slew of them that they became
a politically demanding mob. But Bech had a tender regard,
if not for wealth as a Marxian steamroller, a brute mass of
figures in the asset column, then for the delectable artifacts
wealth could purchase—for Tompkins's lush carpets, for his
gilt-brushed Oriental prints, for his kitchen gleaming with
brass Swiss fixtures and green marble countertops, for his
king-size bed and its sheets of sea-island cotton. The couple
was childless; these possessions were their helpless children.
Each tryst in the luxurious duplex—the maid and the cook
tactfully dismissed by the mistress but retaining who knows
what low suspicions—had made Bech morally queasy.
Tompkins patronizes art; the literary artist pays him back by
screwing his wife. Is this justice?

Clarissa, to do her credit, felt that the situation was somehow sensitive for her lover. She pressed her physical claims
as if upon an invalid, with the soft yet unretreating voice of a
hospital visitor, coaxing him into vigor; she led him as if
he had been a teen-ager into certain byways of gratification
that left her lipstick stains passed back and forth between
their bodies like the ricochet marks in a squash court. The
route to her orgasms could be tortuous. A yoga adept, she
liked being bent backward over a silk-cushioned stool so
that her head rested on the floor a foot below her hips, her
green eyes groping for his face and the rug's swirling pattern
showing through her teased, expanded hair. She did not
mind, she led him to slowly understand, certain Hindu variations on the standard positions, and with wordless hints
drew his masculine force out of its shell of shyness. His very
reserve and hesitation enabled her, it seemed, to break some
seal on her own inhibitions.

Still, she could not hold him. His sense of himself as a violator of Arnold Tompkins's posh apartment, its delicate silks and blameless satins, led him to write Clarissa a letter of withdrawal, pleading, not falsely, a desire to leave her ensconced among treasures whose beauty and worth, though negligently dismissable by her, were not so by him. In short, he did not want by any consequence of scandal to become responsible for a rich woman's upkeep, ardent for debasement though she had shown herself to be.

As he read at the tippy, ill-lit lectern, plowing on with these forty-year-old prose poems, which suddenly seemed fatally mannered as well as badly dated, and then launching himself into the well-worn anthology piece, the truck-stop brawl in his road novel, *Travel Light* (1955), he scanned the audience between sentences, looking for a stray glimmer from the high airy crown of her hair. She had shifted in the darkness from her initial perch in the back row, near the glowing amber sign that was, he squintingly perceived, a kind of magic lantern, a metal box cut, in one of the elegancies common in the old movie-palaces, so as to form against its light bulb the silhouette of a pompadoured eighteenth-century woman at her toilet, above the cut-out script spelling *Mesdames*.

And when the house lights came up, for the apple-corer torture of the question-and-answer period, Clarissa was quite gone, sunk forever beneath the smiling sea of middle-aged—more than middle-aged, elderly—female book-lovers and author groupies. How mischievous of her to show up so magically and then vanish! Had it been a reprimand for his disappearance from her life, to which he had been granted such unstinting entry? They had not met again, even at an office party, for Tompkins had shortly thereafter withdrawn his patronage from *Displeasure*, and the magazine had limped along a while and then collapsed.

. . .

At the West Side "Y"—so much cozier a venue than the more heavily publicized East Side forum at Ninety-second Street—Bech sought for a friendly face in the audience upon which to pin his reading. He was trying, for far from the first time, to pump life into that scene from his novel *Think Big* (1979) wherein Olive, having discovered herself at last to be a lesbian, confesses her previous amours while lying in the arms of Tad Greenbaum's discarded mistress, Thelma, in the orange sunset light that enters the room horizontally, like bars of music, from beyond the Palisades. This passage, with its shuffling back and forth between two love-drugged female voices, was a precarious one to animate, and needed the encouragement of a willing smile from some female auditor. Tonight the smile, so radiant—luscious, even, in its wide white face—did not have to be sought out; rather, it seemed to have sought him out. As he read aloud, murmuring into the rustling, sometimes woofing microphone, he was nagged by the notion that he had known this encouraging face before. The smile, outlined in a lipstick so dark it appeared black in the auditorium half-light, had a sweet, forgiving tuck on one side that implied former acquaintance, an insight into him that bypassed his theatrical attempt to breathe life into the drowsy confidences of two imaginary daughters of Bilitis. The only thing real in what he was reading was the room itself, an exact transcription of the Riverside Drive apartment he had lived in for years, before his ill-fated marriage to Bea Latchett, Norma Latchett's relatively sweet-tempered sister.

Wait, he thought even as he kept his voice working. There was a cranny, a niche in the era of his life dominated by the Latchett sisters where this disembodied black-lipped smile fit. Burgundy mouth, long-lashed purple-irised eyes, straight black hair falling to glossy wide shoulders, a vivid black arrowhead centered between white, well-cushioned pelvic crests. A woman encountered at widely scattered intervals, a woman a touch too fleshy and dogmatic for him, but whose amazing waxen pallor, lighting up rooms otherwise dim, drew him back, now and again, as he glancingly, skittishly moved through downtown literary circles in those slovenly Sixties. *Gretchen*. Gretchen Folz, the would-be poet. Her pathetic cubbyhole on Bleecker Street, its narrow bed snug against a parsley-green wall, access to its other side limited by tilting stacks of New Directions and Grove Press paperbacks. The bed had an Amish bedspread whose pattern of triangular patches reminded him of stars of David, and an iron head whose vertical pipes dug grooves into his back when Gretchen, in the woman-couchant position, straddled him and teased his mouth with her livid nipples.

The thrill of recovered memory made his voice boom inappropriately as he read Olive's tender summing up to Thelma: "It was all, you know, like Snow White's forest on the path to *you*." Decades ago, he remembered, he had vacillated between "path" and "way" and had rejected "way" as a word with too many meanings and too evocative of Proust, but now "way" seemed the more natural expression, though less incidentally evocative of entangling sexual grapples, with leering male faces on the Disneyesque tree trunks.

Gretchen's poems had wispily trailed down the page, making elliptical jumps that he had taken to be faithful to the way her mind worked, her erratic inner connections. Her orgasms did not come easily either. She had been flustered at first by Bech's rather burly determination to work on the problem with her. "Slam, bam, thank you ma'am is really often the most satisfying," she told him.

"What a cop-out," he said. "Think what an exploitative heel that makes me."

"But what . . . ? I mean how . . . ?"

How lovely, how adorably alight her wide, avidly intellectual face had been in its girlish confusion, its pre-feminist reluctance to think of her genitals in detail. He had piqued her interest, and they clambered together over the pillars of Pound and Burroughs, Céline and Genet, Anaïs Nin and Djuna Barnes, which spilled like a row of dominoes, the topple reaching the center of the tiny room.

Why had his contacts with Gretchen been so scattered, so infrequent, as willing and, gradually, responsive as she had been? Her writing, perhaps, had offended him: his erotic drive generally steered clear of literary women, who might compete or try to touch the aloof, unspeakable heart of his raison d'être. Also, she was large, not lithe and little as he liked women; he distrusted the luxury of her spilling flesh, the creamy slowness of her laboring, amid the swelling smells of brine and estrus, toward sexual release. If she had lost a little weight, if there had been a little less flesh to move, she might have found the way—the path—easier. His ministrations felt awkwardly close to those of a doctor rather than those of a lover, with a therapeutic focus that diluted his own excitement. Also, descending into the cramped quarters and futile literary ambitions of Bleecker Street struck him—already faintly famous, with all four of his titles, up to 1963, having achieved mention in the *New York Times Book Review*'s Christmas list of Notable Books— as slumming. And she was Jewish, which wasn't what he needed at the time. He felt Jewish enough for two. He had something she strongly needed, his sexual patience, and this naked need of hers alarmed, it could have been, the fastidious vagabond in him. Though he neglected her for weeks at a time, she was never indignant for long when he coasted back into her orbit.

Tonight, too, after he had doggedly, absent-mindedly completed his reading, and taken half-hearted swings at a few of the puffball questions the audience tossed up, Gretchen met him with no shadow of resentment for his fitful wooing and unapologetic fading-away, but instead with a matured form of her old wistful glee, her girlish hope of fulfillment at his hands. Her kiss of greeting claimed him with a new authority; her bohemian diffidence was gone. "Henry, I'd like you to meet my husband," she said.

He was a substantial red-faced fellow, sixty or so, dignified but not unfriendly, wearing a pinstriped suit that was more accustomed to board meetings than prose readings. "Good stuff," he said gamely, guessing why he had been brought here. To be shown off.

"Henry, how you still do go on," Gretchen said. "A lesbian is the last thing you want to be. You'd have to give up your balls."

"I don't know. I'm still evolving," he said, regretting that her peck to one side of his mouth had been so brief, so dry. She looked fulfilled. Her wide-hipped weight, next to the bulk of her spouse, was no problem, and she had had her hair cut raggedly short and tinged with a metallic cinnabar red, giving her a rather ravishing futuristic look.

"What ever happened to your poems?" he asked. He never knew quite what to say to these women who showed up.

"Privately printed," she answered. The sharp dark corners of her mouth tucked into her creamy cheeks with the only hint of revenge that her forgiving nature would allow itself. "*Beau*tifully printed. Bob *loves* them."

"Bob," Bech said, prolonging the vowel as if to taste her once again, "is obviously a discerning critic. He likes both our stuff. Stuffs."

You don't expect much to happen in Indianapolis, once you've seen the Hoosier Dome and the Soldiers' and Sailors'

Monument. Their pairing reminded Bech of the closer coupling, in London, of Royal Albert Hall—round and capacious and rosy—and the phallic spike of the Albert Memorial across Kensington Road. Perhaps the world can be deconstructed into these two basic shapes, everywhere seeking the other. Just before his reading at the Marion County Public Library, while he was standing idle and momentarily unchaperoned on one side of the steps to the stage, a crisp, short, pleasant-looking woman in a magenta tweed suit came up to him starry-eyed.

He had encountered starry eyes before, in the visages of women who had read too much into one of his novels, casting themselves as his sketchy script's heroine. This woman's approach, however, was not that of a fan. "Henry Bech," she said, in the fearless flat accent of the great American inland. "I am Alice Oglethorpe. You may not remember, but we once travelled from New York to Los Angeles on the same train."

Her handshake was like her voice, firm, and neither cold nor warm, but he detected a slight tremble. Then, her identity dawning, Bech's heart surged forward in his chest and he, the professional spielmeister, felt his mouth open and nothing come out. Her blue eyes, with their uncanny silvery backing, clung to his attentively while his brain groped. He would not have recognized her at all. She seemed too young to be his Alice. Though his blood had bounded toward her, he was ashamed to have become, since they had last been together, an old man. "Oh my God," he brought out at last. "You. Of course I remember. The Twentieth Century Limited."

"Just as far as Chicago," she corrected him. "After that, it was the Santa Fe Super Chief."

His left hand, holding the book that he was to read from

tonight, clumsily tried to caress the hand, the precious piece of her, that he was holding in his right. "How are you?" he asked. "*Where* are you? What happened next?"

Bech's confusion gratified her, and calmed her. She withdrew her hand, with its tremble. Her eyes did not leave his, but her mouth, tense at first, settled into a smile. She had been recognized. "I'm here," she answered. "Or, rather, in Bloomington. I'm well. Still married. I got over it."

She had oddly little aged, just broadened a bit. Her hair was the same light-brunette shade, too nondescript to be a tint—"dishwater blonde" was the phrase his mother used to use—and her wool suit was scarcely saved by its bold magenta from verging on dowdy. Her disguise as an ordinary, respectable woman was intact.

Her husband, he remembered, had been some sort of financial analyst, a middle-level money man. She had been travelling to L.A. to join him at the end of a weeklong conference sponsored by the southern-California defense industry, then in its hearty youth. Oh, she could have gone with Tad and stayed in the hotel, but what would she have done all day—take bus tours to the homes of the stars? Her silvery eyes and dry intonation told Bech that she considered herself, at some level, as much of a star as they. At least she was a proximate presence, talking only to him. She had always wanted to travel across the country, she told him, and hated to fly, though she *could* do it, with a couple of stiff drinks inside her. Bech was going to the far coast on what he intuited would be a futile exploration of the cinematic possibilities of his first, somewhat sensational novel, *Travel Light*. He, too, would rather ride the rails than entrust his body to the bumpy, propeller-driven flights of the late Fifties, before the onset of the big jets. The dashing transcontinental trains were on the way out, and by taking one Alice and he revealed a kindred romantic streak. All this emerged in their first conversation, they having been seated together, two singles, in the crowded dining car.

The shiver of their cutlery on the vibrating tablecloth. The reassuring, fairy-tale solidity of the heavy-bottomed cups and coffeepots, bearing the New York Central's logo. The theatrically deferential black waiters in a world where happy black servitude was also on the way out. Bech sensed as soon as she was ushered to his tingling table that she would sleep with him. There was that pale light in her eyes, a slightly loud shimmer in her teal-blue gabardine suit, an eager electricity in the way she moved and, with a little wine in her, talked. Women who were talkative, the sexual lore of his Brooklyn boyhood had reported and his limited experience tended to verify, "put out" in other respects. He and this woman were as alone on that speeding train, clicking north beside the blue autumnal Hudson, as on a desert island.

His chaperone, the head librarian of Indianapolis, reclaimed him; it was time to go onstage and earn his fee. Alice Oglethorpe said, warmly but formally, that it had been good to see him after all these years.

"You look wonderful—wonderful!" was all he could bring out. She turned away, he turned away. How stupid he had been! No blushing schoolboy could have been more tongue-tied. That clumsy scraping caress he had tried to deliver with a book in his hand. His failure to ask any searching questions. His body felt like a struck gong, swollen by its reverberations. To think that she was near, that she had come to find him! As he dizzily plowed through his reading, the questions he should have asked her flocked to his mind. Where did she live, exactly? Was she happy? Would she run away with him now, now that her motherly duties were done? There had been small children, he remembered, whom she had left with her husband's parents in the Bronx.

But she was not from New York City, her journey had begun upstate, and that made her seem even more of a gift from beyond. Beyond all reason. Beyond all expectations. Under the lectern light his hands looked strange and withered, but for all that rather beautiful. Articulated masses, with hair on the backs of his fingers. He had once been beautiful.

She did not sleep with him the first night. She stood up after coffee and firmly said good night. In those days the Pullman sleepers with green-curtained upper and lower berths had become antiques; the sleeper cars on the Twentieth Century Limited were divided into roomettes, each measuring seven feet by three. Bech scarcely slept, knowing that she was but a few steps away, in another roomette. Perhaps like him she was writhing between the too-tight sheets and flipping the pillow over to its cool side in the vain hope that blessed oblivion would rise from it, mixed with the tireless thud of the rail joints. Toward dawn there was a prolonged bright ruckus that must have been Buffalo.

They found each other at breakfast, in the dining car as it swayed and chimed through Ohio. "How did you sleep?" he asked.

"Terribly."

"Maybe we were lonely."

"I never sleep well on trains, thanks," she said. Her sleepless pallor and the unforgiving morning sunlight as it bounced up from the glittering stubble of the cornfields brought out a slight roughness, a constellation of tiny nicks as if from an adolescent storm of acne, below her cheekbones. The harsh slant sunlight betrayed her and then was slapped down by intervening poles, brick gables, rail-side warehouses. Makeup hadn't quite covered this touching flaw. He had forgotten it, he had forgotten to look for it in the few amazing moments when she had appeared again before him. She had once asked him if he would ever forget her.

He turned the slightly abrasive page under the lectern light. He had chosen—God knows why, perhaps because he believed Indianapolis to be a pious place—that passage from *Brother Pig* (1957) where the Trappist monks, loosely based on what he had read of Thomas Merton, silently plot, with hand signals and written slips, to smuggle in a Jewish reporter from a New York tabloid—a "scandal sheet," one would call it now—to expose the abbot's tyranny and pederasty. How did he, Henry Bech, get caught in this embarrassing tangle of far-fetched, decadent motifs when the most marvellous lay of his life was out there among the shadowy, offended heads of devout Quaylites and Butler University evangels?

Alice and he had breakfasted together, and sat dozily with books in the club car. Other travellers spoke to them, and they were inveigled into a game of bridge, of which he scarcely knew the rules, squinting at his cards beside the sun-slapped windows, trying to decipher her bids, all the time feeling her with him in a dream world of insomniac yearning and wordless anticipation of the night. When, in late afternoon, they pulled into Chicago, for a half-hour shuffle of cars and locomotives, Bech dashed out of the great barrel-vaulted station to buy, in that era just before the Pill's liberating advent, a three-pack of Trojans at a Rexall's on Jackson Boulevard. His heart thrummed as if to break his ribs. The sly, blond-mustached clerk tried to talk him into an entire tin of fifty instead of the pack of three—"You'll use 'em," he promised, on no more basis than Bech's flushed, panting face—and with spiteful slowness, the economy size declined, counted out Bech's change. Suppose the train pulled out without him?

Now, in Indianapolis, he was compelled to make his way

through pages he had felt obliged, decades ago, to write, in order to give his scabrous, irreligious journalist a family background and a professional history satiric of post-war New York literary circles. Had ever a selection been more ill-chosen, more maddeningly prolonged? A few nervous titters in the audience tried to rise to the cultural occasion. Did he hear Alice's laugh? She had laughed, telling him once, "You're safe."

At dinner, as the train hurtled into the darkness of flat farmland where a few distant houses pricked the night, she rose unsteadily from her coffee, smoothing some crumbs from her lap, and said, "I must lie down. I feel sick."

"Oh dear, why?"

His new friend smiled. "The constant motion. The long day. Not you. I like you." She hesitated, fighting a bit for balance as the Super Chief slammed over a patch of rocky roadbed. She bent toward him above the chattering silverware and said, softly but matter-of-factly, "Give me an hour. I must rest a little. Roomette sixteen. Knock twice."

" 'Klein found himself fascinated by the Trappists,' " he heard himself reading. " 'Like Hasidim, they seemed to possess an archaic secret of joy, a secret coded in their grotesque hairdos. The monks' tonsures framed a pink circle of scalp, and their faces had a childish sheen polished to a bright daze by the cruel hours of their devotions and their dawn rising to the dreary duties of farmers.' " Too many dentals, Bech thought. And then his captive tongue was launched into a long and dated description of Klein's brother, a labor organizer when such men still wielded a power that could bring a country to a halt.

After an hour of staring at the flat, loam-black land— were they still in Illinois?—Bech had had the porter make up his roomette, number 5. In pajamas and pinstriped cotton robe he ventured out into the carpeted aisle, alone with its rigid, retreating perspective. He feared she would be asleep, but her answer to his two knocks was quick. Her hair pulled back, her face clean of makeup—his impression was of a nun or a prisoner in her cell—she was kneeling in a nightgown on the bed; there was nowhere else in the tiny cell to be. So that twenty-four roomettes could be fitted into the length of a car, they were dovetailed, with two steps' difference in height between each adjacent pair; the bed of the slightly lower chamber slid in daytime under the floor of the raised room beside it, and the feet of its occupants extended under an overhang which somewhat inhibited their movements. But Alice was small and flexible and he not tall, and at times they seemed to stretch their allotted space to the size of a ballroom. Between times they raised the shade, gingerly, as if watchdogs of Midwestern puritanism might be posed in the black air streaming outside. The vast sleeping landscape would be shattered by a rapid garble of silhouetted architecture, or by lowered crossing gates where headlights patiently burned, or a local station platform like a suspensefully empty stage set. The small towns with their neon signs and straight strings of streetlamps wheeled and fell away to reveal the main visual drama, the abysmal void of farmland. Low streaks of cloud hung in a faint phosphorescence, like a radioactive aftermath.

They must be in Missouri now, if not Kansas. Her pliant nakedness, unified to his senses of touch and smell, flickered in curved short circuits as the train roared past lights defending a water tower or a set of grain silos. When the train hissed and slid to a stop, at a platform holding only a bare baggage-wagon and one loudly reuniting family, he raised the stiff green shade a few inches so he could ponder his companion's supine beauty as a continuous, calm, exultant entity, with rises and swales and dulcet shadowed corners. The curious silvery light of her eyes now lived all along her skin. In the small space carved from the surrounding, upholding clatter and mutter of the rushing train, she was a giantess who met him, his sensation was, wherever he thrusted, with an embracing cavity. She did it all, and had to keep suppressing moans which would disturb the unknown fellow-passengers presumably sleeping an arm's length away. "Will you forget me?" she at one point whispered, a cry come softly from afar. There were fits of dozing amid a constant rejoining. The sly druggist had been right: Bech had underbought. The couple's closet of satisfied desire became nicely rank with a smell that was neither him nor her. "We're all mixed up together," she whispered, after she had swallowed his semen and caught her breath. The heartland they endlessly poured through seemed no vaster than territories laid open within them. "You're *perfect*," she sighed toward morning, sadly, like a distant train whistle, in his ear. She was not quite perfect, he had observed by the hard morning light in the dining car. In the dark he touched her cheeks, which had looked abraded with tiny nicks. A miracle. They were perfectly smooth. "So are you," he told her. It was the truth.

As he read aloud, he kept remembering that it was his unhappy sister-in-law's boss, a self-important thug in a double-breasted camel-hair topcoat, who had reluctantly filled in the young author with details of how labor unions operated. At the time, Bech thought he could, in the long future before him, assemble all America as a mosaic of such research. Now these details, as they passed through the microphone into the air, seemed worked-up and tinny, and his antihero Klein's cynical take on the Trappists—misfits, defectives, cop-outs—adolescently callous. With relief he at last ended the reading; but there were still the questions from the audience to face. Do you use a word processor and, if so, what kind? What authors influenced you in your youth? How did you like the movie of *Travel Light*, starring Sal Mineo? What—his least favorite question—is your personal favorite of your books? The auditorium lights had been turned up, so he could see the waving hands, the eager respectful aggressive faces. He scanned them for Alice, and failed to spot her, but the crowd was large, with restless, ill-lit edges over by the walls, and there was nothing about her, not even the magenta suit, to keep her from blending in.

Dawn had brought them into gauntly irrigated farmland yielding, mile by mile, to desert. He had scuttled out of her roomette like a gopher, and snatched a few hours of sleep in his own. The Pullman car had an ecology they were fitting into. The other passengers accepted them, by now, as a couple. They were invited again to play bridge—Bech timidly failed to bid a small slam though Alice had given clear signals that her hand was loaded—and a beefy pair of middle-aged Texans sat down at their table for dinner, not appearing to notice that the other couple was too groggy to make small talk and conversationally lacked a common past. At some ten-minute stop, where the Spanish adobe architecture squatted as if stunned under a sky full of vaporous thunderheads, Bech ran off the train to find a drugstore and replenish his supply of Trojans. He saw nothing near the station but pottery and buckskin souvenirs of the West, and heard the conductor call "All aboard." The train had become a conscience to him, a home he hurried back to in a panic that it would pull out and disappear.

"That's all right," Alice said that night. "I wouldn't mind having a baby of yours."

"But—" he began, thinking of her unsuspecting husband. Tad. The name suggested an insecure glad-hander, with an affected clipped accent.

"It's my body," she said, a woman ahead of her time. He

wondered if inside every conventional housewife there was such a sexual radical. She took mercy on him: "Don't worry—I'm about to have my period. You're safe." She laughed then, a brief tough snicker, as if her voice had been lowered by momentary empathy with a man's point of view.

After sleepwalking through the day, they gained a second wind as night fell on the duned, saguaro-dotted desert. "Your place, or mine?" he had asked.

"Yours," she said. Having a choice—a little play in their situation—amused her. "I hate that nasty little overhang; my feet get claustrophobic." His slightly higher roomette had no such feature. They could spread out, relatively. Having mounted the two steps, they felt on top of the world. Their three days, he often reflected, had composed a courtship, a honeymoon, and a marriage. You fuck at first to stake a claim, and afterwards to keep the claim staked. They were less ravenous this second night together, and tender in their genitals, and slept for several stretches of an hour or more. They could hear, in the sudden gulp and changed pitch, as of a great musical instrument, the train entering tunnels, and feel its wheels carefully fumble over the switch points at some crucial junction. They could feel the train climb, and sinuously labor through some pass, on a canyon's curved edge, beneath the unseen stars hanging cold and close above the desert mountains. As he sensed the night tilting and slowly swerving toward its end, Bech in his sexual hysteria and exhaustion began to cry, smearing his tears with his face, like a deer marking a tree, across her belly, her breasts, a kind of spiritual semen, leaving its own slimy glitter. As she submitted to this, she patted and tugged his thick, resilient hair.

The line of people with books to sign had no end in sight. "Would you just make this one 'To Roger'? He's my grandfather, he loves your work, he says you've really spoken for his generation." "Could you personalize this one 'For the Inimitable Lyndi'? That's 'L,' 'Y,' 'N,' 'D,' 'I.' No 'E.' Perfect. Thanks so much. It's wonderful to have you here in the Hoosier State."

By daylight the Mojave Desert yielded, an oasis at a time, to the California paradise. Pastel houses and palm trees multiplied to make a horizontal city, oddly colorless under a sky as blue and unflecked as a movie-set backdrop. The train crept to a final bump in mission-style Union Station, and there fell upon all its length the flurry and sudden hustle of a little world coming apart, with some porters to tip and others to beckon, with farewells to be said or avoided, with baggage to be gathered and safeguarded. Alice, at Bech's side all morning in the club car, sleeping with her head on his shoulder, had squeezed his hand and stood up and said, "I'll be back." The Southwestern sun beating through the window put him in a doze. The train bumped. Where was she? He went onto the platform, into the unreally benign air. She had put the distance of two or three cars between them when he spotted her, leading a porter with his trolley, down beside the locomotive, where the triumphant engineer traded guffaws with a uniformed station official. She merged with a man in a gauche brown outfit—slacks one shade, jacket another—and melted into the crowd, his claim reclaimed. Bech had the impression that Tad Oglethorpe was tall and bald. What happened next? Over the years he forgot why, whenever he saw a woman with a touch of rash or roughness on her cheeks, intended by nature to be silken, he was saddened and stirred.

He had imagined he would somehow see her again. The universe, having witnessed so sublime a coupling, would arrange it. And so it had, in its unsatisfactory fashion. The last fan in line went away with his authentic Henry Bech signature, that tiny piece of him chipped from his dwindling life span, and there was no one left in the auditorium lobby but the bookstore staff, packing all his unsold books into boxes, and the tired but cheery local matron, perhaps herself a secret sexual radical, who had chaired the committee that had arranged to get him here. Alice had vanished, and the librarian of Indianapolis had also gone home.

The sight of his books, the seven thin, passé titles, being briskly stashed in boxes disgusted Bech. No matter how many he sold and signed, there were always bushels left, representing tons of wasted paper. These women who showed up at his readings did it, it seemed clear, to mock his books—clever, twisted, false books, empty of almost all that mattered, these women he had slept with were saying. We, *we* are your masterpieces.

How Was It, Really?

Increasingly, Don Fairbairn had trouble remembering how it had actually been in the broad middle stretch of his life, when he was living with his first wife and helping her, however distractedly, raise their children. His second marriage, which had once seemed so shiny and amazing and new, now was as old as his first had been—twenty-two years, exactly—when he had, one ghastly weekend, left it. His second wife and he lived in a house much too big for them yet so full of souvenirs and fragile inherited treasures that they could not imagine living elsewhere. In their present circle of friends, the main gossip was of health and death, whereas once the telephone wires had buzzed with word of affairs and divorces. His present wife, Vanessa, would set down the telephone to announce that Herbie Edgerton's cancer had come back and appeared to be into his lymph nodes and bones now; thirty years ago, his first wife, Alissa, would hang up and ask him if they were free for drinks and take-out pizza at the Langleys' this Saturday. Yes, she would go on, it was such short notice that it would have been rude from anybody but the Langleys. They were socially voracious, now that psychotherapy had helped them to see that they couldn't stand each other. Everybody's mental and marital health, as Don remembered it, was frail, so frail that women, meeting, would follow their "How are you?" with "No, how are you *really*?"

And then—this with an averted glance and the hint of a blush from Alissa—she had seen Wendy Chace in the superette and impulsively asked her and Jim to drinks tomorrow evening. She had said yes, they'd love to, but they couldn't stay more than a minute, Jim had the Planning Commission meeting, they were fending off this evil out-of-state developer who was trying to turn the entire old Treadwell estate into Swiss-chalet-style condos. Just paraphrasing Jim's flighty, cause-minded wife made Alissa glow. This at least was vivid in Don's memory, the way his former wife's eyes would become livelier and her cheeks, a bit sallow normally, would redden and her lips, usually pursed and pensive, would dance into quips and laughter when Jim was near or in prospect. He couldn't blame her; he had been as bad as she, looking outside the home for strength to keep the home going. The formula had worked only up to a point—perhaps the point, somewhere in their forties, when they realized that life wasn't endless. The Fairbairns had been, actually, among the last in their old set to get divorced. They had stayed on the sinking ship while its deck tilted and its mast splintered and its sails flapped, whipping loose line everywhere.

A teetotaller now (weight, liver, conflicting pills), Don could remember the drinks—drinks on porches and docks, on boats and lawns, in living rooms and kitchens and dens. The high metallic sheen of gin, the slightly more viscid transparency of vodka, the grain-golden huskiness of bourbon, the paler, caustic timbre of Scotch, the sprig of mint,

the slice of orange, the chunk of lime, the column of beer
with its rising flutes of bubbles, the hemispheres of white
and red wine floating above the table on their invisible
stems, the little sticky-rimmed glasses of anisette and Coin-
treau and B & B and green Chartreuse that followed dinner,
whirling the minutes toward midnight, while the more prudent, outsiderish guests peeked at their watches, thinking of
the babysitter and tomorrow's sickly-sweet headache. Don
remembered, from the viewpoint of a host, the magnani-
mous crunch of ice cubes broken out of their aluminum
trays with an authoritative yank of the divider lever, and the
pantry's round-shouldered array of half-gallon bottles from
the liquor mart beside the superette, the cost of liquor a kind
of dues you cheerfully paid for membership in the unchar-
tered club of young couples. How curiously filling and adequate it was, the constant society of the same dozen or
so people. Western frontiersmen, he remembered reading
somewhere, said of buffalo meat that, strange to say, you
never tired of eating it. The Fairbairns' friends would arrive
for weekday drinks at six, harried and mussed, children in
tow—the women bedraggled by a day of housework, the
men fresh off the train with their city pallor—and be slowly
transformed into ebullient charmers. Become dizzyingly
confiding and glamorous and *intimes*, they would not leave
much before eight, when the time had long passed to get
the children, who had been devouring potato chips and Fig
Newtons around the kitchen television, decently fed and
into bed.

"How did you and Mom *do* it?" Don's sons and daughters
asked him, with genuine admiration, of his old servantless
four-child household. His children as they homed in on
forty lived in city apartments or virtually gated New Jersey
enclaves, with one or two children of their own whose nur-
ture and protection required daily shifts of women of

color—tag-team caregivers, one to achieve the dressing and
the administration of breakfast and safe passage to nursery
school, and another to supervise the evening meal and
bath and bedtime video. Nevertheless, his daughters were
exhausted by motherhood, which had come to them late,
as a bit of progenitive moonlighting incidental to their
thriving professional careers; conception had been rife with
psychic tension and childbirth fraught with peril. His sons
spoke solemnly, apprehensively to him about the education
of their children and, even more remote, the job prospects
available to these toddlers in the year 2020. They both,
his two sons, performed some inscrutable monkey-business
among computers and equities, and they thought in long-
range demographic curves. Don had to laugh, being inter-
viewed by them as a kind of pioneer, a survivor of a mythical
age of domesticity, when giant parents strode the earth.
"You were there," he reminded them. "You remember how
it was. Our key concept was benign neglect." But they would
not be put off and, indeed, half persuaded him that he had
been an epic family man, chopping forests into cabins amid
the wilderness of the baby boom.

Tracking their own children's progress, they asked him
how old they had been when they first crawled, walked,
talked, and read, and he was embarrassed to say that he
could not remember. "Ask your mother," he told them.

"She says she doesn't remember, either. She says we were
all wonderfully normal."

An only child, born in the Depression, Don had been
honored at his birth with the purchase of a big white book,
its padded cover proudly embossed *Baby's Book*, in which
pages printed in dove-colored ink waited for the entry of his
early achievements and the dates thereof. *July 20, 1935.
Donald took his first step. A shaky one. September 6, 1938. Off to
kindergarten! Donny clung and clung. Heartbreaking.* He was

surprised to discover that his mother, in that little curly backward-slanting hand that seemed to his eyes the very distillation of methodical maternity, had entered everything up through his various graduations and his first wedding; she had noted her first two grandchildren but had not bothered with the second two or with his second nuptials. How odd it is, he thought, that America's present prosperity, based upon our outworking the Germans and the Japanese, has produced the same pinched, anxiously cherishing families as the Depression. His children's individual developments had become in his failing mind an amiable tangle while he daily dined on the social equivalent of buffalo meat.

The lack of recall almost frightened him. Did he help the kids with their homework? He must have. Did he and Alissa ever go grocery shopping together? He had no image of it. The beds, how had they got made, and the meals, how had they got onto the table for twenty-two years? Alissa must have done it all, somehow, while he was reading the sports page. Having the babies, now such a momentous rite of New Age togetherness and unembarrassed body-worship, was something else she had done alone, in the hospital, without complication or much complaint afterwards. The baby just appeared in a basket beside her bed, or at her breast, and in a few days he drove the two of them home, two where there had been one, a doubling of persons like a magic trick whose secret was too quick for the eye. The last childbirth, Don did remember, came on a winter midnight, and the obstetrician, awakened, had swung by in his car for her, and she had looked up smiling from the snowy street, like a Christmas caroller, and disappeared into the doctor's two-tone Buick. Left alone with the residue of their children, he had been jittery, he remembered, and convinced that a burglar or crazed invader, sensing his family's moment of being vulnerably torn asunder, was in the big creaky house with him; Don had fallen asleep only after taking a golf club—a three-iron, in preference to a slower-swinging wood—into bed with him, for protection.

He tried to picture Alissa with a vacuum cleaner and couldn't, though he remembered himself, in the dining room of the first house they had lived in, wielding a wallpaper steamer, pressing the big square pan against the wall for a minute or two and stripping the paper with a broad putty knife and, in drenched shorts and T-shirt, wading through curling wet sheets of faded silver flowers. Once a week, in that same room, she would serve flank steak, it came to him, the brown meat nicely tucked around a core of peppery stuffing, and the whole platter, garnished with parsley and little red-skinned potatoes, redolent of bygone home economics, of those touching Fifties-born culinary ambitions that sought to perpetuate a sense of the family meal as a pious ceremony salted with the sweat of female labor. All those meals slavishly served, and in the end he had dismissed her like a redundant servant. Vanessa and he, with no children to feed, had become grazers, snackers, eaters-out, sometimes taking their evening meal separately, gobbling from microwave-safe containers while Peter Jennings injected his personal warmth into the news. She still had a fondness for pizza, hot or cold.

"But what did you do about *sleep*? About children waking up all night?" the elder of his hard-working daughters, with tender blue shadows beneath her eyes, persisted.

"You all slept through, virtually from birth," he told her, suspecting he was lying but unable to locate the truth of it. There had been a child whimpering about an earache and falling asleep with the hurting ear pressed against the heat of a fresh-ironed dish towel. But was this himself as a child? He could not remember Alissa with an iron in her hand. He did remember getting up from bed in the pit of night and bringing a squalling armful of protoplasm back to bed and handing it to its mother, who was already sitting up with her nightie straps lowered, her bare chest shining. He would go back to sleep to the sound of tiny lips sucking, little feet softly kicking. He had been the baby, it seemed. Yet no social workers came to the door to rescue his children from abuse, no neighbors complained to the authorities, the children waited for the school bus dressed like the others—like little clowns in the space-age outfits of synthetic fabrics decades removed from the dark woollens, always damp, that he himself had worn—and ascended more or less smoothly through the passages of school and, like smart bombs, found colleges and mates and jobs, so he must have been an adequate parent and householder. "It frightens me," Don confessed to his daughter, "how little I remember."

The Saturday afternoons of it all, the masculine feats of maintenance, the changing of the storm windows to screens, the cellar workbench where spiders built webs across the clutter of rusting tools. The heating, electricity, telephone, and water bills—he could not see himself writing a single check, but he must have written many, all cashed, cancelled, and stored in Alissa's attic, along with the slides, the scrapbooks, the school reports and tinted school photographs that had accumulated over twenty-two years of days, each with its ups and downs, its mishaps, its sniffles, its excited tales told by children venturing toward adulthood, through a world that on every side was new to them. Don had lost the anatomy. He was like an astronomer before the Voyagers, before the Hubble telescope, working with blurs. He remembered being in love with one or another man's wife, getting drunk after dinner, telling Alissa to go to bed, and playing over and over again "Born to Lose," by Ray Charles, or maybe it was the Supremes' "Stop! in the Name of Love!," lifting the player arm from the LP repeatedly to regroove the band, and being told with a shy smile the next morning by his older son, "You sure listened to that song a lot last night." The curtains for a moment parted; there was a second of shamed focus. His son's bedroom was above the den where Don had sat mired in himself and the revolving grooves. He had kept the boy, who had to get up for school, awake.

And what of his girls' dating, that traditional tragicomedy, with its overtones of Attic patricide, in the age of the sit-com? His older daughter had gone off to boarding school when she was fifteen, and his younger daughter had been but twelve when he left the house. He could scarcely remember a single hot-rod swerving into the crackling driveway to carry off one of his trembling virgins.

Now this younger daughter invited him to have drinks on a boat. He didn't have to drink liquor, of course, she explained. More and more people didn't; it interfered with their training routines. She herself was slim and hard as a greyhound, and entered local marathons; her hair, which like Alissa's had begun to turn white early, was cut short as a boy's, to lower wind resistance, he supposed. The deal was this, Dad: the husband of a friend of theirs was turning forty, and she, the wife, was giving him as one of his presents a sunset cruise in the marshes, and since *his* parents were coming the friend, the wife—are you following this, Dad?— wanted some other members of the older generation to be there, so the question is could you and Vanessa come, since you know I guess the husband's father from apparently play-ing a few golf tournaments with him?

Actually, when he shook his peer's hand, under the canopy of the flat-bottomed cruise boat, he remembered him as an opponent who had illegally switched balls on the eighteenth green and then sunk the putt to win the match. At the time, he hadn't wished to undergo the social embarrassment of complaining to the officials, but he had avoided club tournaments ever since. Now the man—one of those odious exultant retirees with a face creased and thickened by an all-year tan—crowed over that remembered triumph. His wife, who was somewhat younger than he, and preeningly dressed in clothes that would have appeared less garish in Florida, fastened onto Vanessa as her only soulmate. Don drifted away, trying to hide among the drinking young couples, to whom he had nothing to say. Not drinking did that—it robbed you of things to say.

How strange it was to be once more at a party where the women were still menstruating. Lean, smart, they moved and twittered and struck poses with an electricity like that in silent movies, which look speeded-up. The men in their checked jackets and pastel slacks were boyish and broad—relatively clumsy foils for their wives' animation, which in the shuffle of the party kept sprouting new edges, abrupt new angles of slightly startled loveliness. Don inhaled, as if to extract from the salt air the scent of their secretions, their secrets. It had been at parties like this that he had gotten to know Vanessa Langley, her and her socially voracious husband. The similarity of her name to Alissa's had been one of the attractions; she would be a wife with a "v" added, for vim and vigor, for vivacity and vagina and victory. He had fallen in love with her, she had fallen with him, and here they were, on board together, more than twenty years later.

The boat trundled, with its burden of canned music and clinking drinks and celebrating couples, out through the winding channel between the black-mud banks of the golden-green marsh toward the wider water, where islands crammed with shingled summer houses slowly changed position, starboard to port, as the captain put his craft through a scenic half-circle. There was a white lighthouse, and a stunning sunstruck slope where some American grandee of old had decreed a symmetrical pattern of trimmed shrubs like a great ideogram, and a marina whose pale masts stood as thick as wheat, and a nappy blue-green far stretch of wooded land miraculously yet undeveloped, and the eastward horizon of the open sea already darkening to receive its first starlight while the undulating land to the west basked under luminous salmon stripes, the lean remains of daylight. Don silently gazed outward at all this, and his fellow-passengers gave it moments of notice, but the main thrust of their attention was inward, toward each other, in bright and gnashing conversations growing shrill as the drinks sank in, a feast of love drowning out the canned music. That was how it was, how it had been, the living moment awash with beauty ignored in the quest for a better moment, slightly elsewhere, with some slightly differing other, while the weeds grew in the peony beds, and dust balls gathered beneath the sofa, and the children, unobserved, plotted their own escapes, their own elsewheres.

A few children had come along with their parents and, after being admonished not to fall overboard, fended for themselves. To one boy, rapt beside him at the rail, Don on the homeward swing pointed out a headland and a rosy mansion whose name he knew, beyond the marsh grasses now drinking in darkness as the tide slipped away from their roots. Vanessa, on the drive home, volunteered, "The birthday boy's father's wife and I have a number of mutual acquaintances, it turned out. She said an old college roommate of mine, Angela Hart, just had a double mastectomy."

Don thought of confiding in turn how magically strange he had found it to be again among fertile women, with all the excitement that bred. He might in his youthful cruelty have once said something like this to Alissa—anything to get her to respond, to get the blood flowing—but between Vanessa and him there had come to prevail the tact of two cripples, linked victims of time.

Scenes from the Fifties

YES. Time does pass. The other day I read that Harold "Doc" Humes had died. I knew Doc slightly; hundreds of people did. He was a writer and conversationalist famous, or bucking for fame, in the Fifties—a short man with a merry, thin-skinned face and more intellectual energy and love of life than a writer needs, perhaps. He had published a long novel, *The Underground City*, in 1957, and then, in 1959, a shorter one, *Men Die*. That title, described by a friend of mine at the time as "bald and bad," was not untrue, as his own death shows. The last time I saw him he was playing chess with Marcel Duchamp at the party that sealed my departure from New York City.

It was 1959, and my vision of the moment seems now very time-specific—this living relic of High Modernism seated at a chessboard like some surreal raft upon which he had washed up on the breadfruit island of Eisenhower's America. Around him, dozens of artistic aspirants and operators drank and nibbled and chattered, hungrily circling in search of the immortality Duchamp already enjoyed. Art was big in the

Fifties. We were full of peacetime's rarefied ambitions and uncurtailed egos. I, who have become a silver-haired antique-dealer in Boston, picture that party—held in the high-ceilinged duplex of an art-patronizing couple called Berman—as a display window organized around its most precious ware, the inventor of the descending nude and some other death-less, celebrated trinkets of ironic disaffection. Duchamp was a handsome man, ascetically slender, with an anvil-shaped head. He might have been wearing socks and sandals. There certainly were a pipe, large and hairy ears, and a silk foulard.

I remember wondering if Doc's chess was up to this. "Howie, hi," Doc said to me affably. "You probably know Marcel."

"*Of* him, of course," I said. As I shook both men's hands, I made a youthfully conceited, slyly ostentatious attempt to appraise their positions. In my agitated celebrity-consciousness the board looked like a jumble. I did have the decency to move away quickly, genuinely regretting any dis-turbance that holding out his hand to me had wrought in the great man's cogitations. The popular journals, which in the Fifties still devoted considerable space to the arts, had reported how Duchamp, elegantly disdaining to create any more art, was concentrating his powers, for the remainder of his life, on chess, much as Rimbaud abandoned poetry for gun-smuggling. I could not believe Doc was giving him much of a game, but had to admire the way my bumptious contemporary had thrust himself forward into the radius of greatness and was cheerfully basking there.

The Paris Review, of which Humes had been a founder, reported in its fond obituary that his own abstention, after his two novels, from artistic practice had stemmed from a supposed run-in, in the early Sixties, with British intelli-gence, which had implanted in one of his teeth a micro-scopic radio device that rendered him painfully, obsessively privy to the secrets and subtle clangor of the Cold War. The CIA and KGB had both, he thought, bugged his room, and he would sit swivelling his head to address first one and then the other of the hidden microphones, narrowly averting, with his remarks, an impending cataclysm. He spoke of a black box, called Fido, sent aloft by MIT engineers, which broadcast warnings that only he could interpret. He grew a gauzy big beard, I see on the obituary photograph. He ceased to write. The low thrum of global anxiety became for Doc a deafening static; he was as much a martyr to Cold War tensions as, say, Gary Powers.

Myself, nothing bores me more than conspiracy theories, international espionage, or novels in the portentous paranoid mode. For me, the long stretch of history between Churchill's Iron Curtain speech and the fall of the Berlin Wall, containing most of my adult life, was a blessed interim, a Metternichian remission of the usual savageries—which have been, I notice, resumed. The Cold War deprived men of the infernal heroic options. I deal in antiques, on Charles Street, with a longtime partner, and the peace of my fragilely loaded shop is what I gratefully owe to the atom bomb, the Marshall Plan, the SAC, and Soviet tanks. Believe it or not, readers of the year 2000, the 1950s were a sweet time of self-seeking, brimming, like my shop, with daily expectancy and quiet value.

In New York, Abstract Expressionism was happening, Pop was about to happen, and my wife and I, who had met in art school, were on the verge of happening, or so we felt for three years. It was as if we gave a party and no one came. We had the loft, the devotion and asceticism, the paints, brushes, canvases, and welding equipment (I painted, she sculpted)—everything, in short, but the patrons, the audience, the profit. We had, in one of our few sexual successes, added a female infant to our baggage, and in a drastic attempt to lighten our expenses had moved to a seaside hamlet north of Boston, where once-thriving boat yards building wooden clipper ships had dwindled to a row of clam shacks and, along the hamlet's central causeway, a kind of perpetual yard sale. Here, amid magnificent salt marshes and taciturn Yankee yeomen, my wife and I would definitively ripen our talents. In time, in triumph, we would return to New York. I had temporarily returned on this occasion for two days to close out the legal details of our sublease, and to arrange for the shipment of our horribly bulky, sadly unwanted works of art.

It all sounds more dismal than it was. I was twenty-five and felt that virtually all of my life was ahead of me. Just being in the same high-ceilinged room with Marcel Duchamp made everything seem possible and worth any amount of trouble. There was also at the party a woman I imagined I was falling in love with. We talked together a good hour, posing this way and that on the arm of a giant chrome-frame sofa covered in nubbly Haitian cotton. I forget the woman's name but not the tint of her skin, a neutral calm color like that of a plaster cast "from the antique," as they called it in art school. She was a Venus de Milo with arms. She wore a low-cut dress of bottle green, in one of those shiny stiff fabrics—taffeta, I suppose—considered sexy in the Fifties. Everything was in place, including my geographical distance from my wife and a nagging, hostile sense of insufficiency that had entered our marriage with its northern move. Yet I couldn't quite deliver the punch, the pass, that might have made this Venus mine for the night. Instead we agreed I would swing by her workplace tomorrow; she was an underling in the newly opened Guggenheim Museum. When I arrived, blushing and baggage-laden, she was out to lunch, the front desk informed me; I wandered up the ramp, looking at the big smeared canvases. Abstraction

was getting tired, but there seemed nothing else to do—
like the void at the center of Wright's magnificent, hollow
temple.

When the lady returned, wearing black stockings and carrying a pocketbook over her shoulder, she waved me into
her office, a tiny room in the crammed basement. I sat on a
blue canvas director's chair and she perched at her desk,
waiting for me to make my move. She knew I was married,
and fleeing the city; I had said that much when our inter-
course had been lubricated by the party. Now my gears were
sticking. We smoked, gingerly talked about the art market,
and gossiped about our hosts the night before. She knew
Sally Berman well enough to say firmly, "She is not happy."

I was startled, and somehow took it personally. "What
should she do about it?"

"That's for her to figure out."

"Well," I said lamely, "I'm sure she will."

"What's in your little paper bag?" she asked.

"Oh—a toy for my daughter. A toy brush and comb. She's
not quite three, and has just learned to brush her hair."

"She sounds ravishing, Howard. I wonder if I'll ever have
a child—they say it's worth it."

"It's wonderful, but it doesn't solve problems. It *adds*
problems."

She grew a bit more distant at my implication that she
had problems. I, her woman's eye could see, was the one
with problems. "Good luck up there," she said stoutly in
parting, like a headmistress wishing me well. "I hope it's
not too lonely." She had that Manhattan faith that only
New York people were real, and the rest were laughable
phantoms.

"Oh—there are a few congenial spirits, even up there."

"How often do you plan to get back to New York?"

"I don't know. Not often. It's a long way."

"Please come see me when you do."

"Yes. I'd like to. Very much." But, though she held out a bare, plaster-pale arm toward me with almost a beseeching grace, we hadn't happened, just as New York hadn't happened for me.

Airlines existed in those days, yes, but one didn't think of flying what would become a shuttle route, a bus in the sky for gray suits. One took trains back and forth, a five-hour trip with the layover in New Haven while they switched engines. From Boston's South Station I took a cab to North Station, and found it would be nearly two hours for the next train to my town on the North Shore. But a train for Haverhill was leaving in five minutes, and in my ignorance of New England geography—we had moved just a month ago—I thought that, since Haverhill was also to the north, it would be a time-saving move to get there and then telephone my wife.

I boarded the train and for an hour stared out of a black window at inscrutable, hurrying lights and at my own flickering, murky reflection. It was night; my awkward call at the Guggenheim had delayed my escape until three. New York is always sticky to get away from, like a party where something wonderful may happen the minute after you leave. In the grand and largely empty Haverhill railroad station, there were several pay telephones, but none of them worked. When I made the call from a drugstore a block away, my wife was incredulous. "Haverhill! Sweetie, who ever told you to go *there*?"

It was after nine o'clock and I was groggy and irritable with sitting and swaying in overheated railroad cars. I had brought to read only the Everyman's edition entitled *The Travels of Mungo Park*, and the jiggling small print had hurt my eyes. "Nobody did. It was my own idea. I thought you'd like it; I thought it showed real powers of acclimation." She was a New England native; I was from Maryland. Moving here had been in part an attempt to make her happier.

"Pookie," she said, "Haverhill's twenty miles away, it's the end of the world. I can't possibly come get you—Annie's had a fever both days you've been gone and I don't want to get her out of bed and put her in the cold car. But don't give up. Malcolm's right here, he cooked us our dinner. Let me ask him. He probably wouldn't mind, he's up till all hours anyway, listening to music." She covered the mouthpiece but I overheard her say, "Would you believe it?" and then a short length of laughter, wound of two strands, male and female.

Malcolm lived in Manchester-by-the-Sea, next to our less fashionable Essex. He was a friend of a slight New York acquaintance, and thus far our only cultural companion in this briny fastness. We had both taken to him, my wife more readily than I. To me he seemed a little fey. He had enough money, evidently, to avoid regular employment. He painted watercolors of marsh and dune, played a harpsichord he had made, listened to records of classical music and Forties jazz, read several books a week. He was *dying*, he said, to write a novel about his awful parents, but they were still alive, in their giant summer house on Coolidge Point. Somewhat older than we, with soft muscles and very white skin, a keen cook and domestic decorator, Malcolm made my wife laugh and even purr, as he sat there in our living room, slowly soaking up bourbon and letting his hair down, so to speak. His hair was romantically black but thinning, with a bald spot in the back. As with the late Doc Humes, there was nothing he didn't know or at least wasn't willing to talk about. Bubbly, smooth-tempered Malcolm made me uneasy, a little, but he was all we had, and my wife needed company. He and she half sincerely discussed opening, together, an antique shop on the Essex strip, which already held several.

"Malcolm says allow forty minutes, it's all back roads," she said. "He's being a saint, I think. Haverhill, really, darling—nobody goes to Haverhill!"

Maryland was full of places nobody went to; I wasn't bothered. I had a Coke and doughnut at the drugstore, which was closing up, and walked back through the cold to the railroad station. I suppose it's gone now, long torn down; I have never been back to see. It was a piece of the nineteenth century marooned in mid-twentieth, scaled, like the city's churches, to disappointed expectations. Inside, vandalized telephone booths and coin-operated lockers blocked out sections of the beaded wainscoting and flourishes of carpenter Gothic. Above the lovingly wrought grille of the ticket windows a rough sign was nailed: CLOSES 6 P.M. I was alone with pews of ghosts, travellers that would not return. From far off, somebody was complaining, in the carrying tones of a railroad conductor. Two men passed through the waiting room's great space and went into the lavatory together. Beneath the stained-glass windows brown radiators clunked and sang, warming the varnished boards behind them. Settling to enjoy the stretch of privacy ahead of me, I sat in the center of an empty pew, placed my suitcase at my feet, and opened up the Mungo Park. I was near the end, in the journal of his fatal second trip:

> We kept ascending the mountains to the south of Toniba till three o'clock, at which time having gained the summit of the ridge which separates the Niger from the remote branches of the Senegal, I went on a little before; and coming to the brow of a hill, I *once more saw the Niger* rolling its immense stream along the plain!

Yet I could not keep my mind's eye on the African scenery. I could not shake a sensation for which my present predicament supplied a metaphor: my life was *off the tracks*. My high-rise ambitions and hopes had evaporated somewhere around New London. I would have to get a job, something repetitive and demeaning, to support my painting. Which would wither away. And my marriage: it, too, through no one's fault, was one of those things that were not happening. My wife's excited attraction to Malcolm was indication of that. And my little girl: Annie's very wonderfulness frightened me. So proud now of being able to brush her own hair, she would stroke it clumsily until it fanned out from her head in long floating wands, and then come to me, imagining it was beautifully smooth, her face fat with conceit, saying, "Lookit, Daddy. Lookit."

I was not totally alone in the station. Mine must have been the last train for hours. One of the men who had been in the lavatory had not left the waiting room, and he stood by the door staring out into the dingy small-city darkness. A car wheeled its lights through the station lot and bit the curb with a screech; I glimpsed several heads, including the tufted shadow of a woman's, and imagined that my wife and daughter had relented and driven here with Malcolm. They had been quicker than predicted—miraculously quick.

But it was a young man in an old athletic jacket who slammed through the double doors and raced into the lavatory. Too much beer, I supposed. He had left his motor running and his lights burning. Light poured into the face of the man waiting by the door, washing a halo into the rim of his flimsy fair hair. *Lookit. Lookit.*

The athlete dashed back to his car, the motor roared, and the lights backed off and sped away. The man by the door said to me, "Not bad, huh? Two guys and one cunt." He shuffled forward a few steps, a slender man with a stooped neck. He was not young, and yet not old either—merely hard-used, and poor.

"Yeah," I said, and fixed my eyes pointedly on the book.

It was in the afternoon, and we fastened it to the tree close to the tent, where all the asses were tied. As soon as it was dark the wolves tore its bowels out, though within ten yards of the tent door where we were all sitting.

The little shuffling steps came closer. "How d'ya bet she'll take care of 'em both?"

I refused to answer. I was trembling hideously inside. "I bet she blows one of 'em." Stoop-neck shuffled by close to my knees, paused, shuffled around the back of the pew, paused, and moaned as if to himself, "Nothin' doin' around here tonight." Then, to my immense relief, he went out the double doors into the night.

For all of its Victorian elaboration, the interior of the station lacked a clock. Surely Malcolm's forty minutes was used up. It was one of my artistic affectations in those years not to wear a watch. I kept on reading:

We saw on one of the islands, in the middle of the river, a large elephant; it was of a red clay color with black legs.

The sad stoop-necked man came back through the station doors, with their brass crashbars polished by generations of hands. "Gettin' to be a cold night out there." Shyly keeping his eyes fastened above my head, he wandered closer, his feet scuffling grittily on the marble floor and his little head tilted to one side. "Nothin' doin' around here tonight," he repeated.

I explained, "I'm waiting for somebody. I wish to hell they'd come."

"Yeah, well," the other replied, with an oddly cynical, reedy lilt.

I realized that my responding, whatever the words, was a mistake—encouragement. Stoop-neck had paused ten feet away, transfixed by some scent. I stared rigidly into the book, as if like a campfire its white page made a circle of safety. A foot scratched one step closer, and then the man had seated himself beside me. "You like books, huh?" The thighs of his unpressed cotton trousers were inches from mine. "Hey," he continued, on the same conversational level, "was you ever blowed?"

I jumped to my feet and ran out of the station, abandoning my suitcase. My heart was swollen bigger than an elephant's and pounding with terror and indignation. Remember, I was very young. Not quite twenty-six—a stranger to myself. I restrained myself from running up the stony valley between the railroad embankment and a row of dark shops. The drugstore where I had had the doughnut was at the end of this row, and itself dark. But a taxi-stand shelter opposite the drugstore was still lit inside, waiting for whatever scrap the dying railroads might throw it. Behind a dirty picture window, in a little room papered with calendars, two old men sat on opposite sides of a worn desk that held a telephone and a radio. The radio, with a crackle of static, was playing, I seem to remember, a Benny Goodman quintet. One of the men, wearing a lumberjack shirt, pushed open the door to ask me, "You want a cab, son?"

I said no, I was being picked up by a friend, was it O.K. if I waited outside here? My voice sounded boyish and tinny, and I knew I must look queer, in my big-city suit and artistically shaggy hair and with my finger still marking my place in the Everyman's volume that was still in my hand.

Yes. How young we were, how little it took to stir us up, in 1959. Malcolm came not long afterwards, in his marine-blue MG convertible. Foreign cars were still unusual then—what we now call a statement. I had edged halfway down the hill toward the front of the station, so as not to miss him. Pantingly I described how I had been assaulted and had fled, and he looked at me rather incredulously, there in the half-light, on the steep cold street. He parked in front of the station and went in with me to retrieve my suitcase. The stoop-necked man was gone, but my suitcase was there, in the center of that spread of empty pews, while rusty radiators knocked and hissed along the wainscoted walls. Even the little paper bag with Annie's toy hairbrush and comb in it was still there.

As we began the ride home, Malcolm did not seem his usual blithe self. "Howard," he said, in almost a scolding tone, "that kind of man was no threat to you. They are almost never violent. Violence is not the problem, and in any case the problem was his, not yours."

I felt chastised, and silly for having felt such terror. Everywhere I had gone, on these travels of mine, people had been sending me messages, though my teeth weren't wired to receive them.

Malcolm didn't let go of the subject; he seemed to have given it a lot of thought. He cited to me, from a book he had read, statistics in regard to male homosexuals: their unaggressiveness, their low crime rate, their creativity and forbearance. They were the model citizens, it turned out, of the liberated, diverse, depuritanized world to come. His voice, with its exotic New England twang, held something I had not heard before, an earnest edge. With my wife present, he was all flirtatiousness and idle fun.

"Yeah, well," I said. "That's all very fine. But why *me*? Why did he pick on me?"

Malcolm said, "The obvious answer is, because you were there."

Then, uncharacteristically, he said no more. Was there an unobvious answer? The dim lights of Haverhill sped by; we crossed a river into Groveland. The inside of the convertible was as surprisingly warm as the inside of the station had been, and I relaxed into it. He was wearing a little fuzzy checked hat, perhaps to protect his bald spot. I was touched, and dimly felt my relative youth, my full head of hair, as an advantage, a plume, a source of power. I told him about meeting Duchamp at the party, about Doc Humes having somehow inserted himself at the great man's chessboard. Malcolm laughed, and pressed me for details; I supplied them, but left out my attraction to Venus, and my visit to her after lunch hour, and the gesture of her long arm that benignly released me from my attraction. Malcolm volunteered that last week he and his sister had been present at a local dinner that included John Marquand, who had been handsome and gracious. Marquand was a big name back then.

Memory fades, but it must be that, after the long cozy drive through the winding wintry dark, over the back roads, through Groveland and Georgetown and Ipswich, Malcolm delivered me safely to my house and my wife. Somehow embarrassed about it, as if the fault had been mine, I didn't tell her about the man in the train station. It stayed a secret between Malcolm and me. Years went by, in which he continued as a friend of both of us, seductive to us equally, gently exerting the pressure of love against the one of us who would fall. Nothing happens overnight. By the time he and I had moved to Boston together and opened the shop on Charles Street, the Sixties were well advanced.

Metamorphosis

ANDERSON, something of an idler and a playboy, had spent too much time in the sun; these sunny hours, as his years on earth passed fifty, came back to him in the form of skin cancers, on his face and elsewhere tender and overexposed. His ophthalmologist, a conscientious man with a Brooklyn accent, was troubled by a keratosis near the tear duct of his right eye—"If it invades, you'll be crying for lack of tears"—and sent him to a facial plastic surgeon, a Dr. Kim, who turned out to be a woman, a surprisingly young Korean-American who even in her baggy lab coat evinced considerable loveliness. She was relatively tall, nearly as tall as Anderson, yet with the low waist and sturdy bow legs and rounded calves of Asian women. She moved with a kind of suppressed athleticism, her gestures a little swifter and larger than the moment demanded, so that her lab coat fell open and the white halves of it swung. She spoke a perfectly natural, assimilated American English, except that there was a soft, level insistence to it: the image came to him of a moon buggy, determinedly proceeding across uneroded terrain, in conditions of weak gravity. Her face was lean, widest at the cheekbones, and in color a matte pallor, a tinged ivory, of a smoothness that made him ruefully conscious of his own spotted, blotched, scarred visage. Yet she was a doctor, he need not be embarrassed. He could repose under her examination as an infant does beneath a mother's doting gaze.

She examined him first with her naked eyes, then with a loupe, and lastly with an elaborate mechanism in which he rested his chin while lenses clicked in and out and arcs and spots of light overlaid his half-eclipsed view of her face, posed inches from his in a darkened room. He could hear her breathe, when he held his own breath. Finally she pushed the apparatus between them away and announced that, yes, she would operate, and saw no major difficulty. There were several types of lesion, actually, in the inner part of his socket and along his lower lid, but they could be excised without complication. "It looks as though you have at least a millimeter of unaffected tissue between the basal-cell carcinoma and the tear duct."

He was still seeing spots and fireflies. "What about the other eye?" he asked, less out of curiosity than a desire to hear her talk some more. There was a curious drone underlying her enunciation, a minor undertone which faintly persisted when the sentence was concluded.

"The other eye seems fine. No problems." *Problemmmmss.*

"Isn't that odd, that one eye would and the other wouldn't, after being exposed to the same amount of sun? Or do you think I always scrunched up one eye, like Popeye?"

She smiled at so unscientific a query, and did not deign to reply. Instead she filled out a number of slips, which she gave Anderson as he left. When he stood beside her, he took pleasure in the inch or two that he was taller than she. Her black hair was parted in the middle and gathered behind into a pinned-up ponytail, like a handle to an exquisite jug.

"The front desk will make the appointment for the surgery," she said. "Only a light breakfast that morning, and not too much liquid. It will take a total of two hours." *Hourrsss.* She left the room ahead of him, hurrying to the next appointment, in another examining chamber, with that flighty, gliding walk of hers, her round calves gleaming below the swirling lab coat.

He could hardly wait—the carcinoma was marching toward the tear duct, for one thing—but the soonest appointment the front desk could give him was ten weeks away. "Dr. Kim is a very busy girl," the middle-aged receptionist told Anderson, having read his infatuation at a glance. Dr. Kim was as priceless a part of the clinic, Anderson saw, as its fortieth-story view, this sparkling morning, of the East River and the twinkling low boroughs beyond.

She was pregnant. This fact had been invisible to him during their consultation, and even ten weeks later it had to be drawn to his attention, by one of the attending nurses in the operating room. "I must say, Doctor," the nurse said, while Anderson's face was being prepped with Betadine and framed in antiseptic paper, "nobody would *dream* you were in your thirty-third week. When I was that far along, I felt like a bumper car. I was a *house.*"

There were two nurses, and the three women talked over Anderson's head as if it were a centerpiece of wax fruit. "The first one was like this, too," the doctor said, with her thrilling offhand thrum. "Nothing showing, and then bang." *Bannggg.*

Anderson tried to raise his head, to see Dr. Kim's belly, but she was behind him, upside down in his vision, a glinting syringe in her hand. "It is very important," she told him, "that you keep your head still. Do you mind having your arms strapped down?"

"I don't think so. Let's try it."

"Some people panic," she explained.

Anderson had had facial surgery before, but not stretched out on an operating table. He had sat in a padded chair which tipped back while a preppy young man, wearing a white shirt and necktie as if boasting how small a role blood played in his procedures, carved away at this or that small keratosis. The only pain came with the injection of the painkiller, especially in the upper lip or the bridge of a nose. The tear ducts would overflow. But Dr. Kim's needle, preceded by a swab smelling of cloves or cinnamon, slipped in imperceptibly. A nurse buckled light straps across his chest, and he relaxed into a bliss of secure helplessness.

The three women rotated around him. One of the nurses periodically took his pulse and inflated the blood-pressure cuff, while the other fed instruments to the surgeon. Dr. Kim's bulging belly, now that he was aware of it, rubbed against the top of his head, or one of his ears, as she bent over and confidently broke his skin with tools he could scarcely imagine, since they approached his face along the periphery of his vision. There was a knife shaped as acutely as a sharpened pencil, but also a kind of exquisite corer, whose cut he experienced as a gentle punch, and a cauterizer, producing passing hisses and whiffs of smoke. The touch of her fingers in their latex gloves felt like fairy feet shod in slippers sewn from the skins of baby moles. There were fits of dabbing, to stanch the flow of blood, and sometimes a pinch of pressure and a tugging as the stitches in their several sizes, colors, and degrees of solubility were inserted, pulled taut, and closed with a knot that involved a rapid, mesmerizing twirling of the angled forceps.

Conversational topics came and went among the women— Hillary Clinton's likely or unlikely, spunky or ridiculous challenge of Mayor Giuliani in the next Senate race, the hopelessness or hopefulness of the situation in Kosovo, the chemistry or lack of it between Hugh Grant and Julia Roberts in *Notting Hill*—and at moments Anderson attempted to insert, from within his wimple of sterile paper, his own opinion. "Too skinny," he said, of Julia Roberts. "And he stammers too much."

"When you talk," Dr. Kim observed, "it makes all the muscles of your face move."

"I couldn't believe," the instrument-handling nurse said, "when I was taking anatomy, how many muscles the face has. Eighty-four, I think the professor said, depending on what you count. I mean, are the throat and eyeball ones extra?"

Anderson felt the surgeon's hands and tools move to the lower lid, a ticklish, twitchy area.

The nurse handling his pulse and blood pressure asked above his head, "Are you tired, Doctor? It would kill me, standing this long on my feet in your condition."

"I never get tired operating," came the surprising avowal. "I totally forget myself." *Mysselff.* "I could go all night."

"Couldn't you sit on a stool?" Anderson asked gallantly, trying not to move his lips, like a ventriloquist.

"It never works for me," she deigned to answer. "I need to stand, to feel free in my arms." Her round, smooth *armmms*.

"Most barbers feel the same way," he said. "Standing with their hands up in the air all day, it would kill me."

"A bit more lidocaine," Dr. Kim said in a perceptibly sterner voice. "Don't move or say even a single word." She was playing with him, Anderson thought. They were beginning to learn to play with each other.

When they parted—he with flesh-color bandages dotting his eye socket and she, despite her protestations, wearing shadows of fatigue below her eyes—Anderson wished her well with her accouchement. *Accouchement:* he prolonged the French nasal seductively. She warned him he would have a black eye for a week and asked him to make an appointment at the front desk for removal of the stitches in one week and for a six-month checkup. The East River, broken into fragments by intervening Manhattan skyscrapers, glistened below. A barge full of orange scrap iron was being nudged toward the sea by two tugs, and its slow black wake was overlaid with the rapidly fanning white wake of a police launch. Next to his tear duct, little prickles of pain were beginning.

She removed his stitches in seven days, humming with pleasure at the beauty of her work, and then nearly a year passed before he saw Dr. Kim again. She was still on leave with her baby when his checkup appointment came due, and in a kind of sulk he put off making another. His surgery had been slower to heal than he had expected, oozing for weeks, and an odd bump of gristly tissue on one side of the bridge of his nose was irritated for months by the nosepiece of his reading glasses. When the wounds finally settled, and the red spots blended into his face's patchwork of pink, he then noticed a new wrinkle—not exactly a wrinkle but a sort of raised tendon, a parenthesis of flesh near his tear duct. Anderson's girlfriend, one of a long and querulous series, thought it made him look slightly evil. When he pointed out this minor abnormality to a newly slender Dr. Kim, she reached forward and gently prodded it, not once but several times. "You should have massaged," she said. "But now it may be too late."

"Too late?"

She smiled and reached out again, touching the offending bit of anatomy, and firmly caressed it with a small circling motion. "Like that," she said. "Two, three times a day for thirty seconds."

Her touch numbed his brain, but he clung to reason. "I can't believe that will do much good."

"Try it for six months. Be patient."

"Can't you fix it surgically?"

"It troubles you so? Cosmetically it is very minor, but the operation to change it would not be simple or certain of success." *Successs.* It was as if her voice were not quite hers, ventriloquistically projected from an ideal world elsewhere.

Anderson edged forward in the examining chair, as when fitting himself to the metal chin rest. "I'd like to try it," he said, "if you're willing."

"The insurance—"

"I have a very generous medical plan," he assured her. He imagined the operation—the fitful pressure of her sheathed fingers, like dancing fairy shoes; the painless sizzle of the cauterizing instrument; the blithe topical chatter of the attending nurses; the rustle of the antiseptic paper on his face as he attempted to join in; the rub of her bulging stomach on his skull.

The experience, when it came on its scheduled day, was not quite as he had imagined it. She was not pregnant, the operating room was smaller, and there was only one nurse, who wandered in and out. The procedure this time involved more strenuous tugging and a series of stitches that extended to the verge of the anesthetic's wearing off. But the intensity of the contact was undiluted. This time, he felt freer to use his eyes, and boldly watched her eyes, upside down in his vision. They appeared to brim from the chalices of her upper lids, underlined by the thin black smiles of her eyebrows. Elongate amber flecks like needles in an emulsion gave her irises a rayed, starry depth as her attention poured through the apertures of her contracted pupils, holes through which the world in all its brilliance passed. Whenever she blinked, the action seemed monstrous, like a crab's mouth.

When it was over, and she lowered the pale-green paper mask, her mouth seemed pleased. She pulled off her mushroom-shaped scrub cap and shook her head so that her hair tumbled free, its thick body squirming with waxy gleams. "It went very well," she said. "It is not easy, to persuade slack tissue to reconform." *Reconforrrmmm*—the "r"s were so throaty and the "m"s so prolonged he wondered if she was teasing him. But the professional manner she resumed was impeccable and impervious; she provided solemn instructions to go with the prescriptions she wrote, and a carefully spelled-out prediction as to the course of his healing. "This time, be sure to massage." She demonstrated little circles on the side of her own flawless, straight, taut, matte nose. As she moved, with her low-slung, hurried gait, through the motions of post-op routine, her unbound hair continued to hang and glisten down her back, still releasing, like muscles slowly relaxing, the shape of its coils. "These stitches will dissolve," she said. "Come back in six months."

By then, the East River was edged with ice and smoking with mid-January cold. He surreptitiously examined Dr. Kim for signs of pregnancy, and was unable to detect any beneath the baggy lab coat. She reached out and touched the nearly invisible scar near his tear duct. "Snug," she said. "Symmetrical."

"Congratulations."

"Did you massage?"

"Faithfully. But I notice now that the thin skin under that eye has a crease I don't have on the other side. And both my upper lids are sagging. In the morning they feel like they're resting on my eyelashes. In the mirror I can see them sitting there in more or less random folds, like pieces of wet laundry."

She studied him intently, and rested her fingers on this skin, pressing through the lid onto his eyeball, so that his vision distorted and doubled. "You could do with a tuck," she admitted, "but it is not strictly necessary. You still have undisturbed function." She continued to finger his lids, so that he spoke in spaced accents, like a man under torture.

"It disturbs *me*," he brought out, "that they are rumpling up like that. I want something that may be too difficult for you."

Her touch changed quality, became tentative. "What would that be?"

"I want my lids to look like yours."

Her fingertips, resting on the inner corners of his eyes, stayed there. He thought he detected a slight tremor. "With an epicanthus?" she asked.

"If possible."

"It would be as you say difficult. The graft would have to come from a very sensitive area. The body has few sites where the skin is so delicate. The inside of the thigh, the— The color match is never perfect."

"Couldn't you somehow tug the skin that *is* there into a fold? I feel like a rhinoceros lately, with heaps of extra skin. When I bend over, I can feel my face fall away from the bone. And all that under the chin—couldn't that be tightened up?"

Her fingers thoughtfully moved to his jaw, making delicate adjustments. "It is commonly done," she said, "but it is not as easy as cutting cloth. There is musculature beneath, and nerves and capillaries. It would be a long and strenuous operation." She settled back into a lotus pose, her hands folded, palm up, in her lap. He saw her face not only as a glowing oval but as a piece of seamless tailoring, layers of dermis precisely fitted to cheekbone and jaw-hinge and gelatinous eye-white.

"It could be several operations," Anderson suggested.

Little frown lines flitted into the smooth space between her eyebrows, and were quickly erased. "It is better for you if it is done all at once. One session, one recovery."

"I can take it if you can," he said, in the lowered, virtually hostile tone in which, with another woman, in other circumstances, he would make a proposition.

Dr. Kim straightened in her chair, looked him in the eyes with her liquid, opaque own, and spoke more deliberately than ever. "I want to do it. If you want it done to you. Be aware," she said, "that there can sometimes be loss in sensitivity, even a certain stiffness of expression."

"I'll risk it," Anderson responded. "I hate my face the way it is." He had come to hate, though he did not want to scar their pure relation with such a confession, the daily facts of life: shaving his face, combing his hair and enduring a haircut, putting himself into pajamas and bed at night and getting himself out of them, rumpled and sweated, in the morning. He was weary of the way whiffs of staleness arose to him from his lower regions, and of the way his crowned and much-patched teeth harbored pockets of suddenly tastable decay, as if all the deaths in the newspapers and all the years he had put behind him had been miniaturized and lodged in the crannies of his slimy mouth.

The operation was, as Dr. Kim had predicted, arduous— for six hours she stood on her feet, cutting and tugging, injecting this and that section of his face as she moved to it, like a farmer planting her fields. She wore magnifying spectacles above the green paper mask; his face felt tranquil and lunar under her attentions. Even the work on his eyelids seemed to take place at a great anesthetic distance, though he had rather dreaded it. No graft was necessary; she found as much spare skin around his nose as a puppy has at the back of his neck. When it was over, the two nurses gathered around her as if to save her from fainting. He stayed the night at the hospital; the bed was taut and clean.

In the morning, from within his bandages he smiled, stiffly, to see the patients in the waiting room start at the mummylike menace he presented. Through slits like those of Eskimo sunglasses he saw the East River far below, its black skin broken by the passage of a brimming garbage barge and, at a faster clip, a tourist cruiseboat, circling the island. The blue-green CitiBank Building, the only sky-scraper in Queens, thrust up like a crocus. It was spring; the trees were in bud but still transparent; their leafing-out would be a process as inevitable and graciously gradual as his own healing and emergence into beauty.

There were several visits weeks apart, during which she removed her brocade of stitches—more painful, oddly, than their insertion—and then a two-month follow-up. As if they had shared a rapture too keen to be soon repeated, these appointments were prophylactically cursory, hurried: she was always running late, and the traffic of patients at the clinic approached gridlock. Anderson's bruised and swollen face horrified him in the mirror. The reassurances of his girlfriend—a new one—that he was looking better and better every day meant nothing to him; they were the predictable rote of female flattery, its customary irritating stratagems. Only Dr. Kim could be trusted to provide him with the cool, unbiased truth. Verity was in her touch.

At his eight-month visit, she studied him from an arm's distance, and slowly pronounced, "It came out well. Your canthi still show, but the lids are very taut. The yellow bruis-ing on the jaw will diminish"—*di-min-ish*, three even sylla-bles, like a doll talking—"over time, as will the vertical red scars in front of your ears." She leaned forward and lightly stroked them, with bare fingertips. The halves of her lab coat parted, and he saw that she was pregnant again. She handed him a heavy plastic hand-mirror, and said, "You look. You tell me what you see still to be improved. I will go out of the room."

Her rapid rolling gait, in low black heels rather than the universal, deplorable white running shoes of hospital habit, took her out the door, her lab coat floating, her pinned-up hair from behind glistening like a rope of black silk. It was Christmas season, and a little one-piece crèche unexpectedly stood on her desk. In the mirror he saw a face Oriental in its impassive expression, its smooth, hardened surface marred only by a few lingering welts. The faded blue eyes were the wrong color, and his gray hair was gauzily receding, but otherwise he saw little to improve.

He had never been left alone in her office before. He got out of the examining chair, with its bothersome folding footrest, and walked to her desk. The crèche was of plastic, but rather lovingly designed, with identical startled expressions on the baby, Mary, Joseph, the sheep, the ox, and the shepherds. Next to it were tinted photographs of a toddler and a kindergarten-age child—a boy and a girl, both of mixed race—and an old man. Not old, exactly, perhaps no older than Anderson, but craggy, Caucasian, grinning, big-nosed, rather monstrously bumpy and creased.

"Oh!" Dr. Kim's voice behind him sounded girlish in her surprise at finding him at her desk. She regained her level, professional, rather murmurous pitch. "That is my husband." *Husbannnd*, deliciously prolonged, the very concept come from some far and perfect world. Keeping his back turned, as if to hide his foolish face from her, Anderson touched his right tear duct. It was still there.

Rabbit Remembered

i.

J ANICE HARRISON goes to the front door when the old
bell scrapes the silence. Decades of rust have all but
destroyed its voice, the thing will die entirely some day,
the clapper freezing or the wires shorting out or whatever
they do. Whenever she says she wants to call the electrician,
Ronnie tells her it's on his list of home improvements, he'll
get to it. He likes to do things himself. Harry was all for letting other people do them.

A twinge in her hip slows her progress out from the sunny
worn kitchen, through the dining room, whose shades are
drawn to keep the Oriental rug from fading and the polished
mahogany tabletop from drying out, into the front room,
where the reproduction cobbler's bench in front of the gray
cut-plush sofa causes a detour that has worn a pale path in
the carpet. A big brown Zenith television, its top loaded
with her mother's dusty knickknacks, blankly stares where
her father's Barcalounger used to be. They don't sit out here

and watch on the sofa like they used to. Ronnie likes the little Sony in the kitchen for the evening news, watching while he eats, and Nelson when he's stuck at home after work has the computer upstairs that he says is more fun than television because it's interactive. He wasn't so interactive with his wife that Teresa didn't move back to Ohio with the two children over a year ago. He and Roy, who is fourteen now, do a lot of e-mail, mostly rude jokes (one especially shocking joke this summer went *Remember when the Kennedys used to drown only one woman at a time?*), as if e-mail was as good as having a real father under the same roof.

Often Janice doesn't hear the bell at all, even when she's in the house or the backyard garden. She finds pinched in the door these notices from deliverymen who had to go away or cards from salesmen who didn't get to make their pitch. She's grateful for that but still it makes her feel isolated; suppose somebody rang she was dying to see? She doesn't know who that would be, though. So many she cared about are dead.

The heavy walnut door with its tall sidelights of frosted glass patterned in floral arabesques, the door that she has been going in and out of most of her life off and on, has been swollen and sticking all summer with a humidity that never produced rain. Now it swings open more easily, with a dry crack, fall crispness being in the air at last. The girl—woman, really, close to Nelson's age—who stands on the front porch looks vaguely familiar. She has a broad white face, her eyes wide-spaced with some milk in their blue and middle-aged crinkles at the corners beginning to develop. Taller than Janice by a bit, she fills her beige summer dress well, the cotton taut across her bosom and lap. She wears a navy-blue sweater draped over her shoulders like the young women at the Pearson and Schrack Realty office do, manning their glowing computers, giving a businesslike air. She asks, "Mrs. Angstrom?"

Janice is taken aback. "I was," she allows. "My husband's name now is Harrison."

The girl blushes. "I'm sorry, I did know that. I wasn't thinking." The girl's milky-blue eyes widen and Janice feels this stranger is actually trembling, her body aquiver in its careful quiet clothes, a creature somehow trapped on the welcome mat, in the rectangular shade of the brick-pillared porch.

Behind her, cars swish by on Joseph Street with a fresh dry sound. A shiny-new, brick-red Lexus stands at the dappled curb, under the still-green maples. A cloud passes overhead and the shadow is almost chilling: that's how you feel the new season, the shadows are sharper and darker, and the crickets sing under everything. With the terrible drought this summer the leaves are turning early, those of the horse chestnuts curling brown at the edges, and the front yards where no one has watered have turned to flattened straw, a look Janice remembers from childhood, when you are closer to the ground and summer is endless.

"My mother died two months ago," the girl begins again, taking a breath to steady her trembling, both her hands holding a small striped purse in front of her belly.

"I'm sorry," Janice says. Nelson deals with crazy people at his work all the time and says they're not to be afraid of. She deals with people trying to buy or sell houses, the most money a lot of them will ever have to think about, and they can get high-strung and irrational, too.

"I've never married, she was all the family I had."

So, despite her respectable clothes, this is a beggar. "I'm sorry," Janice says again, in a harder tone, "but I don't believe I can help." Her hand moves to swing the heavy door shut. Nelson is off at the treatment center and Ronnie playing golf at the club with some other retirees so she is alone in the house. Not that the girl looks violent. But she is bigger than Janice, bigger-boned, with a dangerous fullness to her being there, as if defiantly arrived at the end of a long wavering, like a client taking the plunge of offering thirty thousand more than she can afford. Her eyes are set in squarish sockets showing the puffy look of sleeplessness and her hair, cut raggedly short the way they do it now, is mixed of light-brown and darker-brown and gray strands.

"I don't think you can either," she agrees. "But my mother thought you might."

"Did I ever know your mother?"

"No, you never met. You knew each other existed, though."

Janice does wish Nelson were here. He could tell at a glance if this person were over the edge, and give it one of those names he had—bipolar, schizophrenic, paranoid, psychotic. Psychotic, you see and hear things, and can murder without meaning it, and then in court seem so innocent. The varnished grain of the door under her hand calls out as a potential shield and a slammed end to this encounter, but the something pleasant and kind and calm about the girl, who is these as well as troubled and trembling, holds the door open. The dry warm air of this early-fall day in southeastern Pennsylvania—children tucked back into school, the mid-morning streets quiet, the vegetables in the backyard gardens harvested or gone to seed—lies on Janice's face as a breath from the past, her visitor having come from this same terrain.

"I nursed her at the end, she didn't like hospitals, they made her feel penned up," the light, considerate, shaky voice goes on.

"This is your mother," Janice says, in spite of herself entering in.

"Yes, and of course being a nurse I could do that, administer the meds and see that she was kept turned in the bed and all that. Only it was strange, doing it for your mother. Her body had all these meanings for me. She didn't like being touched, as long as she had strength. Though she could come on free and easy with some people, she was really a freak about her privacy, even with me. She didn't like telling me anything, except then when she knew she was dying."

The girl as her nervousness eased has skipped a stage of her story without being aware of it. "What did you say this had to do with me?" Janice asks.

"Oh. I guess—I guess you were married to my father."

A mail truck coasts by, one of those noseless vans they have now, white with a red and blue stripe. They used to be solid green, like military vehicles. Mailmen used to be men; now theirs is a mail-lady, a young woman with long sun-bleached hair and stocky tan legs in shorts who pushes her pouch on a three-wheeled cart ahead of her along the side-walk. It is not time for her to go by yet, but across Joseph Street, another young woman comes out on the righthand porch of the semi-detached house opposite. For years and years that address was occupied by a couple that had seemed old and changeless to her. Then they went off to assisted liv-ing, and a young couple has moved in, with hanging plants on the porch they fuss at, and music that booms out over the neighborhood through the window screens, and two small children who go to pre-school.

"Maybe you should come inside," Janice says, stepping back invitingly, though admitting to her home this piece of a shameful dead past disgusts as well as frightens her.

Inside, the girl, her face and arms as white as if summer had never been, hangs in the dim-lit living-room clutter like one more piece of furniture that time's slow earthquake has jostled out of place. She seems, as Harry used to, a bit out of scale. Janice is used to her house with average-sized people in it, herself and Nelson and Ronnie, though Ronnie's Alex is big, when he visits from Virginia, and Judy and Roy when they lived here took up plenty of space with their music and games and sibling competition. Though with one a girl and the other a boy and over four years between them it wasn't as bad as it could have been.

"Would you like any coffee?" Janice asks. "Or tea—that's what my husband drinks now, for his blood pressure, and now I've got the habit."

"No, honestly—I couldn't take anything on my stomach right now. I've been thinking of what I'd say for so long, and then it came out all backward. My name is Annabelle Byer."

Janice is used to hearing the word as "buyer." For every seller there is a buyer.

"Like I said, I'm single. I'm going to be forty next year. I'm a practical nurse, at St. Joe's for thirteen years, and these last five I've been in home care, those that need an L.P.N., though the number that can afford it is going down, with the tightening up of what Medicare will pay for."

"Do sit down at least," Janice says, to reduce the inter-loper's radiant, unsettling bulk. The girl sits on the sofa, where like everybody else she sinks down lower than she expects, her bare knees brightly upthrust. A few hasty tugs on her skirt reduce the amount of thigh that shows. Janice takes the green wing chair, with the matching arm doilies, folding her hands palm-up in her lap as her mother used to do, setting herself to listen, if the thudding of her heart lets her. Her heart is caught in a net of calculation as to how this innocently disgusting intrusion will affect her life and dis-turb her peace. With Ronnie being so steady compared to Harry, she has known peace.

"My mother worried that I hadn't married," Annabelle tells her, from her relaxed voice already more at home than Janice thinks is quite seemly. "She wondered if it had been her fault, making me distrust men, or sex or something, out of her own experience. I would tell her, That's silly. Dad, as I called him, was a wonderful man. He died when I was sixteen, but still I grew up with this good masculine image. He would toss me all around, even when I was eleven or so, and taught me to ride the tractor and whatever all else a child can do to help run a farm—pick apples and strawberries and feed the chickens and whack back the bushes and poison ivy. We even did carpentry together and he taught me to shoot his gun. I had two brothers, Scott and Morris, I always got along good with—being country children, we did a lot together. And then I had boyfriends, normal enough, though I guess compared to city boys they were shy, but after high school I got a job as a nurse's aide in a nursing home called Sunnyside, out toward the old fairgrounds—?"

She is checking to see if Janice is listening. Janice nods and says, "I've heard of it. Sunnyside."

"And then I went for a year's degree and passed the boards and after I entered service at St. Joe's the boys weren't so shy, some of them were even married doctors, but some weren't, and it all seemed normal to me except, you know, lightning never struck, the question never got popped. Maybe I didn't want to hear it. I'd tell my mother, It's no big deal, if it happens it happens, you're still a person, but it worried her sick, somehow, that I stayed independent, as if she were preventing something, especially after she sold the farm and I asked her to move in with me, we could manage a larger place together, over on Eisenhower Avenue—"

Janice's heart jumps. She once lived on Eisenhower Avenue, with Charlie Stavros, at number 1204, back in the Sixties, when everybody was going crazy. But it shouldn't surprise her; the stately street, fallen away from its heyday of one-family mansions staffed by black or Irish servants, was where the better, safer rentals were, for misfits like her and Charlie or then this girl and her mother.

"—she would be so afraid of being in the way, she'd tell me she'd stay in her room if I brought back a man, but actually I had lived alone in Brewer enough to be wary of bringing men back, they can get rough, and I was in my thirties by then and the good men were married to somebody else. When she saw she was dying—by the time the tumors were detected, oat-cell carcinoma of the lung, the cancer had spread to the lymph system and the bones—she told me that I had more family than I knew. She told me that Dad hadn't been my real father, that he had loved her enough to take her with somebody else's baby. I wasn't a year old, my grandparents in West Brewer were taking care of me while she worked in this restaurant over toward Stogey's Quarry, where she met my—where she met Frank Byer. He moved fast—I guess his own mother had died not long before and a farm needs a woman. Not that he wasn't crazy about her— he was. He was in his forties and she in her twenties and I could see when I got to be, you know, observant that they still had a lot going between them. He kidded her about being fat but then he was fat himself."

Janice hates hearing about these very common people. "Didn't you wonder," she asks impatiently, "how you were born before your parents married?" Through the semi-transparent curtain across the front-room picture window— glass curtains they call them, though they're just cloth—she can see that the woman across the street is still out on her porch, fussing idly with a long-nosed watering can, as if she is listening. But at this distance she can't be. The girl's being here seems shameful to Janice. Shameful and shameless.

"Well, they were vague," Annabelle tells her. "You know how it is to be a child, you assume everything around you is

from the back of her neck and her bare arms. "So I expect you've told me about all there is to know," she says when they have settled again, on the same furniture.

Annabelle does not concede this. She resumes, "I was saying about my parents, as a child I never knew when they got married, and when I grew old enough to be curious, my mother allowed that maybe I had come before the wedding, since Dad's mother was still alive but ailing and a marriage might have hastened her death. This seemed to figure, it being back in 1960, before things got liberal."

What got liberal? Janice asks herself. Abortion, she supposes. And young couples living together. But these things happened then too, only deeper in the dark. The year 1959 seems very close, as close as the beating of her heart, which beat then too, back in the tunnel of time, that same faithful muscle, in its darkness and blood. She doesn't want to prolong the discussion, though; she doesn't want to get involved, though there is a tug, back into the past's sad damp pit.

The girl seems to read her mind. "Yes, my mother described it," she says, "the, whatever you could call it, affair. She and my—she and your husband, Mr. Angstrom, lived together I guess on Summer Street for three months. He never knew if she had gone ahead and had me or not. I knew him, you know. I met him a few times, without knowing who he was. I mean, his relation to me. He was once a patient when I was still at St. Joe's. An angioplasty, I think it was. He was a charmer. Full of jokes."

"He died in Florida," Janice says accusingly, "not six months later. Of a heart attack. He was only fifty-six." As if these hard facts, so hard to her at the time, might force Harry and this girl apart.

"He should have had a bypass, it sounds like. They weren't quite as standard then."

"He didn't want it. He didn't want to have his body

meddled with. He was afraid of it." Janice's voice startles her
by cracking, and her eyes by burning near tears, as if accusing herself of not making Harry's life worth living. She
hadn't called him down in Florida, when he had wanted her
to. He had been begging for her forgiveness, and she hadn't
given it.

"And then before that," this girl insensitively is going
on, "when I was still an aide at Sunnyside, a boy I knew
back in Galilee called Jamie and I—we were living together,
actually, in a little apartment on Youngquist Boulevard,
the building went condo and that broke us up, but that's I
guess another story—went to look at Toyotas over on Route
111. We bought one, eventually, though not that day, when
Mr. Angstrom was there. He seemed so nice, I was struck.
He paid attention to me, he didn't just talk to the man, or try
to pressure us the way car salesmen like to."

"It wasn't exactly his calling, selling," Janice volunteers.
"He didn't really have a calling, after high school."

But how beautiful he had been, Janice remembers, in
those high-school halls—the height of him, the fine Viking
hair slicked back in a ducktail but trailing off in lank sexy
strands like Alan Ladd's across his forehead, the way he
would flick it back with his big graceful white hands while
kidding with the other seniors, like that tall girlfriend of his
called Mary Ann, his lids at cocky sleepy half-mast, the
world of those halls his, him paying no attention of course
to her, a ninth-grader, a runt. They didn't begin with each
other until they both worked at Kroll's in Brewer, she
behind the nut and candy cases and he back from his two
years in the Army, having been in Texas and never sent to die
in Korea after all. He often mentioned Korea as if he had
missed out on something by not going there to fight and
coming back home to a peaceful life instead. Nobody wants
war but men don't want only peace either.

"Yes," Annabelle hisses, too eager to agree, not really understanding how simple we all were back then, "he was a wonderful athlete, I remember the clippings up in the showroom, and then my mother said. She had gone to another high school, that used to play his. She talked a lot about him, once she got started, before she . . . went. I know about you, and Nelson, and the time your house burnt down, my mother kept track of all that in the papers, I guess. She was interested. The way she spoke, at the end, she didn't have any grudge. It was the times, she said. He was caught, what else could he do? Anyway, I was no prize, she would tell me."

Ruth and her views, beneath consideration these many years, have invaded the living room. "My goodness" is all Janice can think to say, as the sherry moves into her veins and begins to tint this nightmare a more agreeable color. What harm could what happened forty years ago do her now?

"He visited her, you know," this young woman goes on, her gestures growing freer, her body bigger as she crosses and recrosses her white legs on the sofa, the beige cotton dress riding higher on her thighs. Her hair, too, seems too short, and bounces a bit too much as her head comes forward. There is some vanity, some push, in that hair—its many-colored thickness, its trendy trampy cut, long and short mixed up together. "The year he died, I guess. Somehow he had found our farm."

"He did?" This is horrible. Harry's affair with Thelma she and Ronnie have together buried, never mentioning it once they were past the courtship stage of confessing everything. They had triumphed, they were the survivors, Harry and Thelma were shades, corpses, sinking deeper into bloodlessness in their buried coffins, their skins crumbling, drawing tight like that little sacrificed Peruvian girl they found on the mountaintop, unbearable to think about. But to hear now that at the same time he was seeing Thelma he was chasing that fat old slut all over Diamond County is as if Harry from beyond the grave is denying her peace just as he did when alive. He couldn't just be ordinary, respectable, dependable. He thought he was beyond that. This girl, both shy and sassy, pleasant yet with something not quite right about her, is his emissary from the grave. Janice wants nothing to do with it, with her. She asks, "Why would he do that?"

The girl puts her knees together to lean forward for emphasis but her dress is so short the triangle of her panties shows anyway. "To find out about *me*, my mother said. She wouldn't tell him. She wanted to keep me pure from him. Then I guess when she saw she would be, you know, leaving me, she had second thoughts and wanted me to *know*." The girl's eyes are less milky now, here in the muted living-room light, and flash with importance, the importance her story gives her.

"*Why?*" Janice cries, fighting back a pressure. "Why not let the past lie? Why stir up what can't be helped? Excuse me," she says. "I must refresh my tea." She doesn't even pretend to go into the kitchen, she pours some more dry sherry into the cup right there at the sideboard, where the girl could see if she turned sideways to look. But back in the front room Annabelle sits staring across at the heavy green glass egg, with a bubble inside, on top of the dead television with the other knickknacks Bessie Springer had collected as a sign of her prosperity as Daddy's car business took hold. Mother and her fur coat, Mother and her blue Chrysler—it was a simpler world back then, when your pride was satisfied with such things. The girl, with all that leg bared by sitting low on the sofa and her navy sweater fallen off her naked arms, has a sluttish way of putting forth her body that must be her own mother living in her. And there is a blandness, a fatherless blankness, her face in profile taking the light as mutely as the egg of green glass.

She senses Janice's eye on her and turns her face and says, "It's so embarrassing, isn't it? My turning up like this. Embarrassing to me, embarrassing to you." She has a plump upper lip that gives her smile a childish, questioning quality. She looks easy to bruise.

"Well," Janice pronounces, back in her wing chair with a fortified mug whose healing tang settles her more broadly in the pose of authority. She vowed years ago never to let herself run to fat like her mother did but she did admire the way in her last years, her husband gone, her generation dying off, Mother took charge of things, keeping a grip on the family pocketbook, standing up for her notions of decency and propriety. Living here in this house, Janice feels still surrounded by her—Bessie Springer's adamant unchanging furniture, her fixed sense of her own worth. Koerner mulishness, Mother would call it when being funny at her own expense. "Maybe that was your mother's idea, to embarrass everybody," Janice tells the girl. "What earthly good did she think telling you all this would do, at your age? Make mischief, is the sum of it. And who's to say it's true, any of it?" Though she feels it is—a whiff of Harry, a pale glow, an unsettling drift comes off this girl, this thirty-nine-year-old piece of evidence.

"Oh, she wouldn't have made it up, it *poured* out of her. It wasn't her nature, to make things up. She used to say of these detective novels she was always reading, 'How do they make all this up? They must have a screw loose.' And she showed me my birth certificate, at a hospital in Pottstown. 'Father unknown,' it said."

"Well, that's it, unknown," Janice presses on, like a lawyer urging a case she knows is bad.

"You asked why," Annabelle says. "I think she thought"—

suddenly tears reflect light in her eyes, the plump upper lip quivers out of control—"you people could help me, some- how." She laughs at her own tears, quickly swipes at her face with expert hands, hands used to giving—rubbing, hold- ing, patting, seizing—a nurse's care. "I was so alone, she must have thought. I haven't had a serious relationship for years. And my brothers, Scott went to Seattle and Morris to Delaware—he was the angriest when she sold the farm and moved in with me in Brewer. He had thought he could work the place and live on it but it wouldn't have been fair for her to have left it all to him. Not that a farm that size could sup- port anybody any more. Even my dad—even Frank—had to run the township school buses to make ends meet."

"Is this about money, then?" Janice asks, alert now, the muddle showing its nub. Money is something she has a feel for; it's in her Springer veins. She acted as accountant for her father, and then for Nelson as best she could, until he had so much to hide. Ronnie has his own savings and pension but she handles her inheritance still, when the CDs come due and at what interest and how to keep capital-gains taxes from biting into the mutual funds: the managers of some run up gains just to make their annual reports look good. This girl won't get a penny from her. Janice sips from her mug and looks at the interloper levelly.

Annabelle considers the question, rolling her eyes upward. "No-o, I don't think so. I clear twenty an hour from the agency and often work twelve-hour shifts. My mother left us a fair amount, even divided by three. The farm had only a tiny mortgage on it, in terms of today's money. And she held down a respectable job, the last fifteen years, with this investments advisory firm in the new glass building down- town. She used to laugh at herself, putting on heels and pantyhose every morning, after being such a country slob. She got her weight down to one fifty-five."

"It's wonderful to work," Janice concedes. "Women of our generation came late to it." It disquiets her to link herself with Ruth, Ruth the unspeakable, holding her husband captive on the other side of Mt. Judge, Ruth the treacherous mucky underside of everything respectable.

"No, it's not about money," Annabelle says, edging herself forward on the sofa preparatory to getting to her feet, readjusting the sweater about her shoulders, and regripping her little purse, striped yellow, black, and red. "It was about family, I guess. But never mind, Mrs. Harrison. I can see you'd rather not get involved, and that's no surprise, to be honest. It was my mother's idea, and she was half out of her head with the medications. Dying people aren't the most sensible, often, though you'd think they should be. I did this for her and not for me, because she asked me to." She stands, looking down on Janice.

"Well now, wait."

"You've been patient, actually. I know what a shock it must be." Those deft, solid hands fiddle with her hair, its artful tousle, as if it were she who had felt the shock.

Janice says in her own defense, "You can't just show up and drop a thing like this on a body."

"I didn't know how else to do it. It didn't seem the sort of thing to put in a letter or over the phone." Trained to move fast, she takes the few steps it needs to the door, and puts her hand on the doorknob, an old-fashioned one with a raised design worn shiny with the years, like brass lace. She tugs the sticky door open with a snap that leaves a little reverberation in the air, a cry that dies away.

There is a poignance in this strong female body, the way it moves almost like a man's, like those women soccer players who beat China this summer. Janice keeps losing daughters: Becky, and then Teresa leaving Nelson after nearly twenty years, and Judy at nineteen secretive and surly, living entirely within her whispering Walkman headset, shutting out her grandmother. She begins, "Annabelle, I'm sorry if I seemed stupid—"

"You did not seem stupid. I seemed stupid. You seemed suspicious, and why not? Thank you for the glass of water."

"I need to think, and talk to Ronnie and Nelson."

"Nelson. That's right. My brother. I think of him as a little boy. My mother said how, those months they were together, your husband was always talking about him, upset about him."

Now the girl is out on the porch, standing on the coco-fiber welcome mat, thin late-morning traffic making its whisper behind her, the dusty tired nibbled maple leaves throwing sun-dotted shadow down on the new red Lexus parked by the curb. Bought with her inheritance, Janice guesses. The nosy young neighbor across the street was off her porch at last. "How can we reach you, if we need to?"

Annabelle's feet, in low beige heels, drum on the porch boards, then stop. She turns to say, "I'm in the book. B-Y-E-R. I'm listed as 'A.,' the only one with just that letter. Don't call after nine at night, please. I get up at five-thirty." Her mother's toughness shows. "But you don't have to call at all." Then her bright round face is a child's again; she smiles the way children do, in sudden blurred forgiveness. "I won't expect it. It was nice to meet you. I had thought you'd be shorter."

"When I was married to your father," Janice says, high enough on the sherry to attempt a joke, "I looked shorter."

It feels then that she is sneaking through the rest of the day, flickering through the parched September brightness in her black Le Baron convertible, with gray cloth interior, a 1995, the last year they made this model. She wonders why

Chrysler discontinued it. Janice loves this car, the way it handles, the way she imagines she looks in it, her head in a fluttering headscarf and her DKNY sunglasses. Buying the Le Baron five years ago was the most extravagant thing she ever did for herself, as a widow at least. Not that she was still a widow after she married Ronnie. She was a second wife and he her second husband. There is a kind of racy glamour in a second marriage, though it can never be like the first, so solemn, both of you so serious with the vows and the being together all night every night and nobody saying no, and all your parents still alive and watching if you make a mistake. She had made a mistake, a terrible one, and others besides, if you consider Charlie a mistake, which she never could, really. He freed her up and restored her sense of worth. And the strangest thing was he kept Harry's friendship and even on her mother's good side—he knew how to get around Bessie Springer. Dear Charlie died two or was it three years ago, living alone in an apartment in the southwest section of Brewer, the old Polish and Greek blocks before the Hispanics moved in, they found him on the sofa dead with an unfolded newspaper on his chest, just closed his eyes for a nap and slipped away. Charlie was like that, understated in everything, his poor weak heart that she was always worried about straining during lovemaking just coolly decided at last to stop. Like the death of your parents it leaves you with one less witness to your life when a man you loved dies. Looking back from this distance, she can't think any more that Harry was all to blame for their early troubles, he had been just trying life on too: life and sex and making babies and finding out who you are. Second marriages were lighter. You just expect a little companionship, a little fun that harms no one else. Nelson kids her about the convertible, calls it her Batmobile, but she knows it's just his disappointments talking, his own marriage such a sad fizzle, not even a real divorce. He says he can't afford it, and Teresa doesn't want it until Roy is eighteen. Or until, Janice thinks, the right man comes along, out there in Akron.

Odd, after all those years of Daddy's Toyotas, she has gone back to American cars. Ronnie never left. Married to Thelma, he drove a succession of an insurance salesman's drab, safe cars, modest but adequate like the benefits your loved ones reap when you're out of the picture as they say, she can't remember the makes, Chevrolets or Fords. Just thinking about those years, Thelma having an affair with Harry almost right up to when she died, gives Janice a hollow sore feeling. Now Ronnie drives a new Taurus, a silvery gray like a Teflon skillet, with the 1999 styling turning everything into oval blobs—the taillights and headlights and recessed door handle shaped alike, and the back, where the trunk lifts up, a continuous blob across, like a mustache or a roll of pre-mixed cookie dough being squeezed in the middle. Cars used to have such dashing shapes, like airplanes, back when gas was cheap, twenty-five cents a gallon.

At noon she shows a house over in a new development south of Maiden Springs to a young couple who had hoped for something smaller. They don't build new houses small any more, Janice has to tell them, land is too expensive and people have too much money. And yet this same couple looks horrified at a perfectly nice and well-kept-up row house on the north side of Brewer, with a terraced front yard planted in English ivy and a third floor converted to an apartment (outside stairs) for some additional income until they need the space when their family expands. "Is it a," the young man asks, "a mixed neighborhood?" He may be in his mid-twenties but already looks overweight and soft, and fussy and potentially irritable as fat people are, being pinched by their clothes and strained by lugging their bodies around. So many young people now, even the girl this morning, have a sunless indoor look. Janice has always taken a good tan, one of the few things she could always like about herself. That, and her legs never being piano legs.

She tells him cheerfully, "There may be a few upwardly mobile minorities living a block or so down, but it's basically upper-middle-income families, perfectly safe for you and your children when they come along. It's an area that has kept its corner groceries and little service shops, a lot of people now are moving back from the suburbs to enjoy the convenience of city life, the stimulation of it. They *want* the ethnic variety, for their children as well as themselves. Trendy restaurants are opening up around here, and some new boutiques coming into upper Weiser Street, where the buildings have been boarded up so long. Believe me, inner city is *in* now."

"I can't imagine myself pregnant climbing all those steps," the female prospective buyer says, looking up the long ter-raced slope, with its concrete steps and pipe railing painted a swimming-pool greeny blue to match the gingerbread porch trim. As these blocks, with their industrial repetition of steps, retaining walls, porches, fanlighted doors, and shingled steep gables, passed from the ownership of the Pennsylvania-German working class to that of a more varied population, the trim and window frames and doors were painted more festively, in carnival colors—teal, canary yel-low, purple, a pale aqua like some warm remembered sea.

Generations have, Janice restrains herself from saying. *The exercise would do you good, Miss Prissy-pants.* "Some people build carports out back," she says. "You need a permit but it's legal. If you don't want even to walk up and look, let's see what new listings come in next week. The ones in your range get snapped up pretty quickly. It's hard to believe, considering all the hard times the region has known, but there's a bit of a real-estate boom on in Diamond County.

To be safe buyers offer over the asking price. People from Philadelphia retire here now. They say they love the slower pace, the friendliness." And yet, she does not add, Brewer all the years of her growing up was considered a fast, crummy town, a town run by gangsters and crooked cops and the enforcers for the steel and coal and textile companies, a town where children could buy numbers slips at the cigar store and so-called cathouses filled the half-streets around the railroad station.

It queasily occurs to her that from where she is standing, here on the high side of Locust Boulevard with its big view of densely built blocks—bricks and asphalt shingles and treetops—falling away down to the curving river a mile away, a descending view pierced by the county courthouse with its boxlike glass annex and the other glass box across from where Kroll's used to be, she is only a few streets above Summer, where that girl this morning was conceived, if you can believe her story. The thought makes Janice feel sick yet at the same time exalted, as if she stands on the lip of a canyon that only she can see. She lives; those who had worked her humiliation in that far-off season are dead.

She doesn't go back to Mt. Judge for lunch, where the mail-lady will have left bills and advertisements in the foyer, and the afternoon sun will be swinging around into the living room, inserting a wedge of golden dust motes behind the Zenith. She doesn't want to go back to the house, it's been spoiled by that girl's visit, the past rising up like that. Instead she has a tuna-salad sandwich and Diet Coke at the West Brewer Diner, which is open twenty-four hours a day. They used to come over here after dances in Mt. Judge, and the place has changed owners and generations of waitresses have come and gone, but the layout, the low booths along the windows on two sides and the long counter backed by quilted aluminum with the slot where the cooks serve the orders up and even the little individual jukeboxes with pages of pop and country classics, is unchanged.

A slender dark-browed girl of startling beauty waits on Janice, such beauty among the middle-aged and pudgy pimpled teen-age other waitresses that Janice's eyes sting. Dark hair, dark eyes, straight nose, firm round chin, soft mouth. Greek, Italian, Armenian even: Janice being herself dark-complected responds to such looks. When the girl speaks, the county's comfortable dragged accent—"So, hon, what can I bring ya?"—tumbles out and with it a vision of her sad future: the marriage, the pregnancies, the heavy meals, the lost looks. The blazing beauty dwindled to a shrill spark, a needle of angry discontent lost in these streets lined with row houses and aluminum awnings and little front porches where the patient inhabitants sit and soak in the evening heat and wonder where it all went. The television slowly goes from selling you perfume and designer jeans to selling you Centrum and denture adhesive as used by aged movie stars. It is a mistake to be beautiful when young and Harry made that mistake but not Janice; she still has what Mother called room to grow, back when she thriftily used to buy her daughter's clothes two sizes too big. She leaves the waitress a dollar tip though the sandwich and Diet Coke came to less than five dollars, counting the quarter she put in the jukebox to hear Patsy Cline's "Crazy" one more time before she dies. Patsy Cline, dead young in a plane crash just like that poor Kennedy boy. And then it's not Patsy Cline's version but that of some young pop "diva," so that's a quarter wasted.

West Brewer is on the way to bridge at Doris Kaufmann's in Penn Park, where the streets get curving and expensive, off the Brewer grid. Her name was Kaufmann when Janice first knew her and then Eberhardt, and a few years ago Eberhardt died and Doris managed to land Henry Dietrich, the grandson of the founder of Dietrich Hosiery, which didn't

close its doors until after the war. To get there Janice has to
drive on Weiser past Emberly Avenue, which would lead to
Emberly Drive and then to Vista Crescent, where she and
Harry and Nelson had lived until the house was burned
down by racist neighbors because of what was going on
inside. She could hardly blame them, it was terrible what
Harry permitted to go on, for whatever selfish reason. How
utterly selfish he was she had never realized before marrying
Ronnie, who was so responsible and methodical. Some men
don't think before they jump, and others do. And now this
thirty-nine-year-old showing up, acting just like him, cocky
and innocent.

Janice likes bridge for the socializing and hearing what
real estate is doing in Penn Park but today it gives her a
slight headache at the back of her skull. First she overbids,
and then in compensation underbids, stopping at three
spades when they should have been, it turns out, in small
slam. Doris, her partner in that round of Chicago, is not
pleased, though with pointed good manners she tries not
to show it. "With twelve points in your own hand," she
says, shuffling with that ripping sound expert shufflers
make, "after I opened, showing at least thirteen in mine,
and with four spades including two honors, you might at
least have gone to game."

"Your shift to diamonds confused me. I had only two."

"I was showing you a second suit *in case*. That's called
communication," Doris says, slapping down the made deck
and picking up a red-filtered Newport she left smoking in
her ashtray. She is one of the last women Janice knows who
still smoke, though she is close to seventy if not quite there
yet; she won't say.

Janice defends herself: "I thought it might be a conven-
tion I didn't know." If she has let Doris down in this hand,
Doris has let her down lately by becoming *old:* wrinkled even

in the flat of her cheeks like Clint Eastwood, her eyelids drooping down on her lashes, her long brown hands like two claws scrabbling at the cards. Doris's thick bejewelled rings, accumulated residue of her husbands, sit loose on her bony fingers; her bracelets clatter on her wrists. Janice used to admire her knowingness on all subjects but Doris has betrayed her by becoming an irritable, half-deaf know-it-all hag. Now she snaps, "I would scarcely be going to a weak two after opening one spade."

The two other women at the table, which is set up in the Dietrichs' huge living room like a little life raft at sea, are Amy McNear, who also got into real estate after her husband passed on, and Norma Hammacher, whom Janice when she gets to know her better will ask if she's related to Linda Hammacher. It was Linda Hammacher, a girl she worked with at Kroll's, whose apartment and bed over in Brewer with a view of the gas tanks along the river she and Harry used to borrow when they were both at Kroll's and first going together. Things had happened to her since she was a silly freshman adoring him in the halls. She had let her boyfriend in junior year of high school, Jerry Nagle, feel her up and come against her stomach in his father's Packard, and then in senior year Warren Bixler used to French-kiss her and use her hand to jerk himself off after the movies, it was gross but really helped her understand what *happened*, and then the summer after graduation Daddy had rented for a month a Methodist camp-meeting cottage in Rehoboth, Delaware, where being in a bathing suit all day and taking a tan deep as a Polynesian's made her feel loose and free. She fell in that summer with a pack of Washington, D.C., kids raised wild in homes with their fathers off in the service or the diplomatic corps. They would cruise the boardwalk and Baltimore Avenue all day and at night head in cars up to Whiskey Beach, where a big pink house had been owned by a du Pont and slit-eyed tall towers stared out to sea as if still watching for submarines, and the college boys would make something called Purple Jesus with grape juice and vodka in galvanized garbage cans, it was the first time in her life she had drunk anything stronger than beer. She had decided as the weeks wore on that it was time and she let a wide-shouldered boy with a narrow ass from Chevy Chase do it to her, there in the dunes on a sandy blanket, the bonfire just over the shaggy profile of the next dune. She saw the gleam of light on the rubber of the Trojan he put on: that was prudent and considerate of him but probably made it hurt more than it would have with their natural lubrication, it hurt but it was done, she was a full woman as of August 1954, his first name was Grant, how horrible that she had forgotten his last name, but he had to go back with his family the next day, or the day after, and she wouldn't have let him do it to her again, she was too sore and scared at herself.

"Janice. Your bid," Doris was saying.

"Pass," she says, though there are some aces and kings peeping up from the fanned cards. She and Grant wrote for a while but she didn't like her own handwriting and thinking of things to say and let the correspondence die.

Even then, woozy on Purple Jesus and embarrassed to think somebody from the bonfire party might come up over the dune to pee, she had liked being on her back, supporting the world in the form of this boy's hard-breathing body, knowing she was built to take it, his painful thrusts, his whimper as he came. Men are surprisingly touching when they come, so grateful for a minute. There had been a boy-friend or two after that, while she worked in the office of Daddy's used-car business, filing and keeping accounts, before he got the Toyota franchise and anybody had heard of a Japanese car, but away from the beach sun she seemed to lose something, what little glamour she had, which was why she had liked Florida eventually. To get away from her parents, she was turning twenty and nothing was happening, she took the job at Kroll's, behind the nut-and-candy counter, the white smock they gave her had "Jan" stitched on the pocket when her parents had always called her her full name "Janice," pronouncing it juicily, decisively, their only child, prized, protected. At Kroll's there turned out to be, working at the most menial job, in shipping and receiving, this tall beautiful guy she remembered from Mt. Judge High, where he had been the star of the basketball team when she had been a runty freshman with skinned-back hair bangs couldn't hide. He also ran the 440 and the mile relay for track but it was for basketball that people remembered him by then, those that did. He seemed lost and funny, apologetic almost, after his two years in the Army and a few dead-end jobs. It was with him for the first time, thinking about it all day behind the counter, that she knew, just as certain as falling asleep, as plain as taking a meal or inserting a Tampax, that she was going to make love, fuck and be fucked, instead of just letting it happen against her better judgment the way it usually was. With everybody else on the street doing everyday things, they would drive down Warren Avenue in Harry's old Nash toward Linda Hammacher's pipe-frame bed, which squeaked and jerked back and forth so much they got to laughing sometimes and had to finish on the floor, her back pressed on the threadbare carpet and all the dust mice under the bed a few feet from her face, plus a single flesh-colored forgotten slipper. Harry was less methodical and steady a lover than Ronnie is, less big, not that it matters the way men think, but she was so excited by his shining torso naked above her and her memory of how heroic he had been on the court gleaming with sweat that she would come, pushing up shamelessly once he was rooted inside her. It helped to be down there in the floor grit. She was slow at some things but not at coming. Even now at the age of sixty-three she gets compliments from Ronnie. She smiles to herself at this secret of hers.

Everybody passes. Doris glances around suspiciously and says, "There must have been some points out there. I had only three, a jack and a queen."

While Norma redeals the cards Janice dares ask her, "Norma, are you by any chance a relation of a Linda Hammacher? She and I worked at Kroll's together, back in the Fifties."

Norma pauses, the cards freezing in her hands. "I had a second cousin Linda."

"Where is she now?"

"She died."

"Oh no! Well, I guess we're getting to that age."

"It was years ago. She was young, relatively. It was rather mysterious."

"How so?" Janice asks.

"Some said of AIDS, though the paper said just of a long illness. Her family didn't like to talk about it. She had been married and divorced."

"Oh dear," Janice says, truly shocked; a piece of remembered happiness has been poisoned.

"It was very tragic," Norma pronounces. "Damn. Count your cards. I should have the last one, and I don't."

As if to comfort Janice for having distracted the dealer, Amy during the next deal fills her in on the latest twist in the saga of a great parcel of land in the east of Diamond County, six thousand acres once held by Bethlehem Steel for its low-grade iron content and now sold to a Canadian developer who, tired of battling his farmer neighbors on every proposed development, had, all legally, turned this bit of William Penn's woods into a borough, with forty voting citizens, all but three of them company employees. Already they had voted in a managed landfill that would take four hundred tons a day of Philadelphia's garbage, trucked up the Turnpike in caravans of garbage trucks, and a water park involving a pool the size of a football field and a hundred-fifty-foot-high rubber-raft ride and an illuminated par-three golf course. "Now they're talking of a ten-story retirement-home complex and a half-mile racetrack for these little miniature racing cars that apparently are all the rage in Maryland," Amy says.

"Well," Janice says, "I guess it's the future."

Doris didn't quite hear and crabbily says, "Are you talking about the Y2K bug? Deet says it's all been overblown, to whip up more income for the computer companies."

Norma says, "Two clubs. At least I think that's what I'm supposed to say when I have a powerhouse."

Janice from her hand sees she will not have to bid, no matter what Doris bids, and in quiet celebration eats a few sugar-toasted peanuts from the pale-green porcelain bowl Doris and Deet had bought in China when they took a tour there last fall, set on a round-topped carved table they also bought there—the Chinese love to ship, even stone lions weighing as much as a boulder, in fact they will even ship boulders, they see a lot of beauty in boulders, Doris has told them—and which matches another carved table at the corner opposite for the other two players, to hold Waterford crystal water glasses and these bowls and Doris's ashtray (you can't complain since she's the hostess, blowing smoke into all of their lungs), while she thinks of how Harry used to love nibbly things, to the point where it killed him, and of how women like Doris are so fanatic about keeping a home up, a place for everything and everything in its place. She could never be like that, making a false religion out of your furniture. Even her mother hadn't been like that, though she liked nice things once Daddy began to make money at the lot. It's a kind of bullying, all these expensive shipped souvenirs of their expensive foreign trips on display, stacking up like the jewelry on Doris's hands from her previous marriages, cleaning ladies coming in to dust them like museum attendants.

For the last two rounds Doris offers them vermouth in little glasses with rose-tinted stems from Venice, and by the time she is at the door saying goodbye and see you in a week Janice wonders how she could ever have been so down on dear old Doris, who has had her to her lovely home so often and gave her so much good advice during those harrowing years with Harry.

Harry, Harry, he was the problem, Janice decides, that girl showing up claiming to be his daughter, no wonder she couldn't concentrate on the bridge, losing a dollar seventy cents and going down two on a three-no-trump bid Doris explained to her she could have made easily if only she had kept her diamond stopper. He made these messes but never cleaned up after himself, even now, dead ten years, leaving it up to the living.

Brewer pours by her in her Le Baron, a river of bricks and signage. People use that word in planning-board hearings as to whether or not there is too much of it; real-estate values shoot up when a community cuts down on signage and buries its electric wires. Janice halts at stoplights and then the flow resumes, a stream of sights deepened by a lifetime's familiarity. She crosses the Weiser Street Bridge, with its cast-iron light stanchions and its plaque naming some dead mayor whose name never took. As a girl she always wondered why the bridge didn't arch up in the air like the Running Horse Bridge a half-mile to the south did, or slant down to the Brewer side like the Youngquist Boulevard Overpass to the north did. The river was shallowest here. A ford in this spot started the settlement in Indian days. In her girlhood the river was solid black with dunes of coal silt. They cleaned that up decades back so that now motorboats use the water and some people swim and even the fish are back. Nineteenth-century industrial cities, she remembers sad-looking Mr. Lister telling them in the realty class on Property and Development Law, made a big mistake by turning their backs on their waterfronts. Now soon it will be another century yet, with its own mistakes, no doubt. She drives straight up Weiser past the white brick sprawl of the Schoenbaum Funeral Directors, it used to be a single small office, with gloomy conical evergreens out front. She wonders how much longer she can stay out of their clutches, with Mother's long-lived Koerner genes fighting Daddy's shorter-lived ones. On the west side of Weiser Square the new four-story shopping center with its glass-enclosed atrium for concerts and civic affairs still hasn't attracted the shops and eateries the planners promised. Along the east side the buildings are much as she remembers them from girlhood; though the façades have been changed over the years and a number have their plate glass boarded up or whited out from the inside, she can recognize the broad windows of what had been Schaechner's Furniture and the narrowing shape of the entrance to Arnold's Footgear, where her mother would take her for patent-leather party shoes and where at a machine you could see the bones of your feet move in a ghostly green light that it turns out gave you cancer. These buildings, two whole blocks of them, above the first floor have windows with decorative brick frames and arches and elaborate overhangs at the top, like castles of a kind. The biggest, Kroll's main rival as a downtown department store, still has its name enduring in painted script a story high on the side that shows: *Fineman's*, where the cool basement restaurant was such an attraction for weary shoppers and the teen clothing on the fourth floor was a lit-

tle more "New York" than in Kroll's, a little sharper and
more frisky—tight angora sweaters in ice-cream shades,
broad cinch belts in shiny fake leather, slinky nylon blouses,
wool skirts that came down almost to your socks and tugged
on your hips with their swaying weight, making you feel
more feminine. "New York" was a way of saying "Jewish"
but even Mother with all her prejudices admitted the cut
and fabric of the dresses at Fineman's was better, and she
could never resist the butterscotch sundaes in the basement
restaurant. As a child Janice was enchanted by the open-
scrollwork elevators and the vibrating wire tracks sending
money and receipts rattling around on the ceiling. All that,
all that fragrant luxury of appetizing goods, gone, just a fading name on an empty building, *Fineman's*.

Across Weiser Square a little up from Fineman's still stand
the four great pillars of Brewer Trust, now absorbed into
something called **MellPenn**, a great green sign lit from
within blocking out the old name carved in granite. She and
Harry were so lucky that time, the bottom fell out of gold
and silver a month or so later. Above the Square, between
Sixth and the railroad tracks, where the downtown movie
theatres had been, a row of palaces you could escape into,
mirrors in the long lobbies and paper icicles hanging from
the marquees, there is just nothing—an asphalt parking lot
on one side and a great dirt hole on the other, where some
developer of an inner-city mixed-residence housing complex,
shining towers on the billboarded architect's projection, has
run out of other people's money. There had been a pet store
here, and a music store run by Ollie Fosnacht, Chords 'n'
Records. Janice can scarcely believe so much is gone and she
is still here to remember it.

Daylight drains from this dry September day. The street
is half in shadow. Above Mt. Judge some high thin clouds
are fanned like a hand of cards. The car clock says five-

twenty. The homeward traffic north on Weiser and along Cityview Drive makes as much of a rush as you ever get, now that the stores and the middle class have deserted the downtown. Just the poor are left, white old ladies and young male Hispanics spending pennies at the Rexall's and the McCrory's, the last surviving five and ten. Nelson deals with these people, the less fortunate, at the adult treatment center, they call it Fresh Start, a few blocks west of where she is now, this side of the old coughdrop factory. Strange, how cheerful working with these hopeless people makes him. It's his family that depresses him. She hopes he gets home after she has had a chance to tell Ronnie about the girl. Nelson will get too involved.

The man on the car radio is excited about some multiple killing in Camden, a man shooting his estranged wife and the three small children, the oldest having made it as far as the back yard but gunned down there against the wire fence. How can he be so excited? It happens all the time now. Cornered by police a mile away, the man shot himself in the head. The suspect was white, the announcer feels obliged to say, since around here with violence you think of blacks first. For months there have been mass murders on television, the schoolchildren in Colorado and then the man beheading women in Yosemite Park and the man in Georgia who had lost a hundred thousand dollars at day trading on the Internet and blamed everybody but himself. He left a long pious note asking God to take his dear wife and little ones whereas the teen-age killers in Colorado mocked and killed the girl who said she believed in God. Either way, you killed them dead, sending them straight to Heaven or to nowhere, to an emptiness like that big orange hole in the middle of Brewer. It makes you wonder about belief, if just a little isn't enough, too much makes you a killer, handing out tickets to Heaven like that terrible man Jones in the South American jungle.

Janice has never not believed in a God of some sort but on the other hand never made a thing of it like Mother or in his weird way Harry. They felt something out there, reflecting back from their own good sense of themselves. Exalted. Eternal. The yellowing memorial plaques along the wall at St. John's, the stained-glass Jesus above the altar, His hands out in a gesture of embrace or despair. You need something. Harry could joke about religion himself but didn't like others to, it had been a grief between him and Nelson. Nelson had learned to scoff to get Harry's goat. And then he became a do-gooder laying his life down for others as they say. Another slap at his parents. The whole late summer was soured for Janice, even the two weeks in August at the Pocono place with Judy and Roy visiting their father from Ohio, by the Kennedy boy's having fallen from the sky with his poor wife and sister-in-law, they must have been screaming, screaming, hitting the water like a black wall. The news analysts said it took just seconds but what seconds they must have been, how can you keep believing in a God that would let that happen, it took you back to his father's being shot, so young and leader of the free world even if it was true he had prostitutes brought into the White House, it took her back to the baby's drowning, little Becky, such an innocent, well who isn't an innocent God might argue. All those Turks in the earthquake, tens of thousands sleeping in their beds at three in the morning. Even these men waiting on Death Row are mostly schizophrenics, Nelson claims, and all child abusers were themselves abused, so they're just passing it on, honoring their father and mother.

She is up past the park now, getting free of the city, rounding the mountain. The viaduct is off to her right, its arches and the houses scattered in the valley at its feet sharp in the low afternoon light, shingles and shrubs, and in the distance blue hills whose name she will never know. Halfway to Mt.

Judge, part of a mall that never really took off and now is a failing antique, the four-screen cineplex advertises BLUE EYES BLAIR WITCH SIXTH SENSE CROWN AFFAIR. She leaves 422 and turns off, at the brownstone Baptist church, into her town, going up Jackson Street and after three blocks right on Joseph.

She navigates without thinking under the Norway maples that she can remember half the size they are now, small enough a child could reach the lowest branches with a jump. She climbed into one once that had a hornet's nest, and couldn't climb down fast enough to avoid getting stung. Now the maples are grown so big the sidewalks in some sections of town are buckling. Joseph Street used to be sunnier, in her memory—more open above the telephone wires and streetlamps, which used to be yellow and not blue in tinge. The houses were full of staid older people instead of these young families that hang these meaningless banners from the porches, as if every day was a holiday. She slides the Le Baron to a stop along the curb, too worn-out and worried by her day to drive around to the garage in the alley and come up through the back yard. That awful couple who wouldn't even look at the row house on Locust Boulevard. So snobby, without any basis. If no woman was willing to climb steps pregnant the human race would have died out ages ago. She gets out and stretches muscles stiff from too much sitting. The big stucco house at 89 Joseph has not looked quite right to her eyes since the big copper beech came down. Harry used to say the place reminded him of an overblown ice-cream stand. And there was a bareness, without the tree. It seems an age since this morning and that girl—like a dream except it wasn't one. She lets herself in between the two frosted sidelights—a little clutter of delivered mail scrapes under the door—and inhales the living room's still air, the air of her life, apparently unchanged.

. . .

Poor Ronnie, he is so good. He still has some clients from the old days, people who wouldn't buy insurance or take investment advice from anybody else, who want to up their property coverage as values rise or to rejuggle their Keogh-plan nest egg to include a bigger slice of the stock market the way it has been going up and up, but basically since Schuylkill Mutual took Ronnie's cubicle and phone and company car from him he has little to do, and almost never complains. He has set up a tidy office for himself with computer and fax machine and filing cabinets in that little front room overlooking the street that Mother used to sew in and that then they had a single bed in for a time, when Nelson began to bring his girlfriends home from college in Ohio. After pecking and squinting and fumbling away for an hour or so's business in this crammed little room, and checking stock quotations and the weather on the Internet, Ronnie goes off in his blobby silver Taurus as if there is work for him out there somewhere, somebody to sell to. All summer he plays golf at the Flying Eagle three or four times a week even though he never had the passion for it Harry did—he is too realistic, and his knee hurts. He has stayed active in that low-class church he and Thelma belonged to. And, what Harry never had the patience or focus for, though he did have a little vegetable garden out back for a time, Ronnie makes projects for himself around the house, painting the exterior trim and puttying windowpanes that have been sun-baked and putting all new galvanized mesh on the sunporch screening. Despite his bad knee, from an injury in high-school football, he gets up at full extension on that aluminum double ladder Harry always hated to lift and cleans out the old galvanized gutters. He talks about tackling the chimneys, repointing the bricks, next. It is a cause for conflict. When she says she's afraid he will fall and kill himself he tells her the house is her main asset and has been sorely neglected until he came onto the scene. Her former husband was a cop-out as a householder, he says, and her son was and is no better. Didn't they know they should be protecting their investment in this place? Ronnie has a workshop in the cellar that sends the whine and rasp of power tools up through the floor and sometimes so much fine sawdust that it coats the cups and saucers in the kitchen cupboards. When he put up drywall partitions in that storage room off the kitchen, the plaster dust got into everything, into the dining-room cupboard with Mother's hand-painted Stiegel tumblers and genuine Chester whiteware. The dust even got into the refrigerator, making the food all taste like the calcium pills Janice takes to fend off osteoporosis. She is still getting used, after eight years, to a husband who is so unambiguously *here*, on the premises, and not always tugging to be out, running in his mind toward the horizon.

As she hopes, he comes home before Nelson, so they can develop a position, which Nelson is bound to oppose. "I won three bucks and only hit two duck hooks off the tee. On the seventeenth I sank a putt you wouldn't believe," he says, having come in through the back door to put his golf clubs and clothes in the tidy golf closet he made with all that plaster dust. The space smells, now, of him, of his sweat on the club handles, in the spikeless shoes, even the sour inside of the hats he wears. Each hat hangs on its own hook, and there is one where the glove hangs like a bat drying out, upside down. She likes Ronnie's neatness, but on the other hand feels scolded by it, the same as with her mother. He moves with a certain sluggish pained quality, limping back into the kitchen. "How was bridge?" he asks politely. Maybe there is usually in second marriages a little stiffness, a certain considerate wariness.

"I kept wondering why I was playing," Janice tells him. "I did something that irritated Doris terribly, I forget exactly what. She's getting old and crabby. Deet spoils her."

"What's for dinner? Did you remember to defrost anything?" Ronnie has learned what questions to ask. Thelma was a clever cook and a zealous housekeeper, along with all else she did, teaching school and raising three boys. Janice at first had tried to give Ronnie real meals, but something always dried out or was underdone, and her attempts at seasoning, though she thought she followed the recipe exactly, miscarried into a funny suspicious taste. With the yuppifying of greater Brewer, all these vague industries coming in that didn't make anything you could handle or drive or put in a box really—"the information industry," they said— there were more and more pleasant and not very expensive restaurants to eat out at; you didn't have to go downtown any more as Daddy and Mother used to for a little celebration, usually in one of the two big hotels downtown, the Conrad Weiser or the Thad Stevens. And otherwise the supermarkets sold wonderful frozen meals and sealed salads.

"Well, I forgot, if truth be known," Janice confesses. "I just got back five minutes ago. I've been doing so much else, and this morning, what a shock, Ronnie, this girl shows up at the door—"

Ronnie is not listening, he is opening the refrigerator door and peering in. "There's still some chicken salad from two nights ago, I don't suppose it's turned yet. And those Japanese noodles Nelson likes. Oh, yeah, and way back behind the wilted lettuce a container of three-bean salad we never got to—should it have that cloudy look? I guess we can make do. They say eating less is better for you." He moves to the counter to turn on the Sony. "Lemme just catch the news, for the weather. The radio wants rain tomorrow, I'll believe it when I see it. La Niña has screwed up the jet stream so it thinks we're the Sahara."

"Ronnie, *please* don't turn on TV. Pay attention, this is serious. This girl—'woman' I should say, Nelson's age more or less—rang the doorbell, which still needs fixing by the way, and said she was Harry's daughter. Her mother died this summer and told her before she died. Ruth sicced her on us."

Now she does have Ronnie's attention. He has lost thirty pounds since Janice first knew him, and he has that deflated, slumped look of people you remember as fatter. His hair, which was kinky and brass-colored, is almost all gone, even over his ears, so they stick out as rubbery red flesh. His pale eyelashes are almost invisible now, which makes his eyelids look pink and rubbed. Like Doris Kaufmann's, his face has become pruny, but the wrinkles aren't as deep as in her leathery skin. Ronnie, though Harry always spoke of him as a crude plug-ugly, in fact has thin babyish skin that makes physical contact with him a little silky surprise, which is something Harry couldn't have known. Now the man fastens on what to Janice had been the least interesting of the morning's revelations. "So Ruth Leonard is dead," he says.

Janice remembers that Ronnie knew this Ruth back in the period when Harry did, that he had fucked her in fact, which Harry always resented, which seemed strange to Janice since in this period a lot of people evidently had. Janice had never met Ruth but there had been this slutty kind of girl in high school, their names got written on lavatory walls, SUSIE PETROCELLI SUCKED MY BOYFRIEND'S COCK, and CAROLE STICHTER IS A MORON WHORE, from bad families on the lower side of town usually; no special looks, overweight and quiet in class, they had existed even under Eisenhower when everybody was supposed to be so pure. She cannot believe a forty-year-old fuck could mean much to Ronnie but from the stunned, slumped way he stands there in his sweated-up knit polo shirt and plaid golf pants it does. "On that farm of hers," he says. "The drought killed her." He is trying to joke away that trance men get into trying to remember what it was like entering a certain woman's space. Now that space is nowhere on earth and he will never get back into it.

"Wake up, honey. According to the girl she hadn't lived on the farm for years, she lived in Brewer with this daughter and worked for some shady investments outfit in that glass building across from where Kroll's used to be. Anyway, why do you care?"

"I don't, much. It was Rabbit that got stuck on her. To me she was just a hooer. What proof did this girl have that she was his kid?"

"None—just some confusing facts only she would know, about how her mother lied to her about when she and this man Byer were married so it would seem he was the father instead of somebody earlier. There's more of that went on than we think, back before abortions were easy."

"They're too easy, if you ask me. These black and Hispanic kids have one like an annual check-up. Nobody cares."

"Ronnie, that's not the *point*! We need to discuss this girl before Nelson comes home!"

Harry always thought Ronnie was terribly obtuse—called him an enforcer, a deliberate-foul artist—but Janice doesn't find him obtuse so much as on occasion having a quality of *being in the way*, of not letting anything just glide past if he doesn't absolutely agree with every detail. He has sat in too many living rooms refusing to leave until the man of the house sees the necessity of buying insurance, it's that blunt thereness he has. Harry was fascinated by Ronnie's big prick and it *is* big, flat along the top as if you could rest a wineglass on it at half-mast, but what struck Janice the first time was the relatively little difference between it erect and not. Whereas with Harry it was like night and day, between being curled asleep like a baby and being wide-eyed and six feet tall and up and at it.

"O.K.," Ronnie says in his plodding, relentless voice, "the point is Ruth did a lot of screwing back then—who's to say it was Hotshot that knocked her up? Did the girl look like him?"

She tries to be honest. "It's awful to say this, but I've forgotten exactly what Harry looked like. There was something about her, a kind of, I don't know, pale glow, and a way she couldn't quite sit still, that rang a bell, I thought."

"You thought. You'll have to do better than that before you owe her anything."

"She didn't say I did owe her anything. What she did say was her mother told her to come see us because she'd be alone in the world."

"We're all alone in the world, it turns out," he says. Janice doesn't know quite what he means but it hurts. Harry may have felt it but he would never have said that to her. She wonders sometimes if Ronnie married her just to score somehow on Harry. His lashless, pink-lidded eyes shift in embarrassment past her face, which she knows looks shocked, toward the clock on the microwave, worried about dinner or Nelson arriving home. He tells her, "There'll be money in it at the end, believe me, if you have anything more to do with this bimbo."

"She works as a nurse, and her mother must have left her something, there was all that money from selling the farm."

"I bet. How'd you leave it in the end?"

"We'd get in touch with her. She won't with us."

"Good. Don't. To me, it smells like a scam."

"But I was *here*. When you were a child, did your parents ever tell you the stranger at the door might be an angel in disguise?"

"No," he says. "They never said that. They said the person at the door probably wants to pull a fast one. Suppose you concede that old Fuckbunny *was* her dad, she may figure she can sue us for hundreds of thousands in back child support."

Janice takes a step forward to touch his shoulder and to offer herself to be touched. "Ronnie, honey, why are you so rude about Harry? He's dead. He can't bother us now."

"He bothers me. He screwed my wife. Twice he screwed my wife," he adds, meaning Thelma then and her now, as a softening joke, and she rests her body against his, its comforting blocky golf-sweaty hereness. His hands find their habitual places on her. She would never have believed in her teens what an innocent homely comfort it could be, after sixty, to have your bottom groped. He weighs her two buttocks as if they are precious. It occurs to her they should do more in bed, while they're still alive. But at their age there is so much to do, all these errands going nowhere, all these little commitments.

Footsteps sound on the back porch, the screened sunporch. Nelson must have parked his car, a '94 ivory-white Corolla he traded Janice's Camry in on—she had given it to him when she married Ronnie and wanted to rid herself of her last link with the Toyota franchise—out back in the garage, seeing his mother's Le Baron out front. Guiltily she and Ronnie break apart in the kitchen. Nelson sees that something has been up, his stepfather has been pawing his mother. To cover her embarrassment she tells him, Ronnie interrupting to correct where she tells it differently the second time, about the strange girl's—woman's—visit this morning.

Nelson's deep-socketed, distrustful eyes dart back and forth as he listens. Listening is part of what he does for a living, and he lets them talk while he fishes a Coors from the refrigerator. He is forty-two. He has put on weight, but nothing like Harry did; Nelson learned the lesson there. His thinning hair, dark but with his father's fineness—Harry's blond hair would just lift off his head when it dried from being combed—is cut so short his skull and face are naked in their angles, like a convict's. He wears a kind of social worker's uniform—khaki pants and a white shirt with necktie but no jacket. A jacket would overstate the distance between him and the clients at the Fresh Start Adult Day Treatment Center at Elm and Eighth Streets. The clean shirt and tie establish his authority, as one of those who guard the gates of Medicare and Medicaid, which compensate the day-treatment centers that have arisen to replace the Gothic institutions that used to house what were called the insane. His title is mental-health counsellor; his salary comes to twenty-seven thousand a year. His qualifications are a bachelor's degree (major: geography) awarded by Kent State in Ohio and a counsellor's certificate earned ten years later in a year's (1990–91) course of study at the Hubert F. Johnson Community College, in new buildings along the river in South Brewer, while living, he and his three dependents, at 89 Joseph Street courtesy of the new widow. Still here, he sits with his mother and stepfather at the round kitchen table with their makeshift meal and their beverages. Nelson has the Coors, Ronnie a Miller Lite in deference to his weight and blood pressure, and Janice a continuation in an orange-juice glass of the New York State sherry she nipped on returning home, to wash away the sour aftertaste of the bridge with its realization that Doris was a failing friend, a haughty old half-deaf crab. Like Ronnie said, we're alone. All we have is family, for what it's worth.

Nelson asks, "Mom, did *you* think she was conning you?" Ronnie in concluding the story had given his opinion that this was the case. Nelson generally avoids conflict with his stepfather, though when Janice first announced she might be marrying him he sounded just like Harry, putting Ronnie down.

"Well, I wasn't sure," she says. "She seemed sincere, but then it was kind of brazen, you could say."

"Con artists can be sincere," Ronnie says. "That's what makes them good con artists. They fool even themselves."

"What's worth conning about us?" Nelson asks with his professional mildness, making a question of everything. "We're just scraping by, in a house too big for us, that we ought to be selling. You're retired from the insurance con game and Mom and I work at shit jobs, for not much." His eyelashes, always long for a boy's, flutter in his deep sockets. His hair-cut makes him look like a Marine or monk.

Ronnie's thin-skinned face flushes. He says, "For a guy who snorted an entire car agency up his nose, you're one to talk about con games."

Janice intervenes, "As I told Ronnie, she seemed to have enough money. Her clothes were good quality."

"What kind of car did she drive?" Ronnie asks.

"You know, I was so rattled I forgot to look. No, wait." She tries to remember the morning—the maple shadows on the street, the mail truck passing. . . . "A Lexus," she announces. "A lipstick-red Lexus, brand new."

Nelson flicks a triumphant glare at Ronnie. "A step up from a Taurus," he says. To his mother he urges, "I think it's *great* that she had the guts to come around at all. Not that anything that happened back then was her fault exactly. Did she look like Dad?"

"Oh Nelson, I keep being asked that. It seemed to me so, in a way, but then I was looking for it. You know how these resemblances are, something you can't put your finger on. She had a round pale face and solid long legs."

Ronnie says, "That could fit anybody, for Chrissake."

"Her eyes—they were pale blue and had a little droop toward the outside corner, like Harry's."

Nelson's eyes, brown like hers, widen with interest. It pleases his mother to see him engaged. He must be like this at work. He comes home drained and irritable and untalkative. "I think we should have her here," he says.

Ronnie is firm. "That's a mistake. Give her an in, you'll never get rid of her. Why should we all get our lives disrupted because"—he gropes for a non-insulting name—"Nelson's dad screwed this dead cow back in the dark ages?"

"I thought you went with her, too," Janice says, herself quicker than usual, alert. "Was she such a cow then?"

"She was a big Brewer broad," he states, after blinking, "who would put out for anybody."

"Not those three months," Janice says. "As I remember, Harry moved in. It was a kind of honeymoon. Me pregnant with poor little Becky, and my husband was on his honeymoon." Putting it like that makes her furious, almost to tears. Ronnie is right, of course. The girl is an alien invader, to be repelled.

"I for*bid*," Ronnie says, putting down his fork and forgetting the amount of chicken salad in his mouth, "anybody getting in touch with this twat."

"Ronnie." Nelson almost never uses his stepfather's name, and says it now softly. "This twat may be my *sis*ter. Dad used to hint sometimes there might be a sister. Here she is, come to us, putting herself at our mercy."

"But what does she *want*, Nelson?" Janice asks. She feels better, clearer in her mind, finding herself now on her husband's side.

"She wants money," Ronnie insists.

"Why, she wants," Nelson says, getting wild-eyed and high-voiced, defensive and, to his mother, touching, "she wants what everybody wants. She wants *love*."

Ronnie turns to Janice conspiratorially. "He's as off the rails as his old man. Remember how Rabbit took that Black Panther and doped-up hippie in?"

"Love does seem a bit much," Janice allows.

"I'll go look her up myself, then," Nelson threatens. "A. Byer. You say she's the only one in the phone book."

"Nelson, believe me," Ronnie says, trying to act the father, "there's nothing in it for you but heartbreak. You've been a victim of Harry Angstrom since you were two, why look for more agony?"

"It wasn't *only* agony," Nelson argues. "There were positive elements in the relationship."

Janice chimes in, "Harry loved Nelson, it frustrated him that he could never express it properly."

"Oh come *on*, you bleeding hearts," says Ronnie, in an exasperated voice strong and angry enough to end the conversation. "I knew Rabbit longer than either of you. I knew him since we were kids in knickers snitching penny candy off the counter at Lennert's Variety Store. That conceited showboat never loved a soul outside his own thick skin. His mother had spoiled him rotten."

ii.

"Hello?"

"Yes?" Wary. Single women have to be, the world full of phone creeps.

"Is this Annabelle Byer?"

"Yes." Slightly reassured to be named.

"This is Nelson Angstrom."

"Oh! Nelson! How nice!"

A pause; he had thought from her enthusiasm she might go on a little more. He says, "My mother described your visit."

"Did she? I wasn't sure it went very well."

"Oh, yeah. She liked you. She just isn't sure what to make of the general situation. It took her by surprise."

"Me, too. I mean, I was surprised at first, when my mother told me. It shouldn't matter, my being a grown woman and all."

"Oh, but it *has* to matter." He feels more secure, as the conversation tips toward the therapeutic.

"How do *you* feel about it?" she asks.

"I feel good," he says. "Why not? The more the merrier, isn't that what they say? Listen. I was wondering if we could have lunch sometime. Just to look each other over." That was one sentence too many, but then he might as well get the curiosity issue on the table.

She hesitates. Why would she hesitate, when it was she who had come out of the woodwork? "I think I'd like that."

"Tomorrow? Next day? What's your schedule?" he says. "I work at Eighth and Elm, there's a little restaurant opened up in the block on Elm toward Weiser, it's called The Greenery, but don't be put off, it's decent enough, soups and sandwiches and salads, kind of neo–New Age, but they have booths for a little privacy."

"Sounds cute," she says. That slightly puts him off. This may be an airhead, sister or not. After all, what does she have for genes? Nothing that promising. She asks, "Would you mind not until next Thursday? Until then I'm on day duty, it's an Alzheimer's patient who needs round-the-clock."

"Great," he says. "Thursday the sixteenth. Twelve-thirty O.K.? I'll be waiting outside. Medium height, short haircut these days."

"I'm," she began to say, then giggled, not knowing how to describe herself. "I'll be in fat white shoes."

. . .

Wouldn't you know, they have picked the one day in September when a hurricane called Floyd is supposed to hit. All sorts of wind damage and heavy flooding in North Carolina, and then predicted to come right up the Chesapeake into southeastern Pennsylvania. But these forecasters are paid to whip everybody up, and though the wind kept him awake last night, rattling the window sashes Ronnie had painted last summer and swishing sheets of rain across the asphalt-shingle roof that supposedly ought to be replaced if they want to keep their equity in the house, the morning isn't so bad that cars aren't moving on Joseph Street, slowing down to go around a medium-size maple branch that broke and crashed last night in his sleep. He didn't hear the noise; he slept better than he thought. The branch lies in the center of the asphalt like a big piece of road kill, its leaves' pale undersides up and already wilting.

Nelson thinks of phoning Annabelle to cancel but he doesn't want Mom and Ronnie to know he has this planned. Instead he phones his boss, Esther Bloom, who lives in Brewer, and she tells him the Center will be open at least until noon. "These people have nowhere else to go, Nelson. A weather event like this brings up survival issues they may need to process."

On the way into town he sees two highway crews, with flashing lights and cops in orange slickers directing traffic, cleaning up fallen trees with chain saws—an old willow that had sunk its roots in the roadside ditch by the failing mall with the four-screen cineplex and, on the other side of the viaduct, where 422 enters Brewer and becomes Cityview Drive, a gorgeous big tulip poplar at the edge of the park. The park has always struck Nelson as sinister, slightly. Tough minority kids hang out among the trees, and there is a dim association with the time his father had left home and lived not far from here in the city, on Summer Street. The

World War II tank near the tennis courts has been recently taken away, and a pretty little white-and-green bandstand built, as part of downtown renewal, though it serves mostly to collect graffiti and to shelter thugs from the weather and has never held a concert that Nelson can remember. The car radio is full of this gunman, one more straight-shooting psychotic, who killed seven and then himself in some Texas Baptist church, and terrorist blasts in Moscow killing dozens, and an interesting item which he doesn't quite catch about cocaine addiction linked to a build-up of certain proteins in the brain—it hadn't been his fault, it was brain chemistry—and then another medical item, which interests him less, about how hot tubs may help diabetics. The Phillies beat Houston eight to six in ten innings, but they still aren't going anywhere, not in the middle of September. As he drives across the park's most open stretch, wind shakes his car so hard that he tightens both hands on the steering wheel.

In Brewer around Eighth and Elm the buildings cut down on the wind somewhat. It's an older area, where commercial meets residential. A former hat factory stands empty but for one little photocopy-and-offset-printing establishment named *PRINTSMART* in a lower corner. The treatment center occupies the basement floor of what used to be a three-story elementary school, grades K through six. The parking lot consists of a strip of diagonal places at the side of the building where the neighborhood residents stick their rusty heaps at night, right across two spaces, neglecting to wake up in time to take them away. The neighborhood is shabby but not dangerous, like most of the clients.

As Nelson gets out of his Corolla he sees a sky darkly bruised in patches above the brick cornices, the clouds layered and shredding as they slide swiftly sideways, but the rain appears to be stopping and the air brightens as if to clear. People on the sidewalks, especially the young women who work in the glass courthouse annex a block away, hugging themselves in short sleeves and not even carrying umbrellas, don't appear to know they're almost in a hurricane. Across Eighth Street a cheap big orange façade saying DISCOUNT OFFICE SUPPLIES has been attached above the doorway to an old stationery store that Nelson remembers still smelling of gum erasers and ink eradicator before everything was bubble-wrapped and packaged for bulk sales; the sign makes a shivery noise as a spatter of bright raindrops sweeps by. Farther down Eighth an old-timey, routed, gold-lettered 𝔗𝔞𝔳𝔢𝔯𝔫 sign swings back and forth. Maybe he should have suggested that as the place to eat—a little racier and more cavelike, with a liquor license—but he obscurely wanted to keep his meeting with his sister sober and pure: a solemn occasion.

The radio said Governor Ridge was considering declaring an emergency and sending all state and local workers home, but inside the Center the staff has shown up, all but Andrea the art therapist, who lives beyond Pottstown, almost on the Main Line. She commutes up to Brewer because funds for art therapists are drying up nationwide and the job she had in Philly was eliminated. To snotty, pouty, twice-divorced Andrea, a henna-tinged brunette with big rings she makes herself on nearly every finger, Brewer is a hick town with too many religious cranks and dumb Dutchmen.

As the morning wears on, the rain with renewed vigor whips at the basement windows so hard that water begins to dribble across the wooden sills. Years ago, before Nelson was hired, the floor was gutted and partitioned into suitable spaces—tiny offices for the staff, larger group rooms for the clients, a reception space, a kitchen where the clients make their lunch and a dining area, with six round tables, adjacent to the sofas and upholstered chairs of the milieu. In the milieu the clients not doing a group or having a consultation can read, knit, play games, and hopefully interact. When this was a kindergarten the five-year-olds learned to tie their shoelaces and fit pegs into holes but social interaction, socialization, sitting in a circle and learning to share, was the main lesson; for these dysfunctional adults it still is. There are thirty of them, theoretically present from nine to four, and a staff of eight, headed by Esther, a doctor of psychology. Nelson has resisted suggestions that he go after an advanced license or degree; he doesn't want a private practice or, after the mess he made running the Toyota agency, any administrative responsibility. He learned his limits.

Some clients straggle in, drenched and exhilarated about a hardship they are sharing with all the residents of Brewer, and others have chosen to stay at home with their delusions, anxieties, and television sets. Because of low attendance Nelson's three-times-a-week group on Relationships is absorbed into Katie Shirk's group on Goals and Priorities. Nelson uses his downtime to catch up on paperwork—progress notes, intake forms—and goes around mopping up windowsills with paper towels. Left wet, the paint peels. The rain has intensified again.

The DiLorenzos show up, though, all three of them, hurricane or not, at eleven sharp. They are desperate. Their world has come crashing down because of a few misfiring neurons. In the waiting area they give off a stagnant damp odor of bafflement—graying patriarch, swag-bellied but still powerful in the arms and shoulders; mother, a touch of peasant drab still in her plain dark suit though money talks in her shoes and the silk scarf at her throat; and son, twenty, slim and good-looking, with an almost feminine delicacy, bright-eyed, wavy-haired, but going soft and pasty with inactivity, and the fear of his own strangeness giving his dark eyes an anxious bulge. His eyes fascinate Nelson with their helpless beauty—dark but not black, paler than his thick brows, an ale color, or like the dark jelly bees feed to their queen, freckled with light, life in them like a squirt of poison. He decides to take the boy first, and asks the parents to wait.

"Well, Michael. How are you feeling?" he asks when the door is closed and he is settled at his desk. His desk is of minimum size and with a fake-wood-grain top. The young man folds himself into the one-piece molded-plastic chair, orange in color, opposite. He wants to slouch to show how lightly he takes all this but the chair in its flimsy, scientifically determined form does not permit much of a slouch.

"O.K. Good. The same."

"Voices quiet?"

Michael licks his lips as if abruptly aware of a dryness. "Yes."

He is lying, Nelson knows, but he keeps his eyes down on the young man's folder, opened six months ago. "Taking your Trilafon consistently?"

"Absolutely, sir." This is another lie, Nelson can tell from a certain retraction in the young voice, a telltale flattening, but Michael wants to believe it, he wants to be cured, of an illness that seems to be nothing less than himself, a rot of his most intimate ego, that voice within, where it was nestled supposedly safe in his skull.

"Any side effects from the Trilafon you want to take up with Dr. Wu?" Howard Wu is the Center's M.D., here three half-days a week. Golden in color, stocky in form, he is much beloved, for his hearty Chinese pragmatism and large convex teeth. He is their jolly Buddha.

The boy readjusts his position, perching on the chair's edge and jerking forward. "I feel plugged up. At both ends. It's like a cold in my nose all the time. I feel sleepy all day,

and then I can't sleep at night. I feel shitty," he says, and titters, as if to disown his feeling. A fission, a scatter, in his
young face makes him hard for Nelson to look at.

"Do you want me to write down, 'No voices'? If I do that,
Dr. Wu will see no reason to adjust the medication."

Nelson's deliberate gaze elicits from Michael a flutter of
avoidance, a batting of lashes under the shapely black brows,
which have that touch of a built-in frown Italian men have, a
thickening toward the bridge of the nose. He must have cut a
tidy swath at Brewer High, not to mention summers cruising
among his peers in the convertible his parents had bought
him, proud they could afford it. He peaked too early, like Dad
in a way. There is still a little bravado, mannerly but dangerous, in the boy's smile, and in the slick way his bouncy black
hair was tamed by the comb. The grooming is a positive
sign. Or did his mother comb his hair for him today, for this
appointment, and see to it that he shaved? "There *were* some
voices," he admits, huskily, then smirks as if to dare the world
to make much of it.

"What did they say, do you remember?"

No answer.

"What did the voices say?"

"Nasty stuff."

Nelson waits.

"They tell me what a miserable fuck-up I am. They tell
me to kill myself. Or maybe I think of that myself, to shut
them up. It might be worth it."

"Michael," Nelson said, loud and urgent enough to make
the boy, whose eyes sidle and flutter, look at him. "If you
ever, for a moment, think you might follow through on
these impulses, you must do what?"

A long pause. "I don't know."

"You must get in touch with the Center. At any hour."

"Yeah, well, shit, I'm not apt to be calling any center at four in the morning."

"The recording gives the number for Emergency Services. Call it. Here's the number in case." He writes it out on a Fresh Start memo pad and rips the sheet off. A renewed surge of rain slashes against the window at Nelson's back. He pictures the leaks venturing, trembling, lengthening, out onto the windowsills of this old school, the paint flaky from previous soakings. "Do the voices say anything else?" Nelson can hardly hear the answer against the noise of the rain.

"They tell me to kill my parents."

This is delivered with a mumbled huskiness and yet with some defiance, a twitch of teen-age swagger and a smirk that hangs on his face forgotten. "How does that make you feel?" Nelson asks.

Michael surprises him with a surge of affect: "*Hor*rible. I *love* my parents. They've been great to me, giving me everything I've ever wanted and not putting any pressure on about entering the, you know, fucking dry-cleaning business." His voice is hurrying, to keep up with his brain. "They sent me to college when a lot of parents would have had me go straight into the business. My dad's getting older and hasn't been strong for a while. They sent me to Penn, the finest university in the state. So what did I do? Hey, I fucked it up."

"You didn't, Michael, you got sick. We're trying to make you better. You're better now. You dress yourself, you're no longer violent—"

"I can be violent at home." He begins to brag, to someone imaginary sitting where Nelson sits. "My mother, what a naggy bitch, honest to God. She says to stop watching the old movies on TV, get up, get out, do this, do that. I don't see the use."

"The use is what we call normal psychosocial functioning. It doesn't come without effort. Let's look at your graph. You have not been in to the Center for a week, and then only twice the week before. That's why I've asked your parents to come in with you. They, and Dr. Birkits, and all of us want your attendance to improve." Birkits was the Brewer psychiatrist the DiLorenzos had taken him to on the advice of the Penn psych service after his break. Birkits, one of these demoralized post-talking-cure shrinks, referred this hot potato to Fresh Start. They don't get many clients with an intact home, and who can afford a private psychiatrist.

"I bet you all do," Michael sneers.

"We do, Michael. We want to improve your functioning, and we offer here at Fresh Start a safe environment for you to practice in, with the groups, the activities, the counselling. But you must attend."

"Hey. Sir. O.K. Can I be frank?"

"Of course."

"I can't stand these people. They're fat. They're queer. They're ugly. They're not my type."

"What is your type?" Nelson asks, and instantly regrets the hostility he hears in the question, which popped out reflexively.

"Loser," Michael responds, and laughs, a barking abrupt noise that doesn't belong to his frightened face. "Loser is my type."

"Not so. You or anyone here. We're human, which isn't always easy. The other clients are kind people, here to help each other. They care about you, if you let them."

"They wouldn't if they knew what's inside my head." He jerks forward in the straight chair. His complexion looks a little clammy, moist at the hairline. The poisoned eyes swarm with shame and yet with an excitement that something transformingly strange is happening to him. "The voices whisper to me about girls I see on the street. This one and that one. They tell me to picture her shitting."

"Shitting?" Nelson has been betrayed into confessing surprise. Perhaps Michael intended this. He wonders how much of an enemy the boy sees him as. Does he sense, within his mental-health counsellor, some ethnic enmity, with envy of his easy slender build and dago good looks? When Nelson tries to picture what a schizophrenic sees he remembers Howie Wu telling him, *Their sense of distance has broken down.* Things up close look far away, is how Nelson has framed this—there is no clear depth in which to locate yourself. The gears that notch us one into another fail to mesh, maddeningly, meltingly. Trying to think his way into Michael's head plants a sliding knife inside Nelson, a flat cold queasy sensation below his ribs.

"They show me her squatting down. I want to rub her face in it. I want her to eat it. Does that shock you?"

"No," Nelson lies.

"Well, it does me." Michael slumps back as far as the chair allows him. His affect is flattening; his eyes narrow as he recalls, "Thirty thousand bucks a year, think of it, plus extras and my own car. Pussy everywhere. Hot-shit professors. A bunch of frats rushing me. And I fucked up. I couldn't hack it. I didn't even know what courses I was supposed to be taking. I hid in my room with the shades down until my roommate complained to the dean and they got the psych service on me. They tell me I told the dean or somebody he was the Whore of Babylon. I never heard of her." He snickers a little, testing the face opposite his.

"Michael," Nelson says in firm conclusion. The boy was bragging now, bullying. *When you feel uncomfortable*, Howie has told him, *trust your gut. Get off the horse.* "I can't emphasize enough how important it is that you are faithful with your medications. I've made a note here to Dr. Wu to reconsider the Trilafon dosage."

"I drank beer and tequila at Penn," Michael tells him,

uncertainly standing, sensing he is dismissed and being relieved yet not, unsatisfied, uncured. "My parents didn't know it, but I would get fucking blasted. I think that's what screwed up my brain."

"I don't think so. The human brain can take a lot of beer. Michael, this is not your *fault*," Nelson says, coming around his desk so that in the tiny office the boy—tall when he stands up, his girlish mouth sagging, his face glimmering in the rainy light, begging to be understood—has nowhere to go but out, to the waiting room, where his parents are eager to come in.

"Such a gorgeous child," says Mr. DiLorenzo, when a second chair has been pulled up for his wife in front of Nelson's desk. "Bright, good. A miracle boy. To have this boy after his three sisters and Maria over forty, it seemed to us a miracle." He speaks carefully, with dignity, as one who remembers when he spoke English less well, the child of immigrants who spoke it hardly at all. His hair, brushed straight back, is going white but his bushy eyebrows are still black.

The wife speaks up: "Even as a little boy, though, he stood apart a little. He would play with others, but then wander away and come inside. I'd say, 'What's wrong?' He'd say, 'Nothing.' As if he didn't see the point of people. He was quiet. He never had a tantrum."

"My wife imagines things in hindsight," Mr. DiLorenzo says, sitting back erect, his eyes enlarged by thick spectacles, eyes frayed to death from closely inspecting fabric. "He was a perfectly normal boy. Got top marks, too, all the way up through senior year. Gave the salutatorian speech about how we should help Russia keep democracy and capitalism. Never any trouble to anybody—teachers, me, nobody."

"A little trouble would have been more normal," his wife says. "At the time I wondered if having all those older sisters hadn't taken something out of him. My daughters and me, we had too good a time, always laughing, always busy at the house, always telling each other things. Michael was like a little prince, detached."

"Don't listen to her, Mr.—"

"Angstrom. Nelson if you'd rather."

"Don't listen to her, Nelson. He was fine. He played sports, got the good marks, ran for student council. Said no to drugs, booze. An altar boy, too, until he was fifteen, and we didn't push that. In America religion becomes your own business. Likewise I told him, 'Michael, listen, you want to forget the dry-cleaning business, be some kind of professional—a doctor, lawyer, whatever, sit behind a desk using your smarts— that's O.K. with me, and Mamma too. Whatever makes you happy. This is America.' But no, he wanted to learn dry-cleaning, summers, after school, it was what he loved. From me there was absolutely no pressure."

"There *was* pressure," Mrs. DiLorenzo tells Nelson. "Joe needed him to carry on and he knew it. That he didn't come out and say it made it worse. The girls, they married and got out of here. They'd had enough of it, the chemicals, the presses, the hours until seven, eight. Only one of them even stayed in the state, and she's way out near Pittsburgh, a nice suburb up along the Allegheny. Their husbands, what do they care about dry-cleaning? It was all on Michael, and he knew it. He snapped. Men don't want their whole lives mapped out for them. They want adventure. Isn't that right, Mr. Nelson?"

"She's crazy," Mr. DiLorenzo confides. "He didn't want adventure. He wasn't like these young hoodlums these days, their heads full of, what do they call it, hip-hop, grabbing guns and going off to shoot their classmates to make the evening news. Shooting their parents, no respect for anything under the sun. He wanted to carry on the family business. There was no pressure. At Penn he was taking chemistry

to be on top of the best, the newest solvents, the most envi-
ronmentally sensitive as we say now. Disposal of used cleaners is the number-one headache in this business; a single
cancer lawsuit can wipe you out—defending against it, even
if you win. I love America, but not its justice system."

"Joe, there was pressure." To Nelson Mrs. DiLorenzo
explains, "My husband, he slaved to build up Perfect. He
began by doing dirty work for this old Jew in South Brewer,
just a basement in a row of houses, a little dark slot, his
equipment crowded into the back, a shed built illegally, fifty
cents an hour if he got that, Joe was always being chiseled.
When the Jew died Joe borrowed to buy the business from
the widow and named it Perfect Cleaners himself."

"It's prettier in Italian, *perfetto*," Mr. DiLorenzo said,
drawing out the word, "but this is America. Things want to
be perfect here. Don't mind Maria—Jake was good to me,
he taught me the trade. Had me out on the vats first, breathing in petroleum solvents before the switch to perchloro-
ethylene, then had me as a finisher, on the steam presses, and
then a spotter, that takes skill—you can ruin a silk blouse, a
fine wool suit. After a while it was going so good I opened a
branch in West Brewer, and then one up in Hamburg, and
two years ago this industrial acreage came up for sale in
Hemmigtown. For a long time I'd been wanting to build
a bigger plant, with summer fur storage and equipment to
take anything, to take even old lace tablecloths, they get yellow with age, very fragile, and big velvet curtains where you
could choke on their dust, some of these mansions in Penn
Park and up along Youngquist, the owners *never*—"

Nelson has heard enough about dry-cleaning. "And you
were counting on Michael to take all this over someday."

"Someday, not now. Maybe ten years, maybe less. We
have a little place in Florida, the winters here aren't so good
for Maria—"

"Don't blame me if you want to go to Florida and stick the poor boy with all these plants, all these employees and their benefits—"

DiLorenzo takes this up enthusiastically, telling Nelson, "It's socialism without being called that. It's putting everybody smaller than Perfect out of business—the benefits, the insurance. There used to be a cleaner every other block. I shouldn't complain, it's good for the bigger outfits that can absorb it, but still you hate to see it. Setting out the way I did back then, with no assets to speak of, I couldn't do it now."

"He *slaves*," his wife says, "and he wants to lay it all on Michael. He wants to go to Florida and look at the girls on the beach and make himself dark as a black."

"The boy was eager, I mean it, with no pressure from me."

"Joe, the boy *felt* pressure. Even his senior year, he was drifting away, into his own world. He was bringing home B's."

Nelson intervenes, to stop their love feast. They love each other, and the child of their hearts is Perfect. "Michael is very angry with himself," he tells them, "for what he calls letting his family down. But, I keep trying to tell him, it's not his fault. It's not *your* fault either. It's no one's fault."

"What is it then?" Mr. DiLorenzo asks simply, of this invisible invader, his son's destroyer.

Good question. "It's a," Nelson says, "it's a disorder of the nervous system, having to do with dopamine flow, with the chemical control of the synapses' firing."

"I often wondered about that," Michael's mother breaks in. "When he was so young, thirteen, fourteen, working with his father summers, inhaling all those poisons."

"Get sensible, Maria," her husband says, hoarse from his talking. "Look at me, inhaling all my life."

"It's not that kind of chemistry," Nelson says. "I'm no doctor, I don't really understand it, brain chemistry is very complex, very subtle. That's why we don't like to assign a diagnosis of schizophrenia without six months of following the client and observing his symptoms continuously. What we do know about the disease—the disorder—is that it quite commonly comes on in young men in their late teens and early twenties, who have been apparently healthy and functional up to then. Michael does fit this profile. A breakdown early in college is pretty typical." He looks down at the yellow pencil still in his hand. On the upper edge of his vision, the faces of the parents before him, it seems to Nelson in a little hallucination of his own, rise like balloons whose strings have been released, but without getting any higher.

"What can we do?" Mrs. asks, her voice fainter than he has heard it before.

"Is there no hope?" Mr. asks, heavier, the chair under him creaking with the accession of weight, hopelessness's weight.

"Of course there is," Nelson says firmly, as if reading from a card held in front of him. "These neuroleptic medications *do* work, and they're coming out with new ones all the time. Michael's hallucinations have diminished, and his behavior has regularized. Now—where you can help—he must learn to take advantage of our resources here, and to assume responsibility for his own medications, the prescribed daily dosages."

"He says they make him feel not like himself," his mother says. "He doesn't like who he is with the medicines."

"That's a frequent complaint," Nelson admits. "But, without nagging, without seeming to apply pressure, remind him of what he was like without them. Does he want to go back to that?"

"Mr. Angstrom, I know you don't like to make predictions," the father says, manly, ready to strike a deal, "but will these medications ever get his head so right he can go back to work—keep a schedule, pass his courses?"

Another good question. Too good. "Cases vary widely," Nelson says. "With strong family and environmental support, clients with quite severe psychotic episodes can return to nearly normal functioning."

"How near is nearly?" the father asks.

"Near enough," Nelson says carefully, "to resume independent living arrangements and perform work under supervision." To have a room in a group home and bag groceries at a supermarket that has an aggressive hire-the-handicapped policy. Maybe. "Keep in mind, though, that many tasks and daily operations that are obvious and easy for you and me are very difficult for Michael at this point. He not only hears things, he sees and smells and even touches things that get between him and reality. Yet it's not oblivious psychosis — he knows his thoughts aren't right, and knowing this torments him."

The two wearily try to take this in. Their appointment is winding down. They hear the rain lash at the loose-fitting elementary-school windows in a tantrum, in a world unhinged.

"It's a heartbreaker," says Mr. DiLorenzo. "All those years since the boy was born, I thought I was building it up for him. Building up Perfect."

"Don't look at it so selfishly," his wife says, not uncompanionably. "Think of Michael. Suddenly, where did his life go? Down the drain into craziness."

"No, no," Nelson urges, almost losing his therapeutic poise. "He's still the child you raised, the child you love. He's still Michael. He's just fallen ill, and needs you more than most young men need their parents."

"Need," Mrs. DiLorenzo says, the one word left hanging in air. She pushes herself up, holding on so her black-beaded purse doesn't slip from her lap.

"What we need," her husband amplifies, rising with her,

sighing through his nose, "is peace. And a vacation. And it doesn't look as though we're going to get any. Ever." Like jellyfish changing shimmering shape in the water, their faces have gone from fear for their son to fear of him, of the toll he will take.

Nelson doesn't argue. The interview has shaken him but he thinks it was healthy that some of these facts were faced. Schizophrenics don't get wholly better. That movie starring the Australian as a pianist who keeps playing because some dear good loving woman has taken him on: a sentimental crock, mostly. They don't relate. They don't follow up. They can't hold it together. It makes you marvel that most people hold it together as well as they do: what a massive feat of neuron coördination just getting through the dullest day involves. These dysfunctionals make him aware of how functional he is. They don't bother him as normal people do. There are boundaries. There are forms to fill out, reports to write and file, a healing order. Each set of woes can be left behind in a folder in a drawer at the end of the day. Whereas in the outside world there is no end of obligation, no protection from the needs and grief of others. Disorganization takes its toll: a flopped marriage and two fatherless children in Ohio, Judy at nineteen defiant and estranged and Roy at fourteen trying to keep in touch via e-mail and Pru up to who knows what, the bitch has shut him out, him still living with Mom and Ronnie like some agoraphobic mental cripple himself. Here at the treatment center, he has his rôle to play. The clients respect him. They sense in this short, neat forty-two-year-old in his striped tie and clean white shirt a pain that has been subdued, sins that have been surmounted, absorbed, brought into line. When he has a free moment, as he does today after the DiLorenzos leave, he joins the clients in the milieu—he partakes of their society.

This central gathering space, with its sagging upholstery

and skinny-legged card tables and rickety floor lamps that yet give off light, smells of coffee and cough drops and unfresh bodies and of the meal—baked beans and ham, with Dutch-fried potatoes, from the odors—being cooked in the kitchen a room away. At one of the card tables Shirley, a fifty-year-old morbidly obese depressive, is playing dominoes with Glenn, a suicidal, substance-abusing homosexual of about thirty-five. Glenn is flagrant. He wears fake diamond studs in his earlobes and another above his nostril wing; he blues his eyelids with a vivid grease and rouges beneath his eyes like a geisha girl. His pigtail always looks freshly braided. Nelson doubts that anyone who takes such pains with his appearance would be truly suicidal; Glenn just knows that the surest way to get official attention, with benefits, is to claim suicidal impulses. This pseudo-Christian society will knock itself out to keep you going, whatever the taxpayer cost. Esther Bloom disagrees. Gays are gay but they are also men, she says. Women flirt; they make emotional noise. When men get serious about suicide, they *do* it, not just futz around with inadequate doses of barbiturates or showy but shallow slashes on the wrist. The most successful group of suicidals, statistics show, are men who have suffered business reversals. Next best are men who feel dead already.

But Glenn is alive now, and in a good mood. He and Shirley—whose massive body, bales of dough-colored flesh, emits from its unwashed creases an odor that seems terrible until it surrounds you completely—clack down the white-dotted black tiles with a vigor that punctures the milieu as if with gunshots. A few other clients have gathered to watch. Nelson stands there puzzling at the patterns being made. If he ever played dominoes, he's forgotten it. At the Mt. Judge playground, the pavilion sheltered checkers and Chinese checkers, and he and Billy Fosnacht used to play marbles in a circle in the dirt, in that year or two before Billy's estranged parents got him a minibike and the boyhood phase of innocently modest consumption ended. Nelson feels forlorn, watching Shirley and Glenn cackle and stymie each other, extending and halting the speckled snake that winds its angular way across the metal card table. "Back to the boneyard, sap!" Shirley cries, her mirth sending sympathetic eddies through the onlookers, an idle ring transfixed within the orbit of her familiar BO.

"I'll boneyard you, you little sweetheart!" Glenn says. "Take that!" He slaps a double five crossways at one end of the domino snake.

"What does that mean?" Nelson asks. "Putting the double sideways?"

Glenn squints up askance, one blued lid half lowered, his nostril-stud catching on one facet the fluorescent light overhead. "Didn't you ever play dominoes, Nels?" he asks. For all his gay makeup, he has a rough voice, a Brewer street voice, deeper than you expect, and pugnacious. His tone suggests that Nelson is having a boundary problem.

Maybe so. The other clients are listening, alert as children with nothing else to do. But he has been trained to be frank, direct, and fearless, within the therapeutic persona. "Well, if I did, I've forgotten. The objective is what?"

"To kill time," Glenn says.

"You poor baby," says Shirley to Nelson. "Were you an only child?"

Nelson hesitates. Watch those boundaries. "I had a sister. She died as a baby."

This shocks them, as he knew it would. They have their own problems, that's what they're all here for, not to hear his. Shirley offers, "We'll teach you, dearie, when this game is over." Her vast face holds a trace, a delicate imprint like a fern in shale, of the face she had as a young woman. There is

a small straight nose and a pointy chin—a triangular bit of
bone in the fat.

"Morons can play it," Glenn says in rough encouragement.

One of the likable things about dysfunctionals is that they
don't hold grudges. They don't stand on any imagined dignity, they are focused on the minute or two of life in front
of them. As he sits there for twenty minutes taking domino
lessons from a mountain of a woman in a stained muu-muu,
and being coached by a rouged pervert with three glass studs
in his face—a fourth, brass, sits on the upper edge of
Glenn's plucked eyebrow—Nelson feels his inner snarls
loosening, including the knot of apprehension about his
lunch date, crazily enough, with a girl out of nowhere who
claims to be his sister.

Outside the Center, the rain still comes down but is thin-
ner; it is swirled and rarefied by the wind into a kind of white
sunshine. There is no point in putting up an umbrella, it
would be popped inside out. Instead, he runs, slowing whenever he feels his shirt getting sweaty inside his raincoat, staying close to the brick buildings, and the façades redone in
Permastone, on the south side of Elm Street. Plastic store
signs bang and shudder overhead, tin mailboxes swing by
one screw beside the front doors of four-story town houses
turned into apartments, empty aluminum Mountain Dew
cans rattle along in the gutter, leaves swish overhead as gusts
plow them like keels through upside-down waves. The elms
lining this street died long ago; the Bradford pears the city
replaced them with have grown big enough to need cutting
back from the electric wires. There are fewer people out on
the sidewalk than usual but those that are are oddly blithe.
A black couple in yellow slickers stands in a doorway smooch-
ing. A skinny Latina clicks along in high square heels and
blue jeans and a pink short-sleeved jersey, chatting into a
cell phone. Is this a hurricane or not? The weather is being

snubbed. People are in rebellion at having it hyped on TV so relentlessly, to bring up ratings.

He runs past one of those few surviving front-parlor barbershops, where two old guys are waiting their turn while a third sits under the sheet to his neck, all three thin on top, and the barber makes four. Dad didn't want to wait around and become an old guy. He didn't have the patience. The wind traces oval loops through sheets of rain. The clouds above the roofs and chimneys trail tails like ink in water. The odds are less than fifty-fifty, he figures, that his date will show up on such a wild day. He hopes she doesn't; it will get him off the hook.

But there she is, waiting outside The Greenery (*Salads, Soups, and Sandwiches*) under a sky-blue umbrella, wearing not fat white shoes as she promised but penny loafers with little clear plastic booties snapped over them, like bubble-wrapped toys. "Hi. I'm Nelson," he says, more gruffly than he intended, perhaps because he is panting from running. "You shouldn't have waited outside, you'll get soaked," he goes on in his nervousness, starting their acquaintance on an accusatory note.

She doesn't seem to mind. Her mild eyes, their blue deepened by the blue of the umbrella, take him in as she defends herself: "But it's so exciting out. Feel the electricity in the air? I heard on the radio driving here the eye is over Wilmington."

"I bet it's soon downgraded to just a tropical storm. North Carolina is where it really hit. Pennsylvania never gets the real disasters."

"Well, that's good, isn't it?" Annabelle asks.

Their heads are at the same level. He is short for a man and she is slightly above average for a woman. He wonders if a passerby would spot them as siblings. "Come on, let's go in," he says, still breathless.

There are six or so other customers, and the last of three booths is free. The interior has that cloakroom scent from long ago of wet clothes and childish secrets. The tidy, self-reliant way Annabelle takes off her white raincoat and red scarf and hangs them up on the peg-hooks by the unmarked door to the restrooms touches Nelson; she is an old maid already. But the bright-eyed flounce with which she sits down and slides her way to the center of the table in the booth suggests that she is still hopeful, still a player in whatever the game is.

The waitress, too middle-aged for her short green uniform, comes over from behind the counter and hands them menus prettily printed with leafy borders but already smudged and tattered by many hands. "Also," she tells them, "we've added hamburgers and hot dogs."

Nelson says, "I thought those were against your principles."

She is lumpy and sallow but not above being amused. "They were, but people kept asking for them. We still won't do pizzas and French fries."

"Way out," Nelson says. Laconic responses have become, these eight years, his professional habit, but this occasion will demand more: he will have to give, to lead. To be a provider.

"I love healthy food," says Annabelle Byer.

"Do you know already?" the waitress asks. "Or would you like a few minutes?" Nelson has been coming here once or twice a week since the place opened last spring, but she is showing him new deference now that he has appeared with a companion. Annabelle is a little round-faced and bland compared with the narrow-hipped Latina in high heels and jeans, but she is not an embarrassment as a date; she could be a colleague at the Center, like Katie Shirk.

"I know," he tells the waitress. "A cup of that broccoli soup you make—"

"It's not a cream soup," the waitress interrupts. "It's a clear soup, some of the customers call it watery."

"I want it," Nelson insists, "and then the spinach salad, with raspberry vinaigrette, and don't go easy on the bacon bits."

"That's just what I want," Annabelle says, more gleefully than Nelson thinks she needs to.

The waitress is writing. "You said *do* go easy on the bacon bits, or don't?"

"*Don't*," Nelson and Annabelle answer in unison. Nelson adds, "And, to drink, in view of the horrible weather, a cup of hot tea. Not herbal, caffeine. Lipton's if you have it."

"Me, too," his sister says. He is beginning to see the downside of having one.

"Don't you have any ideas of your own?" he asks her.

"Almost nothing but. If you'd have let me order first, as you should have, you'd be seeming to copy *me*."

"I'd have thought of something different. Their lo-cal Caesar with strips of range-fed chicken can be terrific."

"I love healthy food."

"You said that."

"Well, I'm nervous. This is *strange*, meeting your brother at last, and it was your idea."

"Yeah, and showing up giving my mother the scare of her life was your idea. Sorry about your mother, by the way."

"Thank you. She didn't seem scared, yours. Almost feisty, you could say. She thought I was after her money."

"Well, what else? Not that she has that much." He feels, what he had not expected, at ease enough with this person to be combative, as if they had rehearsed their competition years ago. "You and I met, by the way," he says. "Twenty or so years ago, at a party in an apartment along Locust Boulevard. The hosts were a couple called Jason and Pam and a fag they lived with called Slim." He wouldn't say "fag" at work—he has worked with a number of gays, on both sides of the client-caregiver divide, and has no problem with it, once he outgrew the fantasy that they were going to grab his crotch—but being with this girl brings out an older, less p.c. self. "I was with my wife. She was very pregnant, and got drunk and fell down the stairs." The memory still shames him: he had given Pru the bump that sent her off-balance, and the image of her skidding down the metal-edged stairs, with the legs of the orange tights she had on splayed wide like a sexual invitation on the edge of disaster, has stayed with him as a turning point in his life. *I must do better than this*, he had thought at the time.

"I don't remember any of that," Annabelle says with her annoying, faintly defiant blandness.

"I remember *you*," he accuses, "and thinking how nice you were. I admired your ear. You were going with a boy called Jamie and worked at some old people's place out around the old the fairgrounds."

"Sunnyside," she says. "My ear?" she asks. Self-consciously she touches her right ear, exposed by the fluffy short-cut hair there. Her hair, a touch damp from waiting in the rain, is brown, with auburn highlights that seem natural and a fair amount of gray sprinkled in. Time is pressing on her though her face pretends not to feel it.

"It hadn't been pierced." He doesn't say it reminded him of his own. He had also liked the way she bulged toward him in certain places, her plump upper lip and the fronts of her thighs when she stood. Some would say she is heavy now but in this county the men are accustomed to that. How had she avoided getting married?

"My mother wouldn't let me," Annabelle was saying. "I guess it was superstitious of her, she said she liked me natural, the way I had been born. Boy, I wonder what she would say with some of the girls now. Even the young nurses, the body piercing, navel, nipple, you name it. I ask them, how can it be sanitary, and they say their boyfriends like it. One more thing to play with, I guess." She blushes and lowers her eyes.

The soup comes, the flowery thin soup The Greenery cooks up with broccoli florets and frothy bean sprouts and slices of water chestnut so thin as to be transparent. Nelson and Annabelle bow their faces into the heat of the soups and realize that their time together is being consumed. "I'm sorry," she says, "I don't remember that party better. Maybe I was stoned."

"No, no, it was me who was stoned. Stoned or wired, that's what I usually was back then. After my father died I got religion, more or less, and earned the certificate to be a mental-health counsellor. Don't you think it's strange, by the way, how both you and I are caregivers?"

"Not if we're related," she says. "I believe in genetics. And health care is an expanding field, as the world fills up with people that would have been dead a hundred years ago. Everybody winds up needing care, pretty much."

"Yeah, you wonder if it's worth all the effort. I mean, you're keeping these Alzheimer's wrecks going when they don't even know enough to thank you, and I knock myself out to keep a bunch of depressive loonies from killing themselves, when if they did it it would save the government a fair amount of money."

She looks at him, her mouth prim until she swallows the spoonful of soup, and says, "*Nel*son. You don't mean that. In the abstract, you can feel that way, but not when you're face to face with the patient. I go on these teams Hospice sends around. Even at the very end, there's something in there, a soul or whatever, you have to love."

"Especially when you're being paid to love it," he says, wondering if one of the water-chestnut slices has gone bad.

A specialty place like this, you don't get the turnover to keep the produce fresh; they give it one more day than they should. The other customers here when they entered are one by one leaving, though a small cluster hangs this side of the door, waiting for a sudden sideways squall of rain to let up. The ceiling lights glow as if evening is coming on, though it's not yet one o'clock.

"Tell me about him," Annabelle demands.

"Who?" Though he knows.

"Our father."

Nelson shrugs. "What's to say? He was narcissistically impaired, would be my diagnosis. Intuitive, but not very empathic. He never grew up. It occurred to me just now, passing a bunch of old guys in a barbershop coming over here, that he died when he did because he wanted to. Those of us around him were begging him not to die but he wouldn't listen." Nelson has rephrased Pru's sleeping with his father just out of the hospital as a way of begging him not to die. Not a bad reframe, he thinks.

"Why didn't you want him to die, if he was so awful?"

"Did I say he was awful? He was careless and self-centered, but he had his points. People liked being around him. He was upbeat. Since he never grew up himself, he could be good with children, even with me when I was little. The smaller they were, the better he related. He was a better grandfather than a father, since he could clown around and have no direct responsibility and not give you a sinking feeling. Me he kept giving a sinking feeling. I mean, he *did* things, too. He ran away from Mom to shack up with your mother. He got involved with a megalomaniacal black guy and a masochistic runaway white girl and got our house burned down. He had a crush on this nitwit young wife of a friend of my parents when they were in a country-club phase. Then he had a long secret affair with his oldest friend's wife. I say friend, but in fact he and Ronnie always hated each other. I mean, this is not a constructive personality we're talking about."

"Yet you didn't want him to die."

"What do you want me to say? Hell, he was the only father I had. What am I supposed to do, wish him dead?"

Annabelle smiles. Her soup bowl is empty. "Some would say that would be normal."

"That Oedipal crap, you mean? Freud is fun to read, but in the workplace he doesn't hack it. Nobody in the business uses Freud any more." But he is more stunned by her saying that than he shows. *Would be normal.* He had wanted his father to live, to continue to take care of him, to be a shelter however shaky. There is a louder scream of wind outside, old tropical storm Floyd. The ceiling lights flicker and then go out.

At the same moment, the waitress brings their salads. "Oops," she says. "Can you two lovebirds see to eat, or shall I hunt up some candles?"

"We can see enough," Nelson says. In the gloomy light, flickering as the wind outside lashes the trees, Nelson leans forward and softly explains to his sister, "He was tall, about eight inches taller than me, and had an athlete's nice easy way of carrying himself. It pained him that I wasn't more like him. He had been a wonderful basketball player in high school, back when it was still a white game."

"That doesn't exactly make a life, does it though?" Annabelle asks, lifting the first forkful of salad to her face. She has a slightly eager way of eating, keeping her mouth closed in a satisfied smile as she chews, her upper lip shiny with salad oil.

"That's what everybody kept telling him all his life," says

Nelson. "But I don't know. At least it was *some*thing, to remember about yourself. I have nothing like that to remember about myself."

"What about your family?" she asks, before taking the next bite, being careful to keep the bacon bits balanced on the piece of spinach.

"They left me. My wife, Pru, who you saw pregnant that time at the party that you've forgotten all about, left me over a year ago and took the kids. Back to Ohio, where she's from. Akron. I met her when I was a student at Kent State." He doesn't say she was a secretary, and older than he; he is embarrassed about that. "My girl, Judy, is nineteen, twenty next January, and off everybody's hands except a bunch of boyfriends', and the boy, Roy, and I keep in touch by e-mail. He's fourteen and knows more about computers than I ever will."

"Why did she leave? Pru."

"I don't know. I guess I disappointed her. She thinks I'm a pipsqueak."

She waits to finish chewing and says urgently, "Nelson, you're *not*. You're a caring, intelligent man."

"Yeah, well. You can be that and a pipsqueak too. I can be frustrating. Pru always wanted us to get a house of our own and I could never see the point, my mother sitting on all those rooms over in Mt. Judge. I didn't want to leave her alone. My mother."

"But now she's married."

"Yeah. But then I didn't want to leave her alone with my pretty awful stepfather. Hey—do I sound normal, or do I sound sick? When I'm over with my sickos I don't have to listen to myself. I just let *them* talk. Boy, do some of them babble! Everybody thinks their little story is the story of the universe."

The waitress comes back from the kitchen and puts an

unlit candle in a pottery holder on the booth table and lights it. "You didn't have to do that," Nelson tells her. "We're about to go."

"Why go?" The waitress saunters to the door and looks out its half-window at the whipped, glistening city. "Pitch black in the east," she says. "Over behind the courthouse." A cardboard sign tucked into the molding says on this side in Day-Glo letters CLOSED. She takes this sign and reverses it so that CLOSED faces the street. The couple in the booth hear the lock click. "The stove and grill are out," the waitress explains.

Nearer, Nelson hears this other female voice, as soft, as transparent as the voice inside his head, say, "Tell me more about your father, as you saw him." The girl is trying so hard to be sweet. Maybe she is sweet. But Nelson dislikes talking about his father. It pulls something too obscure and precious out of him. When he tries to think back to what it was like growing up he keeps getting a picture of his father and him in the front seat of a car, both of them having nothing to say but the silence comfortable, the shared forward motion satisfying. Nelson is being driven somewhere. To the piano lessons that gave him butterflies because he never practiced enough during the week, as Mr. Schiffner with his lavender shirts and tiny Hitler mustache always detected. To soccer practice when he was in that weekend league of middle teens and had hopes of being a star, small but agile. To Billy Fosnacht's or some other friend's, there weren't that many, for a sleepover. Meanwhile his father's big head was happy with his daydreams and his hands were light and pale on the steering wheel, with big translucent moons on the nails, usually one hand while the other absent-mindedly patted and stroked the back of his head in a gesture that maybe went back to the days when teen-agers had wet ducktails, like Sal Mineo or James Dean in the old rebel movies Nelson could watch on

TV. His father had been a rebel of a sort, and a daredevil, but as he got older and tame he radiated happiness at just the simplest American things, driving along in an automobile, the radio giving off music, the heater giving off heat, delivering his son somewhere in this urban area that he knew block by block, intersection by intersection. At night, in the underlit ghostliness of the front seat, their two shadows were linked it seemed forever by blood. To Nelson as a child his own death seemed possible in so perilous a world but he didn't believe his father would ever die.

"I saw him, eventually," Nelson says, "as a loser, who never found his niche and floated along on Mom's money, which was money *her* father made. Mom-mom—my grandmother on my mother's side, the Springers—would always say how I resembled Fred, her husband. He was on the shortish side like me, and sharp at business stuff, and bouncy. But being a loser wasn't the way my father saw himself. He saw himself as a winner, and until I was twelve or so I saw him the same way."

"I loved my father, too," says Annabelle, "the man I thought was my father. He could fix anything—you know how around a farm everything is always breaking down, he never let on he was flummoxed, just would sigh and settle down to it. He had this wonderful confident, calm touch—with my mother, too, when she'd let her temper fly. Whenever the excitable of my patients get to acting up, I try to think of him and act like he'd act."

Nelson's inner ear tells him there is something wrong with this. He is being sold something. But it may be that his ear is jaded, hearing all day about families, dealing with all the variations of dependency and resentment, love and its opposite, all the sickly inturned can't-get-away-from-itness of close relations. If society is the prison, families are the cells, with no time off for good behavior. Good behavior in fact tends to lengthen the sentence.

"He sounds great," he grunts. "Every time my father tried to fix anything around the house, it got broken worse." He hears these words and wonders if they are fair. He remembers his father digging in a garden he had made in the back yard, even building a little wire fence to defend the vegetables against rabbits. He remembers his father on one of their car trips somewhere pleading with him not to get married, not to get himself trapped in marriage, even though Pru was pregnant and the wedding day set: he shocked his son by suggesting an abortion and offering to pay her off. *I just don't like seeing you* caught. *You're too much* me.

I'm not you! I'm not caught!

Nellie, you're caught. They've got you and you didn't even squeak.

He had fought his father off, accused him of being jealous, denied the resemblance the old man was pushing. *You don't necessarily have to lead my life, I guess is what I want to say.* Well, he hadn't, exactly, and marrying Pru hadn't worked out, exactly, but what pains Nelson now is seeing that his father had been trying as far as his narcissism allowed to step out of his selfish head and help his son, trying to shelter him from one of those disasters that most decisions entail. He had tried to be a better father than Nelson could give him credit for, even now. He says with an effort, "But he wasn't all bad. We used to have great games of catch in the back yard. And he'd take me to Blasts games out at the stadium. Once we even drove down to Philly for a Flyers game, somebody had given him tickets."

"I met him, you know. At the car lot. He seemed nice. Of course I had no idea he was my father, but he acted fatherly. And funny."

"What did he say funny?"

"Nelson, how can you expect me to remember?" And then it comes to her. The bright June day, the Toyota agency tucked over on Route 111 across the river, the drive with Jamie at the wheel, and the heavy tall middle-aged salesman with his pale fine hair in the front. He sat in the death seat, Annabelle in the back. She says, "It was the time of the gas shortage. He said all the hardware stores in Brewer were selling out of siphons and soon we'd all be standing in line for everything, even Hershey bars, I forget how that came up. It was like he didn't really care if we bought a car or not."

"He didn't. The only job he ever gave a damn about was operating a Linotype machine like his own father. Then Linotypes got obsolete."

"That's sad," his daughter says.

The waitress is standing there in her green apron. "Could I interest either of you in any dessert?"

Nelson said, "I thought you closed up."

"Yes well, I did, but the cook's still out back, he thinks the power may be coming back on. For dessert we have tofu, honied oatcakes, puffed goat cheese baked in little ramekins, and lo-cal frozen yogurt. That's lo-cal, not local. And lately we've put in some home-baked pies, since people kept asking. They *are* local. Let me see—shoo-fly, lemon meringue, and apple crumb. We may have a piece of the rhubarb still left. We can't warm them, though, as long as the power's out."

She is the mother, it comes to Nelson, that he and Annabelle have in common. The waitress is pure Brewer, her face squarish and asymmetrical, like a bun pleasantly warped in the oven. Good-humored suffering—sore feet, errant sons, daily complaints—radiates through her uniform. And yet, though this woman feels old to him, she is possibly not much older than they are—somewhere in her forties.

"The apple crumb sounds good," he says, not wanting this

lunch to end. For what happens next? It's not like a first date, where a second or third leads to fucking.

"I shouldn't," his sister declares, "but let me try the honey oatcake."

The waitress says, lowering her voice confidentially, "It tends to be a little dry. My advice would be to have it with a scoop of the frozen vanilla yogurt. On the house. If the power stays off, it'll all be melting anyway."

"You're wicked," Annabelle tells her. Her plump face beams, her eyes shine like a birthday child's as she assents. She still has, after living twenty years in the city, a country-girl innocence that, if she is taken as his date, embarrasses Nelson. In his embarrassment he studies the wall above the booths, whose theme is greenery—ferns and bushes and overhanging branches, brushed on in many forest shades. What he has never noticed before, all those noons grabbing a bite at the counter, is that a pair of children are in the mural, in the middle distance with their backs turned, a boy and a girl wearing old-fashioned German outfits, pigtails and lederhosen, holding hands, lost.

"So," he says. "I don't think I've told you much about my—our—father. Mom has a lot of photos and clippings back at the house—would you like to look them over some-time?" He wants to give her her father, his father, but when he holds out his hands the dust pours through them, too fine and dry and dead to hold. Time has turned the spectacular man to powder, in just ten years.

"I don't think your mother wants me in the house again," says Annabelle.

"Of course she does," he says, knowing she doesn't, and adding, "It's my house, too," when it isn't, yet.

"I thought one of you said green tea," the waitress says, putting down two cold desserts and two steaming cups. "The water was still hot, and they all claim it's good for you. The Japanese live longer than anybody. They had on the news the other night these two female twins, over a hundred years old each, that are like rock stars to them."

"Green is great," Nelson says, to chase this motherly woman away. When the siblings have their privacy back, he says to his sister, "This is great, meeting you. I just wish my father could have known you. He hated not having a daughter."

"That's unusual, a bit. Weren't all men his age male chauvinists?"

"He wasn't crazy about males, me included. I think he saw other men as competition. For the women. He was very scared of his homoerotic side. He suppressed it. His only male friend, really—do you want to hear this?"

"Oh, yes."

"—was a car salesman who was screwing my mother for a while. That made it all right somehow, to have a little male intimacy. Charlie, that was the guy's name, he died too, a couple years ago. Another lousy ticker, though unlike Dad he went the full route—triple bypass, pig valves, pacemaker, God knows what all. It worked for a while, but not forever, as you would know, being a nurse. My mother kept in touch with him, even married to Ron. That generation, once they"—he rejects the obvious verb—"once they went to bed together, they didn't get over it." This has taken him a long way sideways. It's true, what the psych instructors at Johnson Community said, if you let somebody talk enough, everything comes out, underside first. "So Dad and Charlie are up there in Heaven," he ironically concludes, "seeing us get together."

"When will we get together again, I wonder," Annabelle says, unironically. She has this frontal mode, part of her innocence. How innocent can you be, at the age of thirty-nine, in the year 1999?

"Soon," he promises. He wonders what he has taken on. "I want to work something out. You should meet more people than just me."

"Oh?"

"Sure," Nelson says in confident, big-brother style. In the same style he signals to the waitress, who has been standing behind the counter, looking out at the storm through the window beside the tall aluminum urns of cooling coffee and hot water.

"I keep waiting for branches to fall," she tells them, "but they don't, quite."

"Pennsylvania can't afford a good hurricane," he kids her. "We should all move to the Carolinas." He hungers for a hurricane, he realizes—for an upheaval tearing everything loose.

The twilight gloom in the place does seem to be lifting. Nelson cups his hand behind the flame and blows out the candle. The waitress brings their bill handwritten on the back of a menu card torn in half: $11.48. "I hope you have the right change, because with the power out I can't get into the cash register to make any."

Nelson looks into his wallet and has one one and the rest twenties. The MellPenn ATMs only dish out twenties, encouraging consumers to spend faster. New bills, too. He hates how big Jackson's face has gotten, and the way it's off-center. His expression is more wimpy. They've turned this old Indian-killer into a Sensitive New Age Guy. It looks like play money.

Annabelle sees Nelson hesitate and asks, "Do you want some money from me?"

"Absolutely not."

The waitress may have been motherly, but he's damned if he's going to leave her an $8.52 tip. Nor does he want to take Annabelle's money: it would give the whole encounter a pipsqueak flavor. He is trapped, pinched, squeezed between impossible alternatives: dysfunctional. He could put it on a credit card but that, too, takes electricity. "You could owe me to next time," his sister mildly says. He ignores her and stares into his wallet at the edges of gray-green money as if a miracle will sprout.

And it does: the lights come on. The machinery of the place begins to hum all around them. "I'll have to open up again," the waitress complains. She taps off a dot-matrix slip and he takes a five and two ones out of the change. "*Thank you, sir. You two have a nice rest of the day, now.*"

Brewer is still a place where a tip of more than ten percent wins some gratitude. "Good lunch," Nelson tells her. "Good and healthy. Lots of crumbs on the pie, like my grandmother used to bake."

"Come again," she says, but automatically, moving on sore feet to wipe their booth table and reset it with paper placemats.

Outside, the wind is bright again, whirling the droplets off the Bradford pear trees. Annabelle's booties glisten; she ties the red scarf beneath her chin, making her face look graver and slimmer. A spattering hits it, and she winces, then smiles. She doesn't know what to expect next. He wants to hand her the world but doesn't know quite how. "That was fun," he tells her. "We'll be in touch." And he kisses her on the cheek, tasting the rain, imagining her skin as half his, thinking, *My sister. Mine.*

"She's Dad's, all right," he tells his mother. "That same weird innocence, that way of riding along."

"She wasn't just riding along the day she came here," Janice says. "She was determined, that little scruffy hairdo and showing off her legs right up to the crotch."

"How would you like to have her here again? Invited this time, with some other people."

"What other people? What am I supposed to say—this is my dead husband's bastard daughter from forty years ago? It was humiliating enough at the time, that whole nightmare, Nelson. I don't see why I should put myself through it again. I can't believe you're asking me—aren't social workers supposed to be so sensitive?"

"Not to their own families, necessarily. Mom, she's *family*. We can't just ignore her, now that we know she exists. Just a family dinner, maybe with Ronnie's boys."

Of the three sons Ronnie and Thelma had, two are presently unmarried. Georgie, the middle one, lives in New York, though his dreams of being a chorus-line dancer are faded. Alex, the oldest and nerdiest and most successful, lives in Fairfax, Virginia, he and his wife having divorced. Alex is no Bill Gates but he has done well and is about Annabelle's age. Ron Junior, the youngest, dropped out of Lehigh after two years and is settled in as carpenter for a local construction company. He married a local girl; they have three kids under ten. Nelson doesn't see that much of his stepbrothers except when Georgie, escaping from the stresses of the Big Apple, has to crash in the big front bedroom that until Pru pulled out had been Judy's room. But they generally gather for Thanksgiving, a meal that Thelma always put on in grand style and that Ronnie insists Janice continue with, though she will never be the cook Thelma was. The first Mrs. Harrison had been a schoolteacher and brought to her housewifely duties a sense of order and measure and respect for the holidays, and also a flair, a flourish of excess. It must have been this excessive part of her that latched on to Harry, loving him to her own disgrace. Janice dreads the turkey—how big to buy it, how long to cook it, at what temperature—and never gets it right. Either the breast is so dry that the slices crumble under Ronnie's carving knife, or the joints are bloody and the children at the table make noises of disgust. Family occasions have always given Janice some pain, assembling like a grim jury these people to whom we owe something, first our parents and elders and then our children and their children. One of the things she and Harry secretly had in common, beneath all their troubles, was dislike of all that, these expected ceremonies. Mother had been a great churchgoer and Daddy tagged along but Janice always felt uncomfortable, on the edge of crying when the organ blasted in, especially after Becky died and God had done nothing that terrible time to help. She and Harry were happiest, really, when they were in Florida, just the two of them in Valhalla Village, golf for him and tennis for her and separate sets of friends and most meals taken at the perfectly adequate and pleasant restaurant there, Mead Hall with its modernistic Viking decor.

Janice's brow wrinkles. "I don't quite see it, Nelson, as being anything but forced and awkward. Just because this dead slut wished this girl on us—"

"Mom, she's my *sister*. Listen. If she can't be a guest in this household, maybe the time has come for me to move out. Pru always said I should anyway, for my self-respect."

"She did? Pru said that?" Janice had imagined that she and her daughter-in-law had shared the house pretty well, all those years after Harry died and they agreed to sell the Penn Park house Harry had loved. She had been off most of the day doing real estate, and Teresa had had to be home with the children and naturally had cooked the meals and did housework and some light outdoor work. It was only right, instead of paying rent. After Ronnie came into the household, it was never so easy. There were currents. Ronnie had his own ideas about how things should be done, in the kitchen and everywhere else. The way Thelma had always taken care of him, he was particular. Thelma spoiled men: it was a kind of malice, and lasted after her.

Poor Nelson. He has this bee in his bonnet—doing something for this girl nobody knows. It clutches at Janice's heart, to think that he always wanted more of a family than they could give him—a bigger, happier one. He had loved her parents because from them descended this sense he craved of a clan operating in the world, this big stucco house a fort of sorts. The boy had wanted her and Harry's happiness so. When they quarrelled even without much meaning it his little face would go white with worry like a bubble trying not to burst. And all this healing he still wants for everybody, it makes her heart gripe to think of how they must have hurt him.

"I don't know, Nelson." Janice yields. "Maybe at Thanksgiving. She'd get lost in the crowd."

"Mom, that's forever away."

"Close enough for us to get used to the idea. I'll have to approach Ronnie. I know he'll be dead set against it."

But when, that night or the next, in their bedroom, she describes to her husband Nelson's silly sad desire, and puts forth her Thanksgiving suggestion expecting it to be knocked aside, Ronnie says, his voice dragged into a more youthful, thuggish register, "Well, I guess it wouldn't kill us. I'd be interested to see how Ruth Leonard's daughter turned out."

He pronounces her name, which Janice always has trouble remembering, so easily; it brings home to her that Ronnie and this slut had been lovers, some weekend down at the Jersey Shore, back before Harry got to know her himself, which had always galled him, though Janice could never see that he had the right to mind. But Harry had been like that: he thought he had a lot of rights, just by being his wonderful self.

iii.

From:　　　Roy Angstrom [royson@buckeyemedia.com]
Sent:　　　Friday, October 22, 1999 8:04 PM
To:　　　　nelsang.harrison@qwikbrew.com
Subject:　　Happy birthday jokes

Dad have a great party with whoever!!! Heres an oldie but
new to me and it struck me as pretty droll. President
Clinton was visiting Oklahoma City after the may 3rd
tornado and a man whose house was demolished put up a
sign: HEY BILL HOWS THIS FOR A BLOW JOB? The
Secret Service made the man take it away. I guess this is a
true story what do you think?

Nelson, sitting in the little upstairs front room staring
at the computer screen, shifts in his swivel chair, pained. If
this is the only way his son can communicate, it's better
than nothing, but he wonders how much the kid knows
about blow jobs. Though after this Lewinsky business even
kindergarten kids know about it, it's right at the top of the
news hour. Pru used to do it to him at first, especially before
they got married, but as the marriage went on did it less and
less, even when both were high on something or when he
went down on her, her fuzzy little redhead's pussy, skimpy
compared to, say, curly-haired Melanie's. One such time he
got into position for her to reciprocate and she confessed
outright that she hated the smell. *What smell?* he had said,
feeling himself beginning to wilt. *I wash.*

You can't help it, she had said. *It's a smell that won't wash off.
It's kind of acidy. Anyway, I'm afraid you'll come in my mouth.*

Why, honey? Why are you afraid? That's so nice, once in a while.

For you it is.

You used to like it.

*I don't remember that. I just said it because I knew you wanted
me to.*

You lied to me?

People can get AIDS, you know, that way.

*Well my God. If I have AIDS you'll get it anyway. How could I
have AIDS? I haven't been with anybody but you for ages.*

So you say. What about those coke whores, before you got clean?

*Coke whores, there are no coke whores. There are just women
who aren't as uptight as others, is all.* It was true, back before he
was clean, when he was a regular at the Laid-Back, the girls
who hung around there looking for drugs and action liked to
give blow jobs because it was a quick way to bring a guy off
and less fuss and muss for them. They didn't even have to
take off their pantyhose in the car. Their mouths did smell
afterwards and when he was stoned he liked to kiss them
even though they resisted and said he was sick, basically
queer. Those girls for all their being whorish had very little
imagination, very narrow parameters. *If I was going to get
AIDS it would have showed up by now.*

*Not necessarily. I read where the virus can be dormant for fifteen
years. It hides around the base of the spine.*

Well my God. And this is supposed to be a marriage.

You can fuck me though.

Now there's a rational woman for you. What about AIDS?

Nelson, I said you can fuck me. Take it or leave it.

I'll leave it. I've lost interest.

So you have. What a baby.

And it *was* lovely to have a woman's head down there, all
that hair under your hands, the tips of her ears and back of
her neck, you can't see her face but her shoulders tense up
when you come, and some have said it excited them too, but
according to Pru they were lying because they wanted something else. Women lie the way blacks lie. If you're a slave
race telling the truth gets you very little. They forget how.

He sees that all the time at the Center. Only for the powers that be does knowing things pay off. Only they can afford to know the truth. He doesn't like Roy knowing what a blow job is. The boy is fourteen, masturbation should be enough. The tightness of it, the newness, the feeling of leaning up against a tall white closed door, the sensation Nelson used to get of standing on his head for a second, the tiny muscles going into spasm: the sensation moves you into another world, up and out, chilly like ice cream, private like thought, a metallic taste in the mouth afterwards, the taste of having been somewhere different. But he wants the images in the boy's head to be innocent, bridal, the girl who sits next to him in an Ohio classroom lying under him all lace and crushed flowers in his mind as he comes in his bed's safety. Not this juvenile filth off the Internet. Who would have thought the Internet, that's supposed to knit the world into a shining tyranny-proof ball, would be so grubbily adolescent?

And Dad heres another one. A guys wife on there honeymoon begs off making love and she goes to sleep and gets up at 3am to get a glass of water and sees hes still awake and asks why. He says his dick is so hard their isnt enough skin left to close his eyes with.

This is more like it, Nelson supposes. Straight married sex, at least. Judy has gone off the deep end with boys, he doesn't know when she lost her virginity, it must have been in Pennsylvania, when they all still lived in this house, Judy in the front bedroom, there were some pretty late dates, he remembers, coming in that sticky front door, whose pop woke him up, footsteps slithering up the stairs, when she was just sixteen, seventeen, and still had her freckles. Pru would know. Pru wouldn't talk about it with him. *Well why not?* she asked back one time. *Your Aunt Mim's a tart, all you Angstroms are like rabbits.*

And she herself, with Dad, in this very room he sat in now, his face lit by a computer screen. He could never quite wrap his mind around it. Which was healthy. There is such a thing as healthy denial. Children use it to keep the image of the caregiver benign despite abuse. Pru when he got after her about it would say she didn't understand it either. *It just happened, Nelson. Things just happen. Not everything happens for some deep reason, like you were taught at social work school.*

Oh, is that what I was taught?

Yes, and to keep asking questions, instead of trying to give answers.

I should have answers? What's your question?

Why do you keep bugging me about what happened once between me and your father, when we were both half out of our minds, me with your druggy stunts and him with his poor beat-up heart? He's dead, Nelson, your father is dead, he and I won't do anything again even if we wanted to. Which we don't. Didn't.

Nelson looks out across Joseph Street at the neighbor's second-story windows, hoping to see the woman of the house undressed. There are three windows, the middle one holding a plastic pumpkin with a light bulb in it, the two flanking it dim-lit, the one on the right probably a hall landing but the others giving on the bedroom, which he guesses is a child's bedroom. That semi-detached house for years was occupied by an elderly couple who lived toward the back of it, in the kitchen and TV den, but this young couple with their two little children have different living arrangements and once in a while you see the wife moving around in her bathrobe or underwear, black bikini pants and two beige cups as snug as skin, the kind of bra advertised in the Brewer *Standard* illustrated by models, names like Secret Shaper, Seamless Charmer, Lace 'n Smooth, Nearly Nude. Pru used to wear bikini underpants but as her bottom broadened she went in for old-lady white cotton panties with enough fabric

for a truck-driver's T-shirt. *You can fuck me, though.* He needs
a woman. Doing a job and coming back to his mother and
stepfather and TV comedies made for twentysomethings in
New York City isn't a life. He sleeps badly: not enough skin
left to close his eyes. But at his age as of today forty-three he
would feel silly in single bars or the party circuit, if he could
find it. The action that used to exist at the Laid-Back up at
Ninth and Weiser was ages ago — other lifestyles, other
drugs in fashion. Cold War worries, Japan worries. With the
century ending all this is sinking into the history books. And
he's afraid getting back into circulation might get him back
into coke, or Ecstasy if that's the thing, or the ever-cheaper
heroin; it's so easy to slip back when you don't feel you
have much to lose. Talking to the substance abusers at Fresh
Start, he can't much argue when they argue for it. Happiness
is feeling happy. Maybe it shortens your life but when you're
dead what's the diff? Living to the next hit, the next scrounged
blow-out, gives their lives a point. Being clean exposes you
to life's having no point.

> Things are pretty cool here Dad. 10th grade is organised not
> much differnt than the 9th except that you are a sophmore
> and get more respect then lowley freshmen. There are a lot
> of American African students at North High but you can get
> along if you mind your own busness and don't make slurs
> and the courses are pretty easy. First quarter I got four As
> and a B in biology but the biology teacher Mr. Pedersen says
> he knows I can do even better.

> Judy is driving mom crazy out most nights and some
> mornings her bed not even slept in but she is thinking of
> signing up for training to become a flight attendent for
> USAirways, there hub is in Pittsburg. Mom is working
> longer hours for this lawyer Mr Gekoppolos (spelling close)
> downtown on Buchtel Ave but says to tell you we still need
> your check and its late.

Thats pretty much it for now Dad I want to play one game of TOMB RAIDERS and then study hard for a biology quizz. TTFN (ta ta for now) luv u :-) ROY.

Nelson's eyes sting, reading this in the tiny print the Windows 98 gives you. Even the print and tiny icons are made for very young eyes. The boy is smart, if the grown-ups over him don't fuck up his head. And Judy, maybe she knows what she's doing. She has evidently no fear of flying, though doesn't like the idea of his daughter in the sky all the time. Dad used to be nervous about flying too.

From:	Dad [nelsang.harrison@qwikbrew.com]
Sent:	Sunday, October 24, 1999 9:31 PM
To:	royson@buckeyemedia.com
Subject:	paternal affection

Roy—Great grades, congratulations. Keep it up. Great jokes, though don't they ever have any clean ones? Sex can be funny but it's also damn serious, about the most serious thing we do. It's good Judy is meeting lots of people but tell your sister not to cheapen herself. Other people tend to take us at the valuation we put on ourselves and a woman is always more vulnerable to a bad opinion. I'm glad she is thinking of a vocation even if it's not the one I would have chosen for her. Our family has been pretty earthbound up to now. Tell your mother I will get the check off but Ronnie thinks I should be contributing more to the household expenses since he is retired and on his pension plan and Social Security, meanwhile the cost of everything including real estate taxes goes up.

The big news here, in my mind at least, is that you have an aunt none of us knew about—a girl your grandfather had by another woman when I was a tiny child. Her name is Annabelle Byer. Nobody knew about her until she showed up some weeks ago and told her story to your grandmother. I took her out to lunch last month and we got along very well. We talked as if we had known each other all our lives. She is a nurse just like I work in mental health—how's that for a coincidence? Grandma is going to have her here for Thanksgiving and maybe you can meet her when your mother brings you east for Christmas. I can hardly wait to see you all. August in the Poconos was nice but it was too long ago.

Everybody's health here is good. The drought this summer has been washed away by a lot of rain this fall but it's too late for the farmers. The only thing close to a joke that I've heard is from one of the black clients at the Center, who has a lot of "Yo momma's so fat" jokes. The only ones I can remember are: She can sell shade, she puts mayonnaise on aspirin, and when she goes to the movies she sits next to everybody. We have a very fat lady at the Center and he never tells these jokes around her.

I am very proud of you, Roy, and love you very much. Dad.

P.S.: Notice how when I use a contraction, I put in an apostrophe. Haven't they taught you that yet at school? Also, "there" is a location and "their" is a possessive pronoun.

He pushes the SEND key without rereading it. He sounds like the kind of prissy father he never had but didn't especially want, either. His father used to say, *Whenever anybody tells me what to do, my instinct is to do the exact opposite.* But order and organization must be kept in the world. Ties of affection must be expressed, or nothing holds. Nelson shuts down the computer, gingerly. Sometimes the machine for no reason freezes, with a rebuking message: This program has performed an illegal operation and will be shut down. The only glow from across the street now is the electric pumpkin grin.

The time he did see the woman across the street in her underwear, her stomach looked stark white, and wonderfully long, dented by its belly button, deep like the doctors do them now.

"Aunt Mim? It's Nelson. Your nephew."

"I know you're my nephew, doll—how many others you think I got? Sweetie, what's up? How's life in the old country?"

Her voice is dry and crackled, parched by cigarettes like the desert from the sun, but nice, with family warmth rushing into its old veins at what she takes to be an emergency. Otherwise, why would he be calling? She is six years younger than Dad so she would be sixty now, not old for some professions but in hers ancient, long out of it, even with face-lifts and ass-tucks and the marvels of modern dentistry. Nelson wonders when she turned her last trick. You get the occasional sex-worker at the Center and some of them keep on with a few old customers almost like a marriage. Now, without her brother or her parents to link her to the region, Aunt Mim never comes back. The last time was Dad's funeral. There wasn't a body, just a square, lidded urn made of a composition substance like pressed bran flakes. Mom had him cremated down in Florida because it was easiest transportationwise. She and Nelson, taking turns at the wheel, brought him back north in the slate-gray Celica in which he had made his last run. Pru had flown down with the kids the day after he and Mom had caught a night flight from Philly but by the time she landed Dad was already gone. Gone and his body, six foot three and two hundred fifty-five pounds, whipped from the hospital to the crematorium. Pru was in disgrace because of having confessed, having been raised as a Catholic to confess everything, that she and Dad had committed—what would you call it?—double-barrelled adultery. Incest of a sort, one night only. She and the kids were scrunched into the two-door sports car's inadequate back seat, and the thick composition box, like a Styrofoam cooler but smaller and dense with its distilled contents, rode in the trunk among all their suitcases. It had been a tough tight packing job to get everything in and Nelson had not been especially gracious when little Judy, who was nine then, burst into tears, their first night's stop at a motel outside Savannah, because she couldn't bear to think of Grandpa all alone out there in the cold dark trunk. The two motel rooms didn't have too many high safe surfaces for such a sacred and ominous thing—surprisingly light, baked bone flakes, Harold C. Angstrom concentrate—so they settled on the top of the mock-wood cabinet holding the television set that slid in and out. Mom and the kids slept in that room, and she had to keep talking them out of climbing up and opening the box and looking inside. He and Pru were so upset with each other they couldn't sleep and finally fucked in an effort to get relaxed, which made them both madder and sadder than ever. The next night, in a Comfort Inn beyond Raleigh, Mom and Pru took one room and he and the kids the other. They fell asleep before he did, they were watching *Roseanne* on television, but in the morning he was still groggy, and after he and Pru had some words at breakfast that left everybody feeling they were tiptoeing on broken glass they all drove off leaving the ashes in their big square bran-colored cookie jar on the spare-blankets shelf of a Comfort Inn closet.

It was Judy who remembered, about two exits up the road. Though Nelson floored the accelerator, it seemed to take forever getting to the next exit and reversing their direction on 95. His whole body went watery with guilt and hurry. The black desk clerk, who had just come on duty, looked dubious at Nelson's panting explanation, but let them have the key again. It was strange to be let back in, as if into an empty tomb—as if they all had died or been abducted. The beds were still unmade, the towels wet outside the shower stall. They found a child's toothbrush in the bathroom as well as Grandpa's remains sitting docilely on the cabinet shelf, the square urn blending in like one of those combination safes motels sometimes give you. Nelson felt this tremendous rush of reunion at the time, taking the canister into his arms, a bliss of wiped-out sins. Afterwards, with schooled hindsight, he saw that there had been a certain unconscious vengeance in their leaving Dad behind, as he had more than once left them behind.

Nelson doesn't remember if they all laughed about it, forgetting the head of their family like that, but he does remember that Aunt Mim wore too much black at the funeral, *all* black, gloves and hat and big sunglasses, more a style statement than a proclamation of mourning. She stood out like a swish vampire among the quiet orderly rows of the hillside cemetery, on the back slope of Mt. Judge, where Earl W. (1905–1976) and Mary R. (1904–1974) Angstrom rested beneath a rose-colored polished double headstone one grassy stride away from the smaller, older, duller dove-colored stone saying

REBECCA JUNE ANGSTROM

1959

His sister. He has always blamed himself somehow. If he had been more pleasing to Dad he wouldn't have left and Mom wouldn't have gotten drunk and it wouldn't have happened. At Dad's funeral Aunt Mim seemed an animated, irreverent slash of black among the dowdy mourners (there were some aging male strangers, even, who showed up, having worked with the deceased at Verity Press or the Toyota agency or played with or against the dead man in his teen-age prime

272 :   LICKS OF LOVE

and who felt enough connection to take a morning out of their own remaining lives) but Dad had loved her, and she him, with the heavy helplessness of blood, that casts us into a family as if into a doom.

"The funniest thing, Aunt Mim," Nelson says over the phone. "It turns out Dad had a baby by the woman he lived with that time and she's showed up. It was a girl baby, and she's thirty-nine, and a nurse living right here in Brewer. She grew up on a farm. I had lunch with her. She looks a little like Dad before he got really fat but when his face was turning round—kind of, you know, sleepy-eyed, with very white skin. So as well as a nephew you have a niece."

"Damn," the phone crackled after a pause. "I'll have to rewrite my will. How come she showed up now? Did Harry know she existed?"

"He guessed, I guess, but didn't know for sure. Her mother wouldn't tell him. She died this summer and told Annabelle before she did. She came to us."

"Who's us?"

"The family. Me and Mom and Ronnie."

"I bet Ronnie's just thrilled. And Janice even more so. I think it was you she came to, Nelson. So what's your thought?"

"Well, it's not as if she's not managing, she makes better money than I do, but she seems awfully alone. I think she should get to meet some people. But I don't know so many people since I kicked coke, except for the clients at work."

At her end of the line, Aunt Mim considers. "How long since you've known about this girl?"

"Since September."

"And you're just calling to tell me now?"

"I've been sitting on it, I guess."

"You're embarrassed," the woman concludes. "Don't be

embarrassed, kid. Your father didn't understand birth control. You were born some months early, as I remember. It's not your funeral. Want some advice from your old aunt, whose life is no model for anybody?"

"Sure."

"This little nursie's not your problem. At thirty-nine, everybody's their own problem. You have a family—how are they?"

This is getting to be a disappointing conversation. If there was anybody he thought would see with him the wonder of his having a sister it was Aunt Mim, his father's sister. "They're good, I guess. Pru finally had enough of me and a year and a half ago took the kids back to Akron. She works for a Greek lawyer downtown, near the old Goodrich factory."

"Oh, those Greeks," says Aunt Mim. "They invented democracy, they'll tell you."

"And Judy's out of school and thinking of becoming an airline stewardess."

"Flight attendant, they like to be called. Some of them, the way they carry on is legal only in Nevada."

"I know. She worries me. She's kind of wild."

"You worry too much. Life is wild. When it isn't a total bore."

"And my little boy, Roy, is almost fifteen. We communicate by e-mail. He's bright, it turns out."

"You sound surprised. Your father wasn't stupid, he just acted stupid. So. And now a sister to fill in the gaps. You're quite a family man, Nelson, I don't know where you get it from. The Springer side, I guess. They were good Germans. The Angstroms never quite fit in."

"I thought you might have some ideas."

"Ideas about what?"

"What I should do, about having a sister."

"Well, your father used to hold my hand crossing the street, and he liked to watch me pee, but maybe she's beyond that. What's her name, did you say?"

"Annabelle. Annabelle Byer."

"Who was Byer?"

"Her stepdad. He was the farmer."

"He's dead, too."

"Right."

"More and more is dead, are you old enough to notice? Vegas is dead, the way it was—a sporting town. The people used to come here had a little class—the gangsters, the starlets. A little whiff of danger, glamour, you name it. Class. The guys used to pay cash for everything, off a big roll of fifties. Now it's herds. Herds and herds of Joe Nobodies. Bozos. The hoi polloi, running up credit-card debt. Gambling is legal in half the states so they've built these huge moron-catchers along the Strip, all the way to the airport. A Pyramid, the Eiffel Tower, Venice—it's all here, Nelson, all for the morons. It's depressing as hell. Sometimes I think of going back east, but where would I fit in?"

"You'd fit in here, Aunt Mim," he hears himself saying. "The house is too big as it is."

She laughs, then coughs, then laughs again. "I never had the figure for it, Diamond County life. I was *skinny*, the other girls hated me. What shape is your sister in?"

"She's a little plump, but not, you know, overboard. Some of our clients at the Center—"

"There you have it," Aunt Mim interrupts. "She's letting herself go. You can't afford in life to do that if you're gonna contend." He has used up her patience. She can only give so much time to the past. She lives in a hustling world. "Come on out and see me, Nellie. Bring your sister if you want. They've got the airfares down to nothing, to keep the moron-catchers booked up. If you want to wait till Judy flies the skies, it'll be cheaper yet. I'll keep. I never smoked except for show. Charlie Stavros still aboveground?"

So it falls to him to break the news. "No, I'm sorry to say. He had this triple bypass, and there was a murmur or something, a bad valve, and they opened him up again, but this time an infection set in—"

"You're scaring me, kid. He was a good guy. He had a touch of it. Class. You, you're lovable. Your Aunt Mim loves you, and don't you forget it." And she hangs up, without saying goodbye or seeing if he had a last word. He hadn't even asked her how her beauty parlor was doing, or if she had a husband.

One night in early November, Nelson dreams he is lying in his bedroom, which is true, although it is somehow smaller, like the little front room where Ron's computer sits. He gets out of bed when he hears a distant clicking noise. He goes to the window and sees out in the back yard a tall man practicing chip shots in the moonlight. The man is bent over and intent and a certain sorrow emanates from him in the gray-blue light. His back is turned and he doesn't turn his head to look up at Nelson though Nelson dreads that this will happen—a staring white mask in moonlight. Instead there is just that patient concentration, as if on a task he has been assigned for eternity—the little studied half-swing, a slump-shouldered contemplation of the result, a disconsolate trundling another ball with the face of the club into position at the man's feet, and another studied swing. Nelson feels indignation that this mournful tall middle-aged stranger, in nondescript trousers and a long-sleeved blue-gray shirt, should have wandered into their yard from Joseph Street and be trespassing so brazenly, making that irritating, repeating noise in the middle of the night. Neither in his dream nor when woken by it does Nelson announce to himself who the homeless man is.

He has passed into wakefulness. The door to the hallway, the latch not quite seated, has been swinging back and forth as if at a ghostly touch, clicking, nudged by the drafts that circulate through the house now that the cooling weather has turned on the furnace. Ronnie is always trying to turn the thermostat down; he says the lousy Arabs are putting the screws on oil again and the price of a barrel has more than doubled in a year.

Nelson forces himself from the warm bed, glancing out the window to see if a tall man is really there practicing chipping, and pushes the door so the latch decisively clicks. The sharp noise rings through the silent house. Not quite silent: the furnace sighs, the refrigerator throbs. His mother in the next room sleeps with a man not his father. It used to be his parents' room, he used to hear them cutting up some nights, making more noise than they thought. The two front bedrooms are empty, staring out at a Joseph Street bare of traffic. Nelson wonders why, no matter how cheerful and blameless the day's activities have been, when you wake in the middle of the night there is guilt in the air, a gnawing feeling of everything being slightly off, wrong—you in the wrong, and the world too, as if darkness is a kind of light that shows us the depth we are about to fall into.

Next morning he calls Annabelle at her apartment. She sounds sleepy; he guesses she had been on night duty and he woke her up. Apologetically, he asks her to have lunch with him again, at the same place if that was all right with her. "Oh yes," she says, "that was a lovely place," in the overly sincere voice of someone who is groping to remember. Had she been failing to think of him as much as he had been thinking of her?

This time, The Greenery is crowded. They have to wait

for a booth, and his head jangles with the angry, forlorn, earnest voices of a Relationships group he had led at the Center at ten this morning. The motherly waitress is not here, replaced by a girl young enough to be a clumsy, overworked teen-aged child of their own. Annabelle wears an outfit, blue jeans and a purple turtleneck, that seems to announce to him a new, careless, on-my-own side of her. Maybe she hadn't been up recovering from late duty when she sounded sleepy. She has never claimed to have no men friends.

The fall has turned cooler. On top of the turtleneck she wears an embroidered red jacket from India or someplace. No hurricane sweeps Elm Street with its drizzling fringe; the sun shines weakly, a white blur in a hazed sky above the city's cornices, but enough leaves are down in the Bradford pear trees for a bald light to strike off the macadam, gleaming where the surface was patched by dribbles of tar. The overworked waitress settles them in a front booth that is still uncleared from the last customers, with him facing the window this time. His face feels lit up so that all its imperfections and wormy nerves show. Nelson is used to the Center twilight, the half-windows giving on street level, and the cluttered gloom of 89 Joseph Street. He says, "I dreamed of my father last week. Our father. I think it was him."

"You're not sure?"

"I never saw his face. But the, the affect"—she has to know the word, any nurse would—"was his. His toward the end. Before he ran south and died."

"Is that what he did?"

"Didn't you know? Yes, basically—he got in the car and drove to his condo in Deleon, that's on the Gulf side, rather than face my mother."

"I can see why. She has a mind of her own."

"Funny, that was just the thing he thought she *didn't* have."

"What *was* his affect? You started to say."

Nelson thinks back. "Discouraged. But dogged. Going through the motions. He was practicing golf in our back yard, which was something he never did. There wasn't room— there was a vegetable garden, and a swing set. In fact he never practiced his golf at all. He just got up on the tee and expected to be terrific."

"And was he?"

"Not very, actually. But in his mind he had all this potential."

"He sounds *dear*. Like a little boy who's always been somebody's pet."

"That was him. Do you think it means anything, the dream?"

"You tell me, Nelson. You're the shrink."

"I'm not a shrink. I keep telling the clients that. They keep looking to me to have answers—all the world wants a guru. A savior. I'm nobody's savior."

"Not even mine?" She smiles—he thinks she smiles, her face is in shadow, the big window bright behind her, with the sidewalk trees going bare. "In the dream, did he say anything to you? Did he—did he give you any instructions?"

"None. He never did. Almost never. He didn't even look at me. I think I made him too sad."

"Why was that?"

"Maybe I reminded him of his other child, the one that died. My sister Becky. Also, he hated my being so short, taking after my mother."

"Did he, or did you just think that? You're as tall as I am, and I'm not short. Five seven."

"Really?" He is thinking about something else; he is rattled enough to tell her. "I tried to run my Relationships group this morning, we discussed how to make it through the holidays—everything goes up in the holidays,

cigarettes and he's been on methadone for years. But he'll do uppers, downers, he'd get hooked on M&Ms if there was nothing else."

"Yum," says Annabelle.

"Jim decides to tell us, maybe just to rile us all up, that the meaning of life is sex, and he starts to describe a sexual adventure he just had, with all the words in place, in this sort of eye-rolling philosophizing way, a girl he met in a Third Street bar. . . ."

"Go on."

"She did this, he suggested that, she said why not, dude, the earth began to shudder and shake—I had to cut him off, which I hate to do, but it was pure exhibitionism, Rosa actually walked out, it was so inappropriate—"

"I know," Annabelle says. "I get that with my Alzheimer's patients. They de-inhibit."

"Your father," Nelson says, thinking the subject needed a change. "The man you thought was your father. Did he ever look at you?"

Her eyes lose their sleepy look; a stonewashed-denim blue, they widen like a doll's when you sit it erect.

"I mean," Nelson hastens to explain, "unlike my father, who didn't look around at me in the dream, even though I know he knew I was there."

"Yes," she says. "Frank did look at me. Especially—"

"Especially after you were sixteen," Nelson supplies.

"He died when I was sixteen. He began to look earlier than that. When I was fourteen." Her eyes regain their unimpeachable calm. "But, you know, nothing. He was a wonderful, generous man. My mother wasn't always easy. She had a temper, and wasn't really a country person. She couldn't talk to the other farm women, Mennonite some of them."

More capable than she looks, the waitress brings his pea

soup with the frothy half-sandwich and Annabelle's hamburger with chips and a slice of pickle, cut the long way. The smell of ground grilled meat travels to him across the Formica, reminding him of high school—its cafeteria lunches, its aimless car rides that ended with Whoppers at Burger King. Since his father's death of sludgy arteries he has been careful to watch his diet; his blood pressure is high for his age, and so is his cholesterol. It was aggressive of Annabelle, he feels, to order a hamburger, just as her outfit is aggressive, the purple turtleneck stretched by the push of her breasts. He wonders if as with the woman across the street her bra is beige, a clinging silky Olga or lacy Bali or satiny Barelythere. Her innocence feels learned, a layer. After two bites of her hamburger she confesses, "I dread Thanksgiving. I don't know what you expect of me."

"Expect? I don't expect much, just you to be yourself and the others to be polite."

"See, that's it. Why should they have to make an effort to be polite? A girlfriend of mine from when I worked at St. Joe's has invited me to spend the holiday with her family, over in Brewer Heights. Wouldn't that be better? Easier for everybody?"

He goes into counsellor mode; his voice slows, each word weighed. "Easier isn't necessarily better. You're family to me and I'd like you to be there with me."

"Family to you but not to them. To your mother I'm just a reminder of old misery."

"The misery of the world," he says, reaching into himself to overcome her resistance. "That's what I kept thinking during my group this morning—the pity of everything, all of us, these confused souls trying so pathetically hard to break out of the fog—to see through our compulsions, our needs as they chew us up. I got panicky and let it get out of control. The group ran *me*."

"Several of the old men I look after," she says, trying to join in his drift, "think they're married to me. They want to hold my hand. They think I'm the right age for them, they forget how old they are, when they don't look into the mirror."

"That Egyptian plane that went down," he goes on. "One of the pilots decided to commit suicide and take everybody with him. Children and everybody. Because he couldn't pay his daughter's medical bills. People are crazy. At times when I'm with the clients I can't see the difference between them and me, except for the structure we're all in. I get paid, a little, and they get taken care of, a little."

"So why do you want me to come with your family to Thanksgiving?"

"The same reason you showed up at the house," Nelson says. "Without your mother, you're stuck. You're not going anywhere. You're under a spell, and we've got to break it."

"My savior." She picks up the limp pickle slice with a dainty grip and before biting it with her deceptively pretty teeth gives him a challenging, sisterly look. "Nelson, are you sure it's *my* spell you're trying to break?"

He is nervous on behalf of his mother and sister and his own self, but things at Thanksgiving go pretty well until the four bottles of California sauterne have been drunk and people are restless and irritable from sitting so long at the table, the Springers' polished mahogany dining-room table, two overlapping tablecloths needed to cover it with its extra leaves inserted. The day is unseasonably warm and spotted with fits of rain, showers that come and go. The summer's drought has been forgotten. They need frost now. Daffodil and crocus shoots are coming up and the lilac buds have the fullness they should have in April. Some cog has slipped in the sky, clogged as it is with emissions from all our heedless cars.

Of the Harrison boys, nerdy, divorced Alex has come up from Virginia, and Georgie from New York, still unmarried and no great mystery why, and Ron Junior with his wife, pudgy Margie, and three children from where they live, in a new development off the old pike to Maiden Springs. That makes eleven with Nelson and Annabelle, but because she owes her so much hospitality and fortifying advice over the years Mom invited Doris Dietrich, as she now is, and her elderly rich husband, Henry, whom Doris calls Deet. Janice never dreamed Doris would accept but she did, loftily saying they had given the cook the holiday off and she was dreading trying to whip up an elaborate meal just for Deet. He is eighty, at least, and even deafer than Doris. Still, he holds himself erect and looks distinguished, a Diamond County aristocrat, a living reminder of the days when the vast old hosiery mills were still mills and not discount clothing outlets. After much dithering and debate, it was decided to put him at Janice's right and Annabelle next to him and Georgie, in Nelson's estimation the least menacing of the Harrisons, on her right.

And the old gent did appreciate—the thin red skin on his cheekbones glowed—being seated beside the best-looking youngish woman there. Margie, Annabelle's only competitor, was one of those local girls who with their chunky sturdy legs in white bobby socks and big boobs in the bulky letter sweater are knockouts as seventeen-year-old cheerleaders but don't carry it past thirty, sinking into fat with their mothers. Ron Junior had put on weight, too, and a construction worker's permanent tan. His mother's mouth, with her slightly shy but welcoming smile, had acquired in his face the stubborn closed set of a man who had settled for less than he might have. His two years up at Lehigh had gone into nailing two-by-fours into tacky house frames, rows of them on half-acre lots. He had become a version of his father, meaty and balding and potentially pugnacious, though without an insurance salesman's pallor. Alex, the oldest and tallest, now looked most like their mother — stringy and wry, the way she became in her long illness, and intelligent and prim in his wire-rimmed glasses. Was it working with miniature circuits that had made his mouth the size of a tight buttonhole? He had done the best of the three boys, moving out to the West Coast and back, climbing the computer programmer's zigzag ladder, though since it was a field where the brightest and luckiest made millions before thirty perhaps he felt like a failure; at any rate, he had a slight apologetic stoop, which was also like his mother as her life had wound down.

Nelson does not remember when he realized that his father and Mrs. Harrison were having an affair. He had his own family and problems back then and his parents' friends to him were a bunch of aging crocks who hung out at the Flying Eagle and thought having a third g-and-t was a real trip and saying "fuck" in mixed company a real break-through. Buddy Inglefinger was the worst asshole, but Webb Murkett and his zaftig little child bride were right up there for repulsiveness. Mrs. Harrison he hardly ever looked at, she was so drab, so quiet, so naggingly ill. Yet, when made extra alert by coke, Nelson could feel currents — just the way the grown-ups grouped when he saw them together, Mom standing next to gawky Mr. Murkett or maybe stocky Mr. Harrison and Dad and Mrs. Harrison just hanging back a half-step together, talking so nobody else could hear, a funny tingling sort of extra peacefulness between them. She was nice to Nelson, too, a little too nice, as if to a much-discussed problem child. This sallow, schoolmarmy, calm-voiced woman knew too many things about him, and liked him a shade more than on his own he deserved. It was eerie, the way she was already under his skin. The Murketts split up and the Inglefingers moved away—Buddy had found a woman as flaky as he—but the Harrisons and the Ang-stroms still would see one another, the six months when Mom and Dad were back from Florida, going out to a movie or a Blasts game, though Dad always said he couldn't stand Ronnie and never had, not since Ronnie was a tough kid from Wenrich Alley. And Nelson would notice that in this quartet his father was less noisy than usual, less frisky and skittish in the way he put on to annoy Mom, more subdued and contented: he seemed more grown-up. It was hard to associate this different man with Mrs. Harrison, but what else would explain it? And then she died. And his father showed less grief than he should have, even scrapped with the grieving widower at the funeral. What a hard-hearted thick-skinned showboat his father had been, just as Ronnie said.

The fact of the affair has long since leaked out and poi-sons any get-together with his stepbrothers. Not that they say anything. But they know, and they see him as heir to his father's guilt, to the pollution of their otherwise perfect mother.

"Alex, it's great to see you up here," Nelson lies. "Are you getting a Southern accent yet?"

"It's infectious," agrees the former computer whiz, now a middle-management tool. "Virginia's a funny state—half hillbilly and half megalopolis, at the Washington end."

"Like Pennsylvania and Philly," Nelson offers.

"It has a better sense of itself than Pennsylvania. It had all those Presidents, and the Confederate capital, and now the economy is taking off. The skyscrapers they can't build over in the District are being built across the river in Virginia."

His words issue from his little mouth grudgingly, as if his brain is being made to perform an uncongenial function.

"Have you met my sister Annabelle? Half-sister, actually."

"I heard she would be here. How do you do?"

"Hi," says Annabelle, wondering if this is the brother Nelson wants her to get to know. It must be: of the other two, one is gay and the other already married, she can see. But why does Nelson assume that if she had wanted to marry she wouldn't have, ages ago? It's insulting, for him to think she couldn't have landed a doctor for herself, back when she was younger. This pale man in bifocals, the pride of the Harrisons, reminds her of a doctor—the same chilly neatness, the same superior air of having mastered a language only a few can speak.

"And what do *you* do?" he asks her, as if everybody knows what he does.

"Oh, hang out," she says, to tease, he seems so prissy, so glassily impervious.

Nelson at her side intervenes: "She's a licensed practical nurse, in private practice for now, mostly the elderly."

"Mmm, impressive," Alex says. "The geriatric is a real growth sector."

"They're more lonely than sick, a lot of them," she offers, not sure whether he is being hostile or merely thinks in terms of sectors.

"You wonder how much dead weight society can carry," he goes on. "At some point in the next millennium, governments will have to establish a cut-off point. Eskimos did it, when they were a viable population. Native American tribes did it. In Sicily, they used to make a party of it—everybody piled on with pillows, so when the old person smothered there was no single person who had, so to speak, 'done it.' "

He is hostile, she decides. She says, "I don't know, there's always something worthwhile there, even when they can't remember from one minute to the next. They're easy to make contact with. Maybe the shame they can't express, about being useless, opens them up." His mouth tightens, his glasses glint. He has taken her meaning, that he is not open or easy to make contact with. All this probing and grappling we must do, out in society: how much easier, Annabelle thinks, it is to stay in rooms you know as well as your own body, having a warm meal and an evening of television, where it's all so comfortably one-way.

Seated at the table, she feels comfortable next to Mr. Dietrich, with his handsome long head and little fake-flesh hearing aid and sharp high cheekbones blotched by a stately excitement. He tells her about his travels—the bulky souvenirs his wife insists on buying, the number of times they have been cheated—in Mexico, in Egypt, in Sri Lanka. He conveys his pleasure in being able to support an acquisitive wife and legions of cheats. "Most of these foreigners are rascals," he says, "but you can't blame them, since they labor under the misfortune of not being Americans." And he looks down at her sideways slyly, to see how she takes that, and turns to Nelson's mother on his other side, asking, "Isn't that right, Janice? Did you hear what I said to the delightful young lady?"

"No, Deet darling, say it again to me!"

Mrs. Harrison is tense. Her dark eyes—like Nelson's, but moister, female, and less lashy, shrunken by age—have been shuttling up and down the table, watching all those faces connected to her. With a stepgrandson on her other side, she has lurched at the old man's overture. They know each other; they have between them that toothless intimacy of the more-than-middle-aged—they can banter without any chance of follow-up.

"I said, my dear, that you can't blame foreigners for being

rascals since they labor under the misfortune of not being Americans!"

Janice puzzles. "I'm not sure I get it. If they're foreigners, of course they're not Americans."

"Of course! Exactly!" Deet in deaf triumph rests his big mottled hand on her forearm and fondly squeezes.

On Annabelle's other side, Georgie asks her about Broadway shows. He cannot believe she's never seen *Cats* or *Miss Saigon*. But he obliges her with a description of a show called *Keep Bangin'* that consists of nothing but men playing drums. He offers to get her and Nelson tickets: "People here really live so much closer to New York than they realize. The drive takes less than three hours, and if you don't want to bother with a car to park there's a perfectly usable bus. If you and Nelson don't want to hear all that drumming I know one of the dance coaches for the revival of *Kiss Me, Kate* that's going to open next week. The most a*maz*ing production I've seen lately has the rather embarrassing title *The Vagina Monologues*, a one-woman show by Eve Ensler, and it's really more serious than it sounds. It's about us and our bodies. All of us. Men, women, and in-between."

"Nelson and I don't really go around together like that," she must point out. "We discovered each other just recently."

"What a remarkable thing," he says, eager to follow any lead she gives him. She makes him uneasy, she realizes. A grin is held on his face like a firecracker ready to go off. His face is theatrically large-featured, and sun-wrinkled like a farmer's—from beaches and vacations, she supposes. He has a marathoner's unnatural leanness, to go with his mobile full lips, big beaky nose, and long, ropily veined hands. He asks, "You grew up around here?"

"Sure did."

"And you don't want to get away? I was always dying to. I

wanted to dance and did make a few chorus lines, but never in shows that had long runs, that was just my luck. What I do now, to make ends meet—the city has become ridiculously expensive, even the neighborhoods that used to be grungy—I facilitate sales at a ticket agency. To put it baldly, I take orders over the phone. My brothers and father think it's a gro*tesque* career for a man past his fortieth birthday, but long ago I decided that they and the good folk of greater Brewer weren't going to live my life for me. My agency sets up out-of-town theatre tours, so there are some executive and negotiative skills involved—really, I don't see why I should be apologizing, I get free tickets to any show I want and still do my *jetés* and *pliés* for an hour every day. I haven't given up on dancing; there are more and more good rôles for males well past puberty. The producers are waking up to the audience demographics. The graying of America—we're all part of it."

Annabelle looks around, afloat in this family simmer. Her own family, in her recollection, took life from her brothers as they grew and brought back pieces of the world—games played, skills mastered, sayings and songs—but her mother was an overweight recluse and Frank stingy with his words, running his buses to bring in cash, like all farmers feeling left behind and exploited. Their holiday occasions had something furtive about them, and half meant. The families of her girlfriends at the regional high school had longer, more exotic summer vacations than she and bigger Christmas trees, more presents, a keener and lighter-hearted will to celebrate. It was a relief to her when this moment of holiday exposure—like the baby Jesus in his manger naked to the starry sky—was over and they could again blend into the safe, laborious routines of everyday, the new year begun. A boy called Jamie, the only boy she really knew for years, asked her to the senior prom, and her dress, peach chiffon with a satin bodice, seemed a piece of her parents' flesh she was wearing, carved from their scanty budget, hot and sticky on her skin. She felt stiff as a doll, tarted up, even though her mother, in her jeans and flannel shirt, tried to see her off with a blessing: "My beautiful baby girl," she said. Annabelle had not felt entitled to be the expense her brothers were— their sports equipment, their field trips, their memberships— as if she sensed, in her mother's ruefully loving touch, the hidden truth that she was only her mother's child. She watches this other family with interest, her brother a lamb among his stepkin.

Nelson sits at the far end of the table, between Mrs. Dietrich and the plump, short, opinionated Margie. Between Margie and Janice the two older children, restless boys, sit and stare with undisguised curiosity across at Annabelle. On the other side of Georgie are his two brothers, Alex and then Ron Junior, in turn next to his youngest child, a girl in a high chair, and next to her her grandfather, who as the wine bottle in front of him empties becomes increasingly cozy with Mrs. Dietrich. Her leathery form is adorned with lots of draggy metal jewelry, as if for some other occasion, a gaudier and more fashionable one than this family obser-vance. The Dietrichs bring to the meal the grace of money, the wealth of honest material industry, its machinery sold south, its employees long dismissed and dead of lint and toxic relaxants, but its invested profits still working for the happiness of the founder's heirs, to the third generation.

Janice sits at the table's foot, opposite her husband and beside the courtly Deet, but she has the air less of the host-ess than of a guest lucky to be there, increasingly light-headed as her wineglass is refilled and the meal she has struggled to prepare is dutifully consumed. The turkey was dry and the gravy a little thick and cold but the stuffing, mashed pota-toes, and cranberry sauce all came out of a box and were excellent, save for that last fillip of taste, tart or peppery, that only a fond and confident cook can impart. Janice's bearing breathes relief that she will not have to do this for another year. She sits nodding at Deet's description of the myriad temples of Myanmar, once known as Burma, the country in Southeast Asia least spoiled by Western tourists thanks to its tough little generals, while resting her glazed eyes on the sight of her husband's head nudging ever closer to Doris's dangling copper earring. Yet even thus engaged Ronnie now and then darts toward Annabelle a look that feels like a thrust; it makes her uneasy, it touches her depths.

"And now the bitch is going to run," Doris's harsh, seldom contradicted voice leaps from her tête-à-tête. "They have no shame, those two."

The pair of little boys, ten and eight and bored beyond endurance, have been excused until dessert and can be heard banging about in the sunporch beyond the kitchen. Annabelle watches Janice to see when she will get up to clear the dishes away, so she can offer to help her. The hostess makes no move except to sip from her glass, though Mr. Dietrich's braying survey of his adventures abroad has momentarily ceased. His wife's voice, overheard by all but him, has stilled the table.

Nelson studies his untidy plate. Cranberry sauce has stained the mashed potatoes. Frowning down at it, he asks, "What does she have to be ashamed of?"

"Well, she's a crook, for one thing," Ron Junior volunteers, in case Doris Dietrich has no ready answer.

"And for another she's no more a New Yorker than I am," Alex adds with a surprising quickness, punching in his data.

The third brother has to chime in. "What's a New Yorker?" Georgie asks. "We're all immigrants there."

"You going to vote for her?" Ron Junior asks him.

Annabelle feels Georgie at her side cringe but muster

mettle to reply, "Probably. If it's Giuliani she runs against. He's an uptight control freak who really blew it with this Brooklyn Museum flap. He tried to withhold city funds, it's as bad as art under Communism."

Doris says, the bracelets on her arm jingling as she props her elbow and pulls a smoking cigarette from her mouth, "The city is safer to visit than it's been for twenty years. Deet and I used to be scared to go there and now we're not."

"Maybe that's just demographics," Nelson says. "There are fewer young black men. And thanks to Clinton's boom more of them have jobs."

Alex announces, "Clinton in my book gets no credit whatsoever for the prosperity. It's all due to the American electronics industry. If anything his taxes have held it back. And now the Department of Justice is going after Microsoft— talk about killing the goose that lays the golden eggs."

"And Alan Greenspan," Deet announces, having caught some of the drift.

"Nelson is defending Clinton, dear," Doris calls down the length of the table to him.

"And Mrs. Clinton, too," Nelson says. He has a defiant streak, Annabelle sees—a disregard that might be their father in him.

"I think they're both disgusting," Ron Junior's chubby wife puts it, having returned from the direction of the kitchen to check on her two noisy sons. "I blame her as much as him for the Monica mess."

"How so?" Nelson asks.

"Don't play naïve, Nelson. She's been enabling his affairs for years—without her defending him over Gennifer Flowers he wouldn't have ever got elected."

"She keeps him hard up," their host says at the head of the table. There is a flushed pinkness to Ronnie's head, in the scalp that shows through his skimpy hair, in the tint of his tender-looking eyelids, in the color that glows through his protuberant ears. "Like they used to do for prizefighters." It's another generation speaking, Annabelle thinks. A coarser, more physical, rust-belt mentality. This man knew her biological father—played the same auditorium-gyms, inhaled the same coal-smoky air.

"And what about her and Vince Foster?" Ron Junior asks. "Don't think that's not going to come up again if she runs."

"The king and queen of sleaze," his wife goes on in a kind of rapture. "I can't *stand* them!" This is marriage, Annabelle sees, this joint rapture.

"*Yes,*" Georgie breaks in, his voice tense, having been coiled within him, "I *will* vote for her. She has her heart in the right place, unlike all you Republicans. She's for choice, for freedom of expression, for g-giving the p-poor a break." He is starting to stammer in his excitement; the other Harrisons narrow their eyes and sigh in an old reflex of pity and contempt; he is not the scapegoat they want today.

"Like the poor Palestinians. Like Mrs. Arafat. They loved that in New York. 'Here, honey, have a hug,' " Ron Junior runs on.

"You New Yorkers," Alex says to his brother loftily, "you're all—" He hangs on what seems to be an "f," and Georgie jumps in:

"Fags, you're trying to say."

"Full of shit, I was going to say, and then thought better of it. We have ladies and a little girl at this table." He pinches his mouth smaller yet.

"He has no coat-tails," Ron Senior says, still thinking practically. "The jerk should have been impeached and we all know it."

"He *was* impeached," Nelson says to his stepfather. "What he shouldn't have been was convicted, and he wasn't, if you'll recall."

But Nelson isn't the scapegoat they want either. His step-father says patiently, "Nellie, he *lied* to us, the American people. He said right out on television, 'I did not have sex with that woman, what's-her-name.' "

Annabelle feels compelled to speak up. "I think he's an excellent President," she says.

Her voice, though shy, is clean and pure, startling. The agitated table, smelling of food eaten and uneaten, falls into a hush. She is their guest, just barely. Who is she, come back from nowhere with her pale round face?

"How so, dear?" Doris Dietrich asks, from the other corner of the table. Her gaudy earrings, strips of copper, twitter as she brings her head forward to hear the answer.

Annabelle fights the blush she feels beginning. She elongates her neck to spread the heat. She loves Clinton, she realizes, from all those hours at the television set, letting his A-student earnestness wash over her, his lip-biting pauses for the judicious word, his gently raspy hillbilly accent. "Oh, the usual things people say," she says. "He really does make you feel he cares—that he *sees* you. He's been there, poor in a crummy town, with an abusive stepfather. And his cleverness, knowing all those facts, and being always right. All those experts on television like George Will saying bombing Kosovo would never work and then it did. And the way he went into Haiti. And has brought peace to Ireland."

"He's a *draft* dodger!" Ron Junior cannot keep in. "If I was a soldier I'd tell him to stuff his orders. Don't send *me* to Bosnia!"

"She was asked a question, let her answer," Nelson says; he is used to running groups.

She goes on, hating making a speech, blushing hotly now, but—having handled the mortally ill so often, knowing what waits for us, all of us, including all of us here at this table—not afraid of speaking her mind, when after all her President had kept going doing his job with the entire country full of cheap and ugly cracks, "He loves people, he truly does. And he has nerve. He knows when to gamble and when to hold back. And he doesn't hold a grudge, even against those in the Congress who hated him and tried to ruin him. Yes, it was too bad about—about his needing a little affection, but maybe he was entitled to some. Aren't we all?"

"A blow job is a little affection?" the host asks, giving her again one of those looks, a thrust from some past where she didn't exist.

"Well—"

"Of course," Nelson intervenes. "That's just what it is."

"That right, Georgie?" Alex asks his younger brother.

"Drop dead, Lex. Go back to the Bible Belt. Though as a matter of fact I agree with Annabelle, I think it's pathetic that this idiotic puritanical nation reduced its President to acting like a sneaky teen-ager. Any other country in the world, he could have a harem if he does the job."

Deet has heard enough to know they are talking about Clinton. He says in that commanding deaf voice, "The man may have his good intentions, but he is too extreme, giving all this government money to those who refuse to work. Raising taxes on the rich hurts the economy over all, history shows time and time again."

"He's *for* workfare," Nelson says, almost suffocated by the ignorance around him. "The liberals hate him for it."

"He makes me ashamed of being an American," Margie volunteers. Something in her akin to sexual passion has been tripped; her face shows spots of outgrown acne. "He makes America look ridiculous, drowning us in sleaze and then flying around all over the world as if nothing whatsoever has happened. It's so *brazen*."

Her little girl, two or so, is too big to be penned into a high chair this long; hearing her mother's voice strain, feeling her mother's blood boil, she begins to kick and whimper. With an irritable backhand she flicks her peas and cut-up turkey off the tray onto the floor. "Hey, take it easy, Alice," says Ron Junior, who has been hit in his necktie by some of the peas.

"Well," his father says, "I'll say this for Slick Willie, he's brought the phrase out in the open. When I was young you had to explain to girls what it was. They could hardly believe they were supposed to do it."

Janice thinks Ronnie looks tired—blue below the eyes, his hair just a gauze up top, his ears feverish. Having lost one husband prematurely, she is watchful of this one, with his silky skin, his steady ways.

Nelson says to Margie, softly, between them, "Brazen, he's still President, for Chrissake," and to Deet, loudly, "Actually, Mr. Dietrich, fiscally he's about as conservative as a Democrat can get. We're feeling the pinch at the treatment center, I can tell you."

"Face it, Nellie, the guy stinks," says Ron Junior, while his daughter wriggles in his lap, glad to be out of the chair but not wishing to be confined by her father's embrace either. "He's dead meat. He's a leftover going fuzzy at the back of the fridge."

Alex opines primly, "He makes Nixon look like a saint. At least Nixon had the decency to get out of our faces. He *could* feel shame."

"Nixon? I never heard him admit anything except how sorry he felt for himself," Nelson says.

"It's the *sleaze!*" Margie cries in a kind of orgasm, visibly quivering. Alice starts to whimper in sympathy. Her mother gestures toward her. "What are children supposed to think? What do you tell Boy Scouts?"

"Boy Scouts!" Georgie exclaims, a big grin creasing his face. "Keep your mind out of the gutter, that's what our scoutmaster used to tell us. But none of us did. Boy Scouts are no saints. He was no saint either, it turned out."

"A much-maligned man," Deet announces, having heard the word "Nixon." "What he did then would be shrugged off now."

"Like Reagan shrugged off Iran-Contra," Nelson says. "Not that he had a clue what they were talking about. Talk about senile dementia!"

"He made the Russkies bite the dust, I'll tell you. He brought the damn Wall down," says Ron Senior, lifting the bottle in front of him and finding that it is empty. "Janice, is there any more wine? Is it all drunk up at your end?"

Doris Dietrich beside him also calls down to Janice. "Janice, what do you think? What do you think about Hillary's running?"

Janice tries to focus. She had been thinking of how much like Harry Nelson was, defending Presidents. Her son has that expression on his face Harry used to call "white around the gills." Why do they do it, care so about those distant men? They identify. They think the country is as fragile as they are. Her father, who hated Roosevelt to the day he died, would get so excited, saying the Democrats were giving the country away. She tells the expectant table, "Oh . . . she should run if it makes her feel better. Let her get it out of her system. Ronnie, you've had enough wine. It's time to clear, but everybody except Annabelle stay sitting. She may help me."

Her attempt to protect the girl fails, for everybody except the Dietrichs and Margie and Alice picks up dirty dishes and crowds into the kitchen. Ron Junior's two boys, Angus and Ron III, have taken Ron Senior's golf clubs out of his closet to the sunporch and set up a kind of putting course among overturned summer furniture. They are taking fuller and fuller swings, and their father gets to them just before some-

thing is broken—the rippled glass table where they sometimes eat in the summer, or a panel of screening he has just
fitted with new Fiberglas mesh. "We're going to have pies,
boys," Janice promises them, and then remembers that she
should have been warming the apple and mince in the oven
instead of just sitting there listening to them all argue.

There is a milling about at the kitchen counter as the
guests deposit the plates and glasses and silver. Annabelle
starts rinsing the plates into the Disposall and stacking them
in the dishwasher, whose baby-blue interior is new to her.
Her host comes over to help, which is his right, it being his
kitchen. But it brings him very close, his sports jacket off
and his sleeves rolled up so the blond-white fur of forearm
hair shows; he lightly bumps her aside and takes the wet
plates into his hands. There is a density to him, a fullness of
blood that her own veins feel. "We'll load all the big plates
into the lower rack and save the saucers for the next load."

"I can move away, Mr. Harrison, if you'd like to do it."

"Why? This works. You rinse, I load." He is close enough
that she smells the sweet sauterne around his red-eared head.
"So," he says, "a blow job's just a way of showing affection."

"That's what I said." She has dealt in her life with so many
older men coming on to her that she feels calm with it, confident she can fend.

"You're your mother's daughter, all right."

"I am?"

"I knew your mother, once. Before she got involved with
that jerk Angstrom."

"Oh?" Fear and fascination twitter together inside her. Her
hand trembles, setting the delicate old wineglasses, family
treasures with etched designs, into the upper rack. He takes
them from her two at time, and rearranges those she has set
in place.

"Otherwise, they rattle around and break," he explains.

"What was she like then?" She asks this but has already decided she doesn't want the conversation to continue. She half turns away from him, looking for a towel to dry her hands.

Ronnie keeps his voice low, so Janice, putting her pies belatedly into the oven, doesn't hear. "She'd fuck anybody," he says softly into the fine hair at the side of Annabelle's neck.

"Why didn't you do that before?" Nelson is whining at his mother.

"Oh, it slipped my mind," she says, "everybody getting so excited about Clinton. Isn't his term about up, in any case?"

"Not soon enough," Ron Junior shouts from the sun-porch, where he is trying to restore order.

"It must feel funny," Ronnie murmurs to Annabelle, "being the illegitimate daughter of a hooer and a bum."

Tears spring to her eyes as if at the lash of a twig while walking in the woods. Nelson sees the change in her face, sees her wheel from the sink with her wet hands still up in the air, and in two steps is at her side. "What happened?" he asks, his breath hot, his eyes sunk deeper into his skull.

"Nothing," she gasps, struggling not to sob.

"What did he say?"

"He didn't say anything."

"I asked her," Ronnie tells his stepson conversationally, "how it felt being the bastard kid of a whore and a bum. I didn't ask her for a blow job, though."

"Ronnie!" Janice exclaims, letting the oven door slam.

"Well, shit," he says, only a bit abashed, "what's she doing here anyway, telling us what a great guy Clinton is?"

Nelson squares up to him, though he is a bit shorter and was never an athlete. "You *told* Mom she could come. You said you wanted to see how Ruth Leonard's daughter turned out."

"Now I know. Looks just like her, without the ginger in her hair. And cunt, my guess is." Buried years of righteous resentment surface in the cool guess.

"You couldn't stand it, could you?" Nelson says. "My father beating you out every time. Every time you went up against him, he beat you out. That's how he was, Ronnie. A winner. You, you're a loser."

"You'd know," Ronnie says.

Others have pushed into the kitchen, the older two Harrison sons. "What's going on?" Georgie asks.

"*Mom*," Nelson asks his mother. "Why did you marry him? How could you do that to us?" The "us," he realizes, must include his dead father.

Janice looks as though she has had this conversation with her son before, and is weary to death of it. "He's good to me," she explains. "He's had too much to drink. Haven't you, Ron?"

"No," he says. "Not quite enough in fact. You drank it all at your end."

"Please forget whatever he said," she says to Annabelle. "Let's go for a walk, some of us. While the pies warm up."

"The rain has started up again," Alex points out.

Ron Junior, in from the porch, wants to defend his father but doesn't quite know from what. "You squirt," he says to Nelson. "This was all your crazy idea, bringing *her*."

"It's thrown him for a loop," Georgie offers to explain, from his New York angle, seeing his father with a detachment the other two haven't managed yet, as an old man getting older. "She got him stirred up, remembering." His young-old face with its exaggerated big features reveals, in the tug of a smile crease at a corner of his lips, what he shares with his brothers, satisfaction that at last some sort of counterblow has been struck for Rabbit Angstrom's leading their mother into adultery.

"I am not stirred up," Ronnie says, with the oblivious stolidity of the insurance agent who will not go away, who will not leave the house until a policy has been sold. "This is my house and I like to have some control over who comes into it."

"Well, we're going," Nelson tells him. "This is it. Mom, I'll come by for my things when this pig isn't here."

"Nelson, you have no place to stay!"

"I'll find one. Come on, Annabelle. Here," and he dodges around Ronnie, startlingly, and rips a generous length of paper towel from the rack under the old-fashioned wooden cabinets and hands it to his sister, to dry her wet and soapy hands with.

Numb, heaped with disgrace, she follows him back into the dining room, past the tall breakfront where Ma Springer's precious Koerner china trembles at their double retreat. Annabelle has to hurry with her choppy small steps to keep up. She dressed for this occasion in a white cashmere cardigan and cinnamon-brown skirt, perhaps a little tight and short for the company. But that's how skirts come now, from New York via the buyers for the malls.

Only Margie, little Alice, and the Dietrichs are left at the Thanksgiving table. A cloud of Doris's cigarette smoke lies up against the ceiling, around the brass-plated dome fixture. Nelson stops to bend down and say loudly, "Mr. Dietrich, I'm sorry, but something has come up and we must run before the pies. Happy Thanksgiving. You too, Mrs. Dietrich. Keep being a friend to Mom, she needs you. Margie, I guess we don't agree entirely about Clinton but that's a very cute little girl you have there."

"Goodbye," Annabelle says to the table in a scarcely audible croak, her throat sore from her choked-down sobs. She dabs at her wet cheeks with the paper towel, held in the hand that Nelson isn't squeezing as he pulls her along. The two small boys have made their way ahead of them into the living room and have turned on the Zenith television. A football game: blue-and-silver uniforms deploy on a bright-green ground with a yellow ten-yard line supplied by computer graphics. The top of the set is crammed with knickknacks, including a heavy pale-green glass egg that since his earliest childhood seemed miraculous to Nelson. How did they get that tear-shaped bubble in there? He has no coat and her jacket hangs in the hall. The front door with its thin panes of ornamentally frosted glass sticks in the dampness of the day, but with a screech pops open, releasing them to the porch and its fresh air. It is raining; the air is chilly, alive. As a child he always loved this porch, his Springer grandparents' porch, where there was a cushioned glider that squeaked and smelled like the oilcloth mattress in his playpen. And there had been an armchair of unpainted wicker. People don't use their porches any more; the furniture was taken to the Mt. Judge dump, now closed, in some decade when he wasn't paying much attention. Being adult, it seems, consists of not paying much attention. The wicker smelled to his childish nostrils of its vegetable origin, of a willow tree in a storybook, leaning beside a pond, trailing its drooping branches and feathery leaves in the crystal-pure water. His senses feel clean again, the rain sharp on his face, the patter in the maple leaves overhead distinct, each drop, as he tugs his sister toward the tired white Corolla he brought her in. The house across the street, where the pumpkins and the woman in her bra have shone forth, is dark, empty. The neighbors are away for the holiday, and thus miss seeing the heir leave 89 Joseph Street for good.

iv.

"O.K., O.K., I lost it," Ronnie admits to Janice. "There was no reason to be rude, people can't help how they got born."

"You should call and apologize." This incident has given her an edge, and anger enough to use it. He had seen in the girl this dead woman he had fucked, and moved toward her, and made an assault in his frustration. This did not speak well of what his wife meant to him. What she meant, she saw when she cleared her head, was a kind of revenge on Harry, and the possession of this house. *This is my house*, he had said, but it was not, it was her house, the house she had been raised in, the house her mother's pride had cleaned and polished and her father's money had maintained. They were surrounded by Koerner and Springer things; the Angstroms and the Harrisons had contributed hardly a stick of furniture, they were nobodies in the county, they would leave nothing behind but their headstones.

"I'm not ready," Ronnie tells her. "I can't trust myself to do the right thing. She's a Clinton-lover, for Chrissake. She must hang around with a bunch of North Brewer weirdos."

He wanted to fuck the girl, Janice perceives, and is wife enough to feel sorry for him, thinking of his burdensome prick that hangs at such loose ends below his furry pot belly, a prick with a flat upper side, a heavy mournful club, circumsized, unlike Harry's. Nowhere to hide its head. "Then call Nelson at least," she says.

"We don't know where he is, do we?" He is correctly guessing that she knows more than he. A long weekend has gone by since Thanksgiving. Nelson came over while Ronnie was at church Sunday. Ronnie faithfully goes to that no-name fundamentalist church beyond Arrowdale that he and Thelma used to attend. Once when Janice asked him why he bothered, he snapped, "The same reason anybody goes. Because we're all sinners." Janice felt this as a slap in her face. Harry would never have said it; he never thought he sinned. She tries not to hate Thelma now that she is dead but she shouldn't have to share both husbands with her. Janice has inherited Episcopalianism from her mother but without Bessie Springer's habit of attendance. There has been for years too much to do on a Sunday morning, her women's tennis group at the Flying Eagle in the summer and in the winter her sessions on the Stepmaster at the Fitness Center at the dying mall on the way to Brewer. She is determined not to get fat like Mother. Her trim little figure is the thing she likes best about herself. Anyway, Mother had friends to go with after Daddy was gone—Grace Stuhl, Amy Gehringer—and Janice has none. So she stays home Sunday mornings with the Brewer *Standard* in all its color-printed sections while her husband communes with the dead.

Knowing this, Nelson called five minutes after Ronnie stepped out the door and was there in his car fifteen minutes later. He took away two armfuls of clothes and said he'd be back for one of the television sets and a couple of upstairs chairs when he had a place of his own. He was sleeping on Annabelle's floor over on East Muriel Street until he could begin to look for a room on Monday. She was fine, just cried a lot because all of the Harrisons hated her. He had told her that Georgie didn't hate her, and the others were out of touch with their true feelings. Anyway, it had been his mistake. Another mistake, he realized, had been hanging on in this house so long, for lack of a better idea and having the delusion that his mother needed him. "You don't need me, Mom. You're doing fine. Ronnie's fine, for being a fat-headed bozo. Tell him sometime that he was good to put up with me so long."

She couldn't argue, really. She loved Nelson for all they had been through together but she was past the age when she could oblige his neediness. She and Ronnie left alone tended to each other's needs, one of which, never stated, was getting ready for death, which could start any time now. A pain in the night, a sour number on the doctor's lab tests, and the skid would begin. They had seen their spouses go that way. She had felt her baby slip from her soapy hands and for some few seconds be unfindable in the tub's opaque gray water. If there was any truth in what the churches said she would be reunited with her baby, not so far from now. Death had that to offer her.

She had given Nelson a piece of mince pie that she had saved in the freezer for him and said how sorry she was about what had happened. Everybody felt terrible about it, except Deet and the three children, she guessed. "No," Nelson said, "it was clarifying. It showed me what a pipsqueak leech I tend to be. There was no reason to drag you all in, my sister is something that concerns Dad and me, not you."

That was yesterday. She tells Ronnie now, "You could call him at work." He understands it as a command, for his having overstepped.

It is not an easy call to make, but no worse than hounding a prospect into buying insurance. You construct a shell for yourself, and speak from within it. "Nelson, got a minute?"

"A minute, yes." He has the Relationships group in ten minutes.

"Listen, I feel rotten about the way I spoke to Annabelle."

His using her name offends Nelson, but he listens.

"I must have been drunk," Ronnie goes on.

"Were you *that* drunk? Mentioning her mother's cunt?" The clients at the Center may be dysfunctional but they have rabbit ears. Through the open door of his tiny office Nelson sees several heads out in the milieu turn, including that of Rosa, who talks to Jesus. She is with a new client, a forty-seven-year-old female obsessive-compulsive. During the intake he was struck by the new client's hands, so painfully scrubbed and chapped, and the fingernails nibbled down to the pink parts. Pru had had such long red hands, he remembers—gawky in the wrists, tender at the tips.

"Look," Ronnie's voice presses on, "I'm calling to say I'm sorry, you're not supposed to make it harder."

"I'm not? Some would say that you owe the apology not to me but to Annabelle."

"I don't trust myself to talk to her. Her being such a bleeding heart for Clinton still pisses me off."

"Was it really Clinton that pissed you off? Tell me, Ronnie, when you looked at her, what did you see?"

"I saw a bleeding-heart broad too big for her miniskirt."

"Anything else? Come on. Help yourself. Think."

"I saw Ruth Leonard back in the Fifties. She'd fuck anybody."

"More. Who else did you see?"

Ronnie is silent, but his silence conveys less animosity than an attempt to think. This is the best conversation Nelson has ever had with Ronnie. His moving out has done that, in just four days. For the first time, Ronnie owes him some respect. "You want me to say your father," he comes up with.

"Only if it's true."

"It's true. She has more of him in her than you do. Stop asking all these questions trying to make me spill my guts. You're sore at me and always have been because I ball your mother."

"Are you sure about that? Maybe I like you for it; *I* can't do it. The fact is, I don't dislike you, Ronnie. You don't threaten me the way you did Dad, for some reason. I like you. I like the way you take care of Mom and care about that big homely barn of a house. You're a caring guy. Insurance salesmen are caring guys, worrying about the loved ones when the breadwinner packs it in. You try to make the dead effective just like I try to make the crazy effective. We're not hotshots but we're responsible citizens. What bugs you about Clinton is that he seems to get away with everything. The same with my father. Let me tell you something, Ronnie, something I've observed: nobody gets away with anything. Those that escape punishment inflict it on themselves. We all do it. We keep our own accounts."

Ronnie is silent, weighing this, looking for the hook. "What b.s.," he says at last. "Nellie, you've become a bull-shit artist."

"Another reason I like you, Ronnie," Nelson rushes on, the insight having just come to him with a force that needs to be vented, "is that you and I are about the last people left on earth my father still bugs. He bugs us because we wanted his good opinion and didn't get it. He was worse than we are but also better. He beat us out. You look at Annabelle and see living proof that he beat you out—you may have fucked Ruth but he knocked her up and he stares out of her face at you. Right?"

"You've lost me," Ronnie admits. "Tell me, what does this kid do for you?"

"Me, it's like she's something my father left me to take care of, and I don't have a clue how to do it. Thanksgiving wasn't the answer. Your sons sure weren't the answer."

Ron Harrison's voice becomes pious. "Nellie, I'm going to speak the truth in love. What I say is going to help you. She's a slick little twat and can take care of herself. Let me tell you something that will shock you. Back in the kitchen, I turned her on. She wanted me to ball her. I felt it, and I had to get ugly, for everybody's sake. I sacrificed myself."

"Talk about bullshit," Nelson says, and hangs up. While

he has been on the phone so long, Rosa and the new client have been scared off, horrified by what they have overheard. He ventures out into the milieu after them, to find out what they wanted, and to show them how sane and normal and trustworthy he basically is.

From:	Dad [nelsang.harrison@qwikbrew.com]
Sent:	Friday, December 10, 1999 5:11 PM
To:	royson@buckeyemedia.com
Subject:	change of address

Dear Roy—Sorry to let your messages and jokes accumulate. The one about how many Texas A & M students does it take to screw in a light bulb is funny but it seems a little heartless, seeing that twelve young people were killed making that bonfire pile and most were freshmen who had just been told to do this by people who should have known better. Remember when you get to college to trust your own judgment. I wasted a lot of time at beery frat foolishness at Kent State until your mother took me in hand. She was a little older than I and had more of a realistic upbringing.

The reason I have been slow to answer lately is that I moved out of the house where your grandmother and Mr. Harrison live, so I don't have daily access to this computer and am using it now on the sly when they are both out at the mall doing Christmas shopping and then maybe a movie, either the new James Bond or new Tom Hanks. Some rude words at Thanksgiving prompted my departure but I've been thinking of it for some time. Your mother and I used to discuss it while you and Judy were growing up there but we never got around to it, the rent was too good ($0.00).

For somewhat more than that amount ($85 a week, so tell your mother I have this new expense) I have rented a big front second-story room on Almond Street, just off Eisenhower Avenue three blocks from the underpass, where you and Judy and Mom if she wants can stay when you come east after Christmas. We can put mattresses on the floor and borrow sleeping bags from the two girls who live in the other half of the second floor here. They are both in their twenties and what we used to call secretaries but have titles like administrative assistant and corporate input organizer. I hardly ever see them but can hear them with their obnoxious dates sometimes late at night.

I have been living on Almond Street only a week but am pretty happy. The apartment comes with a cable television set and other essential furnishings and a bathroom with shower. There's no kitchen but your grandmother stood me to a little microwave, a 1.2-cubic-ft. Magic Chef, for coffee in the morning and a TV dinner at night. There's a 7-Eleven just down the street. This used to be the landlady's daughter's room until she married and moved away, so there are a lot of frilly nice touches left over.

When you come you must meet your new aunt, a half-aunt if there is such a thing, Annabelle. She is shy but very nice, and knows all about you. Those protests in Seattle reminded me of when I was about your age and people were protesting everything, rioting in the streets. Policemen were called pigs and the President was called worse, just like now. I suppose things move in cycles.

I'm glad your birthday went nicely and I'm sorry it slipped my mind. Let me know what you would like for a present and we can get it when you visit. Your own cell phone seems a bit much even if other kids have them. There is a monthly charge, you know, that you would be responsible for. You can keep using this for your e-mail to me but as I say I can't answer easily. At work they don't want you to use the

computers for private e-mail. But I have a phone in my
apartment: 610-846-7331. Call me when you feel like a chat.
Love to you and all those fabulous Akron Angstroms, Dad.

He is not surprised when Pru calls the next evening. Her
voice is lighter, more girlish than he remembers. "Nelson,
what got into you to leave your mother's at last?"

"It felt crowded. Ronnie's a prick, like my father always
said."

"This so-called sister—did *she* put you up to it?"

"No, Annabelle would never apply pressure that way."

"Well, she got you to do something I never could."

"Oh? You were never that clear. You were ambivalent, like
me. It was a free ride, with a built-in babysitter."

She pauses, checking her memory against his. He can picture her lips, drawn back in thought in her bony face, like an
astronaut's when the G's of force begin to tug. She says,
"Maybe it was Pennsylvania I needed to get out of. It's all
very dear and friendly, but there's this thick air or whatever,
this moral undertone. I think Judy is better off without all
that to rebel against."

"And Roy?"

"He's scary, of course, spending so much time at the computer, but a lot of his friends are like that too. Where you
and I see a screen full of more or less the same old crap, they
see a magic space, full of tunnels and passageways and pots
of gold. He's grown up with it."

He is being invited, he realizes, to talk as a parent, a col-
laborator in this immense accidental enterprise of bringing
another human being into the world. "Yeah, well, there's
always something. TV, cars, movies, baseball. Lore. People
have to have lore. Anyway, Roy has always been kind of a
space man."

"He masturbates like crazy, though. There's all this porn on the Internet. And he doesn't have the housekeeping sense to wipe up the sheet with a handkerchief."

Nelson sighs, seeing sex loom ahead for Roy as a dark and heartless omnivore. "Well, yes. He thinks it doesn't show. I thought the same thing, I guess. How's your life, by the way, in the romance department?"

He wouldn't have dared ask a week ago, but moving out has given him a fresh footing with not only his stepfather but his estranged wife. Pru is a year older than he and that year has figured in their relationship from the start, making her seem a greater prize when they dated at Kent State, enlarged by adult features like a secretary's salary and a car (a salt-rotted tan Valiant) and an apartment of her own up in Stow and knowing how to fuck, muscling her clitoris against his pelvic bone and coming matter-of-factly as if it was her woman's plain right. But then once they were married that year's difference became an embarrassment, as if he had just switched mothers. No wonder she and Dad got together. Then in recent years the year's difference had swung back to mattering less, a slightly awkward fact like her also being left-handed, once they outgrew the year when she was forty and he only thirty-nine. He was forty-one when she left him, leaving in the muggy heat of August to enroll the children in Akron schools. She had complained for years about living with his mother and Ronnie and about his dead-end job babysitting these pathetic dysfunctionals, boosting his own ego at their expense, caring more about them than he did about his own wife and children, but what it boiled down to in his baffled mind was something she once shouted, her green eyes bright as broken glass in her reddened face: *My life with you is too small!* Too small. As if being a greaseball lawyer's input organizer and easy lay was bigger. But the size of a life is how you feel about it. Pru was one of seven children and, though her father, a former steamfitter, is dead of too many Buds and her wispy little lace-curtain-Irish-Catholic mother sits in assisted-living housing, she has six siblings and their broods to give her a big noisy theatre to do an aunt act in. Whereas Aunt Mim had only him. And now Annabelle.

"It's great, Mr. Nosy," says Pru. "Actually, I've given Gekopoulos notice, beginning next year. I'd like something more having to do with people, maybe in public relations. Slapping up injury claims and divorce settlements out of glossarized boilerplate isn't exactly non-repetitive."

He suppresses the insight that life as a whole isn't exactly non-repetitive. "It doesn't sound as if the job uses all your abilities."

"Well, thanks, but *what* abilities? somebody might ask. Still I have this crazy idea I must be good for *some*thing. I mean, I can be pleasant. People like me, at least at first. Maybe I should enlist with Judy in stewardess school. Except my palms get all sweaty whenever I fly. I hate how long it takes to land, skimming in over all these highways and cemeteries."

She is spending Christmas with her mother and siblings and then driving to him, all the way across the great Commonwealth, its mountains and quarries, its mills and farms, along the Turnpike for eight or nine hours, Judy spelling her at the wheel, Roy playing video games at every rest stop. "When you come here after Christmas, where do you all want to sleep?" he asks. "I have only this one room. You could stay with Mom and Ronnie and I'll have the kids here in sleeping bags. Or is Judy too old for that?"

"Let's think about it," Pru says. "The basic thing is they see their father."

"Right. But can I say something? It'll be nice for me to see *you*, too."

"Uh-huh," she says, her tone Akron tough-girl flat.

"Let's try to have some fun when you come," he urges. "Life is too short."

"I'll put on Roy," she says. "Judy's out."

"How's it going?" he asks his son.

"O.K., good," is the guarded answer. Roy has always had this strange deep voice that takes Nelson by surprise. Judy he had no trouble loving from the start—her solemn hazel gaze, little square feet, her ankles flexible as wrists, the little split bun between her legs. Roy with his stern stare and upjutting button of a penis had a touch of the alien invader, the relentless rival demanding space, food, attention.

"You got my e-mail, I guess."

"Yeah. Thanks."

"How's school going?"

"Good."

"Are you learning anything exciting?"

"Not really. The teacher in Computer Skills showed us some faulty programming in Windows 98. He thinks Bill Gates is holding the Net-surfing technology back at this point and the government is right."

This may have been the longest utterance he has ever heard from Roy. He says, "Well, you're way ahead of me. You're more at home with this stuff than I'll ever be."

"It's easy. It's all Boolean logic."

"Is there anything you want to do in Diamond County? Shop at the outlets? Eat at the restaurant on top of Mt. Judge? Go visit that limestone cave again? They may close it in the winter, actually." As he runs through this bleak list it occurs to him that there is nothing to do in Diamond County—just be born, live, and die.

But Roy's grave, resonant voice has picked up speed and purpose. "Dad, you may not know this but one of the greatest new biotech companies in the world is in Diamond County. In Hemmigtown, you know where that is?"

"Yes, I know." Nelson is wearying of being an attentive father. His son is a nerd, he realizes, a bore to his classmates and a nag to his teachers.

"Genomics dot com. They're famous on the Internet. They're learning how to transplant genes so you can make viruses that will eat people's diseases. And counteract the parts of a cell that cause aging. And all this neat stuff."

"Roy, it sounds horrible, frankly. If nobody dies, where will all the new bodies go? But I'll check into it. You want to visit?"

"Well, I'd like at least to go look at the outside of the building."

"If you go inside, you might catch a virus."

"They wouldn't let you into that part of it."

"As I say, I'll look into it. I'm thrilled they're doing something here that you've heard of."

The boy is warming up. "Dad, did you know that eventually computer chips won't be manufactured at all, they'll be *grown*, like bacilli in a petri dish? Single ions will act as transistors."

"Roy, I don't want to keep you from your homework."

"Yeah. O.K. Goodbye." And the receiver rattles down before Nelson has time to say, "I love you."

Christmas lights are up in Brewer, from a string of multi-colored miniature twinkle-bulbs swagged in the window of the 7-Eleven on Almond Street to the green-and-red-floodlit concrete eagles at the top of the twenty-story county courthouse. Nelson can see this top, with its red-tipped flag-pole, from his apartment's side window if he presses his face against the glass. In the commercial area around the Center, Discount Office Supplies has arranged conical stacks of reams of paper and automatic pencils and boxes of computer disks in its display window and drenched them with tinsel and confetti, and PrintSmart has duplicated a picture of a wreath on one sheet each of all the colored papers it can supply and hung these on a long string like wash, like laundry for a rainbow world. Within the Center, the clients, under staff supervision, have made a brave attempt to keep the holiday blues away with cotton snow and lo-glo electric candles in the windows and a seven-foot tree as overloaded with handmade decorations as a disturbed mind is with inappropriate thoughts.

Nelson can walk home from work now, and enjoys these ten blocks west from Weiser Street past the old cough-drop factory, deserted but still smelling of menthol after all these years, and through the blocks of row houses put up, a block at a time, by workingmen's savings-and-loans associations in the century before this one, which is down to its last days. Some of the present residents have decorated their little porches and fanlighted doorways and front windows with a Catholic or Pentecostal fervor—doubled and tripled strands of gaudy colored bulbs and thick fringes of tinsel and here and there a plaster crèche or an oleograph image of the adult Jesus as if to say this is what the starlit baby came to, the bearded God-Man born to be crucified.

Already they know Nelson at the 7-Eleven, and he knows the people who man the counter and guard the till: the slangy, hefty bleached blonde who sometimes has her little brown boy doing homework over in the corner behind the ten-cent photocopy machine; the frowning white girl with indifferent skin and close-cropped hair and a single tuft dyed green, always reading a fat college textbook and acting annoyed if you say anything friendly; the oldish man with a pleading, watery-eyed look and a very modest command of English, some kind of refugee from Communism's evaporated empire; the alarmingly big black guy, his head shaved, who has a rap and hip-hop station turned loud on the radio and is usually on the phone talking unintelligibly in Caribbean English; the tiny Hispanic girl with frizzy hair and a silver tongue-stud. They hardly notice now when Nelson comes in around five-thirty and buys his microwave dinner for the night and a half-pint carton of milk for his cereal, to sit overnight on the windowsill. The December nights have been so unseasonably warm, the milk quickly sours.

Nelson finds TV stupid but likes the technicolor fire of it, the way it flares up within a few seconds of his coming in the door and punching the remote. A genie when you rub a lamp, a multitude of genies. He watches until he feels his intelligence being too rudely insulted or his patience being too arrogantly tested by the commercials, which interrupt at an ever-greedier ratio whenever the program gets interesting. Yet some commercials he waits for eagerly. There is the Nicoderm commercial that features this neat-looking woman about his age, with a slight crimp in her chin indicating maturity and experience, in a straight-shouldered dress, telling you what a sensible, efficient method this patch provides for quitting smoking. He loves the level, not-quite-smiling way she looks at you, implying that once you quit she and you will go on together on a purified basis. And he loves even more the younger woman advertising Secret Platinum, "the strongest deodorizer you can buy without a prescription." She is dark-complected and with utterly no fat on her except in her quite full lips, and as her pitch progresses, and her body jigs and jags across the screen, she sweats in growing torrents and at the commercial's climax pops a muscle, cocking her arm with a devilish sideways look right out at him. She works out hard and would fuck hard, the implication is. He needs a woman, Christ. Some nights, like in the joke his son e-mailed him, there isn't enough skin left to close his eyes. He tries to analyze himself: why do these two women in the commercials get to him? Both are strong, he sees. He wants a woman who will take over. The possibilities at work for him are poor: clients are off-bounds and your colleagues should be, even if they were more appealing than plain, earnest Katie Shirk, or pouty, snotty Andrea, the art therapist, or Elenita, the Dominican receptionist, with her hair dyed orange and heaped on her head in woolly skeins like Sideshow Bob in *The Simpsons*, or Esther, who is Jewish and older than he and married to a downtown lawyer and *too* strong. In the bars he used to go to, the girls have gotten too much younger than he, so young they seem silly, like those two on the other side of the wall. They really do say "like" and "you know" and come down funny on the ends of their words like Valley Girls, tucking the "r"s down deep into their throats. He thinks they are putting him on, imitating Lisa Kudrow, but it's just the way they naturally talk. When one of the two girls on the other side of his wall stops giggling and her voice and the rumbly one of a date entwine with fewer and fewer words into silence and animal sounds, he cannot feel too jealous; it's like undressing a Barbie doll in his mind, and finding her smooth and stiff, no nipples and the legs don't bend.

He is waiting for some woman to call. Mom calls, to check on how he is, but there is more and more space between her calls. Local real estate is lively, as if at the end of the year— the century, the millennium, the world as we've known it— people are agitated and looking for some sort of renewal by changing shelter. She herself is looking forward to Florida, where she still has the condo in Deleon, once Christmas and the visit from her grandchildren is over. "To be frank, Nelson, I almost dread it, it will seem so peculiar, with you not in the house."

He is firm. "Ronnie acted like a prick to my sister, and those other Harrisons weren't much better. You were O.K., but just barely. After all, you were married to Dad for thirty-three years."

"Well, his having a love child doesn't sweeten my memories necessarily."

He smiles at the quaint phrase "love child." Nelson has always been close to his mother. It was drummed into him that he took after the Springers—little and dark-eyed, and something of a smooth operator like his grandfather, and he wonders now if he shouldn't let go of that. This sudden sister, this love child, is a chance to draw closer to Dad, the Angstrom side within him.

Yet his third lunch with Annabelle at The Greenery feels like a pull-back. Elm Street is bleak in December, and part of the bleakness is the uncanny warmth, over sixty today, wiping out any anticipation of a white Christmas and rousing the same fear of global warming as this summer's drought. The planet is being cooked. The oceans will rise, the croplands will become deserts. The Greenery seems demoralized. The only Christmas decorations up are some flattened white spheroids of a glimmering ersatz material in the window and against the mirrors behind the counter: not round real Christmas balls but ones in two-and-a-half dimensions, like some computer graphic. Once again he apologizes to Annabelle for his extended family's bad behavior.

"It was bound to be awkward," she says. "I never should have gone."

"My mistake. I couldn't imagine anybody's not seeing you as I do."

"And how is that, Nelson?"

"As a lovely person," he says. *A love child.* He has an impulse to put his hands on hers where they rest, short-nailed and broad, on the Formica tabletop. She pulls her hands back as if reading his mind.

"I'm not such a lovely person, Nelson," she says. "I've done things, and had them done to me."

"We all have," he says. As the words leave his mouth they sound lamely big-brotherish to him. "That's life," he adds, which is also dumb. But what was she talking about, exactly?

"I think," Annabelle says, "we should rest easy for a while. You're living alone and have things to sort out with your family. I'm not really your family."

Like those white Christmas balls that aren't really balls. "You *are*, dammit."

"I'll be going away before Christmas and some days after. That girl I mentioned, we were at St. Joe's together, she and her husband have invited me to go with them to Las Vegas, and, you know, I figured why not, I've never been there or hardly *any*where. They say if you don't gamble everything else is pretty cheap. There are all these fantastic new buildings you can wander around in for free."

"Hey, you must look up my Aunt Mim. *Your* Aunt Mim. Your father's sister. Seriously. I told her about you and she was enthusiastic. She's a real card, honest. She runs a beauty parlor out there. I don't know what name she uses now, she's had husbands, but Miriam Angstrom is her maiden name and I'll give you her number to call. I'll call her and warn her. Please do it. *Please.* It won't be awkward, I know. Aunt Mim is a real sport." It relieves him to think of Annabelle taken care of on the holiday, so he can sneak over to Ronnie and Mom's without a bad conscience. He wonders if everybody has a conscience like his, crimped early and always uneasy.

"I don't want to, Nelson. It'll be one more thing."

"Suit yourself," he says, sharply. She has rejected one of the few presents he could give her, a treat and treasure out of his own genes. "I'll leave her number on your machine but not tell her you're coming." The dispirited atmosphere inside The Greenery is getting to him. He and this half-stranger keep running out of things to say. Finally he asks her, resorting to television news, "So what do you think? Should the little Cuban boy be sent back to his father in that miserable country or kept in Disney World?"

"Sent back to his father."

"I agree." It was as uncanny as the weather, the way he and she agreed about everything.

The phone does ring one evening, while he's watching a *Star Trek* rerun. It's not a woman but a male voice from the past, Billy Fosnacht. "I got the number from your mother. I heard from little Ron Harrison you moved out. His wife is one of my patients."

"What a bitch she is. She's far Christian right."

"If you knew her jawbone like I do, you'd feel sorry for her. It's chalk. I've done three implants, with my fingers crossed."

Billy went to dental school in Boston, Tufts it was called. He and Nelson, friends in childhood, saw each other around Brewer in Nelson's bad-boy days, up at the Laid-Back and other local hangouts, but since Nelson got clean ten years ago there's been a fading away. "What's an implant?" he asks.

"Nellie, how can you not know what an implant is? It's what I do. It's an osseous-integrated artificial tooth. The best ones are made in Sweden. You pull the real tooth, which is rotten by now right down to the root, otherwise you'd set a gold post in the root and crown it, and you open up the gum and insert a titanium screw with an inner thread as well as an outer, and if the bone bonds with it in five or six months you screw a fake tooth into it and the bite is as good as new. Better than new. I do three, four a day. It's the only time I'm happy, when I'm doing implants."

"You're not happy, Billy?"

"Forget I said that. I'll fill you in later. Let's have lunch. On me. I'm flush, and no wife to spend it for me."

Billy has learned a new way of talking—punchy, self-mocking, rapid. In their shared boyhood he had been four months older, a few inches taller, and the one to get the latest kiddie-fad for a present first. His mother and Dad had a little episode in the sexual mess of the Sixties, everybody splitting up back then. Since then Mrs. Fosnacht has died of breast cancer and Billy's father—a weedy little guy who used to run the music store above the old Baghdad movie theatre on Weiser Street, where the great hole in the ground is now—faded south to New Orleans, where jazz came from. The old playmates' conversation reveals that, though their clienteles rarely overlap, they both work at giving fresh starts to members of the Brewer population, and that in middle age both are at personal loose ends. "Sure," says Nelson, of lunch.

They agree to meet downtown, at the restaurant on Weiser Square that was Johnny Frye's Chophouse many years ago and then became the Café Barcelona and then the Crêpe House and then Salad Binge and now under new management has been revived as Casa di Pasta, pasta supposed to be good for your arteries while having a little more substance than salads or crêpes. The day they meet, as it turns out, is the one after the day when Charles Schulz announced he was ending *Peanuts* and Jimmy Carter went down to Panama to give them the Canal.

"He got to give it away twice," Billy points out. "Once when he was President and now when he's a has-been. You notice Clinton's too smart to show his face. In ten years the Red Chinese will control it, just you watch. Those spics'll sell it off."

Nelson's father within him winces when anyone threatens to disparage Clinton or any sitting President. Dad had never much liked Billy, complaining about the boy's fat lips. Yet, seeing him, Nelson cannot but warm: here is a partner in his childish dreams, the conspiracy of imagined speed and triumphant violence that boys erect around themselves like a tent in the back yard under the scary stars. Billy, who used to be heavy like his wall-eyed, doomed mother, has become weedy like his father, though taller. His hair, a curly black like neither of his parents', has thinned back from his brow even more decidedly than Nelson's straight hair, its convict cut. Billy has a bald spot at the back of his head the size of a yarmulke. There was always something about Billy that kept people from taking him absolutely seriously, and that light something has become Jewish, quick-tongued and self-mocking and hypochondriac, caught from his teachers and colleagues in prosthetic dentistry. Yes, he says, his dad is still alive, filling in on clarinet in so-called Dixieland bands, though being white is a big disadvantage, and making ends meet in various fishy ways. Yes, he, Billy, has been married— twice, in fact, once to a nice girl from Newton he met up there in New England and then to one of his assistants in his practice down here. The second marriage broke up the first and then developed its own twinges. She was twelve years younger and he didn't want to go out as much as she did and she got tired of his night sweats and yelling out in his sleep and his moods.

"Moods?" Nelson asks.

"Depressed, irritable, couldn't sleep. Weekends I'd be so beat and bored I'd pray for an emergency to call. Tooth-structure loss I could handle. Wives," he goes on. "They shut down without even knowing they're doing it. The fancy stuff goes and then even the basics are cut back to once a week, then twice a month, and then just holidays and trips abroad. Portugal, Austria, Acapulco—all that way just to get a little nooky from my lawful wedded."

"Well, in my case," Nelson begins, but Billy overrides him: "And then when you suggest maybe this marriage isn't working, they act stunned and tell their lawyers to go for all they can get, this isn't their idea."

Years of dealing with people with their mouths immobilized has made Billy an easy conversational partner, needing very little prompting. "Yelling out in your sleep?" Nelson asks.

The waitress, who looks almost like the sweaty olive-skinned beauty in the Secret Platinum commercial, interrupts with the day's specials. Billy orders bowties with diced shrimp, and Nelson the mushroom ravioli. Both decline wine in favor of water. "Have the sparkling Pellegrino, it's hyper expensive," Billy says. "This is on me, remember." He tells Nelson, "Yeah, awful dreams. In one of them I'm crammed into the trunk of a car, my face right up against the jack, and I can see the car—you know how in dreams you can see things from inside and out both—being slid into a river, like that mother did to those kids in South Carolina years ago. In another dream I'm in one place and my house is burning in another, and I can't get to it, even though I can see the flames burning through the floor right at my feet." He pauses. "So—what do you think?"

So—this is why he's asked Nelson to lunch, to get free therapy. It wasn't just those good old days tenting out in the back yard. Nelson grudges being a wise man outside the treatment center. He says, "We don't do dreams much in therapy any more. There's no time. The insurance companies want fast action—in because of some crisis, 'Here, take these pills,' out. The second dream, though, has an obvious reference. The night I was staying over at your apartment with your mother and puppy and our house burned down in Penn Villas a mile away."

Billy puffs his lips out suspiciously, and his eyes pop a little, too. "When was that? How old were we?"

"Twelve, maybe you were thirteen. Are you serious, you've forgotten it?"

"Well, when you mention it, it kind of comes back, but as a news item mostly. Listen, Nelson. Forget the dreams. I have attacks in the middle of the day. I break out in a sweat like I'm on a treadmill, I can feel my heart doing double time. I think about death, about being sealed in a little lead box and the whole universe going on, rotating, exploding, whatever the hell all it does, on and on and eventually pooping out while I'm still in there, totally forgotten. I'm going to *die*, I can't get it out of my head. You have to wear these latex gloves now and I have the fantasy a little drop of blood is going to seep through from some gay guy's gums and give me AIDS. All it takes is one little drop from a micro-abrasion. It's taking the pleasure out of doing implants."

Nelson has to laugh, his old friend is so self-obsessed, so solemn in his mental misery. Does he want his fingernails, his nostril-hairs, to last forever? "By our age, Billy, we should have come to terms with this stuff."

"Have you?"

"I think so. It's like a nap, only you don't wake up and have to find your shoes." He is being hard-hearted; there is agony here, even if Billy is a comical old friend. Not only are his lips fat, his nose has gotten fat; it sits there in the middle of his face like something added, its flesh faintly off-color. Nelson advises, more compassionately, "Believe in God and the afterlife if that would help. There's some evidence—people who've gone through an NDE are absolutely convinced and can hardly wait to get back to the other side."

"God," Billy sneers. "How can you believe in God after the Holocaust? What did God do to help my mother? They cut off her tits and she still died."

Nelson remembers Mrs. Fosnacht, her helpless outward-turned eye, her wide-open look and big friendly untidy body with a slip usually showing and shoes that bulged at the sides as if they hurt. She had been nice; she had thought Nelson was a good influence on Billy. "Anxiety disorders," he offers, "level off, usually. The human organism gets tired of sustaining them and finds a distraction."

"Nellie, I can't do *tunnels*. I'm not that crazy about bridges, either, especially the Running Horse, the way it arches up. But how can I go to conferences in New York if I can't do a tunnel? I have to go all the way up to Fort Lee and sweat it out on the George Washington."

"You're lucky," Nelson tells him. "There aren't any tunnels around Brewer."

"No, but there are underpasses. I have to force myself to drive through that one at Eisenhower and Seventh. I have zero tolerance for being enclosed. Even here, you notice, I had to get the chair nearer the exit. Airplanes—I haven't been on one since Moira and I split up. They're tin tunnels that go five miles high."

"How did you handle these fears," Nelson asks, "when you were married?"

Billy lifts his hands, superclean and with wrinkled tips from being so much in latex gloves, to let the waitress put his mound of bowties and diced shrimp in front of him. "Shoshana," he answers, "was kind of jittery herself, and I was the stabilizer. With Moira, like I said, we flew all these places to get her to put out, and I would take a couple of stiff belts in the airport lounge."

The waitress sets down Nelson's hot ravioli, the steam fragrant of mushrooms, of secretive gray-black fungoid growth, of damp earth, of greenhouses.

Billy talks on: "Maybe I was too young in my married period to think I was really going to die. I mean *really*, totally—zip—zero. You will be *nada*. I can't eat." He puts his fork down.

Nelson picks up his own fork, saying, "It's a concept the mind isn't constructed to accept. So stop trying to force it to. Come on, eat. Enjoy. Have I told you, Billy, I've discovered I have a sister? No, I'm not kidding."

Christmas for Nelson feels least phony at the Center. These unsettled psyches and unwashed bodies, burdens to society and to their families, who in many cases have abandoned them to a life of shelters and halfway houses, respond to the dim old tale—the homeless couple tainted by a mysterious pregnancy, the child born amid straw and dung, the secret splendor sensed by shepherds and donkeys and oxen standing mute in their stalls. Glenn, he of the blue eyelids and glittering nostril-stud, can play the piano, a skill left over from a closeted adolescence; he extracts the sturdy standard carols from the out-of-tune upright's keyboard while obese Shirley displays a small silvery voice and Dr. Howard Wu a brassy, enthusiastic baritone. The doctor's joining in, with Esther Bloom a conspicuous good sport beside him, singing the Christian words, emboldens the clients: the substance-dependent and delusional, the phobic and borderline, Rosa with her new friend the compulsive nail-biter, whose name is Josephine Foote, and Jim the lusty, exhibitionist addict, who belts out every first line from memory, but then his brain lets go. Nelson is pleased to see Michael DiLorenzo here, letting his cool be thawed, sharing a song sheet with little black Bethleen, a bipolar. The boy's lips move but his ale-dark eyes beneath their handsome brows are elsewhere, muddled and shuttling out of rhythm; he has not shaved this morning, which Nelson takes as a good sign, that his mother's nagging is letting up. All in their ragged fashion get *with* it, taking comfort in the organized noise, the approach to melodic unison, the illusion of a happy family here before the tree crammed with artifacts produced in Andrea's art sessions. There are cookies and cake and ice cream after the sing, and little presents from the staff, all bought at Discount Office Supplies—phallic four-color ballpoint pens for the men and vaginal pocket diaries for the women. In turn there filters up from the clients to this and that staff member shy tokens, enigmatic thanks for care given. Nelson receives from Josephine an intricate collage, mounted on a lacquered black board, of smiling faces cut from magazine advertisements and arranged, bodiless, as thick as flowers in a bouquet. Or is it more of a snowflake scissored together of smiles? Dr. Wu receives a pagoda made of matchsticks, and a lumpy arch of colored clays which Jim explains is a rainbow, pointing to the "pot" at one end. Everyone, onlooking, laughs. The basement floods with the warm faith that the world beyond these old elementary-school walls is friendly, remembers them, wants them to be well and to rejoice.

This is Christmas Eve, a Friday. Next day, Christmas at Mom and Ronnie's seems perfunctory. Nelson drives over to Mt. Judge in the morning, retrieving the Corolla from the curb on Almond Street, where it sits parked for days. The 7-Eleven is open, even as children are opening the presents brought by an omniscient, omnipresent Santa Claus.

Weiser Square and the city park are deserted but for a blowing plastic bag and a vagrant stooped pedestrian studying his shadow on this wanly sunny holy day. The mall before the viaduct is a dead-empty lake of striped asphalt. GREEN MILE TOY II ANNA KING GALAX QUEST.

Mom is hard to give to and always was. He used to give her candy, knowing she'd right away let him share it. As he got older his mind had to keep darting away from dainty things, underwear and stockings for her legs that he knew she was proud of. In his childhood they were held up with garters attached to a girdle and had darker widths at the top that were stirring to glimpse. Pantyhose on the other hand had that darker patch in the crotch, shaped like a big lima bean. Once in his teens he gave her some L'eggs and even they, pulled filmy from their egg-shaped containers, made him blush. This year he is strapped—eighty-five a week for his room, three sixty a month to Pru as child support, extras like the mini-fridge he bought to keep his milk from going sour don't leave much from a weekly salary hardly four C's after everybody's tax bite—so he settles on a dozen Top-Flites for Ronnie, even though Dad always said he had a sledge-hammer swing, and for Mom a Better Your Bridge computer program, imagining her up there using the machine in the little room that used to be Mom-mom Springer's sewing room. But Ronnie says, here in this living room where everything has been pushed around to make room for the Christmas tree, that he doesn't want to risk overloading his hardware and crashing the whole memory with all his financial records in it, back to the Seventies.

To ease this rejection, Mom says, "Honestly, Nelson, I doubt if I could use the program, it looks too complicated, I have trouble following even what Doris explains to me, so patiently every time."

"All right, I'll take it back," he snaps, "and get you something else. How about a sexy nightie?" To him she has given flannel pajamas and a cable-knit maroon sweater, as if to keep him warm away from her presence.

Ronnie has come up with a strange gift, some kind of a needle: *The Art of Happiness*, by the Dalai Lama and an American doctor. Nelson is startled because, in unwrapping, the saintly Asian on the jacket at first peek suggests his late father, not so much physically as in the aura of sly alertness, a tentative tricky lovable something in the guarded smile. Ron explains, in his insurance-selling voice, "I thought since you disdain the Christian religion maybe something along other lines would appeal to you. It's very important, Nelson, to have a spiritual outlet in our lives. There's a tremendous, worldwide upwelling of spirituality to greet the new millennium."

He sounds like he's quoting somebody. Nelson checks the book for any mark to indicate it had been remaindered, and sees none. Ronnie paid full price for this odd gift. "The Dalai Lama," Nelson says. How kindly the tentative, watchful face, in its tinted square glasses, smiles out at him: a father he might have had. "Thanks, Ron," he says. "I'll look into it during my lonely nights." Maybe it's a peace offering but there's no need; after that phone conversation after the Thanksgiving blow-up Nelson feels right with Ron, as right as he'll ever get. Ron is just one more or less well-meaning American bozo, balling Mom or not. Once the testosterone goes, you're left with a limp and a spiritual outlet.

He wants to get out of the house before Ron Junior and Margie and the three kids arrive for the midday feast. He's feasted enough with these people for one year. Alex is staying in Virginia with his broken family but Georgie is coming over from New York on the Bieber bus. Ron and Mom tell Nelson again he would be more than welcome to stay, they'll set another place, but after Thanksgiving he knows that wherever he's at home it's not with his stepbrothers.

At the door, his mother says, "Oh, I nearly forgot. Some woman called early this morning. That Esther who runs your clinic. I said to her, didn't she know this was Christmas morning? She said she did, but she'd like you to call her nevertheless. She was quite short with me; these Jews are so touchy."

"I can't imagine why. I'll call her from my place. Thanks, Mom. Merry Christmas. My love to all those other Harrisons." He kisses her little dry cheek and thinks how she seems to be shrivelling. Osteoporosis, like they keep advertising on television. Everything leaches our bones. The neighbor couple are out in the side yard with their boy and his new, red-runnered sled, though there's not a flake of snow on the grass. The sun makes all the decorations on the way back to Brewer, all the lights and tinsel and the plastic Santa Clauses and red-nosed reindeer, look washed-out, leached of joy. He stops at the 7-Eleven and picks up a frozen shepherd's pie and coffee in a seasonal plastic cup with a holly-leaf-and-berry pattern. They make pretty good coffee, actually. Drawing on his slender social-work Spanish, he says *"Feliz Navidad"* to the frizzy-haired girl behind the counter. She responds with a smile, dazzling in her dusky face, and a ribbon of responding Spanish of which Nelson only understands *"Muchath graciath, theñor,"* the "s"s thickened by her tongue-stud.

Back in his room, Nelson sips the coffee and dials Esther's home number. He gets the husband—a mellifluous, condescending, lawyerly voice. He is rich; Esther doesn't need the money; she runs the Center because she loves mankind. When she comes on she sounds subdued, even shaky. "Nelson, I thought you should know, since you worked with the DiLorenzo boy."

"Know what?" But the flutter of premonition has already risen in his chest. He just saw Michael yesterday, at the fringe of the crowd around the piano, trying to join in. He had wished him a happy holiday. The boy had responded, "O.K., sir," and looked away. He had neglected to shave. But he had begun to participate in groups, overcoming his distaste for the other clients. He wanted to get better.

"He committed suicide. In the night. They found him this morning. DiLorenzo himself called the Center. He was in shock but talked about suing us and Birkits."

That inner space where he had once felt a knife sliding as he tried to empathize with Michael turns more slippery; Nelson feels he is reaching down to bring something back but his hands are soapy and he cannot bring it back, it sinks. *You will be nada.* "Oh my God," he tells Esther. "No. How did he do it?"

"With a plastic suit-bag. Tied around his neck with a neck-tie. Sending his parents some kind of message, you could theorize. 'You want dry-cleaning, here's dry-cleaning.' "

"We lost him. I feel I lost him."

"Nelson, don't be egotistical. We do our best, but we can't do it all. I just wanted you to hear about Michael before it's in the Sunday papers. Everybody uses Perfect; it'll be news." She is brave and crisp but her Center has taken a blow, a black mark.

"How serious do you think the father was about suing?"

"Who knows? The man is a doer, he needs to act."

"He kept an appointment with us the day of the hurri-cane. He trusted us. I should have spotted something, I did drop a note to Howie about the meds. The Trilafon wasn't quieting the voices."

"Don't do this to yourself, Nelson. It is not your fault."

That's what they all say. That's what *he* said to them. But when she hangs up the boy is still dead. Sealed under black glass, gliding feet first to nowhere. Nelson pictures Mrs. DiLorenzo lying in a darkened room, the daughters flying in from their disrupted Christmases, the girlishly handsome young face smeared on the inside of an adhesive bubble like an astronaut's helmet. The strength it must take not to rip the suffocating plastic with your fingernails, the furious determination to smother the voices and silence their obscenities.

He feels too sick, too sunk, to eat. He needs to call somebody, but Annabelle is in Las Vegas and Pru is in Ohio and should be allowed to have her Christmas with their children and her family. Mom is entertaining her born-again stepchildren by now. Celebration has stifled all but a little of the traffic noise that usually permeates the city, though out on Eisenhower Avenue a few scoffers and loners roar by. The end of this very short day has begun to darken his windows before he has the heart to microwave the shepherd's pie and turn on the Oahu Bowl. Hawaii beats Oregon, twenty-three to seventeen, and on the six-o'clock news Jerry Seinfeld has married at last, the Hubble Space Telescope is back in working order, and some Sikhs have hijacked an Indian plane for no clear reason and are jerking it all around the sky. Michael DiLorenzo is not mentioned. He is strictly local news.

"Hi. You're back. How was Las Vegas?"

"Nelson, it was a blast. It's the future or something. My girlfriend and her husband talked me into gambling and I won two hundred dollars one night and lost it the next, of course."

"I bet you didn't call my aunt Mim."

"Well—surprise, surprise—I did, and she couldn't have been sweeter, or funnier. She remembered my mother dimly, from some encounter in a bar that used to be down on Running Horse Street, and had a lot to say about my father. Our father."

"Yeah? What?"

"Oh, what a caring older brother he was, and how hard he worked to perfect his basketball skills. I mean, it didn't just come to him naturally. And how supportive and non-judgmental he always was of her, even after she became a hooker."

"She said that?"

"Sure, why not? She said my mother was never a real hooker, because she wasn't organized in her approach. She even got us into *O*, at the Cirque du Soleil, if that's how you pronounce it. It beats anything you could ever see in New York—underwater ballet and bungee jumpers and a boat that rises right up into the air! I was absolutely riveted."

"Well," he complains, "while you were having such a great time, I ate Christmas dinner alone and had a young client over at the Center commit suicide."

"Oh, Nelson, no! How terrible! Was he one of yours?"

"We don't divide them up that way, but I had counselled him. I thought he was getting better—more engaged, and reporting no auditory hallucinations. Shows how little I know."

"Well, you shouldn't blame yourself," Annabelle goes on in her practical, kind, slightly out-of-focus voice. "We're caregivers, not miracle workers. Just before I went away Mr. Potteiger died. He was eighty-six and terribly frail, with hardly any use of his legs, but such a sharp, frisky mind. He used to flirt! One morning I showed up at his rooms, he was in elderly housing over toward Oriole, and a little Post-it note on the door said he'd passed away. Just those words. 'Passed Away.' "

"It's not exactly the same," Nelson begins to explain, but she cuts him short.

"How's your lovely family? Did they arrive?"

"Yeah, sort of."

"Sort of?"

"Judy didn't come. She wanted to stay with her boyfriend in his apartment, the roommate is off for the holidays skiing in Colorado, and then go with him, the boyfriend, to this big millennial blast in formal clothes in some fancy home the boyfriend knows the son of up in Silver Lake, old rubber money. The guy sounds like a real sponge."

"I *knew* you'd say 'sponge'!"

"She and Pru had a big fight about it and finally Pru gave up. After all the kid *will* be twenty next month, and she didn't ask to go to Akron, she's just trying to make the best of the situation her messed-up parents handed her. She drove all the way herself, Pru, just with Roy; she was *beat* when she arrived, about nine o'clock Monday night, they had kept stopping at what used to be Howard Johnson'ses." It makes him weary just to think about his aging, uncontrollable family.

"Where are they staying?"

"What's with all these questions? At Mom's. It's too small and crummy here, and the morning traffic out on Eisenhower shakes the place." He does not tell her that last night, Tuesday night, he went over after work for a dinner Pru had made in Mom's kitchen and stayed the night in his old room at the back of the house, while Pru took Judy's old room in front and Roy the little room with the computer, on a cot. They all just fell into place, except that he wanted to be in bed with Pru, or at least see her in her underwear, and had tossed and turned. There were too many people in his head, like that Christmas plaque Jo Foote had made him. Among other things he was afraid if he fell asleep he would see that man practicing chip shots in the back yard again.

"That's *sad*, Nelson," his sister was saying. "Roy at least should be over with you."

"Yeah, but I have to work, the Center is shorthanded this week, the suicide has driven the clients crazier. And Roy and Ronnie get along oddly great. They talk about megabytes and RAMs and sit up there at the computer all day, cruising the Internet for God knows what. Filth, probably. Last night Ron took him to a high-school basketball game. I guess there's this holiday tournament on in the county, a big deal, girls' and boys' teams both."

"And how do you feel about your daughter's not coming to visit? Are you hurt?"

"Relieved, in a way. She's gotten to be a handful. She's a redhead, like her mother."

"But she needs to see her father."

"Pru told her that, and Judy said if he doesn't care enough about me to come out here why should I go there and miss an event that only comes once every thousand years? She doesn't seem to think it'll happen in Brewer, only in Akron."

"Well," Annabelle says primly, "it doesn't sound very satisfactory. When am I going to meet Pru, and my dear little nephew?"

"That's what we need to talk about. What are you doing Friday night?"

"That's the—"

"I know. The last of the last."

"I was just going to go to bed and let it all wash over me."

"Yeah, me too, but Pru is as bad as her daughter. She wants to *do* something. I didn't want you to come to Mom's house ever again, not after Thanksgiving, but maybe we could swing by that evening and pick up Pru and say hello to

Roy and go out to a meal and a movie. I don't want to go to any dance or anything."

"You with two women? That's weird, Nelson."

"No kidding. I agree. But there's this guy I used to play with as a kid, my best friend you could say, now he's a dentist who does Swedish implants, who called me up for lunch the other week and really seems a kind of lost soul. He was married twice but isn't now. Suppose he joined us? His name is Billy Fosnacht."

"It still sounds weird. Two people I never met, and you."

"Listen, do you trust your brother or not? You'll have no problem with Pru, everybody likes her, she used to be beautiful, and Billy's a kind of loser—my father used to call him a goon—but it's not like it's a date, he'll just be along. He makes great money, by the way. You have any better plans? Like with that girlfriend and her husband? Or have they seen enough of you lately?" This is cruel, perhaps.

She doesn't say yes or no. She says, "They say there may be terrorist attacks."

"In Brewer? On what, the pretzel factories?"

"The mayor of Seattle cancelled their celebration today."

"He has the Space Needle to worry about."

"Nelson, I hope you know what you're doing." This is Annabelle's way of agreeing.

"No," he says, feeling cheerful for the first time this terminal week, "I don't, frankly."

"And this is my son, Roy."

Annabelle says in auntly fashion, "What a *tall* boy! It's wonderful to meet you, Roy."

They are all, including Billy Fosnacht, bunched awkwardly in the living room, crowded in the insufficient space between the cut-plush sofa and cobbler's-bench coffee table on one side and the Christmas tree and the Zenith television with its jumbly crown of knickknacks on the other. Pru and Annabelle have shaken hands like two big cats brushing whiskers, and Ronnie and Mom have been excessively friendly to this round-faced girl who first appeared at the door in September. Annabelle is wearing a short red dress with a high collar and a diagonal zipper across the bosom, and dark net stockings on her prominent legs—all a little whorish, Nelson thought when he picked her up in his Corolla on East Muriel Street. Maybe Ronnie sensed something. Pru has found a dove-colored shot-silk dress with a boxy jacket that makes her hips look not too wide and sends out zigzags of shimmer; the gray goes from silver to a kind of purple when she moves. She has thickened in the waist and jaw and has crow's feet and tiny creases on her cheeks and even chin that come and go when she smiles her crooked, dissatisfied smile. Nelson can't remember if her nose was always so hooked, with so sharp a point. The long-limbed, green-eyed beauty he and his father had both desired is cobwebbed over with a certain gauze of age and disappointment yet those who remember can see through it; he thinks for forty-four she is holding up pretty well. Her hair, once lank and long and carrot-colored, wears a tint now that looks suspiciously even and shiny next to Annabelle's many-colored shaggy do, which she is letting grow out, making her solid white neck look less naked. Pru sees Billy as one of the gang who nearly ruined Nelson back in the Laid-Back days and greets him coolly, though in fact Billy was never a big user; his parents had crumped out early and he had had to take care of himself. Mom in her nervousness and maybe boosted by some tipple before dinner squeals "Billy Fosnacht!" and embraces him almost in tears, blurting, "I loved your dear mother so!"

Roy is taller than his grandmother and about the same height as Nelson and Ronnie and Pru and Annabelle, but he will get taller; at fifteen his growth spurt has years to go. The dark Springer genes have overruled the Angstrom pallor in the boy's hair and brows and the long curved eyelashes, like his father's but without the deepset wary look. His upper lip is fuzzy and his ears stick out and his eyes are bright; the new century is his. He puts his knuckly hand in Annabelle's competent soft one and tells her, "My sister is sorry not to meet you this time. She had a message I was to give you: your father was a doll."

"A doll?" Annabelle smiles.

"A neat guy, I think she meant. He died when she was nine so she has a lot more memories of him than I do."

Nelson interposes, "She remembers Dad's saving her life once in Florida, in a Sailfish that capsized. Another way to frame it would be that he nearly killed her."

"Nelson," Pru says in half-hearted wifely rebuke.

Roy volunteers, "I remember going to visit him in the hospital once, the high white bed and all these tubes going in and out of him. Also how when there was any candy or nuts around you had to compete with him for them—he'd steal a candy bar right out from under your nose."

This is a success; everyone laughs. Roy gives his mother's slightly lopsided grin, and Annabelle says, "Thank you so much, Roy. You've helped make him real to me."

"We'll have to have you over for dinner in the new year," Ronnie tells her, in a rehearsed voice, not quite looking at her. "I got a ton of Rabbit stories even Janice hasn't heard."

"We have a reservation at the Lookout," Nelson intervenes. To his elders he explains, "That's the fancy new restaurant in the old Pinnacle Hotel. When I called at first they said they were full up. But Billy got us into the first sitting, at seven."

"The maître d's upper-right bicuspid is all mine," Billy explains. "We had to go back in; the first didn't take. Some people burst into tears when that happens."

"Oh, how beautiful you all look!" Janice exclaims, as something in the occasion, the sudden clumping here of strands going back deep into her time on earth, brims over for her. "You all go and have a gorgeous time!" The teariness conjured by remembering Peggy Fosnacht, earnest wall-eyed clumsy Peggy, who had been Peggy Gring when Janice and she were young, blurs her survey of the four adult children, her son among them, and the mother of her grandchildren, all so touching, dressed up to greet this particular calendrical doom, with Harry and Fred and Mother and little Becky all squeezed inside them somehow, the DNA. "Just think," she says, "the next time we see each other, the year will have all those zeros in it! I can't *stand* it!"

"O.K., Mom," Nelson says nervously.

Ronnie says, husbandly-expansive, covering for her tears, pompously proud of them, "Young Bill Gates here and I are going to have a great time making hotdogs and popcorn and watching the boob tube, watching the future roll our way. It's been 2000 for hours in Fiji and Japan—no Y2K problems in Sydney or Tokyo as far as they can tell. Paris was spectacular a half-hour ago and at seven it's going to hit London, Blair and the Queen and their dumb Dome. For most of the world, midnight is already history! Time is relative, as Einstein pointed out. Isn't that right, Roy?"

"Sort of like that," the boy says, embarrassed by so crudely approximate a truth.

"It stretches," Ronnie obnoxiously insists. "Like a condom." Go to church all he wants, this guy is never going to get his brains out of his pants.

They are de-inhibiting together. Billy announces, "I keep thinking of all those that didn't quite make it. JFK Junior,

Payne Stewart, and the other day the Lone Ranger, poor guy."

"God bless you, Billy!" Janice exclaims, burbling out of some chaotic reserve of sorrow that Nelson, dry-eyed, sees into as into a dark well at whose bottom his own head in silhouette glimmers in a disk of reflected sky. Under the pressure of the momentous impalpable event almost upon them they all kiss, Nelson Roy and Janice Pru and Billy Mrs. Angstrom (as he still thinks of her) and Ronnie Annabelle, who tries to deflect him to a cheek but is nailed on the mouth—the same cushiony kind of lips, he cannot but remember, that Ruth once sucked him off with, down in a shack on the Jersey Shore, salt air making everything sticky, the odors of sex tossed everywhere like their clothes, she going at it as if leisurely reducing a Popsicle, stopping and starting and giving him the eye up across his bare belly with its sheen of golden hairs. They all kiss, kiss there by the door, the door with its rasping, failing bell and oval brass knob burnished by uncountable hands, by uncountable comings and goings in the twentieth century, at 89 Joseph Street. The house across the street, Nelson sees, is ablaze as if for a party; in the upper front room the young woman of the house passes preoccupied in a glitzy blouse, her mouth moving with urgent words he cannot hear.

Hurry, they mustn't be late, the maître d' will give their table away; they scramble in an exclamatory tumble into Nelson's off-white Corolla parked at the curb, as excited as teen-agers to be out and off. The plan is the meal and then a movie, not one of the four at the tired mall on the way into Brewer, though as they pass Billy says wistfully in the back seat, "I'd love to see *Galaxy Quest*. One of my hygienists says there's a great sex scene where one of the humans makes out with an extraterrestrial female who turns back into, like, an octopus when she gets excited."

"Nice," says Annabelle, in the back seat with him.

He goes on, "The most *heart*breaking death at the end of this year to my mind, though, was that woman up in a nursing home in Allentown yesterday who was the world's oldest person, it turns out. A hundred nineteen. If she'd hung on just two more days she would have lived in three different centuries."

"I guess that'd be worth doing," Pru says dryly, not quite accepting of Billy yet. She is intent beside Nelson, silently helping him drive. She senses he is stressed. He is thinking of Michael DiLorenzo, another who didn't quite make it into the third millennium.

"Did any of you *know*," Billy asks, "that the world's oldest person was a Pennsylvanian?"

Annabelle waits for Pru or Nelson to say something rude, and when they don't allows, "I'm not surprised. Old people love this state. Only Florida has more, proportionally."

The movie Nelson wants them to see is *American Beauty*, cited the year's best by a number of big-city critics, but assailed by several of Pennsylvania's defenders of decency, and now playing at a second-run, cut-price theatre called Instant Classics, out beyond the old fairgrounds. And they do see it, getting back into Nelson's car at twenty past eleven in a state of some coziness after five hours together, sitting through the movie and before that making polite talk at the restaurant, thinking up topics, steering the two men away from childhood reminiscences, the women talking about their career dissatisfactions, each of the four in private scared of the millennial moment, trying to absorb its significance from the air, the tepid snow-free air. The view during the meal, up on Mt. Judge, one table back from the windows but nevertheless grand, displayed on reality's wide screen Brewer's grid stretching beneath them to the black swerve of the river and the few great holding tanks still not dismantled and the suburbs receding with an ever-dimmer radiance toward lights that show scattered on wooded indigo hills, the home lights of Diamond County.

Back in the Corolla, the movie uneasily digesting on top of the dinner with its wine and smoked oysters, Pru says, "Well, I didn't think that was so great. Could you believe that ending? I couldn't. Stars at night from a field, his grandmother's hands — that guy never acted like a man who had ever noticed his grandmother's hands or anything except his own selfish itches and threatened ego."

From the back seat Billy contributes, "I must say it made me feel better about death. Didn't Kevin Spacey look happy, dead?"

"He looked spacy," Nelson says. "He looked like a freeze-frame. That's what death is, a freeze-frame. Hey, where do you want to go now? I've run out of ideas. We have half an hour. There's stuff downtown, I know. They've put a heated tent for a Christian-rock concert in the big hole on Weiser above Sixth, where the housing project has stalled. We could go and mill about."

"Ugh," Billy says.

The parking lot at Instant Classics is tricky to get out of, five rows of cars feeding into one exit lane, and Nelson is never very sure of himself on this side of Brewer. They have put in some new bypass highways and mall-access roads that confuse him. He somehow thought they would spontaneously know where to go. Why does everything always fall on him? He says, "I wonder if we could get into the Laid-Back."

Pru says, "That old druggie hangout of yours?"

"It's all clean," Billy pipes up. "It's changed owners, after the last set got busted and put in jail. No drugs now. No smoking of any sort."

"Do I turn right or left up here to get back on 222?" Nelson asks.

Annabelle hears him but can only say, "I used to work out this way at a nursing home but everything's changed."

"Try right, it's easier," Billy says.

As Nelson follows this directive he hears behind him Annabelle ask in a soft sympathetic searching voice she has never used with her brother, "Billy, do you think a lot about death?"

"All the time, how did you know?"

"The way you kept flinching in the movie."

"I thought that neurotic kid with the videocam was going to kill somebody, maybe the girl he was spying on."

"Wasn't *she* a hard-hearted horror?" Nelson chimes in. " 'Kill my father. Do it.' " He remembers Michael DiLorenzo confessing that he wanted to kill his parents, and that Michael killed himself, maybe so he wouldn't do it. Nelson tastes the dead iron at the core of even green planets. No fresh start, no mercy. The headlights are picking up flecks, sparks like mayflies; it can't be snow, so it must be flying dirt.

"I didn't like her," Annabelle announces. "I identified more with the other one, the pretty one who acted like a tramp but then turned out to be a virgin."

"And the whole gay business made me upset," says Billy.

"I thought it was very overdone and unconvincing," Pru states, her profile almost haggard in the strokes of oncoming headlights, as the tangled traffic burns above asphalt hard to see, the arrows and lines obscure.

"Boy," Billy rattles on, "they sure gave you enough blood on the wall when he got shot."

Annabelle chimes in, "I loved the routine the cheerleaders did with the bowler hats."

"Pure Fosse," says Billy. "I was afraid somebody's house was going to get burned down, either the hero's or the military man's next to it."

"It was a picture, really, when you think about it," Pru

persists, "of cheap shots at everybody. Advertising, the military, blah blah. Oh come *on*."

"That was so nice," Annabelle continues on her track, "when she is willing but he doesn't sleep with her and makes her a hamburger instead." Nelson has never heard her voice like this, free-associating and childishly trusting. Maybe this evening isn't such a failure as it felt. He has the persistent sensation that there is one more person in the car than the four of them.

"Hey Nelson," Billy's voice whines from the back seat. "Aren't you on this road the wrong way?"

He had been wondering why the traffic was so thin. They have become the only car on the highway, speeding between dark slopes of farmland and distant Christmas lights.

"You're heading toward Maiden Springs!" Billy tells him. "Brewer is behind us!"

"Son of a fucking bitch," Nelson says. "I asked for directions coming out of the parking lot and nobody helped."

"Nelson, you've lived here all your life," Pru points out.

"Yeah, but not around the fairgrounds. I hate this area. The fair always depressed me, the way the school made us go every September."

"Me, too," Billy says. "I was terrified of the freaks. And those rides used to do a job on my stomach. I remember once with Betty Majka in one of those that roll you around opposite each other being afraid I was going to throw up in her face."

"Take the next exit," Pru says, in a low, sharply aimed wife's voice. "Go left at the overpass and then right to get you back on the highway going the other way."

"*I* know how to reverse direction," Nelson snaps at her.

"And the animals in cages," Billy goes on. "I have a nightmare about being in a cage that gets smaller and smaller, like an egg slicer."

"You poor dear worried thing," Annabelle says silkily.

Pru says to Annabelle, as Nelson angrily whips the car up and around the exit ramp, "I think that was unrealistic, too. Most men would have just screwed her anyway. I mean, he'd been dreaming about almost nothing else."

But it is hard for her to break into the cocoon of mutual narcissistic regard being woven in the back seat. From the little overpass road, dark farmland seems to stretch in every direction, broken only by a Gulf station, its towering oval sign aglow, level with the profile of the hills. Nelson asks the back seat, "What do you think, Annabelle? How far would the older man have gone? The father figure?"

Her gentle voice arrives: "Nelson, what are you asking?"

"How far did Mr. Byer go with you? My gut tells me," he says, recklessly wheeling through the entrance ramp and heading down the highway toward where Brewer's dome of light stains the sky, "he went pretty far. That's why you're always saying what a great guy he was. He wasn't. He was into touchy-feely. A good thing he died when you were sixteen, it might have got a lot worse."

"*Ba*by," Pru says to her husband, but there is no stopping him, now that he and the Corolla are headed in the right direction. He needs to undress his sister, in front of Billy.

"And your mother was no help, was she? She was a savvy old tramp, she must have guessed. She'd been through the mill, why not you, huh?"

"That's not true!" Annabelle cries. "She never knew anything! And he never—what's the word?—"

"Penetrated," Nelson offers.

"Exactly!" she says. "He just groped, all in the name of parental affection, of course." This bit of sarcasm pries her open; she makes a strange shuddering prolonged sound of upheaved regret, then pours out, sobs making her gasp, "I didn't dare ask him to stop, he'd handled me since I was a baby, it didn't seem right, yet how could it be very wrong? It was as if he couldn't help it, he was, like, sleepwalking. He'd tuck me in afterwards."

"He knew what you didn't know," Nelson points out. "That he wasn't your real father. And your mother knew it too."

"She had no idea what he was doing, I'm positive. But it was so much a relief when he died that I blamed myself. It had got to be a secret between us, as if I wanted it too, when I *hated* it!" Her tears are coming freely now, pent-up, accusing. Nelson squints into the high headlights, trucks and those fucking SUVs, that afflict his eyes from behind and ahead. The traffic is hurrying in both directions toward some disaster, the end of time as they've known it. Annabelle goes the next step, crying, "I felt I'd killed him! Good for me!" Her round face flashes in his rearview mirror, one teary eye meeting his.

"Right," Nelson says calmly. "It really screwed you up with men since, didn't it? How come, do you think, you've never married?"

"Oh *stop* it!" she protests. "Why do you want me *mar*ried, why do you *care*?" She sinks back, sobbing now with a muffled, burbling quality that suggests Billy is comforting her. Nelson can't risk turning his head to look into the back seat; his sensation of a fifth person in the car is so strong he needs to strengthen his grip on the steering wheel.

Billy says, "Great going, Nelson. So that's psychotherapy."

"It helps to get things in the open," he sulkily says. "Then you go from there." He stares ahead. He has always disliked this flat side of Brewer, as opposed to the tilting Mt. Judge side. Serve-yourself gas stations with ranks of pumps, fast-food franchises with plastic mini-playgrounds for obese toddlers, dismal six-store strip malls, carpet-and-linoleum outlets, vegetable stands boarded up for the winter, cutesy

Amish cut-outs beckoning ignorant tourists from the inner cities to *Real Pa. Dutch Cuisine*. He knows where he is now. If he stays on this new improved 222 a bypass will hurl him right around Brewer southwest toward Lancaster and the Turnpike; instead he turns off, by the mattress warehouse with the Aurora Massage Parlor tucked in behind, on old Route 111, which runs parallel to the river, the silhouette of Mt. Judge far to their right, crowned by the distant lights of the Pinnacle Hotel, where they had been, the four of them, sitting and eating and making polite conversation, a few hours ago. Time does wonders.

Pru says, twisting her head to talk to Annabelle, "So you got pawed. So did I. My father was a crumb-bum, when you think about it. It's not the end of the world." She is tough. Her nose looks sharp as a witch's in profile but he senses her bulk, her body in the shimmery silk dress and rust-brown overcoat, as radiating warmth. Her long hands lie idle in her shadowy lap. He reaches down to adjust the car heat, and his own hand and Pru's knees show similarly pale in the dash-light glow. He remembers how once when she was new to their family she surprisingly comforted him by telling him, *Why, honey. I think from what I've seen your parents are quite fond of each other. Couples that have stayed together that long, they must have something.*

In the back seat, his sister is sniffling and Billy is saying, "Easy, easy. We're talking ancient history."

The road has stoplights now, and up ahead somebody, a car dealer or club owner, has gone to the expense of renting a bank of searchlights; three of them stir the sky to the limits of the local haze.

"We are passing," Nelson announces in a tour guide's droning tone, "the former site of Springer Motors Toyota Agency, now derelict."

Mom sold the acreage and building to a computer-components company that never took off; a sudden turn in technology left it behind. By inner moonlight Nelson sees the ghosts of his father and himself and Charlie Stavros and Elvira Ollenbach standing at the boarded-up windows looking out at Route 111 for customers that will never come.

"My father's!" Annabelle says, sitting up with a rustle. "I remember. With Jamie. He bought an orange Corolla, eventually."

"It was my mother's, more," Nelson says. "It's sad to see. The company that bought it from her is still in bankruptcy proceedings, ten years later. They've probably forgotten that they own it. I heard a Barnes and Noble was interested, to make a superstore."

The searchlights are a little farther down Route 111, in front of what was once a Planters Peanuts store and became, added on to, a disco in the Seventies. The tall thin silhouette of Mr. Peanut outside, a twelve-foot billboard, became a nearly nude dancing girl with her naughty parts covered by bubbles, but that was too sexist to last. Now the humanoid shape holds a cowgirl in short white skirt and high white boots advertising PURE COUNTRY MUSIC. Country music keeps coming back. Or is it just slow to go away? The parking lot looks only half full. People with sense are staying home tonight, exhausted by the hype, petrified of fanatic Arabs sneaking in from Canada.

"Hey, Nellie," Billy pipes up. "It's getting close to midnight, and we're nowhere."

"I know, I'm going as fast as I can. If you hadn't got me lost—"

"Did Nelson ever tell you the story," Pru asks Annabelle, "how he lost the agency up his nose?"

"No, not really." Her voice sounds dried out, for now.

"Say, thanks a lot," Nelson complains to his wife.

"Siblings should have no secrets," Pru says, and makes, he

knows without looking, that prudish little mouth of hers, as if sucking on something tart. "Nelson wasn't always such a saint."

"He was a pill of a sissy, in fact," Billy contributes, making the fun rougher. "A real little mamma's boy, terrified of his father, who was a pretty nice guy, actually."

"Unlike yours," Nelson tells him. "What a sleazebag."

"Very musical, though," Billy tells Annabelle. "He could play anything, any instrument, by ear."

"Oh, I've always wanted to be able to do that!" she responds, snuggling from the way her voice squeezes down. Does Nelson imagine it, or is there the purr of a zipper being unzipped, that long diagonal zipper on the front of her dress? His sister giggles, and a hand is lightly slapped.

Nelson drives the Corolla through West Brewer. Those new-style icicle lights hang like bright napkins from the little porches of the row houses that slant down to the river and the Weiser Street Bridge. The Bridge has old-fashioned lamp standards, yellow glass balls and iron curlicues going green with age, but the light falls cold and contemporary from tall violet tubes on aluminum stems. At the far end of the bridge sits an upscale coffee bar that used to be a black hangout, Jimbo's Friendly Lounge, before the blacks were chased out of South Brewer by gentrification. Then there unrolls beneath the wheels of the Corolla Brewer's main drag in all its Yuletide glory: the trees rimming Weiser Square are looped with necklaces of white lights, scribbles in three dimensions. The square, an open farmer's market originally, was decades ago blocked to form an ill-advised pedestrian park to revive the downtown, but it turned into a dangerous forest, and by a newer plan has been reopened to automobile traffic. They pass Fourth Street, and the bronze statue of Conrad Weiser in Mohawk headdress in the center of the traffic circle at Fifth Street. Trolley cars used to go east, west, north, and south from this point, to amusement parks and picnic groves. The human traffic thickens; the city fathers have laid on a Millennium Ball in the atrium of the glass-enclosed mall between Fifth and Sixth on the left side of the street, as well as the Christian-rock concert a block up on the right, in the great hole. A dim din penetrates the car windows.

"Hey Nelson," Billy says. "The Sunflower Beer clock says it's midnight! Here it's the millennium and we're all stuck in this little Jap jalopy! Nothing's moving!"

"Don't panic," Nelson tells him. "That clock never told the right time. The Laid-Back is only up at Ninth, we'll be there in a minute."

Then Nelson sees the dire occur: at the intersection of Sixth and Weiser, where Kroll's Department Store used to be, two cars ahead of them, the traffic light goes out. Hanging high above the asphalt, the light was green, and now is dead. Not red, dead. The sticky traffic halts completely. Revellers, mostly Hispanic kids in jeans and windbreakers, dart among the cars. A shout is going up, but here and there, as if nobody knows exactly what is happening. The cars behind them honk, in celebration or exasperation. The street-lights flicker.

"Oh my God," Annabelle says, "terrorists just like they said," and begins to cry again.

"It's a little glitch," Billy says, feigning calm, though this must feel like a tunnel to him. "These lights are all on computers."

"Son of a bitch!" Nelson says. Decades of wrongs, hurts, unjust deaths press behind his eyes. He pushes down on the window locks. Hooded kids with sparkle dust on their faces are crowding around the Corolla, and looking up the street toward Mt. Judge. The city's fire alarms begin to wail; church bells are dully ringing. At the top of Mt. Judge, fireworks ignite, one slow bloom after another, mingled with staccato gashes, potassium white and barium green, sodium yellow and chlorine blue, dying, blossoming, dying in drifts of dismissed sparks as the dull concussions thud through the windshield. "We're missing it!" he cries.

The Corolla was the third car from the intersection when the traffic light went out. The first car glided through, unaware of the breakdown, and the next waited for the car on the right to come out and cut across. Sixth is one-way here, so there is no traffic from the left. The cars behind are in the dark, but up this close to the intersection the problem and its solution are plain: take your turn, in democratic American style. The car ahead of Nelson, a little cherry-red specimen of the remodelled VW Beetle, cute as a bug, with oval slant taillights like Disney animal eyes, creeps out and through, and the car on the right, a serious, four-ring, square-cut tan Audi, takes its turn like a good citizen. Then it is Nelson's turn, his dirty white Toyota's turn, to pass through the doused light and continue on, up Weiser toward the mountain and its fireworks, past where Kroll's used to be and where Mom and Dad got together (if they hadn't, he would not exist, think of that) and on across Seventh, where mile-long trains of coal would drag through from Pottsville to Philly and once upon a time there was a Chinese restaurant, and on up to look for a parking space in the blocks beyond the Laid-Back, around where Dad used to set type for the Verity Press. It will be jolly, to walk, the four of them, out in the air. He has an image of a frozen Daiquiri, or should it be a Margarita, with salt all around the rim?

"Hey!" he exclaims. Tailgating the Audi, a black-and-silver Ford Expedition, a huge SUV with truck wheels and a side mirror the size of a human head, keeps coming, trying to barrel through out of turn, against all decency and order. Some brat of the local rich, beered-up and baseball-hatted, with his smirking airhead buddies, gives Nelson a glazed so-what stare. Nelson sees red. "That fucker," he says. *This program has performed an illegal operation and will be shut down.* Pru shrieks when she realizes that Nelson's foot is firm on the accelerator and that nothing short of ramming into the Expedition will stop their forward motion. Its fat high bumper—two-tone, the lower half chrome—reflects their right headlight in a flaring smear; she braces for the bump, the crazed windshield, the crumpled metal, the thud of pain. But the cocky brat in the baseball cap sees with widened eyes that Nelson isn't kidding; and brakes hard, so his buddies' empty heads all bounce in unison. The Corolla skims by, still accelerating, missing by an inch. The dig-out smell of hot rubber fills the interior. The couple in the back seat cheer, a bit breathlessly. "I *hate* SUVs," Nelson explains. "Pretentious gas-guzzlers, they think they own the road."

High in the tinted windshield, so it looks greenish, a ball of twinkling fire expands. The Christian-rock music thumps away in the vast illumined excavation on their right. Nelson shivers, as if a contentious spirit is leaving him. And now Pru is attacking him, trying to hug him, her nose poking into his cheek, her breath fluttering warm on his neck. "Oh honey, that was *great*, the way you made that asshole chicken out. I think I wet my pants."

"Me, too, almost," says Annabelle.

"It's funny about death," Billy contributes from the back seat. "When you actually face it, it's kind of a rush."

To Nelson Pru says, so softly the others could hear only if they were to ignore each other and listen hard, "Let's not hang around too long at the Laid-Back. I thought I'd stay at your place tonight."

v. *And Beyond*

From:　　　Roy Angstrom, Esq. [royson@buckeyemedia.com]
Sent:　　　Saturday, January 8, 2000, 8:29 AM
To:　　　　ron.harrison@qwikbrew.com.
Subject:　　Thanking you

Hi Grandma and Ron—Its been a week so its "high time"
to check in and thank you for the great time we had
together New Years Eve. I really enjoyed seeing all those
fireworks around the world moving across all the time
zones. It made me feel how small the planet EARTH is.
Mom said there were even some on Mt Judge we could of
seen. The thing I remember best was on David Letterman
the three slobby guys where the one hit a golf ball off the
fat ones belly button and the third guy caught it in his
mouth. He could of broke a tooth doing that.

The reason Mom didn't come back to the house at all was
that they nearly had a fatal accident when the traffic lights
went out and it left them all exausted. She says Dad will be
coming out to live with us here in Ohio and thats great too.

Heres a joke—how do you tell when a islamic terrorist is
scared? Answer—he shiites in his pants. Actually it was
nice that in Iran they let them go except for the passenger
who had his throat cut for looking funny at the one they
called the Doctor. What really took my interest in the news
is this Tibetan boy just my age who was the second most
important lama in the world and escaped by walking
several days through a blizzard in the Himmelayas, hes
called the KARMAPA. On the same website I read where
the Dolly Lama (the most important lama) said of YK2
"Millennium? The sun and the moon are the same to me."
You can look all this up Ron at www.tibet.com. A lot of

jokes are at www.ohyesyouare.com. Sample—How do you
tell Al Gore from Bill Bradley? Answer one is a bore and
one sags badly. ROTFL (rolling on the floor laughing).

Thanx again for a really great time and teaching me
3-handed pinockle. I dont expect to stay up playing
pinockle past midnight again until I get to college, maybe
to Kent State like Dad. Its the best.

luv u both ;-) (wink) ROY

"Hi? Annabelle? It's—"

"Nelson! *How* is it going?"

"Not bad. Good, actually. Her apartment is pretty roomy,
though eventually we might look for a house. Roy would
like a house in Stow."

"He must be thrilled."

"Thrills at that age wear off in about half an hour, but,
yeah, he seems pleased. And Judy is pleased. She says boyfriends take you much more seriously if you have a father on
the premises. She's broken up, thank God, with that creep
who kept her in Ohio to go to some very stuffy party, as she
described it. She wishes now she'd come to Brewer."

"Is she still going to be a stewardess?"

"Well, that's a little, where you'd expect, up in the air—"

"I *knew* you were going to say 'up in the air'!"

"But I think so. If one of these jerks doesn't talk her into
living with him instead. But girls now—they're not so easy
to talk into things. They're, what's the word, empowered.
Judy teases me, the way I keep looking at her, but it's amazing to me, how beautiful she's become, even since I saw her
last summer. Every tooth, every eyelash, you know, just so
ex*act*. She has Dad's and my cowlick in one eyebrow. And
there's a new switchy quick way she moves and does things.

She's smaller than her mother, though her hair is like Pru's used to be, but she doesn't have that sort of awkward broad-beamy semi-helpless thing Pru does. Judy is *knit*. She went out for all these sports at high school, and works out at this health club. She lets me feel her biceps."

"She sounds like *your* mother."

"Really? Mom's such a misfit, and Judy's such a smart fit, but, yeah, maybe in a way. Bonewise." *Those little Springer hands.* "I love looking at her hands, they're almost childlike, but have this kind of graceful, what can I say, com*po*sure, and long half-tone fingernails. One half purple, the other yellow. I said to her, USAirways isn't going to let you get away with that. She says, 'I know. It's a *fling*, Dad. You've heard of *flings*.'"

"And Pru?"

"Good news. She saw this ad for 'Human Resources Assistant' for one of the big banks down on Market Street saying 'people-oriented individual' and they liked her; she's one of three they've narrowed it down to. Her experience wasn't quite what they want but I guess this guy Gekopoulos wrote her a raving recommendation."

"I meant you and Pru."

"Oh. Oh. That's O.K. You've met her, you know what she's like. She isn't one to make a big show of her feelings, usually. She says having a man in the apartment is as bad as having two untrained dogs. She should talk, we're surrounded by her relatives out here, they keep calling up and dropping around."

"You certainly are more talkative, now you're back with her."

"It's *you* I like to talk to. Too much, huh?"

"Oh, no. But why do you call her Pru? Your mother calls her Teresa."

"How'd you know that?"

"She called, to invite me to dinner. Just her and Ronnie. And Billy if I wished."

"Billy. That goon. I'm sorry I saddled you with him that night. He got me lost, in my own county, and then stuck in traffic at the greatest moment in history."

"Yes, it was terrible the way he did that. He cries about it in his sleep."

A pause, while he wonders how much he's supposed to make of this disclosure. "About Teresa," he says. "That's her name, but in high school everybody thought she was prudish, and there was another Terry in the class. You're right, though, it's nice to be back with her. I love her, I guess."

"Of course you do."

"I've begun to check around, for jobs in mental health. Akron's a lot like Brewer except it's three times as big. It has the same river, and miles of row houses, and abandoned plants turned into something else—they've turned a huge Quaker Oats factory into a Hilton Hotel with round rooms in the old grain silos—and no shortage of misery. I was thinking of looking for something in a drug-rehab place. Addicts may freeze to death but they don't do suicide."

"That was too bad. I could tell how upset you were."

"I wasn't that upset. Esther told me not to take it egotistically. She asked me when I gave notice if that was the reason. I said I hoped not. Hey, Happy Birthday! Forty. Wow."

"You remembered."

"How could I forget? I even have a quotation to give you. 'The very motion of our life is towards happiness.' End quote."

"What's that from?"

"From a very dumb book Ronnie Harrison gave me for Christmas. It's on page one, which is as far as I've gotten."

"Maybe you should go on to page two."

He has broken the lovely flow they were having. Ronnie Harrison still frightens her. He asks, "How's the weather in Diamond County?"

"*Cold*. Winter! Inches of snow, and some more tonight. We all thought it couldn't do winter any more, because of global warming."

"I know. Here too. The same weather, basically the same everything. But I like it. I like seeing different license plates."

"Your mother said over the phone she and Ronnie are going down to the Florida condo and thinking of selling the house and moving there for good. They both have aches and pains warm weather might help."

"For *years* I've told her to sell. But listen. If you do go to Mom's for dinner, take Billy or somebody with you, for protection from Ron. You're too —"

She waits.

"Delicious. Sweet. Innocent," he finds himself saying.

"Nelson."

"Yes?"

"I *have* been seeing Billy."

"Surprise, surprise."

"You're teasing, aren't you, when you call him a goon?"

"Well, he was a *boy* goon. Anyway, in this country even goons have their rights."

"I think he's darling."

"In what way?"

"He thinks I'm wonderful. After those horrible things you got me to admit in the car at least I don't have anything to hide from him. He says when he's with me his anxieties go away."

"Well, is that a good reason—?"

"Nelson, *no* reason is perfect. But then neither are we."

"O.K., I'll buy that." Happiness for her is already rising in him, like water trembling upward.

"I have a serious question. Don't be flip, it matters to me. Ever since I was a little girl I've thought if I ever got married it would be in a church, with all the formality." Annabelle asks, "If Billy and I get married, will you give me away?"

Says Nelson, "Gladly."

A Note About the Author

John Updike was born in 1932, in Shillington, Pennsylvania.
He graduated from Harvard College in 1954, and spent a year
in Oxford, England, at the Ruskin School of Drawing and Fine
Art. From 1955 to 1957 he was a member of the staff of *The
New Yorker*, and since 1957 has lived in Massachusetts. He is
the father of four children and the author of fifty or so books,
including collections of short stories, poems, and criticism.
His novels have won the Pulitzer Prize, the National Book
Award, the American Book Award, the National Book Critics
Circle Award, and the Howells Medal, bestowed by the Ameri-
can Academy of Arts and Letters.